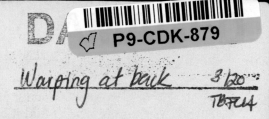
FOREVER WITH YOU

He lifted his head as my hands slid down his sides. His lips pressed against my temple, a heartbeat later gliding over my brow. There was a quick peck on the tip of my nose and then he kissed me sweetly.

And something about that lazy, soft kiss was more powerful than any of the others.

Out of past experience I expected him to hop out of the bed and the awkward search and rescue for clothes would begin. But he didn't. With his one arm still under me, he tugged me along with him as he rolled onto his back, gathering me up so my front was pressed against his side and my leg tangled with his. We were damp and flushed, but as my cheek came down on his shoulder, there wasn't a place more comfortable. His hand idly roamed up and down my back. Neither of us spoke.

As I lay there, my heart pounding and my breaths still coming too fast, an earlier thought resurfaced. Was I falling for him?

Nick turned his head toward mine and his lips brushed my forehead.

No. I wasn't *falling* for him.

Because there was a good chance I had already *fallen* for him.

JENNIFER L. ARMENTROUT

FOREVER WITH YOU

AVONBOOKS

An Imprint of HarperCollins*Publishers*

This is a work of fiction. Names, characters, places, and incidents are products of the author's imagination or are used fictitiously and are not to be construed as real. Any resemblance to actual events, locales, organizations, or persons, living or dead, is entirely coincidental.

AVON BOOKS
An Imprint of HarperCollins*Publishers*
195 Broadway
New York, New York 10007

Copyright © 2015 by Jennifer L. Armentrout
ISBN 978-0-06-236276-6
www.avonromance.com

First Avon Books mass market printing: October 2015

Avon Trademark Reg. U.S. Pat. Off. and in Other Countries, Marca Registrada, Hecho en U.S.A.
HarperCollins® is a registered trademark of HarperCollins Publishers.

Printed in the U.S.A.

10 9 8 7 6 5 4 3 2 1

For the readers.
None of this would be possible without you.

Acknowledgements

I can't start off these acknowledgements without thanking my agent, Kevan Lyon, who has always tirelessly worked on my behalf. A huge thank you to Tessa Woodward, my awesomely awesome editor, who helped whip *Forever with You* into shape. Thank you so much to my publicity team, especially Caroline Perry, and not because of your awesome purple streaks and glasses. Thank you to my other publicist with the most-est K.P. Simmons for helping do everything to get the word out about the book.

I would go crazy if it weren't for these following people: Laura Kaye, Chelsea M. Cameron, Jay Crownover, Sophie Jordan, Sarah Maas, Cora Carmack, Tiffany King, and too many more amazing authors who are an inspiration to list. Vilma Gonzalez, you're an amazing, special person, and I love you. Valerie Fink, you've always been with me from the beginning, along with Vi Nguyen (Look, I spelled your name right), and Jessica Baker, among many, many other awesome bloggers who often support all books without the recognition deserved. THANK YOU. Jen Fisher, I heart you and not just for your cupcakes. Stacey Morgan—you're more than an assistant, you're like a sister. I'm probably forgetting people, but I'm currently stuck at a hotel and my brain is fried.

A special thank you to all the readers and reviewers. None of this would be possible without you and there isn't a thank you big enough in the world.

FOREVER WITH YOU

Chapter 1

The overpacked moving box teetered precariously in my arms as I stepped sideways, using my hip to close the back door of my car. I held my breath, completely immobile in the parking lot, next to a massive motorcycle, the box rattling dangerously.

One. Two. Three. Four. Five . . .

The box finally stopped moving and shaking when I reached six, and I let go of my breath. What was in the box was way too precious to drop. Something I probably should've thought of before I packed a billion things in it.

Too late now.

Sighing, I peered above the cardboard edge so I could see the sidewalk and the entrance to my apartment, then I started forward, determined to not drop the box or break my neck in the process. Thank God and all His—or Her—trumpet blaring angels that my place was ground level.

I really hoped I wouldn't have to move again for

a while. Even though I didn't have that much stuff I had to pack up, this was still a huge pain in the butt. Thankfully the big stuff—the bed, couch, and other furniture—had been shipped and delivered. I just had no idea I could collect so much crap while living in a dorm.

I'd made it to the sidewalk, near the wide stairway that led up to the upper floors, when the burning in my arm muscles grew in its intensity. The box started to shake again, and I swore under my breath, a blistering curse that would've made my father and his father so very proud of me.

Only a few more steps, I kept telling myself, *just a few more steps and I—* The box slipped out of my grasp. My knees bent as I tried to regain my grip but it was too late. The box full of totally breakable stuff started to fall.

"Son of a bitch-ass, rat bastard, mother fu—"

The box halted suddenly, a foot from the cement, startling me so strongly that my string of curses was cut off. The weight of the heavy box was completely gone, and my obviously weak arm muscles wept with relief. At first I wondered if I'd developed some kind of superpower, but then I saw two very large hands that weren't mine on either side of the box.

"I admire anyone who can successfully use the words 'rat bastard' in a sentence."

My eyes widened at the sound of the incredibly rich voice. I rarely blushed. Ever. In fact, it was usually me making others blush. But I did then. My face heated like I'd pressed my cheek against the sun. For a moment I got hung up on staring at his hands. The fingers were long and elegant, the nails filed down to blunt ends, giving away to skin a few shades deeper than mine.

Then the box moved up, and as I straightened, I let my gaze wander above the box, over broad shoulders and then to the very source of that voice.

Holy hot guy . . .

Standing before me was the living embodiment of tall, dark, and handsome. I'd seen a lot of sexy, but this guy was simply off the charts. Maybe it had to do with his unique coloring. His dark brown hair, trimmed close to the sides and slightly longer on top, framed high cheekbones and a cut, angular jaw. His skin tone had a deep, olive tint, hinting toward some form of ethnicity. Possibly Hispanic? I wasn't sure. My great-grandfather had been Cuban, and there were some lingering traits of his that had been passed on to me.

Striking eyes peered out from behind a fringe of thick lashes, and those eyes were truly something else. They were light green around the pupils and almost appeared blue along the rims. I knew that had to be some kind of optical illusion, but they were stunning.

This guy was impressive.

"Especially when those words are coming from a pretty girl," he added, his lips curling up at one corner.

I snapped out of it before I needed a bib to catch my drool. "Thank you. There was no way I was going to save that box."

"No problem." His eyes roamed over my face and then dipped, lingering in some areas more than others. Since I'd been knee deep in unpacking boxes and running around, all I was wearing was gym shorts and a fitted T-shirt despite the chilly weather. And the gym shorts could barely be considered shorts. "You're welcome to finish that 'Son of a bitch-ass' sentence. I'm curious about what other combination you were going to come up with."

My lips twitched into a smile. "I'm sure it would've been epic, but that moment is now long gone."

"That's a damn shame." He stepped to the side, still holding the box. We were side by side, and although I'm a pretty tall girl, he was still a good head taller than me. "Tell me where this goes."

"That's okay. I got it from here." I reached for the box.

He arched a dark brow. "I don't mind. Unless you plan on cussing again, then I might be swayed."

I laughed as I lowered my lashes, checking him out. He had a leather jacket on, but I was willing to bet my savings account that there were some nicely defined muscles lurking under the coat. "Okay then. My apartment is right over there."

"Lead the way, madam."

Grinning at him, I brushed the long ponytail over my shoulder as I headed to our left. "I almost made it without dropping the box," I told him as I opened the door. "So close."

"Yet so far away," he finished, winking when I shot him a look.

I held the door for him. "So true."

He followed me in and stopped. Things inside my apartment were kind of a mess. What I had managed to unpack was scattered across the couch and on the hardwood floors. "Anyplace you want this in particular?"

"Right here is fine." I pointed to the only empty space near the couch.

Walking over, he carefully placed the box on the floor, and like a total horn dog, I couldn't help a perusal of the assets when he bent over. Nice. As he straightened and faced me, I smiled and clasped my hands together.

"You just moved in?" he asked, glancing around. Boxes were stacked near the galley kitchen and on the small dining table.

I laughed as the lopsided grin reappeared. "I moved in yesterday."

"Looks like you have quite a bit to go before you're finished." Stepping toward me, he dipped his chin as he held out his hand. "By the way, I'm Nick."

I took his hand. His grasp was warm and firm. "I'm Stephanie, but almost everyone calls me Steph."

"It's nice to meet you." His hand still held mine as his lashes lowered, his gaze dipping again. "It's *very* nice to meet you, Stephanie."

Warmth curled its way into my belly at the sound of how he spoke my name. "Mutual," I murmured, lifting my gaze to his. "After all, if you hadn't happened along, I'd probably still be out there cussing."

Nick chuckled, and I liked the sound of it. A lot. "Probably not the greatest way to meet new people."

"Seemed to work just fine with you."

The half grin spread slowly, becoming a full smile, and if I had thought he was handsome before, it was nothing compared to what I thought now. Wow. This guy was as gorgeous as he was helpful. "I'll let you in on a little secret," he said, squeezing my hand before slipping his hand free. "It wouldn't take much for you to make it work for me."

Oh, my little ears perked right on up. What a flirt. "That's very . . . good to know." I stepped closer, tilting my head back. A faint cologne clung to him, a crisp scent. "So, Nick, do you live in this condo?"

He shook his head and a strand of dark hair toppled across his forehead. "I have a place on the other end of town. I'm just here, waiting to help pretty ladies carry boxes into their apartments."

"Well, that's a real shame."

His eyes flared, deepening the light green irises. A moment passed as his gaze held mine, and then his lips parted. "That it is." Lifting his hand again, surprise shuttled through me as he touched my cheek, dragging his thumb to the corner of my mouth. "You had some dust there. All gone."

My pulse kicked up, and as I stared at him, for the first time in my life I was absolutely dumbstruck. I was bold. Hell. My pappy said I was as bold as brass balls. Not the greatest imagery there, but it was true. When I wanted something, I worked for it. That mentality had been ingrained in me since childhood. Grades. Dance squad in high school. Boys. A degree. The career. But even in all my boldness, this man rocked me a little, and right off my game.

Interesting.

"I've got to get going," Nick said, lowering his hand. The smile on his face, that crooked half smile, said he clearly knew the effect he had. He headed for the door and glanced over his shoulder. "By the way, I bartend at this place not too far from here. It's called Mona's. If you get bored . . . or want to rethink your ability to string curse words together on demand, you should come visit me."

I knew how to read guys. It was definitely a honed skill, and he was extending an invitation. Just like that, he put it out there, and I liked that. My own smile was slight and most definitely mirrored his. "I'll keep that in mind, Nick."

* * *

A fine layer of dust coated my arms as I stepped back from where I'd piled the last of the broken-down boxes, lifting my hands to my face just in time. The sneeze powered out of me with enough force that my ponytail flipped over my head and nearly smacked me in the face.

Bent over at the waist, I waited a few seconds. Another sneeze was building, and I wasn't wrong. I sneezed again, surprised that I hadn't knocked over the stacked boxes with that one.

Straightening, I flipped the ponytail over my shoulder and took a moment to let it all sink in, past the dust and the skin, even all the way to the bone. I'd finally done it.

I'd moved.

Not to some apartment in the same town I grew up in or went to college in, but to a clear, different state, and for the first time in twenty-three years I wasn't within a twenty-minute drive of my mama. Even at college, I'd lived in a dorm that was no farther than a quick trip to her house. It had been hard—harder than I realized it would be. Since I was fifteen, it had been just my mom and me. Leaving her, even though that was what she wanted, had been difficult. There were tears, and that had been a big deal for me. I rarely cried. I just wasn't that . . . emotional of a person.

Unless one of those damn ASPCA commercials came on the TV, especially the one that featured that "Arms of an Angel" song. Ugh. Then there were tiny ninja onion peelers lurking under my eyes.

Bastards.

After two whole days of unpacking, I was done, and when I looked around me, I felt damn good about what I'd accomplished.

The one-bedroom condo was pretty sweet even though I'd really wanted a two-bedroom. I needed to be sensible for once in my life, though, and by sticking to a one-bedroom, I was saving bank. It had a great galley kitchen, stainless-steel appliances, and gas stovetop—a gas stovetop I'd probably never use due to my irrational fear of blowing myself up.

But the living room and bedroom were spacious, and I was also pretty sure a cop lived here, because there was a cruiser in the parking lot on and off since I moved in two days ago.

And someone who lived here had a really hot friend named Nick.

Score.

Walking over to where I'd left a framed picture on the kitchen counter, I wiped my dusty hands off on my cotton shorts and then picked up the picture. I carefully undid the bubble wrap, revealing the photo that rested safely underneath. Pressing my lips together, I ran my thumb along the silver frame.

A middle-aged, handsome man in beige fatigues smiled back at me, the endless golden desert in the background. A message in a black Sharpie was scrawled next to him.

Not nearly as beautiful as you, Stephanie.

I bit down on the inside of my cheek and walked the picture into my bedroom. The gray bedspread and the white, aged furniture had been a gift from Mom and my grandparents. It gave the whole room a comfy, cottage feel.

Heading for the shelf I installed just above the TV that I'd centered on the dresser, I stretched up, giving the photo a new home next to another special photo. It was of the girls from college and me, at

Cancun during our last spring break. A grin tugged at my lips.

The black bikini I'd worn barely covered my boobs. Or my butt, if I remembered correctly—actually, that was about all I recalled of that spring break. Well, that and those twins from Texas A&M. . . .

Everything was definitely bigger in Texas.

On either side of the photos were gray candles, and I thought it all looked good.

Like they belonged.

I stepped back and for a few moments I stared at the photos and then turned away with a heavy sigh. The clock on the nightstand told me that it was way too early in the evening to call it a night, and despite unloading everything, I wasn't tired. My mind wandered to Nick and what he had said yesterday about the bar he worked at. When I drove out to get groceries last night, I had seen it.

Biting down on my lip, I shifted my weight from one foot to the next. Why not go out and have a drink? And a drink could lead somewhere quite fun. I was a hundred percent full supporter of no-strings-attached hookups. However, I never understood, and never would, the double standard that existed. It was okay for the guys to take charge of their pleasure, but not women?

Not in my world.

If Nick happened to be there and he happened to be as flirty as he was yesterday, then tonight . . . well tonight could become very interesting.

I was *so* going to take Nick home with me tonight and do all kinds of bad things to him—naked and fun things that should burn my ears right off my head. Or at least cause embarrassment since I was visualizing said things in a public spot.

I wasn't.

Not in the very least.

A case of instalust had hit me hard. I was attracted to this guy on a pure primal level, and I was woman enough to admit that.

Moss-colored eyes met mine once more. Thick lashes lowered, shielding those extraordinary light green peepers. God, I've always had a thing for guys with dark hair and light eyes. Such a startling contrast that did very unhealthy things to all my interesting pulse points. I'd never really seen someone with his eye color. They were definitely green, but whenever he stepped out from under the bright lights over the bar and into the shadows, the color seemed to shift to an aqua blue.

Those eyes gave him some great bonus points.

"I'm way too curious, so I've got to ask. What in the world brings you to Plymouth Meeting, Steph?"

At the sound of the familiar voice, I twisted around on the bar stool and looked up, finding myself staring into the baby blues that belonged to Cameron Hamilton. When I first walked into Mona's, I was shocked to see a few people I'd gone to college with. I was still stunned over the fact that Cam and crew were here, several hours away from their normal stomping ground, which had been Shepherd University.

I'd said hello and quickly skedaddled my butt over to the bar even though I could tell they had a ton of questions, but honestly, seeing them had knocked me off guard. I wasn't expecting to find anyone I knew and I sure as hell wasn't expecting it to be not one but two guys whom I'd . . . well, been *real* close to at one point in time.

Talk about a wee bit awkward, considering I never really knew where I stood when it came to Cam and Jase Winstead's girlfriends. I'd discovered, a long time ago, that a lot of girls inherently weren't fond of other females their boyfriends had been involved with, no matter the seriousness of the prior relationship or lack thereof. Not every girl was like that, but most . . . yeah, most were.

Which was something I found . . . well, really fucking stupid.

Most girls were some guy's ex at some point in their life. So they were just hating on themselves.

So I tried to stay out of their paths when we were all at Shepherd, and that worked right up until the night I'd found Teresa—Jase's girlfriend and Cam's little sister—screaming hysterically after she found the body of her dorm mate. Ever since then, even though Jase and I hung out casually for a little while, Teresa had been bound and determined to be my friend. It did weird me out, and reminded me of a girl I had become friends with my junior year at Shepherd—Lauren Leonard.

Ugh. Just thinking her name made me want to throw my drink in someone's face. She had pretended to be friends with me when she really just hated my guts because the guy she dated had kissed me a year before they even met.

And it hadn't even been that remarkable of a kiss, surely not worth all the drama Lauren brought to my doorstep.

"I could ask you the same question," I said finally, picking up my glass.

An easy grin appeared as Cam leaned against the

bar, arms crossed loosely over his chest. "You know Calla Fritz, right?"

"I know *of* her." I glanced over to where the pretty blond girl stood with her arm around the waist of a guy that had military written all over him. I would know. My dad had *that* look. The look that screamed, *I know how to break every bone in your body, but I have a strong moral code that prevents me from doing that . . . unless you threaten one of my own.* The guy with russet, wavy hair was really rocking said look.

"Her boyfriend Jax owns this bar. Used to be her mother's, but that's a long story." Cam paused. "Anyway, Teresa's good friends with Calla, so when she comes up to visit her, we tag along. And since it's so close to Philly, it makes for a good trip."

"Oh," I murmured. Small world. "I just took a job at the Lima Academy and I'm renting a condo not too far from here."

"For real?" Nick said, drawing our attention and causing my stomach to dip in a pleasant, twisty way. "You're working for Brock 'the Beast' Mitchell's trainer?"

My lips twitched at the evident awe oozing from Nick's voice. Anytime Brock's name was mentioned, that was pretty much the standard response. Brock was an up-and-coming mixed martial-arts fighter and he was a local boy. Everyone seemed to worship him. "Yes. But I haven't met 'the Beast' yet. He's actually in Brazil right now, from what I understand."

Nick rested his elbows on the bar, his eyes drifting over me in a blatant perusal. "So, are you a mixed martial-arts fighter then?"

I tipped my head back and laughed. "Uh, no. I

took a job in the offices. I'll be assisting their executive."

"Nice," Cam replied. "That's what you majored in, right? Business management?"

I nodded, not entirely surprised that he remembered. We had been friends, and Cam was a good guy. So was Jase. Speaking of which, when I glanced over to where the crew was crowded around a pool table, it looked like Jase had Teresa in a . . . headlock?

Okay.

I grinned.

"So how long are you guys staying up here?" I asked, taking a sip of my drink as a female bartender with pink-rimmed glasses zoomed past Nick, shooting him a look I didn't quite understand.

Nick ignored it.

"We're heading back Sunday." Cam pushed off the counter. "Don't be a douche," he added, grinning when I rolled my eyes. "Get your butt off the stool and visit with us, okay?" When I nodded again, he looked at Nick. "You're coming over to Jax's tomorrow night, right?"

"Depends on what time I get out of here, but I'll try."

Interesting. So Cam and Nick were buddies. I was relieved to hear that. Cam was a good judge of character, and I already knew Nick was a helpful little charmer, but I felt like I could safely say that Nick wasn't a serial murderer.

I cradled my drink as Cam sauntered back to the pool tables. My mind wasn't made up on the whole visiting them thing yet. Maybe I would. Maybe I wouldn't.

"Want another rum and coke?"

My lips curled up at the sound of Nick's rich, deep voice. We'd been chatting on and off since I plopped my butt down on the stool, and he had seemed happy that I was there.

Total bonus points lottery with this guy.

"I'm good, but thanks." The last thing I wanted to be was drunk. I smiled at him, pleased when his heavily hooded gaze dipped again. "Are you guys usually this busy on the weekend?"

I could see that small talk was something Nick excelled at, which made sense, considering his occupation. He was an equal opportunity charmer. Women flocked to him at the bar. The other bartender, the girl with the pink glasses, seemed to take it all in stride.

"Not sure if you really call this busy, but Saturdays usually bring a larger crowd." He glanced down the bar before continuing. "So you went to school with them?" he asked, jerking his chin in the direction Cam had roamed off to.

"Yeah." Leaning forward, I placed my elbows on the bar. "I had no idea they had connections here. Total surprise."

"Small world," he said, echoing my earlier thought. "But you're not very close with them."

It was a statement, not a question. "What makes you think that?"

"Well, if you were, I guess you'd be over there with them. Or . . ."

Nick was observant. "Or what?"

One side of his lips curled up as he folded his arms across his chest. The movement drew my attention. I was *such* a visual creature. Not that anyone would blame me right now. The black shirt he wore stretched around well-defined biceps. "Or you'd rather spend the time with me."

The twisty motion in my belly cranked up a notch. "Am I that transparent?"

"In the best possible way." He picked up a bottle. "I'm glad you did stop by. Every time the door opened last night, I looked up and hoped it was you."

"Is that so?"

"I speak the truth." His smile was lazy. "Did you finish unpacking?"

"Yep."

"Were there any more rat bastard combinations?"

I laughed. "There were a few more."

"Kind of mad I missed out on them."

"There's always later." I toyed with my glass as I met and held his stare. "So, Nick, do you have a last name?"

"Blanco," he replied after a brief hesitation. "Do you?"

"Keith." I grinned as he unfolded those arms. "I have another question for you."

Moving in, he placed his hands on the bar. "Ask away."

"Do you have a girlfriend?" My breath caught a little when he leaned in suddenly. Our mouths were close enough that we were breathing the same tiny patch of oxygen. "Or a boyfriend?"

Nick didn't bat an eyelash. "Nope to both. How about you?"

Bonus points explosion!

"None," I said, welcoming the tingle that swirled down my spine as his breath warmed my lips.

He tilted his head to the side, lining up his mouth

with mine with just a fraction of an inch between us. I started to feel a little flushed. "You have plans tonight, Stephanie Keith?" he asked, voice deeper and rougher.

I shook my head as my pulse tripped all over itself in a happy little dance.

Nick's grin spread into the kind of smile I knew left a trail of women in its wake. "You do now."

Chapter 2

"*M*ake sure you're waiting for me," he said with a slow grin, picking up two empty glasses as I rose from the bar stool. "I'm off at one. I'll be there in twenty minutes or less."

I didn't respond as I backed away from the bar, giving him a little wave. There was no doubt in my mind that he would show up, and wicked excitement hummed through my veins. Smiling to myself, I wheeled around.

The girl with the pink glasses stood right in front of me, so close I almost plowed right into her. Behind the bar, she seemed much taller, but my five-foot-nine frame towered over her. A streak of pink in her hair matched her glasses, but that wasn't all that I noticed. Up close I realized that she also had a faint black eye.

What the . . . ?

She shoved out her hand. "Hi, I'm Roxy."

"Hi." I took her hand, shaking it. "I'm—"

"Steph. I know. Your friends told me all about you," she explained, and I immediately struggled to keep my expression blank as I stiffened. God only knows what they'd told her. "You went to college with them."

"Yes." My gaze flicked over her, to where Teresa and Jase were with Jax and Calla. Avery and Cam had already called it a night. "I was surprised to see them here."

"I can imagine." Roxy's smile was warm and surprisingly real as she stared up at me. "Anyway, I heard that you had just moved here, so I wanted to say hi and that I also hope this isn't your last trip to Mona's."

Okay. That was an odd statement. "I like the . . . vibe of this place, so I'd probably come back."

"I'm thrilled to hear that." Brown eyes brightened behind her glasses. "It's got to suck moving to a new town and not knowing anyone."

I nodded. "It kind of does. I don't think you realize how important your friends are until you're somewhere and none of them are there."

Sympathy flickered over her face. "I know this sounds random, but every Sunday, Katie—a really cool albeit weird chick—and I get breakfast. You're more than welcome to be a part of our threesome and sometimes foursome. Then you won't be somewhere without any friends," she finished with another wide smile.

Huh. She was really . . . friendly, but for some reason, I sort of felt like I was missing something. Like I walked into the middle of a conversation.

Before I had a chance to figure out how to respond to that offer, Roxy continued, "And also, Nick's a really good guy."

My expression started to lose some of its blandness. Was her overly friendly welcome linked to Nick? Obviously. Perhaps she liked him and had seen us chatting, making plans to get together later. There had been that weird look I'd seen her pass in his direction. Keep your enemies/competition close kind of thing? Some of the excitement that had been buzzing around in me dulled.

Goodness, I was so cynical. I was going to blame past experiences.

"Are you interested in him?" I asked, because even though I didn't know her, I was new to this town, and the last thing I was going to do was step all over someone else's shoes.

Roxy stared at me for a moment and then threw her head back, bursting into giggles as her ponytail swung. "He puts the 'oh-la-la' in the swoon, but I have a man I love very much, so no. Nick and I are friends. I just want to let you know that he's a good guy and, well . . ." She trailed off, shrugging her shoulder. "I just wanted to say that."

I really had no idea what to say to any of that. "Okay. That's . . . uh, that's good to hear." I glanced over my shoulder, finding Nick staring in our direction. I turned back to Roxy. "Well, I'm going to head out of here. It was nice meeting you."

"All right," she chirped, smiling brightly. "Don't be a stranger."

Smiling, I stepped around her and waved in the general direction of where Teresa and Jase were and then hightailed my butt out of there. Crisp air greeted me, and I had to actually crank on the heat inside my car. Autumn was most definitely here and winter wasn't too far behind it.

On the short trip back to the condo, my focus kept

moving from the unanticipated run-in with everyone from Shepherd, to the very unexpected quick chat with Roxy, to what was most likely going to happen tonight.

I had no idea what to make of the conversation with Roxy. I still felt like I was missing something, and honestly, I wasn't used to a complete stranger being that friendly or welcoming, especially to me. More than once I'd been accused of being standoffish and bitchy.

The truth was, it wasn't that I was mean or unfriendly. I just generally sucked at small talk with people I didn't know, and most important, I had a severe case of resting bitch face.

If I had a dollar for every time some random person told me to smile, I would have more money than the Queen of England.

As soon as I entered my apartment, I gathered up the boxes by the door and quickly carried them out to the large Dumpster behind the condo. As I tossed them into the opening, I stared out over the neatly manicured lawn. There wasn't a lot of land since the tall trees were thick, stretching into the night sky, their bare branches reminding me of skeletal fingers. Turning around, I hurried across the parking lot. At night, with the sound of distant traffic, it was kind of creepy back here.

When I returned, I checked the clock on the stove and then hopped down the hall, toward my bathroom. There was time for grooming—there *always* had to be time for grooming.

Grinning, I grabbed a fresh razor from the cabinet below the sink and got down to business, all the while my stomach dipping and twisting into pleasant little knots. I felt a little crazy as I got ready, as if I had downed a case of energy drinks.

Nervous excitement hummed through me like a persistent hummingbird. I wasn't unsure about what I was doing. Hell, I'd known people who'd hooked up after even less time between the first hello and good-bye. I wouldn't be stupid about tonight. If we got to the point where our clothes came off or a condom was required, I had them if he didn't.

The nervousness came from the fact that I was brutally attracted to him on a purely physical level. Nothing more.

A one-night stand only left you feeling empty when you expected more, and I wasn't expecting anything beyond a really happy smile on my face from this. To be honest, I hadn't once in my life wanted anything more from a guy except the required things, like mutual respect, safety, and sometimes, friendship.

I'd never been in love.

Not that I didn't believe in it. Oh, I so did. But I wanted the kind of love my parents had shared for one another—that everlasting, to the end, kind of love, and I had yet to get anywhere close to experiencing it.

And until I did, I had no problem sampling along the way. I mean, would you buy a car without test-driving it? Didn't think so. I giggled at myself.

I pulled the jeans back on, left my feet bare and settled on a cami with a built-in bra. Leaving my hair down, I padded back into the kitchen, snatching a lighter off the counter. I lit the candle I'd placed on the end table. Pumpkin spice filled the air as I walked back to the kitchen, placing the lighter in the basket.

A loud engine rumbled outside, and I whirled around, glancing at the clock on the stove. Fifteen past one. Could it be him already? I dashed over to the large window and oh so carefully peeled back the curtain and peered outside, like a total creeper.

"Hot damn," I whispered.

It was Nick.

It was Nick on a motorcycle.

I remembered seeing it parked outside Thursday but had totally forgotten about it. He'd parked right outside, near the front, and as he stepped off the bike, he tugged his helmet off. One arm went up and he scrubbed his fingers through his hair. I watched as he turned to the back, behind the seat. He started to lift something and that's when I forced myself to turn away from the window.

Pivoting around, I took a deep breath and waited while my heart rate kicked up, doing a tap dance in my chest. Less than a minute later there was a knock at the door. Slowing down my steps, I went to the door and peered out through the peephole just to make sure it was him before I opened it.

"Hey," he greeted me, his lips curling up. A blue plastic bag dangled from one hand and a helmet was shoved under his other arm.

I stepped back. "You said twenty after."

He followed me, nudging the door shut behind him with his booted foot. "Or less. You're forgetting that part."

"Ah, I am."

Nick lifted the bag as he strode past me, into the kitchen. "Brought us something." He placed the bag down on the counter and reached in, pulling out two bottles. "Got an opener?"

Flipping on the overhead lights, I went to the

drawer near the stove and pulled out an opener. "Apple ale? I like that. How'd you guess?"

He took the opener from me and flipped off the lids with expertise. "I figured you'd like something sweet." He offered a bottle.

The glass was cool against my palm. "I also like it hard. . . ." His gaze cut to me, and I grinned. "My drinks, that is."

Nick chuckled. "You seriously just said that?"

"I seriously did." I grinned as I lifted the bottle to my mouth, taking a small sip.

He shrugged off his leather jacket, tossing it on the counter beside the bag. "I think I like you."

"You need to remove 'think' from that statement," I told him. "For it to be accurate."

Another rough chuckle rolled out of him as he picked up his bottle. "Well, since we're being completely honest with one another, I wasn't really hopeful when it came to you showing up at the bar."

I raised a brow as I lowered my bottle. "Oh really?"

"Yep." His throat worked on the drink he took. "I knew you'd show up. It was inevitable."

"Inevitable?" I repeated. "That's a pretty powerful word."

His heavy gaze met mine, and the twisty motion in me returned with a vengeance. "It's the truth."

"You're a cocky bastard, aren't you?"

"And you're a cocky chick?"

I laughed then as I leaned against the counter, across from him. "Maybe."

"I like it. I can tell you're the kind of person who doesn't play games."

Nursing my drink, I crossed my legs at the ankles. "And you can tell this already?"

He nodded. "The moment your eyes met mine yesterday, I could tell you were the type of girl who knows she fucking stops traffic just by walking outside. You own it. There isn't a single bashful or coy bone or muscle in your body."

"And you could tell that just by looking in my eyes?" I snorted.

"Actually, I could tell that by those tiny ass shorts you had on yesterday," he remarked, surprising me. "There is not a single female out there with legs as long as yours who doesn't know that every guy they come into contact with is picturing them wrapped around their waist."

I blinked, knocked off my game once more with him. A moment passed before I recovered. "So, you like my shorts?"

"I fucking loved those shorts." He grinned as he lifted the bottle to his mouth.

Perhaps I should have worn them instead. "Well, it seems like you got me all figured out after two brief conversations, and here I am, not nearly as observant as you. I don't know anything about you."

"Not true," he chided softly. "You know my first and last name. And where I work."

"Wow. I could totally do a bio on you now." I watched his lips twitch into a half grin again. "How about we play a game? A question for a question."

He tilted his head to the side, lips pursed. "I think I can do that. Ladies first."

Brushing my hair off my shoulder, I took another drink. "How old are you?"

"Twenty-six."

"You're still a baby then."

He frowned. "How old are you?"

"Twenty-three," I replied.

"What?" he laughed, the skin crinkling around his eyes. "That makes no sense." He paused. "Unless older guys are normally your thing or something?"

I tsked softly. "It's not your turn to ask a question. It's mine. Have you lived here your whole life?"

"On and off. I was born near here." His eyes glittered. "Answer my question."

"Older guys aren't typically my thing, but I don't think I have a 'thing,' to be honest."

"Equal opportunity player then?"

"I don't think you understand how this game works, Nick."

He smirked. "My bad."

"Did you go to college or are you in college?" I asked.

Nick arched a brow. "Isn't that two questions?"

"Oh, you got me. Pick one then."

His chin dipped. "I did go to college. Is this your first time living away from home?"

I took a drink as I watched his thumb move along the bottle. "I lived in the dorm while I was at school, but this is the first time I've lived out of state. So, did you graduate?"

He nodded. "I did."

The question formed on the tip of my tongue. I wanted to know why he was bartending. I was curious, but not in a judgy way, because there was nothing wrong with bartending. He'd probably made more money than I did, but I pushed the question down. That was too . . . personal for me. Tapping my finger on the bottle, I searched for a good one. "What's your favorite hobby?"

"Besides fucking?" he said, his gaze hidden behind his thick lashes.

My stomach hollowed. Dear God, that was definitely putting it out there, and certain, important points in my body got all kinds of excited upon hearing that. "Yeah, besides that?"

"Hmm . . ." His gaze flipped to the ceiling as his lips pursed and then his gaze slammed into me. "If I had to pick one, I'd have to go with working with my hands."

A sharp swirl of pleasure rattled me. "For some reason, I think that has a double meaning."

One shoulder rose and he took a drink. "What about you? Favorite hobby?"

"Besides fucking?"

Nick's laugh was deep, but his stare was no longer lazy. "Yeah, besides that," he said, repeating my words.

"Um . . ." His thumb was moving up and down the neck of the bottle, and I couldn't help but picture that hand on me, that thumb moving likewise. My mouth dried and my mind was skipping around in dirty, dirty places again. I lifted my gaze. "I'd have to say watching movies. I've probably seen thousands and thousands."

"Interesting." He eyed me over the opening of the bottle.

I set my beer aside and clasped the edges of the counter on either side of my hips, waiting for his next question. He was taking his sweet old time.

"You know what?" Setting his own bottle aside, he pushed away from the counter, and I straightened, my hands slipping off the counter. "I didn't come here to play twenty questions."

My head tilted to the side. "Well, no shit." I smiled sweetly, even as a heaviness settled in my breasts and my blood felt like it thickened.

He was grinning that half smile again. "And you don't want me here to answer questions either."

I met his stare as he stepped forward, stopping right in front of me. Every cell in my body became super aware of his proximity. "If I say no shit again does that make me repetitive?"

"Only a little," he murmured, leaning in and placing his hands on my hips. "So let's say fuck the questions and answers and get down to what we both are anticipating."

The flutter moved from my chest and then down, low in my belly. "You're not the kind of guy to beat around the bush, are you?"

"Nope." His hands settled on my hips and my eyes flew to his. He held my stare. "And neither are you. You're done with these questions, too."

"I am?" My breath caught as his grip on my hips tightened.

"Yeah, you are." He lowered his head so that his mouth was near my ear. "Want to know how I know that? You started to get hot from the moment I said fucking was my hobby." He lifted one hand and without breaking eye contact brushed his thumb over the tip of my breast, unerringly finding and grazing my nipple. "And these have been getting harder by the second."

Oh, sweet Jesus. The bolt of pleasure shot out from my breast and scattered, lighting up every nerve. I was struck speechless, which was a new thing for me.

"And I just want to thank you for wearing this top." Both hands were at my hips again. "I like it almost as much as I liked those shorts."

I placed my hands on his chest and slid them down the length of his stomach, the tips of my fingers following the hard planes of his abs. "Then I think you might like what I have on under these jeans."

A deep sound rumbled out from him as his hands slipped around to my lower back and then down, cupping my ass. "I cannot wait to find out."

"Then don't." I tugged on his shirt, and his answering chuckle was rough. Glancing up, I let go of his shirt. "This is only about tonight."

"Then we're on the same page, aren't we?" He stepped back and reached around to his back pocket. He pulled out his wallet, flipping it open. Out came a silver foil, and I had to laugh.

"A condom in a wallet?" I said. "So damn cliché."

"And so damn prepared," he replied with a wink. He tossed his wallet and the condom on the counter. Grabbing the hem of his shirt, he tugged it up and off. Muscles along his shoulders and upper arms flexed and rolled as he threw the shirt to where he laid his jacket.

Good God, all I could do was stare. Boy took care of himself. His chest was well-defined and his waist was trim. His stomach was a work of art. His abs were tightly rolled but not overdone. He reminded me of a runner or swimmer, and I wanted to touch him.

"Your turn."

My breath shuttled out of me. I wasn't necessarily a self-conscious person, but my fingers trembled nonetheless as I wrapped them around the hem of the cami I wore. In a weird way I didn't understand, the fact we really didn't know each other made it easy to take the top off. Maybe it was because there were absolutely no expectations between us or because this was only about tonight.

Nick's gaze slowly left mine, and I stopped think-ing in general. The taut set to his lips and jaw was like stepping too close to an open flame, but the heat and intensity in his gaze was what started the fire. The look was hungry, and it was a punch to the chest, stealing the air right out of my lungs.

Silently, he lifted one hand and cupped my breast. The gasp that came out of me sounded strangled. He ran his thumb over the hardened tip and then he caught it between his fingers. My back arched and a smug half smile graced his lips.

"You're beautiful," he said, voice gruff. "I bet the rest is just as fucking stunning."

My heart was pounding and my voice was throaty when I spoke. "You want to find out?"

"Do you even need to ask that question?"

I smiled as I reached up, wrapping my hand around his wrist. I drew his fingers down my stom-ach, to the button on my jeans. He needed no fur-ther explanation. Nick broke records when it came to how fast he had me out of my jeans.

"You were right." His fingers skimmed along the thin strap over my hip as he turned me around, his hand following his movements, slipping under the lace along the center. "I really do like this, too."

The thong was nothing more than a scrap of flimsy material, no barrier against his heat as he slipped his hand between my thighs. "God," he said, his voice a thick whisper. "You're already ready."

I was.

I'd been ready from the moment he'd made his intentions clear. With his hand between my legs, he drew me against him, and I could feel him through his jeans, heavy and hard, pressing against me. My back arched and a breathy moan escaped me as his fingers went to work, slipping inside the material and through the wetness gathering there. I grabbed his arm, holding him to me, and the other slammed onto the counter. I braced myself as he curved his body into mine, his chest sealed to my back. Tension simmered to life as I moved my hips against his hand, building on top of itself as his warm breath fanned my temple.

"We can do it here if that's what you want. I can lift you up, get that sweet ass on the counter. Or against the fridge," he said, his lips brushing the shell of my ear. "Or I can take you on the table or the couch, fuck you right there." One hand slid up my side, sending a shiver through me as it closed around my breast. "Or I can just turn you right around, right here, and fuck you from behind." His lips skated over my neck, stopping over my wildly beating pulse. He nipped at the same moment he added another finger, causing me to gasp. "You tell me what you want."

Good God . . .

Those words almost sent me over the edge, and I was close, so close. The guy had magic fingers, and if he kept going like this, it would be over before we got started. "Like this," I gasped out.

"Fuck yeah," he grunted.

My undies were at my ankles and then, over the thunder of my slamming heart, I heard the tinny sound of his zipper going down. The condom was off the counter and on him before I had a chance to grow impatient.

Nick gripped my hips and lifted me up on the tips of my toes, then one hand disappeared and a second later I felt him between my legs. I didn't have to see to know that he was large. Then I *felt* it. He eased himself into me, inch by inch, and so slowly that every nerve ending felt raw as he seated himself fully. The pinch of pain faded and the pressure was almost overwhelming.

One arm circled my waist, drawing me up against him. His groan was deliciously harsh in my ear, mindlessly drugging. He started moving his hips, rocking in and out of me. There was nothing slow about this. Each thrust was deep and fast, wholly precise. This was . . . this was about fucking, and that's what he did—that's what I did. Pushing back, meeting each stroke just as fiercely.

I didn't get a chance to even aid the release along. Both my hands were flattened on the counter and the space between us grew until he curved his body over mine, pushing my upper body down on the counter. The coolness of the laminate was a shock against my heated skin.

The sounds of our bodies coming together, of my gasps and moans and his rough grunts filled the kitchen. The tension built and built, tightening up until my toes started to tingle. One hand slid up the center of my back, balling in my hair as he pinned me there, his hips slamming into mine.

I came in a burst and it was fast, powerful, and damn near blinding. I cried out, my body stilling as if I was being stretched, and his hips kept moving, kept pounding, until he pressed in, grinding against me. Pleasure poured into me, intensified with each thrust. His hoarse shout joined mine and he jerked, his body going still.

Aftershocks sparked. Tiny spasms shook me.

Dazed, I let the coolness of the counter seep through my flushed cheek. After what felt like forever, I opened my eyes and found myself staring at the stovetop. My lips curled up at the corners in a lazy smile.

Huh. Never thought I'd be breaking in the kitchen *this* quickly.

Nick eased off me, his hand dragging down the center of my back, lingering on my hip for a few seconds, and then there was a rush of cool air against my skin. "You still alive?" he asked.

I didn't want to move. "I don't know yet."

His chuckle caused the grin to spread. Pushing myself away from the counter, I bent down to grab my undies.

"Damn," he groaned, and I realized I was giving him quite the eyeful. "No words," he continued. "No fucking words."

Shimmying my undies up, I turned around. His pants were already buttoned as he disposed of the condom in the trashcan. I reached for my top, and as I bent again, I was surprised by the amount of wetness between my thighs.

It had been a while since I'd had sex, but geez, that felt a wee bit ridiculous.

I dragged my top on, straightening out the hem. My gaze lifted to his, and he gave me the lopsided grin. "I don't have words either," I admitted.

"Looks like we're still on the same page." Snatching my jeans off the floor, he came to me, and much to my surprise, helped me put them on, his hands straying in the process. When he was finished, he stepped back. "It's late."

"It is. You good to drive?"

A flash of momentary surprise flickered across his face. "I think I got just enough brain cells left to make it home."

"Fucking your brains out can be dangerous," I replied. "I'm sure there's an operating machinery and driving warning involved."

Nick tipped his head back and laughed as he reached for his jacket, shrugging it on. "God, I really do like you."

"Of course."

Still grinning, he shook his head as he grabbed his helmet. "You're welcome to what's left of the beer." He headed for the door while I slowly trailed after him. He opened the door and then turned to me. His gaze met mine, and the green of his was light and warm. "Tonight was . . ."

"Just tonight," I finished for him. "I had fun."

"Of course," he mimicked, and I laughed.

"Be careful," I told him.

Nick opened his mouth as if he were going to say something, but seemed to change his mind. He moved quickly, swooping down before I knew what he was up to. He pressed his lips to the corner of mine, the touch brief and yet entirely startling. It knocked me out of my bliss and forced my eyes wide as he lifted his head. "See you around."

I didn't respond, was totally incapable of it, as he turned around and walked out the door, closing it behind him. I don't even know how long I stood there, but at some point I had lifted my hand to the corner of my lips. The skin tingled.

That was the closest any guy had gotten to kissing me in a long time.

Chapter 3

"I'm good. I'm great." In the rearview mirror my blue eyes seemed way too wide as I clutched the steering wheel until my knuckles bleached white. "I got this. I *totally* got this."

Ignoring my pep talk, my stomach churned uneasily. I let go of the steering wheel and reached over, grabbing my purse. Prying it open, I pulled out the small bottle of Tums and popped one. The last time I'd been this nervous was eight years ago, and I ended up hurling all over my best friend's open-toed shoes.

I would not hurl today.

Not on my first official day of the rest of my life.

Okay. That was a bit overdramatic. Today was a big deal, though, as it was my first day as an executive assistant at Lima Academy. After all the education, I really had no idea what to expect. I could actually be doing the work I had spent years in college preparing for or I could be stuck with getting coffee and dry cleaning for my boss. If the latter was the case, it would suck, but I would do it. No matter what, you had to start somewhere. You had to put your time in.

Taking a deep breath, I snapped my purse closed and stepped out of my car. I smoothed my hand over my pencil skirt, drew in another shaky breath, and started across the parking garage, the clicking of my heels echoing my pounding heart.

Lima Academy was in a huge building downtown that had once been a factory but now was completely upgraded and converted into one of the premiere training facilities in the United States.

I'd already been to the building several times, during the interview process and then afterward, getting a basic layout. The first floor was a state of the art gym, equipped with practically every cardio and weight machine one could think of. On the second and third floors there were multiple rings, cages, and areas where mats covered the floor as far as the eye could see. Lima Academy didn't just focus on mixed martial arts or cage fighting. They trained boxers, kick boxers, karate, Brazilian jujitsu, Krav Maga, and during the evening, on certain nights, they offered self-defense classes to the public. The fourth and fifth floors were currently under construction. Andrew Lima, the owner and founder of the academy, planned on adding more training rings. The offices were all on the sixth floor, with the exception of Lima's office, which was the seventh.

At no point during the interview process did I meet the actual Andrew Lima or any of the members of his family, who apparently all worked for him at the academy. I'd only interviewed with Marcus Browser, whom I'd be assisting.

I took the elevator from the second floor hall, which fed into the parking garage, up to the sixth floor. My stomach was full of knots, and anticipation bubbled through me as I stepped out, coming face-to-face with frosted-glass doors that read: THE OFFICES OF LIMA ACADEMY.

Mr. Browser's office was in the back, past the field of cubicles and closed door offices. Fixing a small smile on my face, I headed down the center aisle, eased by the hum of conversation radiating around me.

Before I reached Browser's office, his door opened and he stepped out. Middle-aged and fit, Mr. Browser looked at home here, with his pressed pants and company marked polo. He wasn't alone. Another man was beside him, dressed in nylon sweats and a T-shirt also with the company logo.

"Ah, perfect timing." The dark skin around Mr. Browser's eyes crinkled as he smiled. "This is Stephanie Keith, our new assistant. Ms. Keith, this is Daniel Lima. He oversees the training facilities here."

Switching my bag to my left hand, I extended my right. His grasp was firm and warm. "Nice to meet you, Mr. Lima."

"Just call me Dan. There's too many of us Limas running around to go with formality." He dropped my hand, smiling. "And Marcus is exaggerating."

Mr. Browser scoffed but his smile didn't fade as Dan continued, "I only oversee the kick-boxing and boxing training."

"And Dan is way too modest," Mr. Browser explained as he folded his arms. "He helps out in all the areas. Without him, Andre and Julio would be rocking in a damn corner somewhere."

I had no idea who they were talking about, so I nodded and smiled. If I had to guess, Andre and Julio were also a part of the massive Lima family.

"I have to get going," Dan said. "It was nice meeting you, Stephanie. Good luck." He ran a hand over his bald head. "Working for this guy, you're going to need it."

Mr. Browser rolled his eyes as Dan made his exit. "He's actually the easiest of the Lima horde to deal with. Keep that in mind."

"How many are there?" I asked.

"That work here? Five, including Andrew. There are numerous cousins and nephews and God knows who else—because I swear, they are related to half of Philadelphia—but most of them you will never see. The brothers, though, are the only ones who have more say than I do," he explained. "Now that you're an official member of the academy, I'm going to cut the bullshit."

Um . . .

I blinked slowly. "Okay. I'm good with bullshit cutting."

His dark eyes glimmered with amusement. "What the Lima brothers say is what goes around here. Besides me, they are the only ones you answer to and who have authority to give you tasks."

Out of the corner of my eyes I could see that some of the heads in the cubicles were turned in our direction.

"The marketing guys are going to be climbing up your ass, I'm sure," Mr. Browser went on, "asking you to do stupid shit, like making copies and doing office supply runs. That's not your job. They have a person for that." He glanced to our left. "Yeah, Will, I'm talking about you and your lazy ass."

A deep chuckle rumbled out from somewhere behind the cubicle walls, and I guessed that was Will.

"Now, Deanna Cardinali, who you met when you filled out your paperwork, runs HR. You will be assisting her, and she'll be coming around soon to chat with you. This." He gestured at the wide U-shaped cubicle behind me. "This is your new home. You'll be within easy reach when I need you."

Turning to the desk, I got a little giddy inside. I was a total goober, but the desk, the computer and phone, the printer and the file holders, were mine. Okay. Well, they belonged to the company, but they were mine.

From here I would field calls and take notes, throw together manuals and set up calls and business trips, organize files, and according to Mr. Browser, ignore the sales and marketing team. From here I would begin my career at the bottom and climb my way up to the position Mr. Browser held. Maybe not actually here, at Lima Academy, but somewhere. This was all experience that would someday pay off.

I smiled widely as I placed my purse on my desk. "Got it."

"Good." Mr. Browser stepped back and reached into his pocket, pulling out a slip of yellow paper. "Now, I need you to pick up my dry cleaning."

It took approximately two days and three hours for the guys in sales to give credence to Mr. Browser's warning. There were two of them, and I honestly had a hard time telling them apart at first.

Identical hair styled in that messy on-purpose way, employing a week's worth of hair gel in one day. Both wore white polo shirts that were at least two sizes too small, as if they were shopping at Baby Gap. Both worked out . . . excessively. Their muscles were hard core. Shoulders thick, necks wide, biceps like bowling balls, and their hands were meaty fists.

And both spent more time staring at my breasts than actually speaking to me.

I had no idea what they thought they saw when they stared at my chest. Unless they had X-ray vision, none of my dress shirts revealed a damn thing. And if they weren't staring at my chest, it was my legs or my ass. They didn't even try to be stealthy. Whenever I caught them, their grins took on a leering quality.

They also tried to get me to pick up their dry cleaning, their coffee, print their reports, call to set up sales meetings, and just about everything under the sun. Normally I'd have no problem picking up coffee for them or anyone if I was already out doing it, but they always waited until I got back to the office.

Thursday morning, when I returned from getting Mr. Browser his double shot of espresso and, randomly, fresh peonies for his office, one of the Steroid Twins was hovering near my desk. I was pretty sure it was the one named Rick.

I pretended to not see him as I closed Mr. Browser's door behind me and walked to my desk. I set my cappuccino down, sending a hopeful glance toward the phone. There were no blinking lights signaling a message. Dammit.

Placing my purse under the desk, I powered up the computer and clicked on the Word document. The new employee packet was being revamped, and Deanna had me working on the welcome letter and the company policy sheets. Both needed to be updated with the information she had given me the day before. I scanned my notes, my gaze tripping on a few words that were so hastily scribbled I had no idea what I'd meant to write.

Heavy footsteps drew closer.

I focused harder on my notes as I picked up my cappuccino. The tiny hairs along the nape of my neck rose. I could practically feel his gaze boring into the back of my skull. How long would I have to ignore him before he went away? My eyes widened as the seconds ticked by. Would it be too obvious if I picked up the phone and pretended to be on a call?

Rick eased up on the other side of the cubicle, directly across from me. "Hey, Stephanie."

Obviously, ignoring him wasn't going to work. I sipped my steaming, caramel goodness and forced out, "Hi." I didn't want to be a bitch, but he and his Steroid Twin tripped my creep meter big-time.

He plopped heavy arms on the wall. "What you doin'?"

I kept my expression blank as I pointed at the screen with my pinkie. "Working."

"I can see that," he replied, undaunted. "What are you workin' on?"

Swallowing a sigh, I put my styrofoam cup down. "I'm working on the employee welcome packet."

"Sounds borin' as hell." His fingers tapped off the wall. "You doin' anything after work?"

Oh no. My gaze flicked up, and yep, he wasn't

looking at my face at all. His eyes were zeroed on my chest like they held the answers to life. "I have some things I need to do this evening."

His gaze didn't move. "A couple of us are goin' out to Saints down the street. If you change your mind, you should come."

"I'll keep that in mind." I waited another second, and when his gaze remained fastened to my chest, I cleared my throat.

Rick's eyes flew up and he had the decency to look a little embarrassed to be caught ogling. Pink flooded his tan cheeks. "So, yeah, what you workin' on again?"

I had to wonder how well Rick did his job. Luckily, he and his wonder twin weren't in the office a lot. Normally they were in the gym, securing new memberships or off lifting weights or something. "I'm working on the employee handbook," I reminded him with a hopeful glance at the phone.

"Ah yeah, borin' as shit right there," he repeated.

If I could have had any superpower at that moment, I would have chosen to make my phone ring on command.

"I don't know why they hired you to work up here," he went on, and I slowly raised a brow. "I mean, shit, you're hot as hell."

I started debating how weird it would be if I just, I don't know, slammed my face into my keyboard.

"If they had you down on the floor, we'd sell a shit ton of memberships, especially to the guys." He laughed, a high-pitched squealing sound, and I now contemplated the face into computer screen method. "Seems like a waste, havin' you hidden up here. It's obvious why you were hired."

I blinked and glanced up at him. "Come again?"

He winked, and my hands curled into fists. "Anyone with two eyes knows it's because of how you look, so it seems like a waste to have you sittin' up here, doing borin' shit. We could use someone like you on our team."

Shock struck me speechless as I stared at the guy. Did he seriously just say the only reason why I was hired was because of my appearance? Like he legitimately said that to my face?

"Hell, it made sense why the last chick was up here. She wasn't much to look at, if you ask me. Shit, though, hopefully you don't end up like her. Anyway," he said, smacking his hand down on the cubicle wall as he backed away. "If you change your mind, we'll be at Saints. I'll buy you a drink."

I'd rather get stuck at an airport during a snowstorm.

Rick ambled away, obviously feeling very confident about our conversation, while I turned my gaze to the screen. The words blurred as I stared at the computer. Numbness was like ice in my veins. I knew, without a doubt, I wasn't hired because Mr. Browser thought I was pretty. I was hired because I had a 3.8 GPA when I graduated. I was hired because I aced the fucking interview. I was hired because I was qualified.

Placing my hand on the mouse, I clicked on the screen and shook my head, dispelling the thoughts the conversation with Rick had left behind. Well, almost all of them. Who was the girl who had this position and what the hell happened to her?

Chapter 4

The black and white pointed heels with the dainty bow on the back were absolutely darling, but they were brutal. My poor toes were pinched and I was sure almost all the skin along my heel was missing.

Contrary to popular belief, beauty should not equal pain, and no matter how cute the shoes were, they were not worth the stinging bite of pain every time I took a step.

I tossed those suckers toward the back of my closet and slipped on a pair of flats that my feet welcomed. Wiggling my toes, I lifted my hands and ran them through my hair.

My first two weeks at Lima Academy had been exhausting, but in a good, fun, and productive way if I didn't count the run-ins with the Steroid Twins. They were jerks—relatively harmless jerks—but they were easy to ignore for the most part. Especially since I'd learned to be quicker with the pretend phone calls when I saw them enter the offices.

Every day there was some form of grunt work that involved me navigating the congested streets of Philadelphia either by foot or car to track down something Mr. Browser just had to have. But I was also learning, and the excitement of the new job was nowhere near wearing off, even if most of the guys on the sales team were total assholes who spent more time staring at my ass or breasts than working.

Swallowing a yawn, I closed my closet door and gave my bed a long, lusty look. I started toward it but stopped myself. Last night I had sat down around eight in the evening, for a few minutes, and ended up passing out, sleeping straight through the night.

I was not falling for that trick again.

Besides, I wasn't exactly sleepy per se, just weirdly tired. I really hoped I wasn't coming down with a cold or something. The last thing I needed was to potentially miss work for being sick, and because of that, I knew I should be staying in that night and resting, but I was bored out of my mind. And it was Friday night.

And I missed my girls.

For now, I Skyped with Yasmine and Denise, two girls who'd been with me my entire college experience, whenever we were free, which wasn't as often as I liked. Yasmine had moved to Atlanta and Denise was in Baltimore, which was too far from here. Once I was situated, I wanted to make a little trip to see Denise.

Grabbing my purse, I headed out to my car. Truthfully, I was feeling way too lonely and I needed to get out. Back home, there was always someone to hang out with or someplace to go, and I really hadn't connected with anyone here.

Well, except Nick, but that wasn't really a long-term connection. At least not yet. Who knew, though? We could become friends, but I wasn't going to meet anyone sitting in my apartment, marathoning all the seasons of *Supernatural*.

Mona's parking lot was pretty packed, and as I headed in, I wondered if Nick was working . . . and yeah, I also wondered if he had plans later. That last thought brought a smile to my face.

Music and pool balls clanking off one another greeted me as I stepped through the door. Grateful I didn't wear anything heavier than a cardigan, since it was rather toasty inside, I moseyed on around two guys and approached the bar.

I saw the girl with the glasses first—Roxy. She'd changed the color of her glasses and the streak in her hair. Tonight, both were blue and they matched her shirt. A laugh burst out of me when she turned, and I was able to read what was on her shirt.

A BARTENDER KNOWS HOW BAD HEAD IS.

The other guy, the one with the short bronze hair and military written all over him, was also behind the bar. If I remembered correctly, that was Jax, the owner. Near the well, Roxy was working; I squeezed myself in between two stools.

Only a few seconds passed before her bespectacled gaze drifted past me and darted back. Surprise widened her eyes. "You came back."

What an odd statement.

Roxy whirled toward the owner and shouted, "She came back!"

Um.

Jax arched a brow as he glanced in our direction and then shook his head. Unperturbed by the lack of interest on his part, Roxy looked like she was seconds away from doing a cartwheel. "I'm so glad you're here," she said, leaning against the bar in front of me. "What can I get you?"

Pushing aside the strange greeting, I flicked my gaze to the bottles beyond her and then gave up on trying to think of a drink. "I'll go with whatever you have on tap."

"Coming right up." Roxy whirled around, and like a little tornado, she moved behind the bar, returning with a full glass. "Want to start a tab?"

I shook my head and handed over cash. Opening a tab always ended with me drinking way too much. "Keep the change."

Roxy smiled, and I realized the bruise that had been on her face before was completely gone. She returned from the cash register after getting a guy sitting two stools down a fresh bottle. "I was starting to think I'd never see you again. It's been, what? Two weeks?"

"I started a new job," I explained. "I think it kind of wore me out a little."

"Totally understandable." She propped her elbows on the counter. "You're enjoying it here?"

I nodded. "It's taking a little bit to get used to the city. Where I come from, we don't have anything like that."

"Yeah, Calla—Jax's girlfriend—has said that, too. But she's actually from here, though she goes to Shepherd." She paused long enough to take a quick breath. "But you don't know her very well, right?"

"I just know of her. She seems like a really nice girl, though." I took a sip of my beer. "You've lived here your whole life?"

"Born and raised. I love it. It's really the perfect

locale. Super close to the city but still has a town feel to it—one sec." Roxy buzzed down the length of the bar, handling someone who walked up with an empty drink.

Taking another sip, I turned around and scanned the bar. There was such a unique mix of people here, young and old, all different ethnicities and backgrounds.

"There's a lot of hipper bars in the city," Roxy said, returning. She grinned when I turned back around. "Sorry. You had that look on your face. Not a bad one," she quickly added. "Mostly just checking everything out kind of look. I'm surprised we actually get a younger crowd here. There're so many more options in Philadelphia."

"But Mona's is nice," I told her, meaning it. "Yeah, it's not . . . the most in style." I glanced at the neon Coors sign over one of the pool tables. "But I like it."

"You need to get out more," came a voice from behind me.

Roxy folded her arms as she raised her brows at the intruder. I turned sideways. A tall man stood there, his close-cropped dark brown hair matching his classically handsome face. He winked in Roxy's direction.

"It reminds me of home," I replied, raising my glass to my lips.

The guy laughed. "Then I'm kind of worried about your home."

Before I could respond, Roxy sighed. "Shut up, Reece."

A smile broke out across his face as his gaze shifted toward her. "Oh, I love it when you get bossy with me."

"You're ridiculous."

"You love me," he replied.

"I don't know why." She sighed again, much more dramatically. "But I do."

So this was the boyfriend she'd mentioned last time. Nice. Roxy had good taste. Reece tapped his fingers on the shoulder of the guy on the stool. The man looked over at him, and Reece raised his brows. "Why don't you be a gentleman and let this lady have the seat?"

"That's not—"

Before I could voice my protest, the man was out of the seat. "All yours, officer."

Officer? Roxy's boyfriend was a cop? For some reason, I had a hard time picturing her with one. "All yours," Reece offered.

"Thanks." I sat down, and my feet thanked me. "You didn't have to do that, though."

Reece took the spot I'd been standing in. "A guy shouldn't be sitting when there's a lady standing. It's as simple as that." Stretching at the waist, he leaned over the bar and tapped one finger off his lips.

A pink flush spread across Roxy's cheeks, but she planted one on him. As she started to lean back, Reece's hand snaked out and curved around the nape of her neck. Holding her in place, he tilted his head to the side and really went to town.

Good Lord.

Watching them, I felt my eyes widen, and also felt the need to start fanning myself. That was a kiss and then some, and it just kept going and going. One of Roxy's arms had gone around Reece's shoulders, and I half expected him to drag her across the bar. A slow grin pulled at my lips, but underneath the amusement, there was a sliver of unsettlement. Almost like unease, but tinged in another emotion I had tasted earlier. I wasn't sure why I felt that, at this moment, but I sat my beer down on the bar, next to my purse.

From a few feet away, Jax turned to us. "Really, guys?"

With a deep, rumbling chuckle, Reece let go of Roxy, and she settled back on her feet, her eyes unfocused. Someone catcalled, and she blinked rapidly. Narrowing her eyes at her boyfriend, she straightened her glasses.

"You're terrible," she admonished. "And you make a horrible first impression."

"I think I make an awesome first impression," he replied, sending a grin in my direction. "I'm Reece Anders—the love of Roxy's life."

I couldn't resist that grin. "I'm Steph Keith."

"Ah, the infamous Steph." He glanced at Roxy. "Where is—"

"On break." Roxy's smile was too bright, too wide. "Sorry about his rude interruption. He's socially damaged."

"I'm also very thirsty," he replied, eyeing the tap.

Roxy cocked her head to the side. "You see Jax over there? Why don't you get him to serve you?"

"That's mean," he murmured, but he was still grinning as he pushed off the bar. "I'll be back." He wheeled around, heading toward Jax, who stood farther down the bar. As he rounded me, he tapped my shoulder with his fingers. "I like it when she's feisty."

I laughed outright as Roxy let out an exasperated groan that Reece largely ignored. "He seems like a handful," I said once he was over by Jax.

"Girl, you have no idea." Her eyes widened behind the glasses. "But he's . . . he's a great man, and I'm so incredibly lucky, like more than you can realize."

"Oh, sounds like there's a story there."

She smiled softly. "There is. I would . . ." She trailed off as another smile nearly split her face. "Perfect!"

Realizing she was staring at something behind me, I looked over my shoulder. My mouth dropped open. A woman had just walked in, and I . . . I didn't even know what she was wearing.

It was a dress. I think. A dress made out of . . . black duct tape, maybe? That's what it looked like. Skintight, it was nothing more than strategically placed stripes of some kind of black material. It crisscrossed her svelte body, leaving very little to the imagination with the amount of side boob that was visible. Her heels were high enough to make me feel like a wimp for caving in and going with flats.

She strutted in our direction, her hips swaying in a way that drew the attention of nearly every man in the bar. The tall, statuesque blonde had confidence for days.

"You know what I need," she said to Roxy, who was already grabbing a bottle of tequila. She glanced in my direction and her bubble-gum-pink lips pursed. "You're hot. Wow."

I opened my mouth, but I had no idea how to respond to that. At all. Nope. Nada.

"This is Steph." Roxy placed a shot on the bar. "Steph, this is Katie."

"Hi," I said, wiggling my fingers.

Her gaze dropped and she checked me out more

boldly than most of the guys there had. "Wait." Her pink-tipped, super long nails grazed her shot glass. "Is this *the* Steph?"

"The Steph," Roxy agreed. "She was the next one to walk into the bar after Aimee." Heavy meaning dripped from her words. "And . . ."

I started to frown. First, Reece referred to me as the "infamous Steph," and now I was "the Steph"? What in the world was going on here?

"Wow. This is awesome." Lifting the shot to her mouth, she slammed the drink like a pro. "This is so freaking awesome. I knew it. I totally called it." She tipped her fingers off her temple. "I'm psychic."

Wordless, I shook my head as I glanced at Roxy. The bartender's cheeks were turning red as she gave a lopsided shrug. "Katie has been dead on when it comes to her predictions."

"It's a gift. A curse. I fell off a greased-up pole one night. Hit my head. Long story that I'm sure I'll have time to tell you later." She propped a hip against the bar while I simply stared at her. "Is that your purse?"

When I nodded, she reached for it and, completely shell-shocked, I watched her open it and pull out my phone. Normally I would've been all over that, but all I could do was gape at her as her fingers flew over my phone.

"I've texted Roxy and me from your phone. So you now have our numbers and we have yours. There's no escaping us. We're going to adopt you as our new best-est friend-est in the world-est." She slipped my phone back in my purse and plopped it down on the bar in front of me. "You're going to get breakfast with us on Sunday. Of course, you're probably thinking 'Oh hell no,' but you're totally going to come."

I was still gaping at her.

"There is so much we need to tell you." Turning back to Roxy, Katie started to speak, but stopped, clapping her hands together. "I have the best timing. Ever."

For a moment I didn't know what she was talking about, and then I saw him. Nick. My heart did a little flop, and that shocked me as much as Katie did. My heart rarely flopped, and I hadn't really thought about Nick during these two weeks. All right, that wasn't a hundred percent true. I had thought about him a time or two or ten, but those thoughts were fleeting. So my reaction, the way I felt my cheeks flush and how my spine stiffened, surprised me.

Nick strolled out from a hallway on the other side of the bar. Wearing another dark shirt that seemed to be seconds away from bursting at the seams when he lifted his hand, thrusting his fingers through his hair, he looked as yummy as I remembered.

He went to where Jax stood talking to Reece, giving us an eyeful as he lifted a case of bottles onto the bar, his muscles rolling and flexing under the shirt. Reece said something, and Nick stepped back, laughing. The sound was loud and infectious, and my lips tugged up at the corners in response. He replied as he turned in our direction, his smile easy. His gaze lifted, drifting over the bar.

Our gazes collided in an instant.

Nick stopped in his tracks, as if he'd walked straight into an invisible wall. A strange tension seeped into his features as the smile slipped off his face. Shock splashed over it, and then he was heading in our direction on his side of the bar, ignoring Roxy as she stepped aside with a look on her face that said the only thing she was missing was a bucket of popcorn.

"Hi Nick," cooed Katie.

She was also ignored as he stared across the counter at me, his eyes as cool as winter mint. Tiny knots formed in my belly as he placed both hands on the bar and dipped his chin. All I could think about was where his fingers had been the last time I'd seen him and whether they'd end up there again, because why not?

"Stephanie," he said in that deep voice of his, and wisps of pleasure coiled tight. "What are you doing here?"

Chapter 5

His question squelched the budding tendrils of pleasure as if he had reached inside me and caught them in a fist. I drew back, inhaling sharply as my stomach clenched. "Excuse me?"

"Oh no," whispered Roxy, turning to the side. Someone waved a twenty dollar bill like a white flag of surrender and it caught her attention.

"You're a dumbass," Katie said to Nick, and then twirled toward me. "Give him hell. The payoff is so much better in the end. See you on Sunday. Tootles!"

As Katie pranced off, a faint pink crept across the center of Nick's cheeks. He lowered his voice. "I thought we had an understanding."

Perhaps, when I'd walked into Mona's tonight, I'd fallen into some kind of alternate universe? Every conversation I was in felt like I was only hearing half of it. "An understanding of what?"

He tilted his head to the side. "You haven't come back to the bar in two weeks."

"Uh. Yeah. I've been busy." My hair slid over my

shoulder as I leaned forward, the edges brushing the top of the counter. "I don't think I'm following where this conversation is heading."

"You haven't been back since the night we hooked up," he explained, his moss green eyes cool. "So I figured we were on the same page."

"Obviously we're not."

Nick glanced over his shoulder briefly, scanning the bar. His shoulders tensed when his eyes met mine again. When he spoke, his voice was low enough that I could barely hear him. "That night was just that night. One time. There's no reason for you to come back here, especially you."

Whoa. There was so much wrong in that statement I didn't even know where to start. Anger rushed to the surface, crowding my senses, and for that I was grateful, because beneath the fiery emotion was a keen sense of . . . of disappointment. I didn't know Nick that well, but from the brief time we'd spent together, I thought we had been on the same page. Not his page, obviously. His page had asshole written all over it, over and over again.

"Let me get this straight," I said, my voice surprisingly level. "You thought that I would not come back to the bar, because we'd hooked up?"

He didn't reply for a long moment. "That's how it's always been. One night. You said so yourself."

That's how it's always been? Wow. I almost laughed, except nothing about this was funny. "And just to make sure we're completely on the same page, you think I came back here solely to see you?"

One side of his lips curled up. "Well, why else would you come here? Someone like you is much better suited for the bars and clubs in the city."

My lips slowly parted. "Someone like me?"

"You know you're gorgeous. You know—"

"Stop right there," I ordered, placing both my hands on the bar countertop. "We are not and obviously never have been on the same page, Nick. You don't know me. I don't know you. And frankly, how I look has absolutely nothing to do with what *bars* I go to."

Nick blinked as surprise crowded his features again. "Hey, I'm—"

"You're unbelievable." I pushed to my feet, grabbing my purse off the counter. "The last time I checked, this bar wasn't your oyster and you sure as hell aren't the pearl in it. You may get to tell other people—other women—what they can and cannot do, but that will never, *ever*, work with me."

He drew back, brows furrowing, but I wasn't done. "I've never regretted anything that I've done. Until now."

Admitting the truth stung more than it should have. I turned away before I knocked him upside the head with my purse. I made it two steps before I heard him call my name.

"Stephanie. *Steph*." There was a pause and then, "Shit."

Gasps rose, and I looked over my shoulder, just in time to see Nick vault over the bar like a damn gymnast. He'd cleared the bar by several inches. My jaw hit the floor as he landed in a perfect crouch and rose fluidly. Was he some kind of superhuman? That move was rather . . . impressive.

Roxy stood next to Jax behind the bar. Both had stopped in the middle of handling drinks. Liquid sloshed over the glass Roxy had been pouring. Jax looked torn between laughing and yelling at Nick.

Tension seized my muscles as Nick stalked right

up to where I stood. He wrapped his hand around mine, the hold gentle. A good head or so taller than me, he towered over me, and all that made me want to do was punch him in the solar plexus. "We need to talk," he said.

"I think that's the very last thing we need to do," I snapped.

His eyes softened. "I'm going to have to disagree. Let's talk." A strand of dark hair fell across his forehead. "Please."

A huge part of me still wanted to whack him with my purse, or better yet, introduce my knee to a sensitive part of him, but most, if not all, of the bar was staring at us. We—actually, Nick—was already causing a major scene. Eyes were fastened on us. Heat crept up my neck.

"Are you going to make me get down on my knees and beg?" he asked, those lips curving up at the corners again. "Because I will. Right here."

"You wouldn't."

His eyes glimmered in the low light. "I would."

My jaw ached from how tightly I was grinding my teeth. "Fine. We can talk."

"Perfect." Nick winked, and turned around, leading me.

"We don't need to hold hands."

"But we do." He looked over his shoulder at me, his eyes widened with innocence. "I'm afraid you'll change your mind and run off on me, then I'll be all kinds of sad."

I shot him a dirty look as he guided me out. Everyone was watching. One quick glance told me Roxy had recovered enough to stop watering the bar. We headed toward the hallway.

"Nick." Jax appeared at the side of the bar closest

to us. "Don't make me have to clean down the office later."

My jaw snapped open. Fire was seconds away from bursting out of my mouth. "Yeah, that won't be necessary."

"I like her. A lot." Jax grinned as he turned back to the bar.

"Of course you do," Nick muttered.

I flipped him off with my free hand, but he didn't see it as he pulled me down a narrow hall. He opened a door to our right, and after I walked in, I immediately yanked my hand free as he kicked the door closed behind us.

Tossing my purse on a black leather couch, I spun around to face him. Now that we were somewhere private, every F-bomb known to man was about to make an appearance. I stepped toward him, my hands balling into fists as I opened my mouth.

Nick crossed the distance between us in a blink of an eye. He was so fast that I stood there like an idiot as he got right up in my personal space, placing his hands just below my jaw. His hands were large and warm, and he spread his fingers out, his thumbs smoothing over the skin on either side of my lips.

His eyes met mine and they were heated like they had been the night at my apartment. "I'm going to be brutally honest right now."

"Like you haven't been already?" I shot back, reaching for his wrists. I wrapped my fingers around them.

Nick smiled, flashing even white teeth. "See. It's that."

"What?"

"The attitude," he explained, drawing me closer. "When you throw it at me, all I can think about is getting deep inside you again."

My mouth dropped open once more. Honestly, I was just going to walk around all night with my jaw flapping open.

"I normally don't go back for seconds. Things always get . . . complicated when you do, but with you . . ." His voice dropped and his breath was warm against my lips. My body was a dumbass because an illicit shiver of pleasure coiled tight low in my stomach. "Yeah, I'd be willing to make an exception to my rules."

At first I wasn't sure I had heard him right. He couldn't honestly be suggesting what I thought he was, but his hands did a slow slide down my neck to my shoulders. The space between us vanished. His hips pressed against my lower stomach, and oh yeah, he was being serious.

Planting my hands on his chest, I shoved him hard. Nick stumbled a step, and in the back of my head I knew it was only because I'd caught him off guard. "Are you for real?" I demanded.

"That last time I checked I was," he replied.

"Then you have got to be the dumbest son of a bitchy bastard," I retorted, feeling the prickly rise of irritation and latching onto it.

The lines around his mouth twitched and he looked away, compressing his lips.

"You think this is funny?" I planted my hands on my hips and glared up at him. "What's funny is the fact you think you're going to 'get deep in me' again. I'd rather pluck each stray hair on my body one by one instead."

His gaze swung to mine. "You sure as hell didn't have a problem with getting naked with me two weeks ago."

"I didn't. Then you opened your mouth with your chauvinistic pig shit and ruined all the warm and fuzzies."

"Chauvinistic pig?" he repeated, brushing the hair back from his forehead. "Okay. I know I'm a dick. Trust me, but you and I—"

"We had one night. You're right. We hooked up. You left my place without an ounce of expectations between us, and I was cool with that. That's what I wanted. But you obviously think the whole damn world revolves around you." My eyes narrowed. "I enjoyed what we did, but just because I like sex doesn't mean I'm desperate, a whore, or stupid."

He took a step back as his hands dropped to his waist. Surprise flickered across his face. "I never said you were those three things."

"You didn't?" I laughed dryly. "You might not have said those three words exactly, but the fact that you think I came here looking for just you insinuates that I'm desperate. The fact that you think you can get with me after speaking to me the way you did tells me you don't think very highly of me. And after one night with me you think you can dictate to me where I can go and what I cannot do? You must think I'm stupid."

His brows flew up. "Steph—"

"Don't." I lifted a hand, stopping him. My middle finger might have been extended as I stepped around him and snatched up my purse. "This conversation ends with a—how about you go fuck yourself."

Chapter 6

Dressed in cotton sleep shorts and an old Shepherd University sweatshirt, it was a little after one in the morning. I'd returned from the bar and eaten half a carton of ice cream. Now I clutched the gray chevron pillow to my chest as the countdown began on TV and the camera zoomed in on Drew Barrymore. Her eyes were big, reflecting all the hope and anticipation every girl has ever felt when it came down to the moment you'd find out if your one true love felt the same way.

God, this—*this*—was one of my all-time favorite scenes in all the movies in the whole wide world. The moments leading up to when Sam appears at the baseball field, proving that he cared for Josie despite her betrayal.

Man, I was such a goober.

But I had no regrets. None at all.

One of my girlfriends from college, Cora, absolutely hated Drew Barrymore. It was the most bizarre thing ever, but her rage had never been able to dampen my love for this movie.

Granted, there was very little romantic about a twenty-something going back to high school and pretending to be a teenager while falling in love with her über hot and sensitive English teacher. That movie would so never be made nowadays, but there was just something about that first kiss between them that caused my heart to turn to goo.

I sat up, squeezing the pillow as the clock ran out of time and poor Josie looked heartbroken. Cameras panned on the audience, capturing their expressions of sympathy, and then a low murmur rose, turning into cheers. Everyone turned and there he was. Sam. A.k.a. Michael why-won't-you-be-my-baby-daddy Vartan. He hurried down the bleachers, and I could feel a girly squeal building in its intensity as my hold tightened on the pillow—

"Ouch!" Dropping the pillow, I folded my arm over my breasts and pushed against the sudden ache in them. They'd also been tender this morning. "Owie."

I had started to mentally calculate when my period was due when there was a knock at the door, jarring me. "What in the world?"

A sliver of unease brewed. It was damn near one-thirty in the morning and someone was at my door? Hell. The time didn't really matter because hardly anyone knew me well enough to know where I lived.

Snatching the remote off the arm of the couch, I paused the movie right when Sam hit the field. The knock came again just as I stood. I tugged down on my sweater and crept toward the door, visions of serial killers dancing in my head. Stretching up, I peeked through the peephole.

"What the hell," I muttered.

Nick stood on the other side of my door, his hands shoved in the pockets of his jeans as he looked around the empty hall. I dumbly stared at the distorted view of him. I had no idea why I realized he didn't have his helmet with him, because that wasn't important. What was he doing here? I was sure my parting words earlier in the night made it clear that we were so not on friendly terms. Nick was arrogant, but he couldn't be stupid enough to come here to hook up.

Curiosity overrode my common sense in about a nanosecond. Knowing I should just turn off all the lights and ignore him, I reached down and opened the door.

Nick turned to me, pulling his hands out of his pockets. Those light green eyes dipped briefly, all the way to the tips of my fluffy sock-covered feet and then back up. Seriously? Pressing my lips together, I folded my arms across my chest and cocked an eyebrow.

A faint pink bloomed on his cheeks and he offered a sheepish grin as he extended his hand. "Hi. I'm Nick Blanco."

Uh, what? I eyed his hand and then my gaze flicked up.

"I was thinking that we could start over," he continued, wiggling his fingers. "We kind of have gotten off to a bad start."

"I think we got off . . . to a very good start."

The grin became amused. "Okay. That's a good point. We did get off on a very good start."

"But then you ruined it." I shifted my weight from one foot to the next. "Really ruined it."

Now the grin slipped a fraction. "You're right. That's why I'm here." His fingers wiggled once more. "I want to start over."

Suspicion seeded. Normally I wasn't a paranoid or distrusting person, but I didn't get the point in this. "Why?"

"Why?" he repeated, his hand still hovering between us.

I nodded. "Yeah, why? We hooked up. That's all. And it seems to me that you'd be fine with never seeing my face again. That you prefer that, so why would you want to start over?"

My statement must've caught him off guard, because there wasn't a faint flicker of a grin on his face now. "I . . . I don't know."

Both my brows flew up. "You don't know?"

He shook his head. "Normally, I would be fine with never seeing a girl's face again. That's the way it is—the way I like it."

My eyes widened. "Well . . . at least you're honest, but that kind of just reinforces my question."

"I know." Nick's fingers danced again, beckoning me. "I just . . . look, can I come in and talk? It's kind of chilly out here and I really don't think your neighbors appreciate our one-in-the-morning conversation."

I glanced over his shoulder and shifted my weight again. "I don't know . . ."

"You're a hard one to crack." He lowered his hand.

"I'm uncrackable, that's why."

His lips tipped up. "I don't think uncrackable is a word."

"What are you? The grammar police?"

The grin was now back, softening the harsher lines of his face. "I am that person who silently corrects everyone's grammar."

"Oh. Wow. So not only are you a dick, but you're also an annoying dick."

Nick laughed deeply, surprising me. It was the same kind of laugh I'd heard at the bar tonight, before he realized I was there. A deep and infectious laugh. "And you really do say whatever is on your mind, don't you?"

"Pretty much," I replied. "You have a problem with that?"

"No. Not at all." He sounded surprised. "So you're going to let me in or is this it?"

I mulled over what to do. Nick had been a jerk to me, and his view on hookups was beyond archaic. He thought that he could tell girls that once they had sex they weren't allowed back in the bar? What in the hell? But then again, maybe the girls fully knew that going into it. I hadn't, but for some reason, Nick thought I had.

People made mistakes and screwed up all the time, and it wasn't like me to hold a grudge, but *this* had just happened. And truthfully, underneath the anger there was hurt. While I hadn't expected much from Nick, I wasn't expecting that kind of greeting. It stung. I was only human.

"By the way, not sure if you've realized this yet or not, but Reece lives in the same condo. Upstairs," he said, flicking his gaze up. No. I had not known that. "And Roxy spends a lot of time here. They're probably on the way here once she gets off, so it's going to get real awkward, me standing out here and them strolling on by."

My eyes narrowed into thin slits. "I haven't seen

either of them, but that makes sense. I've seen the police car a bunch of times."

Uncertainty flickered across his handsome face until I sighed and stepped back. "You're not getting any," I warned.

His thick lashes lifted. "I didn't come here for that. No. Seriously," he said when he must have read my doubtful look. "As hard as that is to believe— and I'm not going to lie, when I look at you, sex isn't too far from the brain—but that's not why I'm here."

"You always say what's on your mind, too."

"Guilty." He stepped inside, and I closed the door behind him. "I know it's late, but I don't have your number or I would've called you."

"You could've just waited till the morning."

He glanced at me as he shook his head. "Actually, it would've driven me crazy all night if I didn't come and at least try to talk to you."

Unsure of what to make of all of this, I bit the inside of my cheek and stepped around him. Nick glanced at the TV and raised a brow. "*Never Been Kissed*?"

"You say one bad thing about this movie and you can walk right back out that door."

He raised his hands in surrender. "I wasn't going to say a thing."

"Uh-huh." I plopped down on the couch, placing the pillow in my lap. "So are you going to apologize or something?"

Nick sat on the couch, his gaze fixed on the paused TV. For a moment I got kind of lost in staring at him. The guy didn't have a bad angle. His profile, with the high cheekbones and cut jaw, could launch a thousand razor blade campaigns. "I am . . . I am sorry about the way I acted. I'm kind of a dick about certain things," he said, letting out a deep breath. "I know that's not a good enough excuse. I do know you didn't do anything to deserve the way I acted. That was all me."

I decided to drop a little of the attitude. "When I went to Mona's tonight, I honestly wasn't going there just because you worked there."

"I know."

I took a deep breath. "But you were an added bonus of going there."

His gaze cut to mine and held.

"Not a huge bonus. A small one," I added.

Nick smiled as he leaned back against the couch. "A little bonus, huh? I'll take what I can get." Lifting his left hand, he knocked the hair off his forehead. "You . . . you surprised me."

Hugging the pillow close, I averted my gaze. "How so?"

"I don't know," came his now familiar response. "I don't really know you, so everything about you should surprise me, but it runs . . . deeper than that."

"I surprised you because I didn't think it was cool of you to expect me never to step foot in the bar again?" Incredulity seeped into my tone.

"I know how it sounds. Trust me. I know." Suddenly, the weariness was evident in his voice, dragging my gaze back to him. He was staring at the TV now, his brows knitted. I quickly looked away as he exhaled deeply. "I don't do relationships."

A laugh climbed up my throat and I cut it off. "That sounds . . . cliché."

He chuckled, and out of the corner of my eyes I saw him smooth his long fingers under his mouth. "Yeah, it is. But that kind of shit . . . well, it's not my thing. The . . . the women I get with, they know it. I don't lead anyone on."

"You didn't lead me on, but I honestly didn't know you'd flip out if I came to the bar."

"I guess I thought you wouldn't. I mean, I knew you'd come to the bar the first time, but I didn't think you'd come back." He paused, and I could hear the wall clock ticking. "I'm probably making no sense right now."

Not really, but I wanted to try to figure him out. Some people said curiosity killed the cat, but I was on the side that believed knowledge brought it back. "You said something at the bar—something about having rules?"

"Yeah."

My gaze slowly drifted back to his profile. I really needed to stop staring at him, but I couldn't seem to help myself. "You really have rules about these things?"

"Don't you?" he replied.

"No. I . . ." I trailed off. That was a good question and he had gotten me. I did have rules. "Well, I guess I do. Always use protection. Make sure I don't have different expectations than the other person. I have to like them. There has to be some kind of connection," I rambled on. "But I don't have to never see them again."

He rested the back of his head against the couch and turned his cheek toward me. "I have that rule so no one gets the wrong expectation. I don't like for things to get . . . complicated or messy."

I considered that. "Or you just don't like to get close to someone."

"Do you?" he asked quietly.

"Yeah."

"So why do you have sex with some guy you just met? Look—I don't mean that as a bad thing. I'm thrilled that you do—did with me. But that doesn't seem like a way to get close to people."

I shifted, curling my legs up against my chest as I pushed the pillow away. "Maybe it's because I have no problem hanging out with or getting to know someone I had sex with."

His grin turned wry. "Okay. You got me there." There was a pause. "But why don't you have a boyfriend? Someone like you can't be single for long."

"I'm not sure I like how you keep referring to me as 'someone like you,'" I admitted.

"It's not an insult." His serious stare met mine, and my gaze skittered away. "I mean it, it's not."

Wrapping my arms around my knees, I decided to let that go for now. "I haven't had a boyfriend in a long time."

"Bullshit."

I laughed. "Totally by choice."

"Explain," he demanded. "I need more details on this."

"Why is it so surprising? You don't have a girlfriend and you're hot. Granted, you are a dick, but a lot of chicks will overlook that for a nice set of abs."

"You think I have nice abs?"

I rolled my eyes. "You know you have a great stomach."

He chuckled. "I told you why I don't have a girlfriend. I don't do relationships."

"Well, neither do I."

There was a pause, and then, "I guess we are a lot alike."

Looking at him, I tapped my fingers off my knees. "I thought so."

"Past tense, huh?"

I nodded slowly. "I don't have anything against relationships. I'm just a firm believer in not wasting your time unless you see a future with someone. That doesn't mean you can't enjoy each other, but why put the effort into something when you know it's not going to go anywhere?" I shrugged one shoulder. "That's my motto."

"And you've never met someone that you thought would go somewhere?"

"Nope."

"Huh," he murmured. A distant look crept into his features.

My fingers stilled. "You have?"

One shoulder rose after a moment. "I did once before. Apparently I was wrong." The smile reappeared and was quickly gone. "Way wrong."

"So . . . like I said, you don't like to get close."

"No," he countered with a frown. "That's not the case."

I arched a brow as I laughed softly. "Okay. Whatever." Unfurling my legs, I stretched them out in front of me. As I wiggled my toes, I could feel his gaze on me, and even though I told myself not to, I glanced over. Our gazes met briefly, and then I looked away, swallowing. "By the way, I accept your apology."

"You do?" he asked softly.

Refusing to look at him, I stared at my socks. "I still think you're a dick, though."

"Kind of hard to believe you really accept my apology if you think that."

"Well, it helps that you're really attractive. I'm

shallow like that." I was lying. I wasn't *that* shallow, but I enjoyed his reaction.

A surprise laugh burst out of him. "I feel like I'm being exploited over here."

"Don't let my shallowness mean more than it does," I advised, fighting a grin.

"So I guess that means you—"

"If that sentence has anything to do with sex, I suggest not finishing it."

Nick chuckled. "Actually, I was going to say I guess that means you . . ." He trailed off, and when I peeked at him, he had the most boyish grin I'd ever seen on a guy his age. "Okay, I lied. Totally had to do with sex."

Smoothing my hands over my face, I hid my grin. "You . . . you are terrible."

"Possibly." A heartbeat passed. "I like the hair, just FYI."

Luckily my hands were still on my face, so he didn't see my smile grow. I'd forgotten that I had put my hair in pigtail braids when I got home. "Thanks," I said, my voice muffled by my hands.

"Can I ask you something?" he asked.

"Sure." I lowered my hands, twisting toward him.

He dipped his chin, causing that damn lock of hair to sweep across his forehead. "You were star- ing at me earlier, weren't you?"

Dammit. I tried to fight it, but I felt warmth creep- ing up my neck. "You're so arrogant. I was not star- ing at you earlier."

"You say arrogant, and I say observant." Nick shifted before I could respond, reaching between us and tugging one of my braids. He tugged gently, his fingers curling around the braid. "You and I cool?"

It took me a moment to answer and I wasn't even

sure why. Deep down, I already knew the answer, so I forced it out. "Yeah, we are."

"Good." He slid his fingers down, smoothing them over the loop, drawing my attention, and I was helpless to not watch his fingers work their way down. "Will I see you at Mona's again?"

Drawing in a short breath, I lifted my gaze, but he was staring at my braid. "Maybe."

"Say yes."

My heart was starting to beat faster. "Yes."

"That was easy."

"To see Roxy," I added, and I smiled when he laughed. "I'll make sure I say hi to you if you happen to be there."

"Make sure you do." Smiling, he tugged on my braid once more and then flipped it over my shoulder. His hand lingered in the space between us and then he cupped my cheek. The move startled me as he dragged his thumb under my lip. "It's really a shame."

I frowned. "What is?"

"Us," he said, his voice low as his thumb made another sweep, and my breath caught. "That you and I are the way we are. It's a damn shame."

Chapter 7

The smell of fried bacon and maple syrup caused my stomach to grumble like a monster straight out of a horror movie. It screamed, *Feeeed meeee*.

Stopping in front of the empty hostess station, I stretched up on the tips of my sneakers and scanned the booths for two somewhat familiar heads. The texts from Roxy and Katie had started Saturday evening, and I would've agreed to meet them Sunday morning right off the bat, but their escalating pleas and messages had been quite entertaining. At one point Katie had threatened to break into my apartment and draw a mustache on my face if I didn't come.

The funny part was, I wouldn't have said no to them. Sure, Katie, whom I'd only met briefly, seemed like she might be missing a few screws, but whatever. Who was I to judge? I missed my old friends and our weekly, or sometimes triweekly, meet-ups. Admittedly, I was a social creature most of the time, and the loneliness I'd been wallowing in wasn't going anywhere.

I spotted Roxy and her blue glasses toward the back of the busy restaurant. The walkways between the booths were crowded with racing kids covered in sticky jelly and older people trying to rein them in as I made my way toward them.

Roxy's hair was pulled up in a messy bun and her eyes squinted as she glanced up at me. "You seriously went running before you came here. You weren't lying."

"Nope. I try to run every day." I sat beside Katie, who compared to Friday night was dressed down in a baby blue off-the-shoulder sweater that looked like sequins had thrown up on it. Her blond hair was pulled back in a low ponytail at the nape of her neck. "I have to work out," I explained, placing my purse between Katie and me. "I eat like five starving guys in college. It's actually embarrassing how much food I can consume in one sitting."

Katie laughed. "I don't have that problem. I can eat whatever I want and not gain a pound. Actually, I'd probably lose weight." Her shoulders rose in a shrug. "Sucks to be you all."

Roxy scowled at her. "You don't need to rub it in, you know."

"Don't hate me because I was born this way." Katie grinned when Roxy rolled her eyes. "Maybe it's Maybelline. Maybe it's Katie."

I giggle snorted.

The waitress appeared at our table, clicking the pen she'd pulled out of the pocket of her apron. She took our drink order and then dashed off to fulfill it, her white sneakers squeaking across the floor.

"I'm glad you came," Roxy said, propping her elbows on the table. "I was worried I was going to have to search you down and force you to come eat with us."

I laughed again. "I'm pretty sure you'd have a hard time doing that."

"I'm scrappy." Roxy grinned. "I could take you."

Thinking of the shiner I'd first seen her with, I decided she was probably telling the truth. "I'm glad you guys invited me." I paused while the wait-ress returned with our drinks before disappearing again, then I said, "So, I know Roxy works at the bar, what about you, Katie?"

"At the club across the street from Mona's." Katie dumped a packet of sugar into her coffee and then picked up five more, managing to rip the tops off in one impressive swipe. "It's a strip club."

"Oh." How had I not noticed a strip club across the street from Mona's?

Katie dumped the sugar in her coffee. "I strip. I don't dance. I take my clothes off for a living and get paid damn good money for it, too."

I blinked. "That's cool."

Her gaze turned shrewd. "You don't have a prob-lem with that?"

"Um, not if you don't." I glanced at Roxy, who was busy cleaning her glasses, a small smile pulling at her face. I picked up my soda and took a deep drink.

Katie tilted her head to the side, studying me. "Really?"

I lifted a shoulder. "Nope. Honestly. I think it's pretty cool you have the lady balls to do it."

A slow grin appeared. "You should do it. You'd make so much money. Hell, I'd pay to see you—"

"Katie," sighed Roxy, resting her chin in her hand. "Stop trying to recruit rookie strippers. You do this every time you meet someone. No one has agreed yet."

I grinned as I pictured the odd blonde roaming the city, looking for women who wanted to take their clothes off. "I don't think I could do it. I'd get up there and then forget how to take my clothes off."

"Taking your clothes off is the easiest part," Katie replied seriously.

Roxy looked doubtful. "Those spandex running pants leave very little to the imagination. If I had your body, I'd walk around naked all day."

"I have no problem getting naked when it's—I don't know, an intimate situation," I announced, "but doing it in public is a different story."

"That's good to know," the waitress said, pen in hand. "Do you guys know what you want to eat?"

"Awkward," I murmured under my breath as my eyes widened.

Roxy giggled, and we quickly placed our orders. Katie ordered grits and a waffle, and I went with an omelet and a side order of bacon. Roxy went for some kind of fruit thing and a bagel. I watched the waitress zoom away and then said, "Well then . . ."

"I think she needed to know your getting naked preferences," Roxy said, sitting back against the worn red booth. "So how is it working out at the Lima Academy?"

"You're surrounded by hot guys from nine to five, right?" Katie perked up, like a bell had been rung. "Especially Brock. *Mmm.* Goodness. Brock can get all beastie with me anytime he wants," she said, and I almost spit out my drink when she added, "My vagina would have its own personal landing strip for him."

"Oh my God," Roxy whispered as she snickered. "The imagery. I'll never get it out of my head now."

I never wanted that imagery in my head. "I actually don't see a lot of people, and I have yet to meet Brock. I think he's coming back next week or something, but it's pretty cool. I've been doing a lot of running around, but all and all, it's what I expected." I lifted up, sitting with my legs crossed. I always had to. It was weird, but I wouldn't be comfortable if I didn't. "Everyone is nice. Well, except these two guys that work in sales."

"Are they mean or something?" Roxy asked.

I shook my head. "Not really. Just overbearing and douchey. One of them said the only reason why I got hired was because of the way I looked." Flipping my ponytail over my shoulder, I rolled my eyes. "And he meant that as a compliment. For real. Like I should've thanked him for that."

"Wow." Roxy frowned and her glasses slipped down her nose. "What an ass."

"Pretty much." No arguing that. "He said something about the girl who used to work in my position, but I don't remember much other than him saying he hoped I didn't end up like her."

Blood drained from Roxy's face so rapidly I jolted forward. "Oh God, are you okay?" I asked, wondering if she had some kind of medical condition.

"Yeah. Yes. It's just that . . ." She trailed off, straightening her glasses.

"Wait." Katie wrinkled her nose. "Wasn't that girl attacked by the Kip Corbin creep?"

"Yeah," Roxy confirmed quietly.

Something was most definitely going on, and I didn't have to wait too long before Katie expanded on the details. "If you ask me, a guy with two first names as their first and last name just says bad shit is on the way," she said, and I pursed my lips together, because that didn't make a lot of sense to me. "Kip Corbin was this freak who basically stalked Roxy for months and attacked a bunch of other women."

"What?" My eyes nearly popped out of my head as my voice rose a notch.

Our conversation halted while the waitress brought our food, and all the plates of yummie goodness sat untouched while Roxy fidgeted with her fork. "He was this guy who lived above me," she said. "Seemed normal. Obviously wasn't. He was basically a budding serial killer."

My jaw dropped.

"He attacked a lot of other girls. I was lucky." She smiled tightly, and again I thought of the bruise I'd seen on her. That was now explained. Good God. Horror swamped me. "Reece showed up in time and . . ." Color hadn't returned to her cheeks as she stared at her plate of food. "I was very lucky."

"Total white knight right there." Katie stabbed her bowl of grits with her fork. "But that girl who used to work at Lima, she was the last executive assistant."

Holy crap.

And Rick had made the poor woman's exit sound like it wasn't a big deal. God, he was grosser than I had given him credit for. One look at Roxy told me she wasn't doing too well. I reached over and squeezed her hand. "I'm sorry. I didn't mean to bring it up."

"It's okay." She squeezed my hand back. "You had no way of knowing. And it's in the past."

"And Kip Corbin is dead." Katie shoved a heap of

grits into her mouth. "The girl who used to work at Lima was Isaiah's cousin. And of course, you don't know who Isaiah is, but you'll probably meet him at some point at Lima. I think he's a funder of the academy or something, or whatever you call people who pay for stuff." She scooped up another mouthful. "Anyway, Isaiah is like the legit mafia. Everyone here knows that. Don't get on his bad side."

My gaze swung sharply to Roxy. "For real?"

"For real." She forked up a strawberry. "Kip ended up hanging himself in jail, but it was real suspicious. No one crosses Isaiah or messes with one of his own."

Picking up my knife and fork, I started to cut my omelet into absurdly small pieces. Hot UFC fighters. Sexy bartenders. A serial killer. And now a mob boss? This was like a romance novel. Or a Lifetime movie channel. Geez.

"Let's talk about something else," I suggested. Relief eased the taut line of Roxy's shoulders. I searched for something else and settled on familiar grounds—the connection between here and Shepherdstown. "I'm still kind of in shock that you all know everyone from Shepherd. It's a small world."

"I know!" Roxy exclaimed, her eyes brightening. "It's bizarre—amazing—but crazy bizarre. I know they were just as surprised as you were. I know you don't know Calla well, but I hope you get to hang out with her when she comes back to visit. She usually spends every other weekend here with Jax."

"That would be cool," I murmured, forking the omelet into my mouth.

Katie snickered. "You said, as enthused as a kid opening up a package of socks Christmas morning. Why's that? You don't like Calla?"

"No. I mean, I like Calla, but, I don't know her, but . . ."

"But what?" Katie prodded.

Pushing the fluffy yellow stuff around my plate, I didn't know how to respond, because I wasn't sure how much Calla had known and told Roxy. I picked up a slice of bacon and crunched away. By the time I finished, I decided to be truthful, because why not?

Wasn't like I was ashamed of anything Calla could've told Roxy.

"I'm not sure if she likes me," I said, picking up another slice of salty, greasy bacon.

"What?" Roxy's lips parted as she pushed her glasses back up her nose. "Why would you think that?"

"Well, maybe because I've had relations with Cam . . . and Jase at one point." I went for a drink of cool soda. "Not when they were with Avery or Teresa or anything like that, but . . . yeah, some girls don't care if that was in the past, before them. And Calla is really close to Teresa."

"Oh." Roxy blinked once and then twice. "Calla never mentioned anything like that."

Pressing my lips together, I resisted the urge to smack myself in the face. Well, perhaps this was an even worse conversation idea. Go Steph! "Well . . ." I raised my hands with a shrug. "Anyway, I'm not really close to any of those girls for that reason."

"But all of them seemed super excited to see you," Roxy insisted, frowning. "None of them were catty or gave you the side eye. And I notice all cattiness from a mile away. It's like a special radar I have."

Hmm. Maybe they were cool with me? But I wasn't even sure Teresa knew about Jase and my one and only hookup. I knew Avery had found out about Cam, but Avery was always hard to read. Maybe I should've just kept my mouth shut about all of this. I barely knew these girls and I just told them I'd hooked up with two random guys they knew.

I went back to pushing my omelet on my plate. "You probably think that sounds slutty—"

"No. I don't," Roxy stated firmly. "Not to me."

My lips curved up in a smile. "Contrary to what some might believe, the list of guys I've been with isn't as long as my arm."

"Mine is as long as my leg," Katie replied and then tipped her head back. Her brows furrowed together. "Well, wait. Probably as long as both legs and an arm."

"Wow," murmured Roxy, appearing impressed.

"Sounds like you have me beat." My smile raised a notch as I peeked at her. "But it's weird being close to them—Avery and Teresa. Which is strange, because one of my other friends—Yasmine—she'd messed around with Cam, too, and it's not weird for us."

"Was Yasmine in love with Cam and Cam in love with her?" Roxy asked. "Because if not, then that probably explains it." She popped a piece of canta-loupe into her mouth. "And you weren't in love with him either, right?"

"Nope. Good point."

"I bet some chicks think you're a real tramp." Katie laughed.

My smile slipped off my face. "Well, yeah, I'm sure some do. Actually, I know some do." Sud-denly, I thought of Nikki Glenn, a girl who was in my English 102 class my second semester at Shep-herd. "This one girl, a couple of years ago, wrote 'vengeful tramp' in shaving cream on the hood of my car."

Roxy's eyes widened behind the glasses. "Oh, wow."

"In September, during a heat spell." Pursing my lips, I nodded. "Yep. I ended up having to get a paint job. That doesn't come off. And just imagine the looks I got when I drove the car into the body shop."

"Did you sleep with her man or kick her dog into traffic?" Katie asked.

It was my turn to laugh. "No. I've never slept with a guy—at least knowingly—that was involved with someone else. Nor have I kicked any animal. This girl was mad because I was friends with her boyfriend. I'd known him for years, long before she came into the picture. We went to high school together and had gone to homecoming as each other's dates one year. That was it. According to her, based on my reputation, I'd slept with every guy I've ever talked to." I paused, thinking back. "Ironically, they are no longer together and I still chat with the guy whenever we see each other."

I shrugged a shoulder. "The funny thing is, Donnie—that was the girl's boyfriend—he was such a player before he met Nikki. Now he is probably someone who has two legs and two arms worth of girls he'd been with, and she didn't have a problem with him sleeping with an entire zip code worth of chicks, but boy did she have one with me, and I hadn't even so much as kissed the dude on the cheek."

"They never do," was Katie's sagelike reply.

"I don't get it." Roxy slathered a continent-sized amount of cream cheese on her bagel. "Like why would anyone care who someone was with if it was in the past and everyone was safe about it? Consensual sex or whatever between two people isn't shocking. I don't walk around thinking Reece has never been with anyone but me, and he knows I've been with other guys before. And I know damn well Avery and Teresa don't think their guys haven't been with anyone else. That whole mentality is stupid."

"Yeah, it is," I murmured, staring at my plate as an old burning sensation picked up in my gut. What people thought of me, especially virtual strangers who had absolutely no impact on my life, didn't bother me most of the time. But I genuinely liked Cam and Jase, so that meant I liked their girlfriends by extension, and . . . yes, I wanted to be liked by them, too. I didn't want them to think I was lurking in the shadows somewhere, about to pounce on their guys. Truthfully, though, there were times when the opinions of virtual strangers like that of Nikki Glenn did get to me. Moments when whispered words and harsh looks had cut deeper than they should— moments when words like "slut" and "whore" were laced with enough venom to take me down.

I'll never really understand it, I realized as I sat there, staring at the red and green flecks of the left-over peppers, why others' sexual habits bothered people—especially other women—so much. Of all people, you'd think women would be more tolerant of other women's choices, but sadly, a lot aren't. In a lot of ways they could be worse than the guys. It wasn't like I was sitting in judgment over those who waited for marriage or believed sex automatically equaled love. I could care less if someone had two partners or fifty. So why did they have to?

"You know what? Fuck 'em," Katie replied, moving onto the waffle that was as wide as her plate. "That's my motto. Because here's the deal. They hate on you because you had mutual, consensual humping with some guys who weren't even involved with anyone, while they worship the dirty-ass ground the guy walks on, like they slipped and fell into your vagina, for doing the same thing? That's what we like to call dumb double standards, and what we in the business like to also call 'Mind your own business.' No matter how many times it's explained to those kind of people, they aren't going to understand. Never. Dude, that's their problem. Not yours."

"True," Roxy said, nodding.

"Women are each other's worst enemy, you know?" Katie continued. "Wives and girlfriends all the time come into the club, pissed off at *me*, because *their* husband or boyfriend came there on *his* own free will. Like, just because I strip, I want to get with their goofy ass husbands." She rolled her blue eyes so far back I worried they'd get stuck. "And if doing that and having safe and fun times with available dudes makes me a slut, I have no problem getting that tattooed on my middle finger."

Suddenly, without any one reason I could put my finger on, the back of my eyes started to burn, and I think I fell a little in love with Roxy and Katie at that moment.

These were my people.

Roxy's gaze bounced from Katie to me, and her smile turned soft and mischievous. "Speaking of guys who are players, players, I have to bring up Nick."

A strange pressure clenched my chest as I scooped

up the last of my omelet. Nick. Oh, Nicky boy. I was
so doing my best to not think of him and his parting
words.

That you and I are the way we are.

What in the hell was that supposed to mean and
why was it a shame? And why did he have to be
so freaking hot *and* really shitty when it came to
dealing with the opposite sex? Ugh. Double and
triple ugh.

"Yeah," Katie said. "Now let's get to the good
stuff." She twisted toward me. "So you and Nick
hooked up. Congrats on that. I imagine that was a
good and decent hard fucking."

The fluffy egg and diced bell peppers I'd just
eaten almost got stuck in my throat. I swallowed
quickly and then dragged in air. "What?"

Finished with her food, Roxy pinned me with a
no nonsense stare that would've made my mama
proud. "We know you hooked up with him."

"Did he tell you that?" I blurted out.

Roxy grinned. "No, but you just confirmed what
we already knew."

My eyes narrowed. Dammit. "If he didn't, then
how did you know?"

"Because of what he said to you when he saw you
Friday night in the bar," Katie explained. "He didn't
expect you to come back. Therefore, that means y'all
did the nasty. That's his M.O."

"You guys know about his . . . I guess, his rule?"
I started to fiddle with the wrapper the straw had
come in, folding it like an accordion. Although I had
sincerely forgiven him, anger brewed. "Did everyone know about that except me?"

"Well, everyone who knows him does." Roxy's

brows knitted as she studied me. "He didn't set up ground rules or something before you all got down to business?"

This was such a weird conversation, when I thought about it. "Not really. At least not in a way that I understood what he was saying. Having a rule where a girl can't go back to the bar after sleeping with him is about the dumbest thing I'd ever heard of."

"You'd be surprised by how many chicks he's hooked up with who're totally okay with it," Roxy replied dryly, and then leaned forward, placing her elbows on the table. "But as long as they're cool with it, too, whatever, but man, when you told him off at the bar, it was freaking priceless. Don't get me wrong. I consider Nick a friend, and we get along because we're just friends, but I wished I had thought to record that."

I'm glad she hadn't.

"I'm so disappointed I missed that." Katie sighed heavily. "But you gave him hell. He needs that. Hell, most people need that every now and then."

"Oh man, and when he jumped over the bar to stop you from leaving?" Roxy fanned her face with her hand. "I need to get Reece to do that at least once a week for me."

I coughed out a laugh. "Yeah, that was kind of impressive."

"And I also missed that." Katie pouted. "Such bullshit."

Roxy grinned. "So are you going to give us the details?"

"Apparently you all already know everything." I straightened out my straw wrapper and then began folding it again. "Not many details left."

"There's always detail," Katie corrected. "But I don't have to ask if he's good or not, because one look at him tells me he's good at it."

A flush stained Roxy's cheeks. "And that's not the kind of detail we're asking for. I know he went to see you after he left Mona's Friday night. His car was in the condo parking lot."

So he did drive a car. I shook my head. "He did stop by Friday night, but we didn't do anything. He actually came over to apologize to me."

Roxy's brows climbed her forehead as she exchanged a look with Katie. "Say what?"

I glanced at the bedazzled girl next to me. "He came over to apologize for the way he acted." I paused. "Obviously, that must be shocking behavior for him."

"Shocking doesn't really even cover it." Roxy blinked a couple of times. "Did he try to get some after apologizing?"

"Not really," I answered, letting the wrapper uncurl in my palm.

"Whoa," Katie murmured.

I wasn't sure if the whoa was a good or bad thing. "He seemed genuinely apologetic, to be honest. We chatted for a little while and then he left, but he did say something along the lines of me coming back to the bar."

"Whoa," repeated Roxy.

"Is this all really that surprising?" I sat back, dropping the wrapper on my plate.

Roxy nodded slowly. "Yeah, for Nick it is. Look, I don't know how to say this nicely, but—"

"He's a dick?" I finished for her, and when she winced, I had to fight the grin. "Trust me, I know he's a dick. I've never in my life had a guy act like that after we got together. And I've only forgiven him because, like I said, he seemed genuinely sorry. That doesn't erase how he acted, though."

"Yeah, he's a dick," Roxy said. "But he can be a really nice guy. Nick was there for me when I was dealing with that . . . that creep, but he's got relationship issues," she finished.

"I don't think he's a bad guy," I said. "I just think he's not relationship material."

Roxy was silent for a moment as she smoothed her hand over her hair, stopping when she reached the topknot. "I honestly think I'm his only female friend. He hardly talks to Calla. It's kind of weird. It's like she doesn't exist to him."

Okay, that was weird. I thought about how he believed he met the "one" but had been wrong. Was it Calla? I didn't know enough about her to even hazard a guess at that possibility.

"But that's just how he is." Roxy's brow creased as she continued. "And we're not even that close. He's not the most talkative guy. Sometimes he goes through spells when he is, but mostly, he's kind of quiet, like an observer."

Come to think of it, he hadn't been real talkative the first night we got together. Then again, both of us had other things on our minds. "He was pretty talkative Friday night."

"That's pretty telling." Roxy's forehead smoothed out. "When you walked back into the bar Friday night, I just knew something was going to go down between you two."

"Of course you did, because I called it the first night Steph walked in the bar."

I turned to Katie. "You did?"

"Remember. I'm kind of psychic." She tapped her finger off her temple. "I called it."

"She did," Roxy confirmed, grinning gleefully, while I'm sure I had *What the Hell* written all over my face. "Katie told Nick that someone was coming into the bar who he was going to fall for and he was going to meet his match. Guess what?"

"What?" I said wryly.

"You strolled right on in that night." She clapped her hands excitedly. "And here we are."

For a moment all I could do was stare, and then I laughed. Some of the weird comments Roxy and Katie had made when I first met them now made sense. "I don't see why this is such a big deal. Nick's a player who normally doesn't apologize or act decent to chicks he's slept with. Knowing that doesn't make him more alluring in my book. And even you said he was a dick."

"Well, no shit, but the fact that he is acting different with you means something," Roxy countered, and then she squinted. "Unless you don't want it to mean anything."

"She doesn't," Katie answered, and my gaze swung to hers sharply. "She's going to break his heart."

I stared at her, absolutely dumbfounded. "I am not going to break anyone's heart."

"Oh, you will. You won't mean to, but it's going to happen." She was serious, and a sad look crept into her features as she met my stare. "Yeah, it's going to happen."

Shaking my head, I turned to Roxy. She was staring at Katie with this perplexed look on her face. I threw up my hands. "Why are we even having this conversation? Just because I accepted his apology and he appears to want to be friends doesn't mean either of us are entertaining the idea of going *there* again."

"People can change," Roxy said.

I shot her a bland look. "Please don't tack 'for the right person' on the end of that."

She made a face. "No. I was going to tack 'when they want to' on the end of that."

"Oh." I flashed a brief grin. "That sounds more believable, but still, it doesn't matter. Maybe Nick and I will be friends at some point, but that's it. I don't think our paths are going to cross a lot outside of visiting you."

"I don't know about that," Katie said, and when she looked at me, the unwarranted and strange sadness lingered on her pretty face. "I don't think you're going to have a choice when it comes down to it."

Chapter 8

*T*he first day of October slammed into the city of brotherly love, winds blustery and temps that made me rethink the decision to move farther north instead of south. As I worked at my desk, I hoped that I wouldn't have to go out again. The thin linen pants and blouse, even with my jacket and scarf and gloves, did nothing to beat down the cold.

There was a good chance I really was coming down with something.

I bit the inside of my cheek as I flattened my hand on my belly. My stomach churned like a washing machine. It had been that way since I got up. Running in the wind had been hard enough, but adding in the nausea and the lingering fatigue, I barely made it this morning.

Missing any time when I was only in my forth week at the academy was unacceptable. What I needed to do at lunch was swing by the Walgreens down the street and stock up on antiflu meds.

I was going to try to will myself into not being sick, I decided as I started working again. Mind over body and all that jazz.

My fingers stilled on the keyboard as I heard Rick's high-pitched laugh and I gritted my teeth. As I focused on my screen, my cell phone buzzed from where I'd placed it under the monitor. My gaze flicked to it. It was a text, and there was a number in the little box above the message, one I didn't recognize.

Hey.

That was all the text said. Frowning, I waited a few seconds, and when there wasn't another message, I picked up my phone, and clicked on the text, then went to the add photo option. I scrolled until I found an image of a little girl glaring at the camera with a perfect what-the-hell expression on her little face. Grinning, I sent the picture back as my response and then placed the phone down.

Perfect timing, too, because I heard Mr. Bowser's voice—er, Marcus. He'd insisted that I call him Marcus. Stretching up, I peered over my cubicle. My eyes widened. It was Marcus walking with Andrew Lima. The man who owned Lima Academy was shorter than me, but even though he was well into his fifties, the body under the shirt and nylon pants was that of twenty-year-old. He was smiling at something Marcus said, his teeth a brilliant white against skin that reminded me of sunbaked clay. The man was definitely handsome, even with the two cauliflower ears and the thin scar that ran across a nose that had obviously been broken a time or dozen. It was crazy—the older man probably knew exactly where to deliver a blow that would immobilize a person or worse in under a second.

My heart tripped up and the acid in my stomach

started bubbling. I was nervous to meet my boss for the first time.

Andrew and Marcus also weren't alone.

Beside Andrew Lima was the one and only Brock "the Beast" Mitchell. I knew this because it's what his shirt said. Plus the guy was built. Not as overly done as Rick, but those shoulders could take down doors. He wore a dark blue baseball cap, twisted backward, but otherwise was dressed the same as Andrew Lima. His gaze was lowered as he walked along, trussing his right wrist with white hand wrap. I assumed they must be gearing up for training.

Brock glanced up at something Andrew said and his lips spread in a wide smile. His dark brown eyes were a deep, warm shade, and his features intense, almost perfectly asymmetrical. Wow. I'd seen pictures of Brock, but they hadn't done him justice. I totally got why Katie said she'd have a landing strip just for him. The guy was gorgeous, almost too gorgeous to be putting that face in front of punches and kicks.

My phone buzzed again, but before I could glance down to check it out, Marcus was at my desk. Our eyes met, and I fixed a smile on my face as I rose, ignoring the nauseous tumble my stomach decided to take.

The group stopped and Marcus's skin crinkled at his eyes as he gestured toward me. "Ah, Andrew, you haven't had a chance to meet my new assistant. This is Stephanie." Marcus angled his body toward them. "And this is Brock," he said to me. "He just returned with Andrew."

Don't puke on the boss. Don't puke on the boss. I extended my hand, and Mr. Lima's handshake was firm and brief. "It's nice to meet you." *Don't puke on the hot martial-arts dude. Don't puke on the hot martial-arts dude.* I offered him my hand, too. "It's nice to meet you also."

Recognition flared in Brock's brown eyes as he shook my hand with his left. "You're the infamous Steph."

I froze, having no idea what he was talking about. As my wide gaze swung to Marcus, I could feel the bile climbing up the back of my throat.

Marcus arched a brow.

Andrew chuckled as he leaned against my cubicle wall. "Infamous? This is a story I've got to hear."

"I've heard that Stephanie schooled Nick over at Mona's last week," Brock explained, and there was a good chance my eyes were going to pop out of my head. "Brought him down a peg or two in front of everyone."

Oh my God.

"Everyone has been talking about it," Brock went on, much to my growing horror. "Jax gave me a blow-by-blow description on the phone the other night. Wished he had that on tape."

As did Katie.

Andrew looked impressed as he eyed me. "I can only imagine what Nick did to warrant that."

Would it look strange if I dived under my desk and hid?

"What has Nick been up to lately?" Andrew glanced at Brock, who was grinning like a madman. "He hasn't been in the gym. I miss sparring with him."

Nick sparred with Andrew Lima? Oh wow. That sort of explained how he was in the kind of shape he was.

"You miss kicking his ass," Brock replied, chuckling as he started wrapping his left hand. "I don't know." Those dark lashes lifted and brown eyes pierced me. "I have a feeling we're going to see more of Nick."

Oh my word.

All I could do was smile weakly. My stomach had finally settled down, but now I felt out of it for a different reason. Never would I have ever thought that anything to do with Nick would somehow come up while at work. Without warning, Katie's odd statement cycled through my thoughts.

That I wasn't going to have a choice when it came to our paths crossing.

Was Katie really a psychic stripper?

No. I gave myself a good mental bitch slap and focused on the men in front of me. I glanced at Marcus and shook my head. "I'm sort of a . . . combative personality. Sometimes."

Andrew laughed again.

"You'll find that most of the people around here have the same personality." Marcus's eyes gleamed in the bright light. "Did you finish the report I requested?"

"Yes." I clasped my hands together. "It's on your desk."

"Perfect," replied Marcus.

"Where are you from, Stephanie?" Andrew politely asked as he raised his hand, smoothing it over his closer cropped hair. Light reflected off a wedding band. "Local or out of state?"

"Out of state," I answered. "I'm from West Virginia." Pausing, I waited for the inevitable overused and not funny comment or the widening of the eyes. When that didn't happen, I added cool points to all the guys. "I graduated from Shepherd University."

"Really?" Interest sparked in the owner's eyes, and a muscle flickered along Brock's jaw as he secured the wrap on his hand.

"My daughter is leaving in the spring to attend Shepherd," Andrew said. "Of course, I want her to stay closer to home, but you can't keep them at home with you forever, can you?"

"You can try," Brock muttered under his breath.

I glanced at him. "No, sir." There were so many colleges and universities near Philadelphia, but I understood the need to strike out on your own. "Shepherd is a very good school in a great community. She will be happy there."

"I think so." The older man smiled. "I've actually checked the town and surrounding places out. There aren't training facilities there, not the kind that offer the extensive experience and wide variety that we can."

Oh dear.

"My daughter is . . . unaware of my inquiry, but there are several properties there that would fit our needs." Intelligence brewed in the man's eyes. "What do you think of Lima Academy setting up in your neck of the woods?"

"I think there is definitely a market for it," I answered honestly. UFC fights had been a big deal while I was at college. I could picture tons of guys I knew signing up for classes and getting their asses kicked. "And you're right. You won't have a lot of competition."

Mr. Browser nodded when Andrew turned to him and raised his brows inquiringly. "I know," he replied patiently. "I already have several meetings set up with the local Chamber of Commerce. We should hear something before the end of the year."

Andrew was about to speak, but his attention was snagged by the front of the office. The lines of the man's face softened. "Speaking of the little devil," he said.

I followed his gaze and saw a young girl step inside. Her light brown hair looked like she'd walked through a wind tunnel, which I could sympathize with. If my hair hadn't been pulled back, I'd look the same.

A mauve-colored scarf was wrapped around her throat, tangling in the long locks. Her heavy sweater was bulky and her dark jeans loose, even ill-fitting, giving her the appearance of having no shape. As she drew closer, I could see that her features were delicate, but the heavy bangs dwarfed her face.

Her nervous gaze darted over us, hit Brock and then stayed there as she hurried to where we stood, her fingers fidgeting with the edges of her sleeves. Her face pinked the closer she got to us.

"Hi, Dad." She gave a short, awkward wave as she stopped beside Brock.

Andrew went to her, leaning over to drop a kiss atop her head, and there was no ignoring the burst of envy that exploded inside me. "Hey, baby girl, you here to see me?" he asked as he drew back.

My dad . . . he used to greet me like that, always so happy, always so warm. A knot replaced the churning sensation, and I struggled not to look away.

An easy grin stretched Brock's lips as he dropped an arm over the girl's shoulders. He towered over her by a good foot, but he fit her to the side of his large body like he'd done it a million times. "Nah, she came to visit me. Sorry, old man."

Andrew laughed deeply, shaking his head while her cheeks turned as red as a strawberry. She lifted her chin, and I saw it in her eyes at that moment. The whole world had to have seen it. Adoration filled her gaze, but that wasn't all.

Love.

The girl looked at Brock as if he was responsible for putting the stars in the sky at night and was the sole reason the sun rose every morning. The warmth didn't leave her cheeks, but only seemed to heighten, and I didn't think she was aware of anyone else as Brock grinned down at her. The pang of envy resurfaced. Mom used to look at Dad like that every single damn time their eyes met, and my dad had the same look in his eyes.

Brock, however, reached up with the arm he had around her shoulder and messed her hair, an act I imagine 1 an annoying older brother would do.

Ouch.

He dropped his hand to her shoulder, nearly knocking her over. I quickly looked away, and found that Marcus was doing the same thing, studying his groomed nails.

"Jillian, dear, this is Stephanie," Andrew said, drawing my attention. The girl was no longer staring adoringly at Brock, but was watching her father with a degree of hesitation. "She just graduated from Shepherd."

Interest sparked and her brown eyes met mine briefly. "I'm starting there in the spring. Actually, I'm transferring there." Her gaze flickered from mine to her father, and then dropped to my shoes. "In the spring, but I already said that, so . . ."

Brock's hand squeezed her shoulder

"That's what your father was saying," I said. "You'll really like that."

"I think so," Jillian replied, but the lack of excitement caused me to doubt that she believed it.

I glanced at Brock, but he was staring down at her bowed head with a frown. "If you have any questions about the campus or whatever, I'll be glad to help you," I offered.

Approval settled into the lines of Andrew's face. "That's a good idea, actually. Jillian, you could go out to get coffee with Stephanie."

She nodded without looking at me and, well, I could tell that was probably not going to happen. An awkward silence fell, broken by Brock. "You're not in class today?"

Jillian shook her head. "Nope. I had an exam, and I finished early, so I'm done until later this afternoon. I thought I'd stop by."

"Admit it. You heard I was back and you came to see me," he teased, and I bit down on my lip as blood rushed back to her face. Dear God, was he that oblivious? Brock put her in what looked like a headlock. Yep. He was that oblivious. "Come on, Jilly-bean, you can help me set up."

Jillian glanced at her father, and he nodded. "Go ahead and head down. I'll be there shortly."

"Nice meeting you, Stephanie." Brock said, and with his arm still around Jillian's shoulder, steered them toward the doors. "I'm sure I'll see you around."

"Nice meeting you, too," I replied, giving him a tiny wave.

They got halfway down the hall when Jillian stopped and turned halfway around. "It w-was good meeting you."

I smiled at Jillian, but her face looked like a tomato about to burst. Poor girl. "Same here."

When they were at the doors, her father sighed heavily as he faced me. "Thank you for offering to talk to her. I doubt she'll take you up on the offer. It's nothing personal. She just doesn't warm up to strangers well. Hasn't since, well . . . in a long time, but I appreciate it nonetheless."

"It's no problem. I hope she does decide to get coffee or whatever." And I meant it.

Andrew nodded again, and the conversation ended between us. As Marcus and Andrew disappeared into the closed office, I sat back down and reached for the mouse. Just as my fingers brushed it, I remembered the strange text.

Tapping on the phone, I saw another message from the unknown number.

What in the hell? Ha.

Well, that wasn't the response I thought I'd get. At least whoever this was didn't type in text speak, thank God. I debated sending another pic. I had an entire arsenal of them but figured there was no point in dragging this out. I texted back, *who is this*, and dropped my phone in my lap.

A few minutes later it vibrated. One glance down and my lips parted in surprise. The response didn't make sense.

I couldn't believe it, couldn't even figure out how it was possible, but I could read, and as long as something wasn't functioning incorrectly in my head, I saw who was texting me.

It was Nick.

Chapter 9

*I*t's Nick.

When I didn't respond, because I was too busy staring at my phone dumbly, it vibrated again.

I conned Roxy into giving me your phone number.

My eyes widened.

Another text came through almost immediately. *Mainly bc I figured at some point you'd ask for mine. I saved you the trouble. ;)*

Oh my word, the arrogance knew no limit. I hadn't been planning to ask for his number. Okay, it might've crossed my mind, but I had decided it was best to let that sleeping dog lie. Yes. I was obviously attracted to Nick, as he was to me, but I wasn't sure I could be just friends with him while lusting after him, and I wasn't sure I could trust him not to have the same reaction he had last time after we got together.

A fourth text followed. *Please don't be mad at Roxy. She likes you. But she also likes me.*

My brows rose. Irritation sparked, but it was minimal. I'd met Roxy and Katie again this past Sunday for breakfast. We hadn't talked about Nick this time, but part of me wasn't surprised that she'd given him my number.

I hope you're not mad.

Snapping out of it, I picked up the phone and sent back: *I'm not.* And that was the truth. It wasn't like I gave Roxy the impression I would flip my shit if she gave him my number. Though she probably could've asked first, but that was water under the bridge at this point.

Good, he sent back. A moment passed and another text came through. *Did you save my number?*

The corners of my lips curved up. I texted back: *No.*

That earned me a frownie face followed by: *You break my heart, Stephanie. I saved your number.*

Doubtful, was my response. But I quickly saved his number as I glanced up, hearing someone laughing from a few cubicles over.

A couple of moments passed and Nick texted back. *You totally saved my number, didn't you?*

I swallowed a laugh and shook my head. *Yeah, I did.*

Knew it. The three little dots appearing under the text bubbled, and I waited. *So I was texting you with a purpose.*

Pressing my lips together, I sent back a quick reply. *You were?*

Ha. There was a pause, and then, *Reece is having a get-together at his place tonight. A small one. Roxy is working, but I thought you might like to come?*

My stomach tumbled instead of churned, and I wasn't sure if I liked that sensation or not. Hesitation filled me, something I wasn't at all accustomed to. I normally knew what I wanted to do, but for the first time in a very long time, I was unsure.

Chewing on my lower lip, I glanced up and looked around the office. Not like the answer to what I should do awaited me in the light fixtures. I flipped my gaze back to the phone and started to text back.

I haven't been feeling well. That was the truth. *But if I'm feeling okay tonight . . .* What in the hell was I doing? I didn't know, but I was doing it, doing it real hard. *. . . . I could stop by. What time does it start?*

The three little dots appeared. *Around 8pm. You okay?*

Yeah, just stomach kind of messed up. Probably something he didn't need to know. *I'll text you later and let you know.*

Ok. I hope you feel better.

Thanks.

There were no more texts after that, and as the seconds turned into minutes, and minutes into hours, I still had absolutely no clue what I was doing.

And I wasn't sure if I loathed that feeling.

Or if I sort of liked it.

I got home a little after six-thirty and changed into a pair of jeans and a loose sweater that was made out of a soft chenille material. I loved this sweater so much I wanted to snuggle with it, but that would be weird.

Barefoot, I padded into the kitchen and opened the pantry doors. I stood there for several minutes, picking at a packet of tuna fish and then moving onto the boxes of rice. Neither of those things interested me, so I moseyed on to the fridge. Microwavable bacon was somewhat appealing, but the sliced honey ham and Swiss cheese would be more filling. I didn't want those either. Closing the door, I opened the freezer. There was a packet of hamburger meat and a steak, but both were frozen solid, and I hated defrosting meat in the microwave, so that didn't do me any good. Sighing, I closed that door, too. I was hungry but not. My stomach seemed to be feeling better but my appetite was most definitely weird.

Opening the drawer near the stove, I started scanning the take-out menus I'd already started to accumulate since moving here. Chinese. Pizza. Italian. Subs. All of it looked good, but nothing sparked my interest as it should.

I glanced at the clock as I held a Chinese menu and felt my tummy tighten in a mixture of excitement and confusion, which was an odd combination. Whoever was going to Reece's thing tonight would be arriving in the next hour or so. Nick would be arriving.

Nick.

Dammit.

I still had no idea if I was going to stop by Reece's or how I really even felt about Nick getting my phone number, contacting me, and then inviting me to his friend's place.

If he was looking for something casual between us, the invite wasn't strange. That was actually pretty common, but I had a hard time believing he sincerely thought that would happen between us so soon after what went down at the bar.

Turning my gaze to the menu, I let out a deep sigh and then dropped it back on the counter. There was a packet of Reese's Halloween pumpkins. Would that count as dinner if I just ate all nine of them?

Sounded legit to me.

Picking up a thick bobby pin, I twisted my hair into a loose knot and shoved the pin in. I was just about to pick up the menus again when there was a knock at my door. My heart turned over as I closed the drawer. With my pulse picking up, I walked to the door and took a quick peek through the peephole even though I had an idea who it could be.

I was right.

Nick stood in the hallway outside my apartment. Curious, I unlocked the door and opened it. He turned toward me, and there was this squeezing type pressure in my chest. Not unpleasant, but . . . but wholly unfamiliar to me.

His hair was damp, the dark strands curling along his forehead. Drops of rain dotted his powerful shoulders. When had it started raining? God, I'd really had a single-minded focus on those menus, with nothing to show for it.

"Hi," I said, my gaze dropping to the plastic bag he held.

"Hey," he drawled, and my stare was dragged back up. He looked good, but I figured he always looked good, from the moment he woke up to when he rested that head of his on a pillow. "I brought you something."

Blinking, I stepped back. "You did?"

"Yeah. Can I come in?"

I nodded and watched him walk in and close the door. He took the bag to the small bistro table I had set up in the dining area. I was at a loss for words when he started speaking.

"When I was younger and not feeling well, my

mom used to make me homemade chicken noodle soup." Nick pulled out a plastic container and faced me. "It's a lot better than the canned stuff. She used to drop in some herbs that are good for settling the stomach and actually give the soup a good taste so it's not so bland." He headed for the kitchen. "Your bowls here?"

"Above the left counter." I was frozen.

He pulled out a ceramic bowl, put it on the counter and peeled back the plastic container lid. Carefully, he dumped the noodles, chunks of chicken, and broth into the bowl. "It's still a little warm but it needs to be heated up a bit. Microwave okay?"

My lips slowly parted. It was obvious it was not canned soup. "Yes. Microwave is fine." I inched closer to the kitchen. "Did your . . . did your mom make that."

"No." Nick placed the bowl in the microwave. Little beeps echoed through the silence. He placed his hands on the counter before the microwave, his back to me. "My mom died thirteen years ago."

"Oh." I placed my hand on my chest. "I'm so sorry to hear that."

He nodded, but the line of his spine was tense, his shoulders hunched. I opened my mouth because losing a parent was something I could relate to, but beyond what I'd already said, I couldn't find the words. It wasn't something I talked about often. The microwave dinged and he removed the bowl. The aroma was wonderful, making my stomach grumble happily. Finding a spoon, he brought the soup back to the table. His lashes lifted, moss green eyes meeting mine.

I drew in shaky breath. "Did you make the soup?"

Nick nodded once more.

"Oh. I . . ." I couldn't believe he had brought me soup, let alone taken the time to make it himself. All of this was so incredibly sweet and extremely unexpected; I couldn't speak. I just stood there, staring at him like an idiot.

The hollows under his high cheekbones turned pink. "It's not that hard."

"I don't know how to make chicken soup from scratch."

A small smiled pulled at his striking features. "Maybe I'll teach you one day."

"You really made me soup?"

The smile spread as he ducked his chin. "Yeah, I did. You going to sit and eat it? I promise it will make your stomach feel better."

In a daze, I shuffled over to the table. My stomach was twisting again, but it had nothing to do with the nausea I'd felt earlier in the day. I sat at the table, and honest to God, I was moved to the point where I wasn't even thinking of his douchey behavior in the bar.

"Thank you," I said, my voice strangely hoarse. "I mean it. Thank you."

"It's no biggie." He handed over a spoon. "Eat up."

My fingers brushed his as I took the spoon. The shiver that raced up my arm was hard to ignore as I scooped up some noodles, steaming broth, and a chunk of chicken. My taste buds practically orgasmed. "It's delicious." I glanced up, my eyes wide. "I can taste something kind of minty."

Nick folded his arms. "You look so surprised. I'm actually a damn good cook."

"I am not doubting that now." I swallowed another mouthful, biting back a moan.

His lashes lowered, shielding his eyes. "I thought I could bring it by before I headed up to Reece's. I'm a little early, but he'll be okay—"

"You don't have to leave," I said in a rush, and then felt the tips of my ears burning. "I mean, if you want to hang out here for a little bit, you can."

Nick's eyes met mine and then lowered as he slid onto the seat across from me. He rested his arms on the table. "How are you feeling?"

"Better. The nausea settled this afternoon, but this soup is really helping." I was eating like I hadn't been fed in days. "You didn't bring some for yourself?"

"What's left in the container is yours. I ate earlier." He leaned back in the small dining chair, exhaling softly. "I'm glad you're feeling better."

I paused long enough to smile and then I finished off the bowl. Standing, I carried it to the sink, washed the bowl out, and then placed it in the dishwasher. Turning around, my breath caught in my throat.

Nick had gotten up and followed me, moving so quietly that I hadn't heard him. He was only a foot away, and if I moved a little to my right, we'd be in the same positions we'd been in that night.

My stomach hollowed in response. I so needed to stop thinking about that, but once I did, my brain latched on. My chest rose sharply. I could practically feel his hands on my sides, my hips . . . between my legs. God, was it hot in here? I tugged on the neckline of my sweater. I so needed to get my hormones under control. This was ridiculous.

But when I looked up, our gazes collided and I couldn't look away. Heat swamped my senses, and my overactive imagination flooded me with memories of how he'd felt pressed against my back, him inside me, stretching me.

Nick tilted his head to the side, his gaze hooded as he changed his stance, spreading his legs. "Don't look at me like that," he said, voice gruff.

I blinked. "I'm not looking at you."

His lips quirked up. "Besides the fact you're looking *right* at me, you're looking at me in that way."

Some of the heat had faded, but not nearly enough to make me stop thinking about what we'd done in this kitchen. "In what way am I looking at you?"

"Like you want a repeat of that night."

Damn. He freaking nailed it right on the head. I didn't say anything as I crossed my arms under my chest, but I stiffened as he took a step forward. A half foot separated us.

"And you really need to stop," he said again, his voice low as he lifted his hand, catching the strand of my hair that had fallen loose and tucking it back behind my ear. His knuckles brushed over my cheek. "Because I'm trying to be cool over here." He lowered his hand. "I'm trying something different."

"What are you trying?" I asked.

Those amazing lashes lifted once more and his stare pierced me. "I'm trying to be friends with you."

Chapter 10

*W*hat Nick had said was like being dunked with ice water and then shoved into a walk-in freezer. It wasn't so much that he wanted to be friends with me, and I was assuming the kind of friend that didn't have sex, but it sounded like he'd never been friends with a girl before.

And that didn't make sense.

There was Roxy, and there had to be other girls he'd been close to that he hadn't banged. Had to be. Wasn't there? Then again, Roxy had said something about Nick not having a lot of friends. And there was the whole weird Calla thing.

"You aren't friends with girls?" I asked, speaking slowly.

"No. Not really." He paused as he scrubbed his fingers through his hair. "With the exception of Roxy, but I don't think we're really friends."

"She thinks you are."

His brows lifted, as if he were surprised. "Huh."

I couldn't believe this. "What about Calla? She works at the bar when she's here, right?"

Nick choked out a laugh. "We're not friends."

He said that in a way that caused a tiny amount of suspicion to bloom. "Did you two—"

"No. Calla and I didn't hook up. Jax would toss my ass off a cliff if that was the case. He had it bad for her long before she walked through the bar's doors," he said, sighing. "We just aren't close."

"Okay." I leaned against the counter, letting the Calla subject drop. For now. "But you're twenty-six years old. How in the world have you made it this long without having girl-slash-friends? I don't get it."

He cast his gaze toward the living room, a muscle flicking along his jaw. "I did in high school and stuff. I don't know." He raised a shoulder. "I just haven't in years."

The conversation we had before, where he hinted that he'd been seriously involved with someone and it ended badly, resurfaced. I didn't need to be a psychologist to figure the fallout from that relationship had affected all his relationships with women.

Nick had the kind of baggage airlines charged extra for.

Which was another reason for me to get my libido under control when it came to him.

"You feeling up to visiting Reece?" he asked, changing the subject.

Knowing what I did, I should've said no, but he'd made me chicken soup from scratch. How could I? "I think so."

A wide smile transformed his face from striking to breathtaking. "Great. You ready to head up? All you need is shoes."

I glanced down at myself with a frown. "Maybe I should change."

"Not necessary." He turned away, picking up the container and carrying it to the fridge. "You look beautiful as you are."

I stared at his back for what felt like ten minutes and then shook my head. Stepping around him, I walked to my bedroom and grabbed a pair of flats. Back in the living room, I swiped my keys. "Ready."

Nick grinned as he swaggered past me, opening the door. "Ladies first."

Reece lived a couple of floors up, and as we neared his door, laughter could be heard. Nick knocked, and it wasn't the young cop who answered, but an older, more rugged version of Reece. Brown hair cut close to the skull and a heavy stubble across his jaw, his blue eyes as bright as the ocean.

"Hey, bud." The guy shook Nick's hand as he stepped aside and reached back, picking up a bottle he'd placed on a shelf. He gave me the once-over. "And who's this?"

"Stephanie," Nick said, placing his hand on my lower back, ushering me in. "She lives downstairs. New to town. This is Colton, by the way, Reece's older brother."

Ah, that made sense. "Nice to meet you."

Colton smiled as he passed a quizzical gaze at Nick. "It's good to meet you. Come on in. They're about to get started."

I followed Colton into an apartment that was larger than mine. Sparse and tidy, Reece kept good house. Several people were in his living room. I recognized Reece right off the bat. He was standing by the window, a beer in his hand, but not the guy who sat on the couch. Based on his buzz cut, I was going to take a wild guess and say he was a cop. There was a woman sitting on the arm on the other side of the couch. Her dark hair brushed her shoulders as she glanced up and smiled.

Reece looked over and did a double take, quickly hiding his surprise with a slow smile. "Hey guys." Amusement twinkled in his eyes. "Glad you all could make it."

I smiled, giving the small group a little wave. "Hi."

Colton eased past us, dropping onto the couch beside the woman. "I guess I'll do the introductions since Reece is an asshole. This is my girlfriend, Abby," he said, introducing us. "And this other guy over here is Brad."

His brother snorted. "Yeah, I am terrible at that shit."

Brad glanced up and nodded slightly, and curiosity crawled across Abby's pretty face. "I'm Steph," I said. "Nice to meet you all."

Reece glanced at Nick, raising his brow as Brad leaned forward, picking something small and black off the coffee table. The TV screen shifted, revealing they were playing a game.

"Game night," Brad explained, waving a controller. "It's an epic Mario Kart death match. We go in rounds—partners. I'm stuck with that loser." He nodded at Reece.

Reece raised his middle finger.

"Do you play?" Nick asked, turning around.

I nodded. "Not in a while. I kind of suck."

"That's okay." He grabbed two chairs from the kitchen and brought them into the living room, placing them near the couch. "I'm the best Mario Kart player in the world."

"You think he's exaggerating?" Colton laughed, shaking his head. "He's not. It's like he was born playing this game."

"It's because I have a lot of time on my hands," Nick replied as I sat on the chair closest to Abby. "That's why."

Reece snickered as he walked around the coffee table. "That's such bullshit and you know it."

My little ears perked up at that comment, but Nick didn't respond as he sat beside me. So if Nick said he had lots of time on his hands, but Reece called bs on that, what was Nick doing that he didn't want to talk about? I told myself that even if we were becoming friends, it wasn't any of my business, especially right now, but dammit, I wanted to know.

"Do you want anything to drink?" Reece offered, heading for the kitchen. "I have beer and soft drinks. And Roxy has half my fridge loaded with sweet tea."

"I'm fine," I called, shoving my oddly icy hands between my knees. "Thanks."

Reece and Brad started off first, playing against Colton and Abby. Each player was racing against one another, and if either team member won, it counted for the team. Brad won the first round, and he was legit taking score. Abby handed over the controller, and of course I chose the princess as my character, and of course I could barely keep the damn thing on track. I sucked, but it was funny and the sides of my stomach ached from laughing so much.

After a few rounds the death match paused so the guys could get refills. I noticed Nick wasn't drinking, and I wondered if he didn't drink that much at all. The night at my place, he hadn't even finished half the bottle.

I chatted with Abby, quickly discovering that she was a sweetheart and that she and Colton had only recently starting seeing each other.

"Are you and Nick together?" she asked, keeping her voice low. The guys were in the kitchen, but that wasn't very far away.

"No. We're just friends."

"Oh." Her brow wrinkled. "I thought you guys were. I don't know him well, but ever since Colton and I started dating, I've never seen him with someone."

That didn't surprise me. I started to respond, but the guys returned, and Nick sat a glass of water for me down on the coffee table, next to a bowl of chips Reece had planted. I hadn't asked for it, but it was a courtesy and sweet gesture that Abby noticed with eyes like a hawk.

I stayed longer than I thought I would, sucking utterly at Mario Kart, but I was enjoying my time with everyone. The only reason I left a little after ten was because I had work in the morning, unlike the rest of them, who had unorthodox schedules. When I rose and said good-bye, Nick tossed his controller to Colton and followed me out.

"You didn't have to leave," I told him as he closed Reece's door behind us.

"I know." He shoved his hands into the pockets of his jeans as we started walking down the hall. "I'm being a good friend and walking you home."

I laughed as I glanced up at him. "I live here."

"Such a long walk, though. And cold." He shuddered. "Damn, it's cold out here."

He was not lying. A skin-chilling wind whipped

through the hallway. My arms were wrapped around my chest as we headed down to the first floor. We stopped at my door, and I dug my keys out of the pocket of my jeans.

"Thanks again for the chicken soup." I turned to him, smiling. "I had fun tonight."

Nick cocked his head to the side. "So did I. Reece usually does this every other week. You know you're more than welcome to join in."

Reece had said as much as I left, and I would definitely love to do it again, especially if Roxy was there. I imagined playing Mario with her would virtually be like playing against myself. "You're heading back up?"

"Yeah. Just for a little while. Then I'm going to head on home."

"How far do you live from here?" I asked, unsure if I had asked that question before.

"Not that far. About fifteen minutes. I live just on the other side of Plymouth." Nick's brows knitted and his mouth opened, like he was about to speak, but he appeared to change his mind. "Well, I hope you keep feeling better."

"Me, too." I studied him from under my lashes. "Have a nice night."

Nick's gaze flickered over my head, toward my door, and then he stepped back. "Don't be a stranger, Stephanie."

"Ditto," I whispered.

A small grin appeared and then he pivoted around. I watched until he hit the stairwell and disappeared. I went into my apartment, closed the door and then got ready for bed. It was still early, and while I was tired enough to call it night, I lay in bed for too long, trying to figure Nick out.

The boy had baggage and questionable dating ethics, but he was sweet and kind enough to make homemade chicken soup? He still wanted me and yet he was denying the attraction in order to be friends with me? Why? Why, when he hadn't done so before with any other girl? It wasn't because I was a special snowflake. There had to be a reason. Something.

Figuring him out was impossible.

Nick was like a jigsaw puzzle where the most intricate pieces had been misplaced, and deep down I knew that no matter how many times I would shake the puzzle up and start over, those pieces would always be missing and I would never have the complete picture.

The nausea came and went the rest of the week, striking at the oddest moments, sometimes in the morning, other times in the afternoon, and Thursday night right before bed. Friday, I grabbed lunch at a dinner down the street from work, and the smell of grease nearly took my legs out from underneath me. My stomach had never been this sensitive before, and normally I loved the smell of all things greasy.

I was no longer convinced that I was coming down with a virus or something, and when I chatted with my mom Friday evening, I almost brought it up, but I didn't want to worry her. Besides, I'd made an appointment with a general practitioner who had an opening in two weeks at a nearby clinic. I didn't think anything was seriously wrong, but the nausea and fatigue were starting to freak me out. I'd never had any health problems before, and I could count on my hand how many times I'd actually had a cold.

Sunday morning I was feeling fine. A little tired, but my stomach was grumbling happily as I puttered around the apartment. My butt needed to run since I'd missed the last couple of days, but it looked like it was going to rain and . . . and yeah, I wasn't feeling the whole physical exercise thing. Instead, I took a long and drawn out shower and then pulled on a pair of jeans. I yanked my hair up in a quick knot, bypassed the makeup except for a quick sweep of lipstick and mascara. Looping a pale blue scarf around my neck, I headed out.

Tomorrow I would run, like, a million miles.

I left my apartment to meet up with Roxy for breakfast. Katie was out of town this weekend, which was disappointing. She could turn a Sunday breakfast at IHOP into an adventure. The parking lot was full, forcing me to park near the back. Thick clouds blocked the sun, and chilly fall rain was ready to pour down. Before I got out of my car, I checked my phone. No missed calls or messages. I wasn't even sure why I was checking.

Definitely not for any missed calls or texts from Nick.

Nope. Definitely not.

I dashed across the parking lot, slowing to a more sedate pace when I reached the sidewalk instead of plowing into a group of elderly women.

Cute stickers of ghosts had been applied to the glass doors, reminding me that I needed to get a pumpkin and start to stock up on candy, though I had no idea if kids trick or treated near the condo or not.

I hoped so.

Halloween turned me into such a goober.

Once inside, I rounded the hostess desk and scanned the packed restaurant. My mouth dropped open when I saw Roxy in a wide, half-moon-shaped booth toward the back.

"Oh my God," I whispered, stiffening.

Roxy was not alone, like I expected.

Three girls sat with her—blond-haired Calla, the widely smiling Teresa, and redheaded Avery. It was like a freaking rainbow over there. My feet wouldn't move as the air punched out of my lungs. They hadn't seen me yet. I could just turn right around and—

Teresa looked up and started waving enthusiastically. All the girls looked.

Dammit.

Okay. I was not a flight girl when fight-or-flight kicked in. I wasn't going to start now. I did nothing wrong, and if these girls had a problem with me, then, well . . . it would just suck. I couldn't change it. I *wouldn't* change it.

Drawing in a deep breath, I forced my feet to move. Roxy stood, a smile fixed on her face but her eyes pleading. "Glad you made it." She gestured for me to take her seat next to Teresa. "Everybody was in town and—"

"And we wanted to see you," Teresa cut in as I sat beside her. Her eyes were as bright and as blue as her older brother's—Cam. "We really didn't get to chat a lot last time."

"Yeah." I struggled with what to say as I placed my purse between us. Roxy sat back down, and as I glanced around, my gaze met Avery's. She gave me a tentative smile.

Okay. So this was weird. I had something really intimately in common with the girl sitting across from me and another sitting next to me. Really kind of awkward, really kind of—

Pulling the brakes on my stupid train of thoughts, I focused on a normal greeting. "It's nice to see all of you. How long are you guys up here for?"

"We have Monday and Tuesday off. Fall break," Calla answered, and I was momentarily surprised by the fact I'd already forgotten about fall break. "So I'm here until Tuesday night."

"Which means Jax will be in a giving mood." Roxy grinned.

Calla's cheeks brightened to a pretty pink. It was only then that I noticed the scar on her cheek. When she had been at Shepherd, she wore heavy makeup to conceal it. It didn't look like she was wearing any today.

"I think we're heading back Tuesday night, too." Teresa fiddled with the edge of her menu. "Cam wants to head up to New York City tomorrow."

"I've never been." Avery picked at her menu. Sitting straight across from me, she looked much smaller than I remembered. "So, I'm very excited to see it."

"I've only been once. It was fun," I said, resting my hands on my lap. "But a little overwhelming."

Teresa leaned back against the cushion. "The first time there, I ended up having an anxiety attack later that night when I started thinking about all the buildings."

"Really?" Avery's eyes widened.

"The buildings can give you a crowded feel." Teresa shuddered. "Especially when you're not used to it, and it couldn't have just been me being weird, so you'll be fine."

"You better be fine," warned Calla, grinning. "I'm surprised Cam didn't escort you here himself."

Avery's cheeks flushed red as her hair as the waitress appeared, taking our drink orders along with the food.

"Why would Cam escort you here?" The skin between Roxy's brows knitted. "He sounds like Reece."

Calla's shoulders straightened as excitement splashed across her face. "You don't know?"

"Oh!" Teresa squealed, causing me to jump a little. She clapped her hands. "I love this part."

Confusion marked Roxy's face, and I was glad I wasn't the only person who had no idea what was going on. "No. I don't," she said. "What's going on? It's not the wedding, right? We all know about the wedding."

"I knew you guys were engaged, but I didn't get a chance to say congrats for that," I chimed in. "When's the big day?"

Avery's eyes brightened. "We were going to do a spring wedding, but we're pushing for the middle of the summer now. We decided to change the date."

"Why?" Roxy asked, her brows knitting together.

Our drinks arrived, and Avery took a long gulp of her water before she spoke. "I'm . . . I'm kind of pregnant."

My eyes widened. Oh my God, Avery was— Wait, *kind of* pregnant?

"You're pregnant?" Roxy's voice was pitched high.

Teresa giggled as she bounced next to me like a rubber ball. "And she's not kind of pregnant. She's almost four months pregnant."

"Congrats!" I smiled, shocked, but genuinely happy for them. Whenever Cam and Avery were around each other, it was so obvious how much in love they were. Hell, even before they were together. I remembered the night I was at his apartment for the UFC fight he'd ordered. He couldn't keep his eyes off her, and I hadn't been surprised when he left his own place when she'd made an exit.

"Oh my God! Congratulations!" Roxy's glasses slipped down her nose. "Wait. At Jax's cookout, when you said you had the flu? You were pregnant then!"

Avery nodded as happiness filled her gaze. "We weren't sure then. Well, the over-the-counter test said yes, but I was waiting for the official doctor's words, because who knows? Maybe the results were positive due to user error."

"How does one take a pregnancy test wrong?" Teresa laughed, her eyes glittering.

"Don't you just pee on a stick?" Calla looked at Avery. "It seems pretty simple."

"It's easy, but when you're not expecting to get pregnant, you take like a hundred tests, and still don't believe the results." Avery bit down on her lip as she ran her finger along the rim of her cup, her engagement ring twinkling under the lights. "And you still kind of don't believe the doctor, but then it's hard to not believe. The being tired on and off—the puking and being grossed out by smells that didn't bother you—oh, and your boobs . . ." She made a face. "They hurt. Everything starts to make sense. . . ."

"The tortoises are going to be so jealous." Teresa giggled as she pressed her hands together under her chin. They were talking about Raphael and Michelangelo, Cam and Avery's pet tortoises. They were the only people I knew in real life who had pet tortoises. "They're not going to be your babies any longer." Her smile spread. "Maybe I can babysit them more often."

"I'm pretty sure Ollie will come up with some kind of weird playpen where the baby and tortoises can roam together but not touch one another," Avery said, and I laughed, because if anyone could come up with something like that, it would be Ollie, the slacker genius.

Avery continued on, but my mind danced away from what she was saying. She and Cam were having a baby. Wow. I had no idea what she must be feeling, still being in college and all, but I knew they'd make it work. Going through morning sickness and all of that while in school had to . . .

Then it occurred to me, hitting me with the force of a racing truck full of pregnancy tests.

As I stared at Avery's freckled face, my smile faded inch by inch. My stomach dipped and twisted. Ice slammed into my chest. The faces of the girls blurred out. My mind left the table.

Teresa frowned as she leaned forward. "Are you okay, Steph?"

My heart started to pound and blood rushed my head as I started to mentally backtrack over the past days and weeks. If my calculations were correct, I was missing something *very* important, like life and death kind of important.

Oh my God . . .

"Steph." Calla reached over, placing her hand on mine. "You all right?"

I blinked, sucking in air as the faces of the girls came back into view. "Yeah. Yes. I'm totally okay."

"Are you sure?" Concern settled into Roxy's features. "You look really pale."

Avery tucked a strand of hair back behind her ear. "Maybe you're coming down with something?"

Beside her, Teresa nodded. "There's a really bad virus going around. Half of the school seems to have it. I hope that's not it."

"Probably just a little bug." Roxy leaned back, looking like she wanted to pull the collar of her shirt over her mouth and nose.

"I think it might be," I said hoarsely, but those words felt like a lie, a really big one, because the mental calculations I'd just done in a rush meant something completely different than coming down with a bug or a virus.

The girls started chatting again, their voices an excited hum as the food arrived, but I didn't hear what they were saying. As I glanced up, my eyes met Avery's and my stomach twisted once more. I quickly dropped my gaze to my untouched plate of food and started counting again. I counted four more times, and each time I came up with the same thing.

My period was two and a half weeks late.

Chapter 11

The rest of breakfast with the girls was a blur. My food had been mostly untouched and I couldn't follow the conversation. Roxy knew me well enough to be concerned. When we left, she walked to my car, asking if I was okay. I barely managed a mumbled reply before driving off.

It couldn't be.

There had to be another reason why I was having symptoms so similar to Avery's, and my period being late had to be a coincidence. It had been at least six months between the last time I had sex and the night I spent with Nick. Plus, he had used a condom. And double plus, I was on the pill.

But . . . oh my God . . . I knew there were a couple of times when I hadn't taken pills because my head was all over the place. Since I wasn't having sex—didn't have any plans to have sex until I met Nick—I hadn't been stressed out about missing them.

Like one really could just plan sex.

Oh God.

My heart raced sickeningly fast. What if— I cut that thought off. I couldn't even let it finish. The idea horrified me. Not because I didn't want kids. I did want kids, you know, like years from now, when I was settled in my career and married. Yeah, the married part would be nice.

Fuck. Having a boyfriend would be nice.

This was not how I planned my life. Not that I had a detailed plan, but I figured after graduating from college, I would spend a couple of years in my current job, putting my time in, and be one of those über sophisticated chicks who actually traveled when they had a vacation. West Coast. Europe. Asia. I wanted to see the whole world. Eventually I would meet a guy. We would date, get engaged, and have a massive wedding, and maybe by the time I reached my thirties, I'd think about having a baby.

Not now.

Not before I was settled in my career, traveled the world, got married, and my massively, ridiculous wedding.

Oh my God, this couldn't be happening. There was a good chance I was going to puke all over myself.

Now I sat in the parking lot of a drugstore, my knuckles aching from how tightly I was clutching the steering wheel. I stared at the entrance, unable to force myself to get out of the car. I needed to. I needed to go in and buy a pregnancy test, because a pregnancy test would prove that I wasn't pregnant and I was just overreacting. Stress could make your period late. A ton of things could make your period late, not just a fertilized egg.

Oh my God—*a fertilized egg.*

I did not have a *fertilized egg* in me.

Woman-ing up, I snatched my purse off the passenger seat and stalked into the drugstore with a single-minded focus. Bypassing the makeup aisles, I headed straight for the section most women didn't like to linger in—past the tampons and the pads and a ton of other things I never understood why we needed so many different brands for and stopped in front of a slew of boxes.

My eyes widened.

Holy no babies, why were there so many pregnancy tests? I was frozen as I scanned them. E.p.t. Clear Blue. Ovulation Test—what the heck? E.p.t. Early. Why were there so many? My hands shook as I picked one up and flipped it over. My vision blurred as I read the back. I couldn't believe I was buying a pregnancy test.

I'd never had to buy one before.

This could not be happening.

Placing the box back, I blindly picked up another and turned it over. The hairs on the back of my neck rose and my stomach dropped to my toes. I glanced around but didn't see anyone staring at me. I was totally freaking out.

I grabbed another box, started to leave and then whipped around, picking up another box. Just in case . . . I experienced user error.

My face was burning like I'd been under a heat lamp as I carried my purchases to the front and a slim woman with deep grooves in her face, around her eyes and mouth, waited.

Her brows rose when I dumped my armload on the counter and she glanced up at me, a wry grin on lips covered with faded, purple lipstick. Picking up one box, she offered a throaty chuckle. "You can never be too sure about some things, huh?"

I wanted to hide under the bin of candy behind me.

"Nothin' to be embarrassed about, honey." She scanned one pregnancy test and then plopped it in a bag. "Most people buy several boxes the first time."

Was it that obvious this was my first time? Wait a second. Was I seriously having my first time? As the boxes went in the bag and I was given my total, I realized somewhat numbly that whether I was prepared for it or not, this was really happening.

I could be pregnant.

As soon as I got back to my apartment, I placed the potentially life-changing bag on the counter and walked into my kitchen. I kept all medicines, along with my birth control pills, in a cabinet. Anyplace else, I would end up forgetting about them.

Taking a deep breath, I opened the purple plastic container, smoothing my fingers over the rows of small pills. I counted back and then counted back again. Squeezing my eyes shut, I cursed. The dates I missed . . .

They were important dates.

Snapping the container closer, I placed it back and then dropped my elbows onto the counter. I scrubbed my hands down my face. My thoughts whirled in a continuous circle until one main one wiggled free. If I . . . If I was what I feared, did taking birth control pills after . . . after conception effect the baby?

I didn't know.

Frankly, I knew very little about the whole ins and outs of pregnancy. I was an only child. No one I knew at my age, with the exception of Avery, had been pregnant. It wasn't like women were born with this knowledge, and I seriously doubted many moms decided to hand down that kind of information until it was necessary.

Maybe I miscounted the pills.

Lifting my head, I picked up the purple container and counted again. Breathing felt a little iffy as I finally made myself stop. No matter how many times I counted, the end result wasn't going to change.

But even if my missed pills occurred during epically bad timing, Nick had used a condom. He had. . . .

Actually, I had felt extraordinarily . . . wet after we had sex. So much so that I thought it had to do with not getting any in a while. Could the condom have broken and that was what I felt? That had never happened to me before, so there was a chance I wouldn't have recognized it for what it was.

"Oh God," I whispered, my voice sounding incredibly loud in the silent apartment. Reaching up, I tugged on my hair, letting it fall down over my shoulders. "Oh. God."

Unable to stand still or sit, I walked to where I left my purse and dug out my phone. My fingers hovered over the screen. Who was I going to call? I didn't feel comfortable ringing my friends from back home, and there was no way in hell I was calling my mom about this, not when I had no idea what was going on.

Clutching the phone to my chest, I went to the couch and sat. I almost called Roxy, but I knew she would be hanging out with everyone most of the day. I thought about calling Yasmine or Denise, but I'd missed my Skype calls with them both the past week, and how could I just spring that on them? And what could I say to them? That I bought a million pregnancy tests after freaking out over what Avery had said? Granted, I had reasons to be freaking out, but still, I knew how that appeared.

I set the phone down on the cushion beside me and closed my eyes. This was not how I expected my lazy Sunday to go. I knew I needed to get this over and done with.

I didn't move from the couch.

The rest of Sunday afternoon dragged by as I worked up the nerve to even open the first box. It appeared to be a normal run-of-the-mill pregnancy test with a plus meaning pregnant and a minus meaning hallelujah. Definitely no user error there. I started reading the instructions and a choked laugh escaped me.

Do not insert the test stick in your vagina.

Was that seriously an instruction that needed to be given to someone?

Carefully opening the package, I pulled out the stick and walked into my bathroom. I removed the purple cap as my stomach roiled.

My heart pounded like I was running uphill as I did my thing. The only thought in my head was how I awkward this was. Really. When I was done, I snapped the cap back on and gently placed it on the counter of my sink.

Then I ran from my bathroom, like legit *sprinted* out of the bathroom.

Pacing the length of my living room, I knew I

only needed to wait for two minutes, but two minutes turned into five and five minutes turned into ten. I wasn't ready. Running my hands through my hair, I shook my head. I wasn't ready to see this.

But what if there was a little, happy negative sign? But what if there was a really scary plus sign?

I eyed the remaining unused boxes on the counter and kept wearing a path in the hardwood floors. I'd always been so damn careful in the past. I'd never feared the chance of becoming pregnant, and now that there was a possibility I could be, I didn't know what to do.

Never in my life did I feel so . . . so helpless.

Actually, that wasn't true. When I was fifteen and there were two men in pristine, dignified uniforms knocking on our front doors. When I stood on the stairs and the blood had drained from my mother's face when she saw them, I had felt helpless then.

I loathed that feeling, hated the memories it dredged to the surface. Seconds when our whole entire life changed, never to be the same. Air leaked out of me. Coming to a stop in front of the TV, I realized I could be in the very same position, standing on that very razor-sharp edge of monumental change

Or I could just be freaking out.

A good forty minutes had passed since I placed the test on my sink. I needed to go look at it. Get this over with, like I knew I had to. I wasn't a coward. I could face this, no matter what. Biting down on my lower lip, I charged down the hall and into the bathroom. My reflection in the mirror told me I looked as out of control as I felt. My hair was now all over the place and my eyes were wide, pupils dilated.

I looked like some psycho in a hockey mask was after me.

Shoulders stiffening, I slowly dragged my gaze away from my reflection to the white and purple tipped pregnancy test.

I saw the result.

I couldn't un-see the result.

Plain as day, there was a very visible symbol that could only mean one thing. Only. One. Thing.

Maybe I let it sit too long. Or maybe I shouldn't have put a cap on it. I needed to take another one. I had two more.

Hurrying into the kitchen, I picked up the other box. It was more high-tech. Not only did it give you a yes or no, but if it was a yes, it gave an estimated length of pregnancy. I didn't have to go to the bathroom, though. Rushing to the cabinet, I grabbed a glass and filled it up, and when I finished with that one, I drank another, and then another, and then I waited.

I wasn't thinking, hadn't done anything other than force water down my throat. Less than an hour later I took the second test into the bathroom, did my thing, and then placed it next to the first one.

I didn't leave the bathroom this time.

With my heart in my throat, I eyeballed the test as my hands clenched and unclenched at my sides until the pregnancy showed me the results once more.

The first thing I noticed was two numbers with a dash between them: 2-3.

And above that one word.

Pregnant.

Chapter 12

$\mathcal{J}$ust to start Monday off with a bang, I took the third pregnancy test that morning, and it, too, came back positive. Pregnant. Three tests with the same result, but there was still a tiny part of me that wanted to believe that I had done something wrong, that without a doctor confirming I was pregnant, there was a chance I wasn't. But I wasn't dumb nor was I seriously that naive. I knew that when I went to my doctor's appointment next week, what the three tests had already told me and what I'd been experiencing the last week or so would confirm what I already knew.

And according to the really fancy test, I was two to three weeks past my last ovulation. Meaning I was roughly four to five weeks pregnant. The timing was spot on.

I was actually pregnant.

There was a bun in my oven.

I was knocked up.

Monday and Tuesday at work passed by with me in a numb daze. I don't even know how I did my job or how I got through Rick's endless insinuations and leering looks without losing my flipping mind.

My nerves were stretched taut and I felt sick to my stomach when I packed up Tuesday evening. The moment I turned off my computer, my thoughts immediately started swirling around what I was going to do. Should I get in contact with Nick? I hadn't heard from him since last Wednesday. Should I tell anyone what was happening? Did I need to?

Was I going to go through with this—with this pregnancy? And if so, how would I tell my new boss that in roughly eight months I would be needing maternity leave? Better yet, how could I even raise a child on an income that I lived off comfortably, though that wouldn't work if I included the cost of caring for a child.

Unaware of even walking to the elevator in the hall, after pushing the button I realized that I wasn't alone. I glanced to my left. Rick, one half of the Steroid Twins, was standing there. I could barely swallow my sigh of frustration as I eyed him. A black skullcap was pulled down over his ears, and his cheeks were ruddier than normal. As always, his gaze wasn't on my face. It was on my chest, which was absurd, because between my peacoat and my scarf, there was no way in hell that he could see anything.

God, I had bad timing in all things.

"You heading out?" he asked.

Considering it was the end of the day and everyone was leaving, I wasn't quite sure how the answer to that question wasn't obvious. "I'm leaving for the night."

"Uh-huh," he murmured, his gaze dropping to my pelvic area. My lips curled in distaste. "A couple of us are getting drinks. Want to join us?"

I plastered a tight smile on my lips. "Thank you, but I'm pretty tired."

"You're definitely pretty." He leered, and I looked away, barely resisting the urge to roll my eyes. "And you're always tired. You sure somethin' isn't wrong with you?"

My brows knitted. Oh, how accurate he was, and he had no idea. "I'm fine."

"Then why don't you come out with us?" he pressed, and my hand tightened on the strap of my purse. "What? Are you too good to go out and have a little fun? Maybe too uptight?"

I exhaled loudly, my patience wearing thin as I turned a cool gaze on him. "Yes. I'm that uptight."

Thankfully, the elevator doors opened and I stepped in before he could respond, reaching for the button to close the door. Of course, I realized my mistake immediately. Rick followed, catching the door, and I mentally strung together an atrocity of fuck bombs.

He was actually smiling. "You have an attitude."

I shot him a bland look, not even dignifying that with a response. Engaging with pervy Rick was the last thing I needed to deal with right now. Thank God there weren't many floors to go down, and before this confrontation could go any further, the elevator jerked to the stop. The doors opened.

Rick had planted himself in the opening, smiling and not moving.

What a bastard.

Hands clenching into fists, I turned to the side to avoid touching him as I moved past, but at the last possible moment he stepped to the side. His front brushed against my stomach and hip. What I felt, what was so disgustingly obvious, sent a shiver of revulsion through me.

Rick smirked.

That was it.

I stopped with my back to the wind whirling past the cement pillars and parked cars. "Don't ever touch me again. If you do, I will be in Mr. Browser's office faster than you can blink an eye."

His smirk faded. "I didn't touch you."

"Bullshit," I snapped, my jaw clenching. "You know what you just did."

Rick huffed out of the elevator, and I held my ground as he got into my space, his face flushed so red I wondered if he was going to have a stroke. "Are you threatenin' me?"

"No." I held his stare even as a tendril of unease formed in the pit of my stomach. "I'm making you a promise."

He drew back, his eyes beady in the low light. I held his gaze for a moment longer and then I whirled around. My heart pounded as I walked to my car and the back of my neck tingled. Was he going to follow me? No. I reached my car without further annoyances, and I hoped and prayed that he would heed my promise and back the hell off.

I'd dealt with guys like him before. Frat boys who didn't understand personal boundaries. Guys at the gym who thought everyone who looked their way was into them. Normally they backed off the moment they realized you weren't going to be intimidated. Hopefully, Rick fell into that group.

As I pulled out of the parking garage, I heard a text go off. Since my phone was in my purse, I left it there. The streets were congested, and I needed to pay attention so I didn't ram someone's car.

The drive home was as annoying, but expected. The sky was a deep blue, the sun almost gone, by the time I walked through my door. Shrugging off my coat, I laid it over the back of the kitchen chair and placed my purse on the table. I started for the fridge, but remembered I'd received a text. Going back to my purse, I pulled my phone out and tapped the button.

My heart lurched in my chest. The text was from Nick.

You up for game night?

My brain sort of emptied for a couple of moments. I stared at the text until the screen faded to black. Reece was having what I guessed was a bimonthly Wednesday game night, and Nick was inviting me again, but I . . .

I wasn't in the mood to go up there and pretend that everything was okay, because it wasn't. Placing my free hand against my lower stomach, I jerked it away. What was I doing?

I couldn't see Nick right now without blurting out what was going on, and I wasn't ready for that conversation. Right or wrong, it was the truth. I hadn't fully wrapped my head around the fact I was pregnant, I couldn't even begin to talk to someone else about it, especially him, because I knew that was going to be a difficult conversation.

If it was a conversation that was going to even take place.

I didn't respond to Nick's text.

And he didn't text back.

I made it through the rest of the week without having a mental breakdown when I realized a pair of pants that had been loose before now felt a little bit snug, which could've been simple paranoia. The upside was Rick. He seemed to have gotten the message and hadn't come near me since the elevator gross-out.

I still really hadn't come to terms with what was going on inside me.

Friday night I texted and told Roxy I wouldn't be able to do breakfast on Sunday because I wouldn't be in town, which was true. Early Saturday morning I left my apartment and drove the three hours to my mom's house. She was expecting me, but she didn't know why I was coming down.

I needed . . . I needed my mama, and this conversation I had to have with her couldn't be done over the phone. There was no way.

My mom lived in the same house I grew up in, and I knew she would never leave the two-story colonial-style home on Red Hill in Martinsburg. There were too many memories.

It was close to eleven when I pulled into the driveway. The asphalt was cracked, like it had been for the last three years. Mom kept saying she was going to get it repaved, but I didn't see it happening in the near future.

Swallowing hard, I sat in the car, letting the engine idle as my gaze roamed over the front of the house. An autumn wreath hung from the front door.

When I was younger, this close to Halloween, she used to put those ghost and witch stickers in the front windows.

But I wasn't a little girl anymore.

Obviously.

I turned off the ignition and grabbed my purse and the overnight bag I'd packed. I planned on staying the night. Climbing out into the bright sun, I walked up the pathway obscured by thick holly bushes.

The door opened before I knocked, and despite the rapid anxiety building in my system, a wide smile broke out across my face. "Mom."

She stood in the doorway, holding a white and brown ball of absolute terror who was doing everything in its little dog power to get down. Around her neck was a silver chain that hadn't been removed in years. My father's dog tags. "I was wondering if you were going to come in or sit outside all morning."

Laughing, I stepped inside and gave her and the dog a one-arm hug that warmed my chilled skin. "I wasn't out there that long."

She arched a dark brow as she let the dog down. "Uh-huh."

Dropping my bag and purse on the floor, I swooped down and scooped up my mom's Jack Russell terrier, which she had appropriately named Loki. The little dog squirmed in my arms as it bathed my face in kisses for about three seconds and then whipped itself around in my arms until I placed it back down.

Loki tore off through the foyer and into the den before dashing back into the room. The dog ran a circle around me and then darted off down the hall, returning with an orange and black striped, stuffed tiger in its jaws. I shook my head.

"I baked your favorite." Mom started toward the kitchen.

I followed her, inhaling the familiar apple and cinnamon scent that was faintly shadowed by something that reminded me of vanilla. "Pound cake?"

She glanced over her shoulder, winking. "You bet."

My stomach grumbled happily.

Mom always walked fast, like there weren't enough minutes in a day, and most certainly did not look like she was a few years shy of fifty as she moved through the house. She had me and married young, at age twenty-four. Thinking that drove home the fact that I was twenty-three and I—

My mouth dried as I shook the thought out of my head. I looked like my mom. Her black hair was cut shorter, though, brushing her shoulders, and there were more fine, delicate lines at the corners of cornflower blue eyes and near her lips. She wasn't as tall as I was, as my height was something I'd picked up from my father, but my mom was beautiful.

And I knew she had to have guys lining up to be with her, both those younger and older than her, but she didn't date, and I knew she never would.

The kind of love my parents had felt for each other defied reality.

A pound cake was cooling on a rack near the stove, and I could practically feel my mouth starting to water as Mom picked up a knife. "How was the drive?" she asked, slicing into the cake. "Did you have any trouble?"

"Not bad." I sat at the same kitchen table where I'd grown up eating evening meals. "It probably would've been under three hours if I hadn't hit traffic."

Mom placed a plate in front of me, along with a fork. A second later a glass of milk appeared, and I was suddenly thrust back into a time when there was so very little to worry about. Tears burned the back of my throat, and I blinked my eyes rapidly as I cut into the cake.

She sat down beside me, a cup of coffee in her hands. Within a heartbeat, Loki jumped up into her lap. "I was surprised when you said you were coming home. I wasn't expecting to see you until Thanksgiving."

With my mouth full with buttery goodness, I raised a shoulder in a shrug.

Mom eyed me as she sipped her coffee, careful not to disturb the dog curled in her lap. As I concentrated on finishing off the pound cake, I knew my mom was figuring me out just by watching me. She could read me like I had all my secrets written on my forehead. She knew something was up, and I also knew she wouldn't beat around the bush, waste time with banal conversation.

And she didn't.

"You look really tired, honey." She lowered her cup. "You haven't been sleeping well."

Sleeping this past week had been hard. I'd go to bed with my thoughts in so many different places that I'd wake up several times throughout the night, my mind racing as if I hadn't been asleep at all.

"Is it work?" she asked.

I placed the fork on the empty plate. "Work is fine, perfect actually. It's a good job, and I'm happy with it."

"Then what's going on?" Mom's lips curved slightly. "I know something is. The moment you called me, I did. You don't live in a different time zone, but a three hour drive isn't a walk in the park."

Taking a drink of the cold milk, I leaned back in the chair. I lifted my gaze and my eyes met hers. "Do I really look that bad?"

"You don't look bad, honey, but you look tired." She paused, her hand absently smoothing over the top of Loki's head. "And you sounded stressed when you called me."

My stomach churned, and I wasn't sure if it was due to the infamous morning sickness or just nerves, because I came down to see my mom so I could tell her the truth, so I could get grounded and hear her advice. This was probably going to be one of the biggest bombs I would ever drop on her, and I felt sick.

"Stephanie?"

Reaching up with a shaky hand, I tucked my hair back behind my ear. "There is a reason why I'm here. Not that I didn't want to see you."

Her smile turned wry. "Uh-huh."

"But I need your . . . advice." I could feel my lower lip start to tremble. "I need your help."

She sucked in a sharp breath. "Okay. Now I'm starting to freak out a little."

I clamped my hands together in my lap, because I was also starting to freak out a little. Well, I was quaking inside, so I was freaking out a lot. I stared at my bleached white knuckles and forced my hands to relax. "I . . . I'm pregnant."

Silence.

So much so, you could hear a cricket sneeze.

It stretched so long that I had to look up and see

her reaction, and when I did, she was simply staring at me. Her eyes were wide, her lips were parted. Blood had drained from her face, and her hand had stilled along the dog's back.

"I've messed up," I whispered, close to tears. "I know I have. I should have . . . well, I was careful. He was careful, but I missed pills and the condom must've broken." My cheeks started to heat, and even though I'd always been open with my mom, this was an awkward conversation. "I took three tests," I rambled on. "All three of them said I was pregnant, so I know . . . I *know* I'm pregnant. I've been feeling sick and I've been tired and I . . . I messed up."

"Oh, honey." Mom snapped out of it. Leaning over, she managed to keep Loki in her lap while she squeezed my arm fondly. "You didn't mess up. Getting pregnant is *not* messing up."

Sure as hell didn't feel like the opposite. "He's not my boyfriend," I said bluntly, needing her to know the whole picture. "We were together . . . once."

Understanding seeped into her features as she got what I was saying. Pregnant due to a one-night stand. How . . . how cliché. She blinked once and then twice. "It happens," she said slowly, as if she was still processing everything. Her hand squeezed my arm again. "More than people realize, it happens."

Yeah, but I never thought it would happen to me.

Famous last words.

"You know that your father and I weren't married before I got pregnant with you," she said after a moment. "Things don't always work out as planned."

I wanted to smile, because I knew she was trying

to make me feel better about this. "But you two were together and you were in love and—"

"And none of that is required to have a baby, hon. It's nice. It's what we all hope for—what I hoped for when it came to you—but it's not always what happens."

I stared at the scratched surface of the table, my voice barely above a whisper when I spoke. "Are you . . . are you disappointed?"

"Honey, why would I be disappointed?"

A strangled laugh rattled out of me as I leaned forward, running my finger along the grooves in the table. "Um, maybe because I'm twenty-three and I'm pregnant . . . and I'm single."

"Could be worse."

I arched a brow.

"You could be sixteen and this could be happening. Or you could be sick instead," she said, her gaze steady and serious. "You know, Stephanie, things could be worse."

I thought of the knock on our door nine years ago. "You're right."

She exhaled slowly and then patted my arm before picking up her coffee. She took a huge gulp, and all I could think was there wasn't enough caffeine in the world to deal with this. "Do you know what you are going to do?"

My breath lodged in my throat. "I . . . I don't know."

There was another pause. "You have options."

I closed my eyes. The milk had started to curdle in my stomach. "I know."

"Do you know how far along you are?" she asked. "It can't be that long."

"Based on the one test and timing, I'm at about five weeks." I opened my eyes and drew in a shallow breath.

Some of the color had returned to her face. "Okay." Her tone told me she was moving into Mom-can-take-care-of-this mode. "About this guy. Does he know?"

I shook my head. "I just found out this past Sunday and I needed to wrap my head around it first."

"Understandable." Her hand returned to smoothing the dog's back. "Do you plan on telling him?"

My mouth opened, but I didn't have an answer.

She pressed her lips together and then nodded slowly. "If you choose to not go through with this, that is ultimately your choice. No one else's. I believe that, but I also believe you need to tell the father. Sorry, hon. That's just the way I feel."

The father . . .

God, hearing words like that was like getting shocked by a live wire.

But I knew in my heart of hearts that I personally wouldn't feel okay with not telling Nick. Not giving him the chance to at least know what was going on, to weigh in with his opinion. In the end, what he felt might or might not sway my decision. I didn't know, but I didn't believe that everyone else needed to feel the same way I did. To each their own. It was not my business or my place to say, except when it came to me.

And I knew I had to tell him.

"We need more cake for this conversation." Mom woke the sleeping dog and placed it on the floor, where Loki scampered off to the water bowl. She went to the counter and returned with two huge slices, one for me and one for her.

"Thank you," I whispered, my throat scratchy.

"Honey." She reached over, cupping my cheek. "This isn't the end of the world. Yes, this is a big deal. It's a huge one—one that no matter what you decide is going to stay with you for a very, very long time."

A knot formed in my throat, cutting off my words.

"No matter what you choose, no matter what option you're going to go with, I will love and support you either way," she stated, and the tears filled my eyes then. "You decide you're not ready for this, I'll be right there with you if you want me to be. And if you decide you want to go through with this and have that baby, I'm going to be a proud grandmother—a damn good-looking grandmother, too."

I laughed shakily as a tear snuck free and coursed down my cheek.

Mom caught that tear with her thumb. "No matter what, I love you and I will always be proud of you."

Chapter 13

$\mathcal{I}$ made it back to Plymouth Meeting by noon on Sunday, and while I was still freaking out every couple of minutes, I had a better grasp on things. Going home to my mother was the smartest thing I could've done.

Hearing her and being around her, spending Saturday curled up on the couch watching movies and pigging out, had helped ground me. We had talked about it, that evening over sundaes, going over the . . . the choices I had and their ramifications. There was no doubt in my mind that she had meant what she said. No matter what I decided or what happened, she would support me.

Though when I left a few hours ago, I could tell she had visions of onesies dancing in her head as she stood at the door, holding Loki in her arms.

My apartment was chilly when I stepped inside. Taking my bag to my bed, I dropped it off and then turned around, heading for the thermostat in the hallway. I cranked it up and then ate the cold-cut sub I'd picked up on the way back.

When it was close to one, I picked up my phone and brought it to the couch with me. I figured Nick had worked last night and I hoped that I wasn't about to wake him up with my text. Of course, I could call him, but that would seem odd since neither of us had ever called one another before, and I could imagine him pushing until I told him what was up over the phone.

Hey, you around?

I winced after I sent the text, because how lame was *Hey* when I was about to deliver news he could not have ever expected. A handful of moments passed before I got a response.

I thought you didn't like me anymore.

He had to be talking about the fact I'd ignored his last text. I was about to respond but he beat me to it.

I've been living in this dark, dark place.

My brows rose.

Another text came through. *Not eating. Not sleeping.*

"What the . . . ?" I whispered.

So, so sad. I shaved my head bald.

There was a pause. *I'm totally just kidding.*

A startled laugh erupted.

And all of that was probably creepy, huh? Yeah, I'm here. What's up?

Despite everything, I smiled as I shook my head. He was . . . Nick was a handful. I finally sent him back a text. *Is there any way I can see you today?* I paused and then added, *It's important.*

Several moments passed before I got a response. *Sure. I can be there around three?*

I'd texted back letting him know that was okay,

and the next two hours were filled with antsy pacing. When he knocked on my door, a few minutes past three, I nearly jumped out of my skin. I hurried to the door, opening it.

Seeing Nick after almost two weeks had passed was like laying eyes on him the first time. Dark hair brushed his forehead, the ends curling slightly. His hair was growing, I realized. Those light green eyes were warm and curious as they drifted over my face, and his smile was lopsided. The white thermal he wore stretched over his broad shoulders, and as my gaze dipped, I could see that his hard chest was outlined. He had to have one hell of a workout plan, but I wasn't sure how he stayed in shape.

I was pregnant with . . . his kid, and I hardly knew anything about him.

God, that was like dunking your face in ice water.

"Hey," he said, stepping inside. "Sorry I'm late. There was an accident. Took a while to get around it."

"It's okay." I closed the door, ignoring my pounding heart. "Would you like something to drink?"

His curious gaze stayed with me. "Sure. What do you have?"

"Um. Soda. OJ." I started for the fridge, wishing I had something harder for him to drink. "I have sweet tea."

"That'll work."

Busying myself with getting him a glass, I tried to act normal. "Did you work last night?"

"Yeah." Without looking at him, I knew he was just outside the kitchen, watching me. "I got off at one. Right now, I'm only working Thursday through Saturday."

"Is that enough hours?" I faced him, and sort of

wished I hadn't asked that. Then again, it was sort of necessary. "I mean, Roxy works four days there, doesn't she? Ten hour shifts."

"She does." He took the drink, eyeing me. "I only need to work those days right now."

What did that mean? I knew Roxy made decent money bartending, but she also did graphic design and that kind of stuff on the side. How much money was Nick bringing in if he only needed to work three days? Or maybe he didn't need to work a lot because he could still live at home with his parents, for all I knew.

Oh shit. What if he still lived at home?

I recalled him telling me that he had a college degree, so why was he working at a bar, only three days a week? God, I had so many questions.

"Did you call me over to talk about my hours at the bar?" he asked, his lopsided grin spreading.

"No. I . . ." I cleared my throat as I slipped past him and walked to the couch, trying to clear my thoughts. He followed, sitting down on the edge. "That's not the reason why I asked you to come over."

His brows rose slightly as he took a sip of his tea. "I got to admit, the anticipation is killing me."

I ran my hands down my denim clad thighs to keep them from shaking. I figured the best way to tell Nick would be like ripping a Band-Aid off. Make it quick and as painless as possible. My throat tightened. "I don't know how to tell you this." Pausing, I looked over at him. The easy grin had slipped a notch. "I'm . . . I'm pregnant."

There. I said it.

The grin was completely gone from his face and

he was staring at me like I'd spoken an entirely different language. I saw his hand spasm around the glass. He didn't speak, but since I got the most important words out, there it was, like a plug had been yanked out of my throat.

"According to the tests I took, I'm around five weeks pregnant, which makes sense timing wise," I continued in a rush. "I have a doctor's appointment on Thursday, at noon, and I'm guessing they will confirm what I already know."

Nick's mouth moved for a few seconds but there were no immediate sounds. "I used a condom." Those four words were hoarsely spoken. "I *always* use a condom."

The muscles in my back stiffened as something I'd never even thought of just occurred to me. What if he didn't believe he was the father? After all, what reason did he have, given how we got together? My heart started to pound. "I know, but the condom had to have broken, and looking back, it did feel . . . different afterward. I haven't been with anyone else since you and it had been like six months before you. I take birth control pills, but when I was getting ready to move, I missed some," I rambled on. "I didn't pay any attention to it, because I wasn't with anyone until . . . until you."

Nick looked away as he set his barely touched drink on the end table. "You're sure you're pregnant?"

"I took three tests." I waited for him to ask if I was sure he was the father. That question would sting, but I expected it, and couldn't really blame him for it.

"Oh, shit." He pushed to his feet, thrusting a hand through his hair. "Oh, shit."

"That pretty much sums it up."

Nick glanced down at me, his pupils dilated, and then he looked away. He walked toward the door, and for a moment my heart stopped. I thought he was leaving, but he spun around. Pacing. He was pacing. "How long have you known? Is that why you didn't return my text last week?"

His question caught me off guard. "I took the tests last Sunday—a week ago. I didn't answer your text, because I . . . well, honestly, I hadn't wrapped my head around it then. I didn't know what to say to you."

He faced me, his lips thin. "You should've told me the moment you found out."

I jolted. Of all the things I expected him to say, that hadn't been it. "I needed to talk to my mom first."

Nick blinked, obviously surprised. He opened his mouth and then gave a little shake of his head. Lifting his hand, he rubbed the heel of his palm across his chest. I hoped he wasn't having a heart attack. I kind of felt like I might have one.

"I'm sorry," I said, because I didn't know what else to say.

He turned away and tipped his head back, hands at his hips. "All right. I wasn't expecting this. I need a moment."

Understandable. I pulled my legs up, tucking them close to my chest as I rested my chin on my knees. I had an idea what he must be thinking. Lots of confusion and shock, I imagined. I was still shocked and I'd known for a week.

"Are you okay?" he asked suddenly, whipping back around to me. I stilled, surprised, as he sat back down on the couch. "That's why you were sick the other week, wasn't it? How are you feeling now?"

Shocked, all I could do was blink at him.

"Pregnant women get morning sickness, right? That's why you were sick?"

I snapped out of it. "I think so, but it hasn't been severe. It comes and goes throughout the day."

He stared at me a moment and then cast his gaze to the floor. "You're really pregnant."

It didn't sound like a question, so I didn't answer.

"I'm . . . I'm going to have a kid." Shock colored his tone, and I was glad he was sitting down now. "Oh, wow. I don't . . . know what to say—wait." He twisted toward me. "Wait. I'm getting ahead of myself. Do you want this baby?"

My entire body tensed and my throat sealed off as my pulse skyrocketed, turning my stomach upside down.

"Because I do," he said, his gaze holding mine. "We created this baby, didn't we? So I want this baby. You haven't said if you do or not or what you plan."

I felt my jaw loosen. No words rose to the tip of my tongue. I didn't know what to say. Shock rippled through me, floored me. Nick wanted this baby? I hadn't expected that. Oh no. I expected protests and so much surprise that we wouldn't even get to this conversation today. I figured I was going to have to search his ass down after he ran for the hills, screaming.

His gaze sharpened. "I'm assuming you haven't made up your mind or you plan on keeping the baby, because why else would you have told me. You could've just . . . you could've handled it without me ever knowing."

"I couldn't do that without talking to you." My mouth felt dry, and I looked away. Everything seemed so . . . so real, which was stupid, because everything *was* real.

"You haven't decided then?" He lurched to his feet and his hand went through his hair again. A moment passed. "Do you even want kids?" A choked laugh rattled out of him. "Fuck. Listen to us."

I squeezed my eyes shut. "I know."

"Do you?" he persisted.

"Yes. I want kids." I forced my eyes open just in time to catch a flicker of relief crossing his face. "But I thought I had time and I'd be married first. Or at least . . ."

"In love? With someone?"

I blinked and then whispered, "Yeah."

Nick's features softened before he dipped his chin. His shoulders rose with a deep breath. "I can take care of this baby—I can take care of you, Stephanie."

Holy crap.

My eyes widened, and I swore that my heart might've faltered a beat. "I don't need you to take care of me, Nick. That's not—"

"I know that's not why you told me and I didn't mean it like that. I know you probably don't think much of me—"

"What?" My brows lifted. "That's not true."

He went on as if he hadn't heard me. "—being that I bartend, but I can support you and this baby. I will. That's not something you need to worry about."

"How can I not?" The question escaped me before I could stop it.

"Trust me," he said earnestly.

My stomach roiled. He was asking for some major trust there, but in the end, whether or not he could help support this child wasn't going to determine if I kept this baby. Nick was right earlier, but it still hadn't prepared me for his willingness to do this.

Nick actually wanted this baby.

A knot took form in my throat as emotions swirled violently inside me. Normally I was so in control, but everything that was going on had blown through my defenses. Unable to sit, I stood, and before I knew it I was in the kitchen, one hand on the edge of the counter and the other tugging at the collar of my shirt. It felt hot in here. Maybe I shouldn't have cranked the heat up so much.

"Are you okay?" Nick's voice was close.

"Yeah." I cleared my throat. "I didn't plan on getting pregnant. Obviously. And this couldn't have happened at a worse time, and I feel shitty for even saying that, but I just started a new job and there is so much I want to do—planned to do—before having a child. I wanted to travel. I wanted to be stable . . ." Well, the rest of what I wanted was right in everyone's face. "And I . . ."

A hand gently settled on my shoulder, turning me around. I swallowed hard as I lifted my gaze. Light green eyes bored into mine. "And what?" Nick asked.

"I didn't plan on this," I repeated as my heart thumped in my chest. "But I want this . . . I want this baby."

Something I couldn't quite read flickered in his eyes as he wrapped his hand around my wrist, pulling my fingers away from the collar of my shirt. "Then we're on the same page."

"We are," I whispered as my gaze dropped to where he still held my wrist between us. "This . . . this isn't going to be easy, Nick."

"There isn't anything about what is happening that's going to be easy. You didn't have any siblings, right?" When I shook my head, a wry grin appeared. "Neither do I. Any experience with babies?"

My heart was doing that horrible pounding again. "Nope."

"Me neither."

"Oh geez."

Nick laughed, and I couldn't believe he could laugh right now. "It can't be that hard."

"I'm going to have to thoroughly disagree with that," I said wryly.

"We'll figure this out." His eyes searched mine when I lifted my gaze. "We will. You and I. Together. We can do this."

Together.

That one word was like having my entire chest placed inside a juice grinder. Together. Besides my mom and my friends, when had I ever approached anything in unity with someone else—with a guy? Not since high school, and really, one couldn't count that as an example.

My thoughts were still whirling and the knot was lodged in my throat, going nowhere. How I planned my entire life had veered off course in one of the most important ways. I had no idea what to expect now, not a week or a month from now, especially not a year from now.

Everything had changed, and I was . . .

"I'm scared," I whispered as my chest squeezed.

Nick didn't respond. Not vocally. The hand on

my shoulder slid around to the nape of my neck as he dropped my other hand. Without saying a word, he hauled me against his chest and his arms circled me. Stiffening in his hold, I inhaled deeply. He smelled fresh, like spring, and as he dropped his chin to the top of my head, I slammed my eyes shut against the burn.

But I wasn't just scared of having a baby. God, that did scare the living hell out of me, because I wasn't sure if I'd be a good mother, if I would raise a kid right, but the fear swirling around in me like a dusty, dark cloud was twofold.

Because as I stood there, stiff and awkward, my arms clamped to my sides, in Nick's embrace, it was hard—too hard—to look at him objectively. To separate the situation we were in and how that made me feel toward Nick, and what had existed between us before I found out that I was pregnant.

Realization was hard to swallow, but I forced myself to acknowledge what I felt every time someone mentioned his name—that tightening in my chest and stomach, the unnerving and unfamiliar sense of anticipation that always accompanied how I felt. We were obviously very attracted to one another on a pure, visceral level, but I also remembered Nick's words the night he'd came to apologize.

He wished we were different.

Did that mean he wished for something more? But he had wanted to try to be friends with me, something he'd apparently never done before. And how did I feel? Could I feel more for him?

As his hand slowly moved up my spine in a smooth, comforting gesture, I felt my heart trip over itself in response. Yeah, I could . . . I could feel more.

Maybe . . . maybe this was *it*. Maybe this attraction, the simmering chemistry, would transform into something far, far deeper. Maybe he was the . . . the *one*.

Seconds ticked by and my muscles slowly loosened. Tentatively, I lifted my hands and placed them on his waist. The embrace wasn't perfect, but as my cheek eased against his chest, I wasn't sure if either of us were capable of perfect now or if it even mattered. We were virtual strangers, with our own issues and pasts, who believed we were being responsible, only to find out life had completely different plans that neither of us foresaw.

And the hug might not seem like a big deal, but it was a start, a beginning of our linked futures.

Chapter 14

"I would like a rib-eye, medium. . . ." My gaze flicked from the young waitress to the menu. Was I not supposed to eat possibly undercooked foods now that I was pregnant? I had no idea. I needed to Google this shit. Sighing, I closed the menu. Safety over taste. "I'll go with medium well."

"Is that how you normally eat steak?" Nick asked as the waitress moved away.

I shook my head. "I normally eat it like you do— medium rare, but I'm not sure if I should be eating meat like that now."

Sitting across from me, he picked up his glass of water. "Maybe we need to get a manual or something."

"I think we do." Grinning, I fiddled with the edge of the cloth that had been rolled around the silver-ware. "I'm sure there's one out there."

After what wasn't the most awkward hug in history, Nick had asked if I was hungry. Instead of explaining that I just ate, I decided to go with whatever he was suggesting, because we needed to talk. A half an hour later we ended up at the Outback not too far from Mona's.

"You said you have a doctor's appointment, right?" he asked. "This week? I want to go with you."

For the hundredth time today, astonishment winged its way through me. I settled back against the booth. "You don't have to—"

"I know I don't have to." Nick frowned, and damn, even with a pretty decent frown on his face, he still was strikingly handsome. "But I want to."

Something warmed in my chest, but I ignored it. "It's just a general doctor. They're just going to tell me I'm pregnant and that I'll need to see an OB/GYN."

"Then why not go ahead and set that appointment up?" His gaze was steady, searching. "Why go to a general doc when you already know what they're going to say?"

Damn. He had a good point.

"I have a good point, huh?"

My eyes narrowed. "Can you read minds?"

"No." He laughed. "I'm just logical."

"Whatever," I sighed. "Okay. I can make an OB/GYN appointment tomorrow. Well, hopefully find one."

He smiled briefly. "I can be available whenever. You let me know. I can drive you or meet you there."

"Okay." Folding my arms over my stomach, I peeked up and found him watching me. "Are you . . . you going to tell your family?"

The line of his jaw hardened. "No."

His response was so quick it was cutting. "Okay."

"Dammit." He leaned forward, resting his arms on the table. "I didn't mean it like that. I don't have any immediate family—not any that would care."

I tipped my head to the side. "What does that mean?"

"A lot." He rested his chin in his hand and his fingers obscured the well-formed mouth. "I'm not close to my extended family. I don't even know if they still live around here. Are you planning on telling Roxy?"

Knowing he'd changed the subject on purpose, I struggled to let it go. Things were very new to us and our steps were tentative. If he didn't want to divulge that information right now, fine, but he would have to eventually. "I hadn't thought about it. Were you?"

"I was going to leave that up to you, but I don't think it's something I could keep secret from everyone," he reasoned. "I'll have to let Jax know if I need time off or something, but he'd keep it secret."

"He might tell Calla. I mean, they're together and I'm sure they talk. Then if she knows, there's a good chance she'll let it slip." I bit down on my lip. "We don't have to tell them anything right now, though."

He nodded. "Nothing needs to be said at the moment, but what about your job? How do you think they're going to handle it?"

"Ugh." I plopped my chin into my hands. "I don't even want to think about it and I have no idea how they'll respond. I guess I still have some time before I tell them."

Nick raised a dark brow. "I don't think you want to drop a pregnancy bomb on them a few months before you're due."

"I know, but I'm barely a month, so I have time." I wrinkled my nose when he raised both brows. "And I really don't need to tell them for a long time, right? It's not like I'm delaying the inevitable."

"Huh."

My eyes narrowed again. "What does that mean?"

"Nothing." There was a brief pause. "You're not delaying the inevitable here. You don't have to tell them yet. I mean, I think women wait for a while, but you just don't strike me as the type who delays anything. You seem like you meet most things head on."

"Obviously you don't know me well." Immediately, I recognized the snottiness in my tone.

Nick's fingers lowered from his mouth, revealing a half smile. "That's what we're doing, aren't we? Getting to know each other."

Kind of felt like we were just scraping at each other's surface and not going any deeper. "We do need to." I softened my tone.

"Agreed." Suddenly, he reached across the table with his long arm. His hand cupped my cheek, and I stilled, holding my breath as he swept his thumb along my chin. "You had a piece of lint there."

My pulse fluttered. "I did?"

"Yeah." His lashes lowered, shielding his eyes. "Not anymore."

"That's good," I whispered, the fluttering expanding. "Are you searching for more lint?"

Nick chuckled deeply, and the sound elicited a fine shiver out of me. "Maybe." His voice had changed, sluicing over my skin like warm water. "Lint are tricky little beasts. But I think I'd have to do a more thorough search." His lips curled fully as he removed his hand. "Just to make sure you're lint free in all the important areas."

I grinned. "You're so helpful."

"That I am." He tilted his head to the side and the low light glanced off his high cheekbones. "Anyway. We need to figure each other out. We are stuck with one another for like . . . well, forever now."

A wave of prickly heat washed over my skin, eroding the sensual warmth of his teasing. A bitter-edged hurt I didn't fully understand replaced it, and my mouth immediately formed words. "I guess you need to start buying better condoms then, huh?"

The grin twisted into something wry. "I guess you need to pay better attention to taking your pills, huh?"

Touché.

We both scored points there.

"Look. We need to make this work." He pressed back against the seat, his eyes chilly compared to earlier. "And pointing fingers at one another for this isn't going to do us any favors. There's a lot we need to figure out—a lot of important things like child care, how we're going to raise this kid—the money it's going to take. I'm not sure about the legalities involved in all of that, but we're going to need to figure it out."

The prickly heat spread, and I wished I was outside, letting the cold wind chill my body and erase the sting. I felt myself nod, but I couldn't get the word "stuck" out of my head. Being "stuck" with someone didn't allude to anything deeper. What the hell was I thinking earlier, when Nick had hugged me? That we could somehow grow to really care for each other, maybe even . . . maybe even love one another in the way I'd always hoped I'd fall for someone?

I was a fucking idiot.

Nick and I had sex. Now we were dealing with the consequences. Emotions weren't involved in this. Nope. Not at all.

He looked away, a muscle ticking along his jaw. The food arrived, but my stomach had soured.

Well, that new beginning didn't feel too shiny now.

The stack of fresh binders wobbled in my arms as I navigated the cubicles Monday afternoon. The revamped HR manual had been completed, but now they needed new binders, because of *reasons*. The plastic, chemical scent turned my sensitive stomach and I was half tempted to throw them into the stockroom, but once again, there were *reasons* why that wouldn't be acceptable behavior.

I stacked them on the center shelf, spines facing out, and then smoothed down the front of my blouse. A different scent overpowered the chemical one, something too musky. Turning around, I almost threw myself on the floor and started flailing like a two-year-old.

Rick stood in the doorway, his flushed face and beady eyes a very unwelcome sight. He was the source of the newest stomach-turning aroma. Some days it smelled like he bathed in cologne. He smirked.

I sighed.

Today was not a good day.

My shitastic mood kicked off in the morning when I tried to slip on this extremely cute pin-striped pencil skirt. I'd gotten it up my thighs and over my hips but when I tried to zip it up, it cut into my stomach and stretched the seams.

Then, after experiencing the very first pregnancy-related clothing failure first thing in the morning, my stomach was not a happy camper the entire rainy commute to work. Not having had the fore-sight to check on what pregnant folk could use to deal with nausea, I just had to suffer until I got home. My paranoia would not allow me to Google that info while I was at work.

Since my stomach felt like it was just bubbling with bile, I couldn't eat much for lunch, which made me hangry—hungry and angry at the same time. But that wasn't the main source of discontent during lunch. I'd hidden in my car and started call-ing OB/GYNs, and dear God in heaven, was everyone in the county pregnant and in need of a baby doctor? I had to make six different calls to find a doctor who could see me by the second week of November.

The second week of November!

Holy crap, by my calculations, I'd be around eight weeks pregnant by then. Eight weeks! That was two months and some spare change. What in the hell was I supposed to do between now and then?

There were a lot of things I could screw up in two and half months.

But I made the appointment, and then, even though the dinner with Nick last night had gone downhill as quickly as a zombie apocalypse would, I texted him the date and time I'd scheduled my first appointment.

No response.

Not a damn thing.

Oh, he wanted to be involved and we needed to be in this together because we were *stuck* together, but that text message was three hours ago, and he still hadn't responded? We were getting off to a great start.

Granted, for all I knew, something could be going on, but my shitty day was just shitacular and logic wouldn't do anything but make me angrier.

And now I had Rick staring at me like the dickhead he was.

I stalked toward the door, planning to punch him in the balls if he didn't move out of the way or brushed against me again, but as I neared him, he stepped to the side. Rick said nothing as I all but stomped past him, out the door, holding my breath so I didn't choke on the cologne. He just stood there, like a creep, staring at me.

Creeper-mc-asshole.

I'd neared my desk when Marcus's door flew open, rattling the edges. My eyes widened as I jerked to a stop. Andrew Lima raced out of the office, hauling butt to the main doors. Marcus was right behind him. Andrew's daughter—the quiet Jillian, darted out next.

"What happened?" I asked, my hand fluttering to my stomach for some unknown reason.

As I jerked my hand away, the gesture went unnoticed. Jillian's face was leeched of all blood as she hurried past me. "It's Brock," she said, her dark eyes shiny with tears. "He's been hurt."

Chapter 15

*H*ardly anyone spoke of anything else the rest of the day at work. Everyone was blown away by what had happened in one of the training rings down below. From what I could gather from the guys milling in and out of the office, Brock had been training one of the newer fighters, a young guy who had a world of potential in the mixed martial-arts arena.

No one quite knew exactly how the injury happened, but it sounded like Brock was showing the younger man grappling moves. Something had gone wrong, and Brock was flat on his back, clutching at his chest. He'd said that he felt a pop in his chest, and while I didn't know much about MMA-related injuries, that didn't sound good.

And it hadn't been.

By the time we were starting to close down the office, Marcus returned and the news was grim. Brock had suffered a pectoralis major tendon rupture—a tear in the interior muscle that surrounded the chest wall. The tear was so severe that the muscle had been separated from the bone and he was rushed into surgery to repair it. In a handful of seconds Brock "the Beast" Mitchell had suffered what some feared would be a career ending injury.

Horrified, I hadn't known what to say. I didn't know Brock that well, but it was depressing to hear that his entire future could've shifted irrevocably. The malaise lingered well past the time I'd gone home and changed into a pair of warm and comfy sweats. Roxy stopped by for a little bit, and I told her about Brock. She was as saddened as everyone else.

When she left to head up to Reece's, I chatted with Yasmine on Skype for a couple of minutes about nothing in particular before she leaned toward her computer screen, her brown eyes filled with concern.

"How are you really doing, Steph?" she asked, her voice sounding distant over the Skype connection.

I clutched the throw pillow close to my chest as I eyed her back. "I'm doing good. Like I've said."

Her head tilted to one side. "You look really tired, though."

Geez. My lips pursed. "Do I look like a hot mess or something?"

"Kind of," she replied.

"Thanks."

A wide smile broke out, raising her dark cheeks. "I don't mean anything by it. You just look tired."

I'm pregnant formed on the tip of my tongue, but I couldn't get those two words out. I had no idea what Yasmine would think. I doubted it would be the typical squeals of excitement that had gone down when Roxy heard Avery was pregnant. It would probably be a lot of "holy craps" and the like. A weird heaviness settled on my chest. I quickly changed the subject, asking about Atlanta.

Once I was off the call with her, I grabbed a snack and then plopped down on the couch, munching on Cheez-Its as I fell down the rabbit hole known as Buzzfeed.

A few minutes after nine, my phone dinged. My hand froze halfway to my mouth and an orange square fell, plopping off my chest as my gaze swung to where my phone rested on the arm of the couch.

It was from Nick.

Ok. I can be there.

That was it? Nearly nine hours later and that was his response? My hand tightened around the phone. I wanted to text him back and demand why it had taken him so long to respond, but that *wasn't* me. Or at least that had never been me before, but now was it?

I picked the Cheez-It up off my boob and popped it in my mouth, chewing the poor thing like I was a wolverine with a bone. All I wanted to do was plant my face in a pillow and scream.

Scream so many F-words that ears all around the condo blistered.

And that was a wee bit dramatic.

What was wrong with me? Hormones? Didn't women get kind of emotional when they were pregnant? That sounded like as good an excuse as any, but did it happen this quickly?

Tuesday and Wednesday were overcast and dreary, matching my mood and those at Lima Academy. Brock had made it out of surgery and he'd have to be in an arm sling for at least six weeks. It was too soon to tell if he'd heal completely and could return, or the outcome would be what everyone feared.

I hadn't seen Andrew or his daughter since Monday, but I imagined both were distraught, for very different reasons. Brock was essential to Lima's success, but I couldn't forget the way Jillian had looked at him. Even though she was leaving, she clearly was very much in love with Brock.

Nick had texted me back on Tuesday, sometime during the afternoon, and I hadn't responded, because . . . well, I didn't have a good reason. A huge part of me knew I was being childish and that, honestly, this was the time for me to act mature, but I couldn't rattle up enough energy to care.

When I got home Wednesday, I immediately pulled on flannel pajama bottoms and a loose sweater and then chatted with my mom. She was happy that I had told Nick, and while she tried to keep her cool on the phone, I could tell she was thrilled that in about eight months she was going to be a grandmother.

It was close to seven-thirty when I got off the phone with her, and I was currently eyeing the wealth of snack food in my pantry. I'd made a much needed trip to the grocery story after work on Monday, stocking up on foods that I discovered via a very confusing and somewhat overwhelming Web site for moms-to-be.

Eggs. Salmon. Veggies and fruits—colorful fruits and vegetables, because apparently there was a difference. No boring colored fruits for pregnant people! Sweet potatoes. Greek yogurt. And finally, lean meats.

I sort of liked the fatty meats, because, you know, I preferred things that had taste.

I'd also picked up a mammoth-sized prenatal vitamins and acid reflux medicine. Since it appeared there wasn't a lot that was approved for expecting mothers, and the heartburn medicine was, I thought it might help with nausea. I wasn't going to take it now, since the sickness was manageable, but it was good to have on hand.

Cheez-Its or Pringles? That was what I was debating when there was a knock on my door.

I turned around slowly as my heart did a cartwheel. A moment passed and then I approached the door. Even though some instinctual part of me knew who it was, I checked. It was Nick. Biting on my lip, I glanced down at myself and sighed. My sweats were at least two sizes too big and my cropped sweater was not something I'd ever wear in public. A decent part of my stomach was visible, and while there were no noticeable changes, I wished I had time to run back—

Well, wait. Why did I care what I looked like or what he thought? I was mad at him. And I could look worse. I could have a Cheez-It stuck to my chest or something. I opened the door, ready to demand to know why he was there.

Before I could open my mouth, Nick strolled right on in, like he had every right in the world to come in. A helmet was tucked under his arm and a worn leather jacket stretched over his broad chest.

"So you still have a motorcycle?" I blurted out, and man, wasn't that a stupid question.

He placed the helmet on the kitchen table. "Yeah, I do." His brows knitted. "I have a car and a motorcycle. It stopped raining, so I decided to ride the bike."

"But isn't it cold on the bike?"

One shoulder rose in a shrug. "You get used to it." There was a pause as that light green gaze slid over my face. "I need to get you on the back of my bike and take you for a ride."

A tight shiver tiptoed down my spine. Those words dripped with a heavier meaning. Folding my arms across my stomach, I looked away, my gaze landing on the helmet. "Why are you here, Nick?"

Silence greeted the question, forcing me to look at him. His gaze sharpened as he stared down at me, his jaw a hard line. When he spoke, his voice was clipped. "I can't believe you'd ask me that question."

I wanted to point out why I had, but the reasons weren't very good. I could recognize that now.

"So I guess this is why you didn't respond to my text Monday?" he said, his hands settling on his hips. "I've done something to piss you off. I don't know what exactly, so would you be kind enough to let me in on whatever it is?"

The prickly irritation was back, but mostly directed at myself. What was really bothering me, what I didn't have the nerve to point out, was what he had said at dinner Sunday night. That we were "stuck" together. There was the source of my frustration and . . . and yes, the dull ache in the center of my chest. But telling Nick that would be equivalent to stripping down and doing a little dance for him.

"I guess . . . I was upset over how long it took you to respond to my text Monday." I squeezed my eyes shut, hating myself for even saying that out loud, because it was partly true. "I just thought you'd . . . um, respond quicker."

When I opened my eyes, a look of doubt was etched into Nick's expression, but so was . . . amusement. I pursed my lips. What in the world did he find funny about this? He shrugged off his leather jacket and draped it over the back of the chair. Guess he was staying. "You're right," he said.

I glanced around the room. "I am?"

Nick stepped toward me, and I stilled, unsure of what he would do. He was so damn unpredictable, and he did surprise me by taking my hand. Threading his fingers through mine, he tugged me away from the entrance. My heart did an unsteady flop, because for a second I thought he was leading me back down the hall, toward the bed, and while my head said that was a bad, bad idea, my body practically exploded with a rush of hormones screaming hell yeah.

But that wasn't where he was guiding me. He led me toward the couch and then sat, tugging me down so I was sitting right next to him, my thigh pressed against his, and since my head was happily splashing around in the gutter, the contact sent a wave of heat through me.

I needed to get a grip.

My gaze dropped from his beautiful eyes to an area below the belt.

I really needed to get a grip.

Or laid.

"What are you thinking right now?" Nick asked.

"Huh?" My gaze flew to his face. "Nothing."

He turned his head slightly. "Yeah, I don't believe you. Your face is suddenly flushed and your eyes are unfocused— Wait, are you feeling okay? Is it the—"

"I'm fine." Not like I was going to tell him I was horny. I pulled my hand free and clamped them between my knees. "So . . . what was I right about?"

Without looking at him, I knew his gaze was fastened on me, and it was that intensely unnerving gaze that made you feel like he was seeing right through you.

"You were right about the not-texting-back thing. I should've texted you back sooner."

Surprised, I glanced at him sharply. "Are you for real?"

He ignored that question. "But you also should've had the balls to call me out on it immediately. We could've dealt with it then instead of you stewing for two days over it and me having to ask Roxy yesterday if you were dead."

"What?" I leaned away from him. "You asked Roxy if I was dead?"

A completely unrepentant look settled into his features. "Well, I didn't say those exact words, but I saw her at the bar this afternoon when I swung by and asked if she'd heard from you. My point is, you should've had the balls to call me out on it."

"I don't have balls," I said snidely. The crazy thing was, in any other situation I would've called his ass out on it immediately. I wouldn't have stewed over it.

One side of his lips quirked up. "Then you should've had the fertilized eggs to call me out immediately."

I jerked. A laugh roared out of me. "Fertilized eggs?"

His grin spread. "That's the next best thing to balls."

"Oh my God." I smacked my hands over my face as I laughed. "That just sounds all kinds of wrong, Nick. So wrong."

"Yeah, you're right. It does sound weird." He chuckled as I lowered my hands.

Warmth crept into my cheeks and I squirmed uncomfortably. "You're right," I said. "I should've said something or asked, or at least I should've responded. It was childish, and normally I'm not like that. I guess I'm . . ."

"Stressed?" he supplied gently, nudging my leg with his.

I nodded. "Yeah, I am, but that really isn't an excuse. It's not—"

"There was a reason why I didn't get back in touch with you until later, on Monday night. I take care of my grandfather." That statement jarred me. Nick was looking straight ahead, all the earlier humor vanished from his striking profile.

"What?" I whispered.

His throat worked before he spoke. "My grandfather—his name is Job." His full lips twitched into a brief grin. "I know that's a weird name. My family is Romani. You probably know us by the other term. Gypsy. Though most of us don't like that term. At all."

Wow, my guess that he had a Hispanic background was way off target. He was an actual Romani? For some bizarre reason, I was absolutely fascinated by this, probably because I'd never knowingly met one. There were some Romani who lived near Martinsburg, according to one of those reality shows on TV, but I'd never seen them. However, this really wasn't the time for me to ask a hundred questions about his heritage and come across sounding completely ignorant.

"And before you ask, my family has been settled in this area for years. I went to public school and I didn't grow up in a caravan of RVs," he continued, his dark brows knitting. "I know there are a lot of stereotypes about our culture, but most of them aren't true or they've been completely romanticized."

Now I felt entirely stupid for thinking what I did, but I never thought less of Gypsies—er, Romani—or anything like that. "I'm part Cuban," I told him."

He looked at me, his brows raised.

"Well, my grandfather grew up in Cuba. He made it to the U.S. when he was a teenager," I told him, shrugging a shoulder. "Anyway, just thought I'd . . . throw that out there."

The smile that formed on his lips was small, but genuine. "Good to know." He paused. "My grandfather has been very ill, and there's no one . . . left nearby to take care of him, so I do. I live with him so someone can be with him during most of the day. There's an in-home care nurse who stays with him in the evenings to give me a break and also when I'm at work."

I was floored as I listened to Nick. I didn't have a clue about any of this, but something Reece had said the night I'd been at his place came back to me. It was his response to Nick saying that he had a lot of time on his hands. Reece had called bullshit on that, and now I knew why.

"He has Alzheimer's," Nick explained.

Oh no. My heart squeezed with pained sympathy.

"It's been pretty severe this last year or so, but it hasn't always been that way. There were weeks when no one would even know anything was wrong. You know? He'd just have moments of confusion. Like he'd sometimes repeat something he'd said about an hour earlier and then he would show up with his shirt buttoned incorrectly—little things. And then it changed, but that's the way the disease is. It progresses, and he has these episodes when I need to be there for him. He gets pretty stressed when he doesn't recognize the nurse. Hell, most of the time he doesn't recognize me."

I closed my eyes.

"But he's usually comfortable around me. Maybe it's something inherent in him that knows I'm blood. The docs don't think that's the case, but whatever." Nick let out a tired breath. "But when he's stressed, it takes a lot to calm him down. Sometimes he can get . . . violent. He doesn't mean to. I think he's just so confused and afraid. Anyway, he'll throw things, and while the nurse is patient and understanding, I don't feel right leaving her to deal with it. And Monday, I'd left my phone in my car, and I honestly didn't even think about it until that night, and by then . . ."

He'd been too stressed out to really worry about my text. God, I wanted to bitch-slap myself across the face, and the only reason I didn't was because of the feeling of pride rushing through me. Nick was . . . wow, he really was the puzzle I couldn't figure out. Whatever conception I had of him was sorely off base. Taking care of his ailing grandfather was something a lot of people wouldn't do. Being a caregiver, even when you had professional help, wasn't a walk in the park. At times I knew it could be as stressful as being stricken with the disease. The fact that at twenty-six, and for how many years, Nick had been taking care of his grandfather, blew my mind.

Changed the way I viewed him.

I was proud of Nick.

Reaching over, I placed my hand on his arm. "I'm so sorry, Nick."

His gaze dropped to where my hand rested. "I didn't tell you so that you'd pity me."

"I know." I swallowed against the sudden knot in my throat. "I don't pity you. I just feel bad that you and your grandfather have to go through this. I don't have any personal experience with it, but I know how hard Alzheimer's can be. I'm . . . I'm proud of you."

Nick's surprised gaze flew to my face. He didn't speak.

"A lot of people would've placed him in a facility. You didn't."

"It might get to that point," he said, voice low.

I squeezed his arm. "And if it does, it won't be because you didn't care enough for him. I think you know that."

His gaze collided and held mine. "Yeah."

Something occurred to me. "Is that why you bartend? You mentioned having a degree, but is it because bartending allows you to virtually pick your own hours?"

"Partly." Nick leaned back against the couch, causing my hand to slide to his. I left it there.

"Is he doing better now?" I asked.

Nick nodded. "For now."

Pressing my lips together, I drew my hand back. "I am sorry you have to go through this."

He didn't respond right away. "How are *you* feeling? Still nauseous?"

The change of subject was understandable. "It hasn't been too bad. I learned that I could take antacid meds if it gets too bad and it might help. All and all, I feel kind of normal." I scrunched my nose. "Well, I might be a wee bit more emotional than normal."

Nick grinned. "Nah."

I rolled my eyes.

"Nice hair." His hand snaked out and tugged on the edge of one of my braids.

I smacked his hand away and grumbled, "Whatever."

"It's cute." His gaze was bright and soft. "You're like Pippi Longstocking."

I squinted. "How in the hell do you know about Pippi Longstocking? That's from, like, decades ago."

"I know things. Important things." He smiled. "Besides, you're like the grown-up, sexy version of Pippi Longstocking."

My brows rose. "Oh. Wow."

"But I like the sweater better," he added, his gaze dropping.

"I think you like the fact you can see some skin better," I corrected.

"You got me there." Sucking his lower lip between his teeth, he sat forward. "Can I do something?"

I arched a brow. "Uh, sure?"

Nick twisted so he was facing me, and when his hand moved toward my stomach, I realized I probably should've asked him what he wanted to do before I gave him permission. A second later the palm of his hand landed on my stomach.

Sucking in a sharp breath, I straightened. My eyes widened. His hand was large, nearly covering the width of my stomach, and his palm was warm. I felt the touch all the way to my spine.

He leaned in, so close that I felt his breath against my cheek. "I know I can't feel anything yet, but I just wanted to put my hand there."

"Why?" I felt a little dizzy, like I'd been holding my breath.

"It makes me feel close to the baby."

Oh gosh.

Oh man.

I dragged in a deep breath, but the warm and fuzzy feeling was spreading through me, and that wasn't all. He wanted to be close to the *baby*. His hand moved slightly as his fingers brushed the band on my sweats.

"It's right in there," he continued. "A part of you. A part of me. No matter how any of this came about, it's pretty amazing."

My ovaries might've just exploded.

His lashes lifted. "Don't you think?"

"Yes," I whispered and then I said it louder, "Yes."

Nick's lips brushed the curve of my cheek, and I shivered once and then twice. When did he get so close? My breath hitched as my heart thumped in my chest. If I turned my head an inch or two to the left, his mouth would be on mine. Anticipation swelled, and snapping at its heels was confusion. Why did I want him to kiss me? Okay. There were several reasons why I'd like him to kiss me. Lots and lots of reasons, but what was *his* reason?

His palm was still pressed against my stomach and those lips were somewhere in the vicinity of my jaw, and I remembered his almost kiss. The one that had caught the corner of my lips the very first night. Suddenly, kissing him was all I could think of. What would his lips feel like against mine? Would they be hard or soft? With him, probably a little bit of both. If he kissed like he fucked, it would be the kind of kiss that forever changed the way you viewed kisses from the past and the future.

Nick's head dropped a little and the stubble along

his jaw dragged across my chin. I swallowed a gasp as heat flashed throughout me. His palm slid off my stomach, spreading flames as he wrapped his hand around my hip. He pressed his forehead against my shoulder and that warm breath tickled my neck.

This sound came from him, a purely primitive masculine sound that did crazy things to my nerves. My heart pounded as he lifted his head slightly, and then I felt his lips against the sensitive spot just above my pulse. Muscles low in my belly coiled tight. *Kiss me. Really kiss me. Kiss me.* Those words were on repeat as he continued to lift his head.

Nick drew back, and he didn't kiss me, but when I laid eyes on him, I knew his mind was where mine was. His chest rose and fell heavily and his gaze was heavily hooded. Glancing down, there was no hiding the bulge in his jeans.

Holy hell . . .

"So, what are you doing tonight?" he asked, and his voice was deep, rough.

"I had no plans." I wet my lips. "Are you going to Reece's?"

He shook his head. "I didn't come over to see him. I came to see you."

That . . . that pleased me. "I was just going to watch a movie and eat some Cheez-Its. Okay. A lot of Cheez-Its. Maybe some Pringles, too."

The lopsided grin appeared on his lips. It was infectious, and I felt myself grinning back at him. "Well, why don't you pick out a movie and tell me where the Cheez-Its *and* the Pringles are. We'll watch a movie."

A huge part of me was hoping that watching a movie was code word for let's get naked, but as I picked out something I thought he'd be interested in—the movie *300*—and he returned with a slew of snacks, we did just what he'd said.

Sitting side by side, we watched all the airbrushed abs flounce across the screen—or that's what I paid attention to. I replayed memories of all the guys I'd hung out with and even the guy I dated in high school, and I couldn't recall a time where I found myself watching a movie with a guy and eating junk food while wanting nothing more than to just straddle him and get down to business.

Usually I didn't sit and watch movies with a guy I wanted to do dirty, dirty things with, and not do said things. This was a first for me, and I sort of liked it. No. Not sort of. I really did enjoy it.

Nick's warmth seeped out from him and bled into me. Once I stopped shoving food in my mouth, I found myself leaning into him. Not on purpose. It wasn't something I was wholly aware of, but at some point my entire right side was pressed against his left, and his left arm was dropped along the back of the couch.

It felt . . . right.

Eventually my eyelids became too heavy to keep open. I fought the lull of sleep, because seriously, I didn't need to fall asleep on Nick, but it was no use. Snuggled up against him, more comfortable than I could ever remember, I slipped into a peaceful sleep.

Chapter 16

I was warm, not too hot, but the toasty warmth pricked up my consciousness. I was slow to wake up and the cobwebs of sleep lingered even as I blinked my eyes open. My brows furrowed as I stared at the TV. The volume was turned down, but I could tell it was some weird info commercial. Faint light filtered in through the window.

What the . . . ?

It was that moment when I realized I wasn't alone. My breath caught in my throat as my surroundings started to make sense. Curled up on my side, my back was pressed against the source of all the hard heat.

Nick.

Oh my jeebus, I remembered falling asleep on the couch, but in those moments before I had slipped under, I honestly didn't think Nick would've stayed. My eyes widened as I took stock of the situation. Nick's body was curved around mine, and I knew this couldn't be the most comfortable sleeping position for him. He was a tall guy, and this couch was cramped.

But he was here, his hand not resting on my hip, but on my lower stomach. In the pale light of dawn, I stared at his hand in a strange sort of wonder. Had he placed his hand there on purpose? It was such a protective, male gesture. Or had he done it while asleep?

Either way, it did something to me. Sharp tingles shot from where his hand rested and spread below in a warm wave of shivers. It also formed a knot in my chest and in my throat. Like when he asked to feel my stomach last night, I was shocked and my . . . my entire being was moved. Combine all of that with what he told me about his grandfather, I was beginning to see who Nick really was. Some of the missing puzzle pieces were appearing and clicking into place. Not all, but some.

As I stared at Nick's hand, a very important sense of knowledge filled me. Nick would be a great father. I didn't know a whole lot about him, but based on what he did and sacrificed for his grandfather, I had no doubt he would approach fatherhood the same way. Not to mention he didn't see any of what he was doing to take care of his grandfather as a sacrifice. He was . . . he was a good person—a great person.

Tension that had settled in my shoulders and back since I found out I was pregnant began to slowly ease. It was like an awakening. No matter what went down between Nick and I, he would be there for our . . . for our child. I wasn't in this alone.

But as I stared at his hand, I also realized that I

didn't want him to just be the father of our child. I wanted to find the rest of those puzzle pieces and figure him out. I wanted to know what it felt like to be kissed by him, and I wanted to know what it felt like to actually . . . make *love* with him. This sudden need went deeper than the physical.

I wanted him to mean more to me.

I wanted to mean more to him.

Yes, getting pregnant was what really brought us back together, but it didn't have to be the only reason.

Carefully, I shifted so I was on my back. His hand remained where it was, splayed across my lower stomach, the weight comforting. A moment passed and his thumb moved in a slow circle, a very slow and precise circle, just below my navel.

Nick was awake.

I lifted my chin, and my gaze locked with a sleepy, light green eye. My pulse kicked up as his thumb continued to move, now in a half circle. I drew in a deep breath as my body really started to wake up and get on board with the closeness. The tips of my breasts tightened, straining against the soft cups of my bra. With each breath I took, the arousal grew and I became painfully aware of it.

"Mornin'," Nick said, his voice abrasive with sleep.

I repeated the greeting, but I barely heard it. I was too busy staring at him. A faint shadow covered his jaw. His hair was a disheveled mess, the short ends standing up in every direction, and the slight smile on his face gave him quite the boyish look.

Clearing my thoughts, I focused on something to say and then stated the obvious. "I fell asleep."

"You did." Humor filled his eyes as he lifted his head, twisting it side to side as if he was working out a kink.

"You stayed."

His gaze slowly glided over my face as he settled back down. "I did. You were just too cozy and warm to leave. You mad about that?"

"No." Quite the opposite. "I didn't mean to fall asleep."

"I didn't mind. I liked this."

My heart started doing this little dance in my chest. "But what about your grandfather?"

"I texted the nurse. She stayed. Needed the over-time, I guess, because she was really happy about it."

I lowered my gaze. "I hope that didn't cost you a lot."

"It didn't."

That couldn't be entirely true. In-home nurses had to charge a pretty penny, but I was pleased that he stayed. Really pleased.

"By the way," he drawled. "You snore."

My eyes flew to him. "What?"

"Yep." He grinned down at me. "You sound like a baby chain saw."

"I do not snore!"

His gaze was hooded. "How would you know? You're asleep."

I opened my mouth to protest, but he was right, how would I know? I never slept with a guy, not even the one I dated in high school, and while I was in college, my roommate had a habit of sleeping with ear buds in. Oh my God, maybe that was why she did that.

"Do I really snore?"

He looked serious for all about two seconds and then chuckled. "No. You don't snore. I was lying."

"You ass!" I screwed up my face as I smacked his arm. "Here I was thinking I actually sounded like a chain saw."

"A baby chain saw," he corrected.

"Whatever," I muttered, fighting a grin.

His grin was easy as he lifted his hand from my belly and scooped a strand of hair that had escaped my braids, brushing it back from my face. "Come on, you would've had to know if you snored or not. Some guy would've told you."

"I've never actually slept with a guy," I admitted. "So it could've been possible."

He lowered his hand, placing it back on my stomach. "So I'm your first."

"At something," I remarked.

"I'll take it."

I grinned. "I think you need to shoot higher."

"Babe, you have no idea how high I'm shooting right now."

My breath caught. "Tell me."

Our gazes held for a moment and then his lashes lowered, shielding his eyes. A small smile played over his lips as he spread his fingers across my stomach. I felt his chest move with a deep breath.

"I want to do something," he said as his hand inched farther south. "But I don't think you're going to let me."

I curled my hand against the side of the couch. "Depends on what it is."

"Hmm." His fingers closed around the band of my sweats. "I want to touch you."

Oh God.

My pulse tripped all over itself as he tugged on my bottoms. It felt like my tongue was glued to the roof of my mouth.

He lowered his head just slightly and I felt his breath dance against my cheek. "I want to feel you come around my fingers."

There was a good chance that my heart stopped as I shifted. I felt him then, hard against my thigh.

"I know things are . . . different right now," he said, those lips brushing the curve of my cheek as he spoke. "And I thought I didn't want to complicate things, but I've got to be real honest with you, I want to get all up in that complication. I want to get all up in you." The grip on my sweats loosened. "So are you going to make my morning?"

My chest rose and fell rapidly. For a brief moment I thought that Nick and I had a habit of doing things ass backward—sex first, then baby, and now some heavy petting, all before a date? Well, we did have a date last Sunday. Kind of?

The heat in my veins and the dampening between my thighs told the voice in my head to shut the hell up.

I was such a slave to my body, but as I turned my head toward his, and felt my nose brush his cheek, I didn't care. "I'm going to let you make my morning."

He stiffened against me and then said, "Thank God."

My eyes drifted shut as I turned myself over to his capable hands, and he didn't make me wait long. He shifted so his forehead was pressing against my temple, and I realized that in that position he could see what he was doing.

That turned me on even more.

Nick drew his hand back up to just below my navel, lingered there almost reverently, and then his large hand slid under the band of my sweats. "Holy fuck," he growled. "Tell me this whole time you've had nothing on under these?"

"Nothing." Heat turned my blood to lava. "I didn't expect anyone last night."

His fingers slowly ventured south as he used his knee to nudge my legs apart. "So you're like this when you're home alone? No panties."

"Mostly." My breath caught as the tips of his fingers brushed the sensitive nub.

"Damn. I'm not going to ever forget that."

I started to respond, but then he cupped me and all thoughts vanished. His fingers trailed lightly between my legs, moving back and forth in a languid manner that curled my toes. My breathing constricted.

"You're so soft here. I think it's the only part of you that is."

I wanted to tell him that wasn't the case. That I was a big fuzzy ball of fluff when it really came down to it, but one finger grew bold, slipping inside me. My hips arched, taking him deeper, and his answering groan sent another flash of heat through me.

His finger began to move through the wetness, slow and steady, taking his time, and my hips chased the shallow movements. A breathy moan escaped me as he added another finger, gently stretching me. I grabbed at him, curling my fingers around his wrist. Tension built and coiled in the pit of my stomach.

Nick twisted his hand so that his palm pressed

against the bundle of nerves, wringing a gasp out of me.

"Oh God," I whispered. Muscles clenched.

"That's it." His voice was thick, needy. "I can feel you."

The pace of his fingers picked up, going deeper and faster, and that tension continued to coil until the pressure shattered, whipping darts of pleasure through me. My cries were throaty and my hips came clear off the couch as the release burst into tiny aftershocks.

Nick stayed with me, knowing exactly when to slow his fingers, and when he eased them out of me, I watched him, utterly spent and dazed, my muscles nothing more than goo as he lifted those fingers to his mouth.

Holy crap.

A whole new wave of lust slammed into me as those fingers popped out. "Best breakfast I've ever had."

Rolling onto my side, I reached for the bulge that had been pressing against my thigh this entire time, but he reached down, catching my wrist. My eyes widened. "You're going to stop me?"

His expression tensed. "As much as I'm going to hate myself for this, I'm going to have to."

"Why? You had your breakfast. I want mine."

Nick's brows rose.

"Protein shake," I said, and my lips twitched.

A shock of laughter roared out of him. "Holy shit. You went there."

"I did." I tried to reach him again, but his grip tightened.

He let out a short breath. "What time do you have to go to work?"

At first I didn't understand why in the hell he'd bring up that question, but then it struck me. The bliss faded. "Oh my God." I jerked back and jack-knifed into a sitting position. My gaze zeroed in on the clock. "Holy shit! I need to get ready."

"Thought you needed your protein shake?"

I shot him a look as I lurched to my feet and thankfully didn't tumble over. "That protein shake is going to have to wait."

Nick stretched out, throwing his arms above his head as he eyed me from his reclined position. For a moment I couldn't move as I stared down at him. A very irresponsible part of me wanted to say screw it and literally screw it, but I couldn't. I backed away.

"Maybe later?" he offered, eyes hooded.

I drew in a shallow breath. "Definitely later."

Chapter 17

*W*ith Nick working the evenings and me working during the day, there wasn't a lot of time for us to
see one another. I knew I could visit him at the bar,
but what was developing between us seemed too
new and fragile for me to become his personal barfly.

But that didn't mean he was MIA after he left my
place Thursday morning.

He texted that night when he arrived at Mona's,
and checked in on Friday when he got up, which
was a lot earlier than I thought for someone who
worked until one in the morning. Then again, now
that I knew he had his grandfather to watch over, he
was probably operating on minimal sleep.

Saturday night I'd done what was a first for me.
I texted Nick before I went to bed. I'd done so gig-
gling like I was sixteen, and his answering text left
a smile on my face.

While you're sleeping, I'm thinking about breakfast.

I so knew what he meant.

For nearly four days I'd been thinking about "breakfast" and when I could get a second helping, and those thoughts intruded at the most inopportune times. Like when Marcus was rattling off a list of things I needed to do or when Deanna from HR joined me for lunch on Friday. While she'd been talking about her daughter's recent engagement, my thoughts had pranced into uncharted territory. I was wondering what it felt like to go to sleep and wake up in *bed* with Nick.

This was something I never really spent a lot of time thinking about.

Thankfully, the nausea hadn't gotten any worse as the pregnancy progressed. At six weeks pregnant, it was still there, but I grew used to what I now considered a low-alert need to vomit. I knew that I was lucky, because some women had horrific morning sickness. From what I gathered the day I'd found out Avery was pregnant, she was one of those pour souls who spent the better part of the afternoon hurling.

My mom was convinced my pregnancy would be like hers—relatively easy—and I hoped that was the case. Maybe if I didn't miss any time leading up to when I'd need maternity leave, my boss wouldn't flip a lid as much.

But that didn't mean Mom wasn't worried. When I had chatted with her on Saturday, she tentatively asked if I'd given any thought to the future and if I was making any plans. The question jarred me. Beyond keeping the baby and working at getting to know Nick better and possibly being with him, I hadn't made any plans outside of my doctor's first appointment.

When Mom realized this, she told me that I had time, but there was no mistaking the underlying thread of worry in her voice, and that anxiety transformed over to me. What was I missing? I made my first appointment. I was taking prenatal vitamins and eating the right foods.

Well, I was also eating some wrong foods, but the struggle was really with my Cheez-It Party Mix.

Obviously, I hadn't picked up a single drink since I found out, and I'd cut way back on the caffeine intake. But what else could I plan? It was too early to get obsessed with baby clothes or to start picking out baby furniture.

And the thought of baby furniture led to another major stressor.

Where in the world would I put a crib and all that jazz? In my walk-in closet? That sounded like child neglect or something.

As I drove to meet up with Katie and Roxy on Sunday morning, I came to the shaky realization that I was going to have to move again. I needed a two-bedroom. Maybe not immediately, but my one-bedroom wasn't big enough to have everything the baby would need. I could afford a two-bedroom, but it would be stretching it. Definitely not comfortably.

But I wasn't alone.

I remembered that as I parked the car, my grip easing on the steering wheel. Even our relationship never progressed beyond the physical, Nick would help me—help us.

The panic receded as I briskly walked toward the restaurant, chin down against the chill. Katie and Roxy were in their normal seats, and I joined them, rubbing my hands together to burn away the chill.

"I was wondering if you got lost." Katie arched a blond brow.

I shot her a look. "I'm wondering if you know how cold it is outside."

Roxy laughed as she eyed Katie's getup. The latter was wearing magenta—not purple, but really magenta—colored overalls. Underneath them was a sparkly baby blue sports bra.

"Do they make sports bras with sparkles?" I asked.

"What? I wish. Do you know how much easier my life would be?" Katie stuck out a glossy bottom lip. "I spend at least an hour a day bedazzling shit and using a hot glue gun."

My brows rose as I exchanged a look with Roxy.

"I've had severe hot glue gun burns. In places you do not even want to know about."

"Wait." Roxy pushed her glasses up. "I do want to know."

I wasn't sure I did.

"Sometimes you have to be wearing the clothes to make sure the embellishments look right," Katie explained, quite seriously. "It's not like they sell bathing suits with diamonds organized in the shape of a cock on the ass."

My jaw unhinged, and immediately I pictured those bottoms and knew I'd never get that out of my head. Ever.

"Okay then." Roxy smacked her hands off the table and quickly changed the subject. Drinks arrived and then our food was placed down. The steam was still rising off my omelet when Roxy's shrewd gaze landed on me. "So what's going on with you and Nick?"

I paused, a forkful of eggs and peppers halfway to my mouth. Roxy and I texted on and off, and she stopped over if I was home when she was visiting Reece, but I hadn't talked to her about Nick or about the pregnancy. I wanted to, boy did I ever want to, because I wanted to tell someone other than Nick or my mom, but Roxy worked with Nick, and that changed things.

"What do you mean, what's going on?" I asked.

Katie stabbed a piece of sausage. "What she means is that Nick hasn't hooked up with another chick since you strolled into Mona's."

Thank God I'd swallowed my food, because I was sure I would've choked upon hearing Katie's blunt remark, but a deep, almost unsettling relief uncoiled in the pit of my stomach. Whether Nick was still messing around with other people was something I hadn't allowed myself to even think about. A tiny part of me hadn't thought he was, but there were no labels between us, and even though he was attracted to me and we were linked together by this baby, that didn't mean he was settling down.

Roxy smiled slightly as she picked up a piece of bacon. "I can see that you're happy to hear that."

I opened my mouth, about to deny it, but suddenly I was tired of pretending. And that's what I was doing. It was bigger than just letting my friends in, sharing my life with them. Sooner or later they were going to find out the truth.

Nervousness made my stomach queasy. I wasn't sure how they'd respond to what I was going to tell them. I also wasn't sure how Nick would really respond, when it got down to it. "We have . . . stayed in touch," I said.

Roxy's look turned bland. "Yeah, I know that."

Waving half a piece of sausage around, Katie snorted. "In other words, you've been screwing each other's brains out?"

"Actually, no." What he had done Thursday morning didn't count. "We haven't had sex since the first time."

Katie dropped the sausage. "A pig just flew past the window."

I rolled my eyes.

"Really?" Roxy sounded surprised.

Nodding, I cut another piece of omelet with my fork. "No. Okay. Well, we've messed around—once," I added, when a knowing gleam filled Roxy's eyes. "And that was just a few days ago."

"Holy crapola, girl, I don't know any girl that Nick has hung out with after having sex with them and they've—"

"It's because he's fallen for her," Katie interrupted as she picked up her fallen sausage. No sausage left behind, that girl. "So he'll do all kinds of things he hasn't done before."

I slid her a sidelong glance. "Is that your psychic stripper powers at work again?"

"Damn skippy."

I grinned as I shook my head. "We're not boyfriend and girlfriend. I don't know what we are. Actually, that's not really true."

"What does that mean?" Roxy brought her glass to her mouth.

"We're going to be a mom and dad in approximately seven and a half months. Roughly." I dropped the bomb like someone would drop a mic.

Tea sprayed into air, luckily in the direction of the

aisle. I smacked my hand over my mouth, stifling my giggle as Katie sat there and stared at me. Guess her psychic stripper abilities hadn't enabled her to foresee that.

Once Roxy recovered from becoming a human geyser, she whipped off her glasses, lowering them to the table. "Are you screwing around with me right now?"

I shook my head.

Katie still stared at me.

"You are being totally serious?" When I nodded, Roxy sat back. "Oh my God." Her voice dropped to a whisper. "You're pregnant?"

"Yeah," I said, smiling weakly as I placed my fork on my plate. Appetite gone, I struggled to keep the smile plastered on my face, but it was hard. The reaction to Avery's pregnancy was vastly different from mine. Like two different continents different. I nibbled on my lower lip, my brows knitted. "I know Nick and I aren't together. Maybe we will be one day. I don't know. I'm kind of hoping that's the case, but right now we're working at . . . getting to know each other, but we decided to do this."

Katie's mouth popped open but she didn't say anything.

I lowered my gaze, at once very unsure of what I'd just done. Maybe I should've kept my mouth shut. "I'd missed a couple of pills while I was moving, and the condom broke," I said, feeling the need to explain so they didn't think I just ran around having unprotected sex. "I know it's not traditional and—"

"Wait." Roxy raised her hands. "Okay. I'm sorry. I'm just shocked. I didn't expect you to say that. I don't think anything is wrong, and I can tell you think that's how we feel. We don't." She glanced at Katie. "Right?"

"Right," Katie said. "I don't even think my mom knew who my dad was."

Roxy's brows knitted.

"When I was little, I was convinced that my dad worked for the CIA, and that was why I never met him. He was like a spy or something," Katie continued as I bit down on the inside of my cheek. "Then I realized it was like one of the three possible guys and none of them were spies. Unless they were a spy when it came to finding the nearest bar."

"Um. Okay." Roxy blinked, returning her attention to me. "What we're trying to say is that we're just surprised, but we're not judging you or Nick."

My spine was still stiff. "Seriously?"

"Seriously." Contrite, Roxy leaned forward. "And I'm so, so sorry if I gave you that impression. Really."

I nodded, wanting to believe her, but it was hard to forget the excitement when Avery announced her news, compared to the absolute shock clearly written on Roxy's and Katie's faces when I told them I was pregnant. Drawing in a deep breath, I decided to let it go.

"Are you guys happy about it?" Katie asked, as blunt as ever.

The flutter returned to my chest. "Yeah, we . . . we are. As strange as that sounds, we are happy about it. It was a shock, but we're getting used to it." I paused, and my next words sort of just rushed out in a jumbled mess. "Nick did this thing Wednesday night when he came over to see me. He asked if he could, you know, place his hand on my stomach, and when he did . . ." My cheeks started to heat. "He said he felt close to the baby, and I . . ."

"Turned to goo?" Roxy said, eyes unfocused. "Because that's what I would've done."

"Jumped on him and ripped his clothes off?" asked Katie. "Because that's what I would've done."

I laughed softly. "I think my ovaries exploded, but I kind of just sat there. It was . . . there really aren't words when it comes to how that feels, I guess."

"Wow," Roxy said after a few moments. "I can't believe Nick is going to have a kid. That you're going to have a kid."

"He'll be a great father," I immediately said.

Her eyes met mine and she nodded seriously. "Yeah, he will be."

I wondered if she knew about his grandfather, but if not, I didn't feel it was my place to tell. The rest of the conversation centered around all things baby—crazy baby talk. Like if I wanted a boy or a girl. Did I have a name picked out yet? Who knew?

Katie wanted to be the godmother.

I had no idea how to respond to that—to any of what they were saying.

"You know what this reminds me of," Katie said while we waited for our checks. "That movie *Knocked Up.* Except you're less annoying than that one chick and Nick is definitely more attractive than that guy."

The skin around Roxy's eyes crinkled as she laughed. "Did they end up together in the end?"

It had been many years since I'd seen the movie, so I couldn't remember, but as dumb as it sounded, I hoped so. Even far more bizarre, as we got up to leave, I kept thinking about what Katie had said more than once. That I would break Nick's heart.

I scoffed at the notion, because seriously, but nevertheless, an odd sense of unease settled in the pit of my stomach. Once in the car, I pulled out my cell and typed out a text to Nick that I wasn't sure he would be that thrilled about.

I told Roxy and Katie.

"You're going to think it's the most boring thing ever," Nick said, after I asked him what he studied in college. "It actually *is* probably the most boring thing ever. Accounting."

A startled laugh left me as I watched him. *He* was cooking *me* dinner.

That had been his response after I told him that I'd dropped the bomb on Roxy and Katie. He'd pretty much said, "Hey, I'm making you dinner tonight. Hope you like roasted chicken."

I liked food in general, so I was excited.

I also liked Nick . . . in general, so this also excited me.

"That is boring," I replied. "I never would've guessed it."

"I've always had a knack for numbers. Seemed like the logical thing to do. I have a bachelor's degree. Was thinking of taking online classes for an MBA— Wait," Nick said as he paused, a serial-killer-sized knife in his hand. On the counter was a head of lettuce, a tomato, and a cucumber. "What are you doing?"

I was standing by the counter with my forearms pressed against my breasts. Apparently I'd forgotten I wasn't alone. Slowly, I lowered my arms. "My . . . my breasts are tingly. Like really tingly. It's kind of distracting."

He placed the knife on the counter as his lashes dropped. "Yeah, it's distracting."

"Sorry?"

One side of his lips quirked up. "Do you need help with them? Because I volunteer if you need them inspected or rubbed or petted."

"You are so helpful." I grinned as I tucked a strand of hair back behind my ear.

He tilted his head to the side. "That's me. Mr. Helpful. Willing to take one for the team, even if it means I have to touch them."

"Real hardship for you."

"You have no idea." Nick went back to chopping away at the veggies. "Is that normal?"

"According to this one Web site I found, where it breaks down what to expect week by week. They've been sore, but today they just tingle." I paused, leaning against the counter. "The baby is the size of a tadpole right now."

He glanced up from what he was doing, his eyes bright. "That's . . . tiny."

"It'll almost double in size by next week," I told him, inhaling the yummy aroma of chicken and herbs. "I also have to pee a lot. Like I'm a nonstop waterfall."

His brows lowered. "Thanks for letting me know about that."

I folded my arms as I watched him shuffle the lettuce into a bowl. "I thought this was caring and sharing time."

"Speaking of sharing time, I've gotten about five million texts from Reece and Jax." He picked up the tomato and placed it on the carving board. "I'm pretty sure the moment you left Roxy this morning she got on the phone with Reece, who then called Jax."

I cringed. "Um, sorry? I didn't think about the fact she would tell Reece, which is a duh moment. I should've guessed that."

"No need to apologize." He carved up the tomato perfectly. "I'm actually glad you did say something. I don't like keeping my friends in the dark. They're pretty cool about it. Happy for me—for us."

My breath did a funny thing, hitching in my throat. I remembered Roxy and Katie's immediate reaction and I shoved those thoughts aside. Watching Nick finish the salad, I pressed my lips together. The knot was back, lodged in my chest. "I'm lucky," I said, my voice barely above a whisper.

"Of course you are." The tomato slices were scooped up and dumped in with the lettuce. "You were the honorary recipient of my very active sperm."

I laughed as I turned sideways, blinking back the sudden wetness that had gathered in my eyes. Damn hormones. "Well, besides that, Nick."

"Explain." He started slicing the skin of the cucumber with expert ease, unlike me, who always ended up losing half the cucumber during this process.

Drawing in a shallow breath, I unfolded my arms. "You're handling all of this so well. I'm lucky, because some guys . . . they would've been real assholes about it."

"Well, some guys don't need to be engaging in behaviors that can end in reproducing," he commented dryly. "I'm not one of those guys."

"True." I watched him chop for a moment. "But I

didn't really know if you were going to be like that or not. No offense, but you've been so . . . so wonderful about everything—about me being pregnant, me telling Roxy and Katie, and dealing with your friends. So, I'm lucky."

Sliding the diced cucumbers into the bowl, he walked around me, carrying the board and knife. He placed them in the sink and then turned around. Taking one step with those long legs of his, he was right in front of me. He lifted his arms, and his hands curved around my cheeks, tilting my head back so that our gaze met.

"I'm the lucky one," he said, his eyes searching mine. "You didn't make a decision about this baby without involving me. You didn't take that choice away from me. And this is something I know you don't know, but I never thought I'd have a child. Not because I didn't want one, but because I just . . . I just never thought it would happen. I wasn't screwing around when I said I didn't do relationships, but with you—with this—*this* is different. Yeah, it was a big damn surprise." His thumbs smoothed along the line of my jaw. "But there's not a single part of me that doesn't realize how lucky *I* am."

I lowered my gaze, willing the stupid wetness to go away. "There you go again, being all great about this."

"It really isn't that hard to be this awesome," he teased.

My lips curved up, and when I raised my gaze, I figured it was time to really figure out what we were doing, what both of us expected from this. "Can I ask you something?"

His gaze dropped to my mouth, and the tense,

hungry look that settled into his features was hard to ignore. "You can do whatever you want."

Reaching up, I wrapped my hands around his wrists. "Is it true that you haven't hooked up with anyone since you met me?"

Those heated green eyes flew to mine. "I'm going to go out on a limb here and say Roxy's been very chatty lately."

"Actually, it was really Katie."

"Girls," he murmured, and then he laughed softly. "They're right. I haven't been with anyone since I've met you."

The relief from earlier resurfaced. "Why?"

"Why?" His brows rose. "I don't know."

"You really don't?"

Nick's forehead wrinkled as he seemed to seriously mull my question over. He dropped his hands but didn't step away. "I just . . . there's been opportunity . . ."

"I'm sure there has been," I replied wryly.

A quick grin flashed across his face, but it didn't dampen the confusion etched into his features. "I just haven't been interested, and I . . ." Trailing off, he closed his eyes. "Fuck it."

My head jerked back as I blinked. Fuck it? That was not the response I was looking for, but before I could say anything, his hands had clasped my cheeks and he'd tilted my head back again. He lowered his mouth to mine.

And he kissed me.

Chapter 18

The first contact of his lips against mine was a shock to my system. It had been so long since I'd been kissed, really kissed, that I'd seriously forgotten how it felt, but even with the lack of memories, I knew this was going to blow every other kiss out of the water.

His lips glided over mine once and then twice, as if he were mapping out the layout, committing the feel to memory. When he tilted his head to the side, I felt his tongue sweep across the seam of my mouth. There wasn't a moment of hesitation on my part.

I opened for him, and he took that kiss deep. My hands settled on his arms and my body sank into his. The kiss branded me, dug in below the skin and muscles, and wrapped around my bones. I didn't think I'd ever been kissed like this. Not that I could remember.

Not that it even really mattered.

Clutching his arms, I kissed him back. I chased

after him, staking my own claim. A soft groan rippled out of him, and I knew he was also branded. Our tongues tangled, and the touch of his mouth against mine increased. Raw. Fierce. Those were the two words that came to mind as he started to back me up. My hands slid down his taut sides, reaching the low hanging jeans. One of his hands slid around to the nape of my neck, tangling in my hair as—

The one minute warning went off in the oven, breaking us apart. Both of us were breathing heavy as we stared at one another. My lips were pleasantly swollen and I felt thoroughly kissed.

"That's why," Nick said thickly. "That right there is why I haven't hooked up with anyone else."

"A kiss?" My chest rose and fell sharply.

"Not just a kiss." He shook his head as he dragged his thumb along my lower lip. "It's the way you feel against me—the way your body just softens right into mine. It's those tiny sounds you make when you're liking what I'm doing. It's the way I get as hard as a baseball bat if I even think your name. And it's been that way since I saw you in those damn little shorts."

My mind zoomed back to the day I was moving in. "Those were some little shorts."

"No shit." His voice dropped a level. "I'm going to be honest. After we hooked up, I wanted to get right back inside you, and it was real hard not to *accidentally* run into you again in those days afterward. I didn't think it would happen again. That's just my practice, but when you tore into my ass in the middle of the bar, you caught my attention, and it isn't going anywhere."

In my chest, my heart started jumping around.

"I know I said I wanted us to be friends, but obviously, I'm shitty at the boundaries that friends have," he continued, his gaze never leaving mine. "Things are different now than they were then."

Because of the baby.

"I don't know what's going to happen between us, but I know we can't be just friends." His forehead dipped to mine, and I sucked in an unsteady breath. "And I know—yeah, I know—you can't just be friends with me. Friends don't kiss like that and friends sure as fuck don't come like you did around my cock and my fingers."

Oh dear.

Those lips curved up at the corners. "So that's why I haven't been with anyone else, and I don't plan on changing that. Not when you and I are going to try to make the best of this."

Make the best of this? My thoughts spun those words around and around in my head. They weren't the most romantic or the most promising, but they were the truth, and more than that, they were realistic expectations, and that was something I valued higher than pretty words.

Even though pretty words were nice to hear from time to time.

"Yeah." I smiled up at him, feeling a bit shaken. "We'll make the best of this."

Making it work between us was immediately tested not even five minutes after we finished the yummy dinner. The in-home nurse had called.

Nick answered right away. "What's happening, Kira?" Whatever she said on the phone wasn't good, because his eyes closed and he pinched the bridge of his nose. "No—it's okay. I'll be right over. Yeah—no, it's fine."

When he hung up the phone, I spoke first. "You have to go. I understand."

"I'm sorry. My grandfather is having another . . . thing." He started to rise.

"Like I said, I totally understand." I'd popped up. "Do you want me to go with you?"

The look on Nick's face wasn't something I'd forget in a long time. He looked horrified by the idea of me joining him. "No. That's not necessary. Not at all."

I didn't take it personally, but I'd wanted to tell him that I could handle whatever was happening with his grandfather. However, I didn't want to delay him further. Nick had started for the door, shrugging his jacket on. But before he left, he returned to where I stood and kissed me. Much like the first one, the sensations it evoked were shattering and devastating, with all the feelings it stirred to the surface.

I felt that kiss the whole time I was cleaning up.

The week leading up to Halloween ticked by with a weird feeling of things moving too slow and yet too fast at the same time. Being pregnant made me hyperaware of the passing of time, something I hadn't really paid attention to before. Now everything in my head was catalogued by weeks.

Dan, one of the Lima brothers whom I'd met on my first day, had taken Rick and another salesperson on a business trip to the West Coast. I wanted to throw a little party at my desk. Maybe I'd get lucky and Rick would end up staying on the opposite coast. My heightened sensitivity to smell and to jackasses approved of such a move.

I was busy at work the entire week, helping Marcus prepare for his own business trip in November. He would be going to my hometown to help get all the approvals necessary for expanding the academy. I still wondered if Andrew's daughter had an idea that her father was setting up shop there. I hadn't seen her since the day Brock was hurt, and I hadn't see him either.

On Thursday, Nick had surprised me with a text saying he was going to be in the city in an hour and asking if I wanted to get together for lunch. What shouldn't have been a big deal had my stomach tumbled in knots. How crazy was it that it was the first time I'd ever done something like this with a guy I was interested in?

I had all this experience, but a lot was still unknown to me.

Grabbing my purse off the desk, I headed down to the gym level and immediately saw Nick crossing the street, heading toward the academy. I stepped outside and waited on the sidewalk.

His dark hair was growing, and I liked it that he was wearing it down. It was artfully messy and suited his striking face by softening the harder lines. Wearing his worn leather jacket, he hopped up on the sidewalk and stalked toward me. I couldn't stop the smile from forming. I was such a goober.

"Hey," he said, stopping in front of me. Pulling his hands out of the pockets of his jeans, he attacked the buttons on my coat. "Were you so excited to see me you couldn't put your jacket on correctly?"

I rolled my eyes. "Yep. You got me."

He chuckled as he finished with the last button near my neck. "I don't want you getting sick."

Since that was kind of cute, I didn't undo the last

button even though I felt like it was one inch away from choking me. "I thought we could hit up this diner two blocks down. They're fast and I've always been able to find a seat.

"Fine with me."

Nick fell in step next to me as we headed toward the crosswalk, navigating the steady stream of people. Our arms brushed every couple of steps, making me aware of how close our hands were. Would he hold my hand? Should I initiate the contact?

Why was I even thinking about any of that?

Mentally kicking myself, I glanced over at him as we waited for the little person in the box to turn green. "So what brought you into the city?"

"I was shopping for a Halloween costume."

"What?" I laughed.

He grinned. "I'm kidding. Though Roxy has Jax convinced that we all should dress up for Halloween this Saturday."

"Are you dressing up?" Excitement bubbled up. I loved Halloween, and every year, I always got into it, dressing up and finding a party to go to. This year was going to be different, though. Even if I did know someone who was throwing a party, going to one felt weird knowing that I'd be six weeks pregnant. Or maybe that wasn't weird and pregnant chicks still went to parties and bars and stuff. I had no idea. I needed to Google that later.

"I'm going as a bartender," Nick answered.

I grinned as we crossed the street. Wind caught my hair, tossing it around my face. "That's real creative, Nick."

"I know, right? I think Roxy will be shocked," he replied, grinning. "I actually came in this morning to talk to the admission people over at Strayer University about their online masters program."

"Really?" I reached up, snagging a piece of hair that was trying to get in my mouth. "You're seriously considering enrolling?"

He nodded, and I thought that either the cold wind was pinking his cheeks or he was flushing. "Yeah, I'd been toying with the idea for a while and right now seems like a good time to make that move. Financially I'm doing okay, but with the baby coming, I need to . . ." His brows pinched, and my breath caught in my chest. "I need to really start thinking about the future. There's no excuse for me not to do online classes, and with the way things are going with my grandfather, the flexibility of bartending isn't going to be necessary for that much longer."

The chill that skated over my skin had little to do with the cold. "What are you saying?"

Nick glanced over at me, his expression blank until I saw his eyes. Pain surfaced there, clearly visible. "I don't think he has very much longer."

"What?" My step faltered on the middle of the sidewalk outside the diner. "Nick—God, I'm sorry. Are you . . . are you sure?"

He stood, shoving his hands back in his pockets. "Yeah, on Tuesday I had to take him into his doctor, and with the episodes becoming more and more frequent, it's kind of like the writing on the wall, you know? He was kind of hovering between the last two stages of the diseases, six and seven, the last year, but he's definitely in the final stage now and he's started having problems swallowing and . . . yeah, it's happening."

I pressed my hand against my chest, above my heart. "I don't know what to say."

"I know. It's not easy to even think about him passing, because no matter what fucked up things happened growing up, he was always there for me." He cut those words off abruptly and looked away. "I don't want to take him out of his home, so I'm meeting with . . . with Hospice next week." Nick cleared his throat. "Then they'll come out and see him. I think I've got time with him, but . . . it's nearing the end. I just know it is."

There really weren't words for things like this, so I stepped forward and placed my hand on his arm. His gaze shot to mine, and I stretched up, pressing my lips against his cheek. When I settled back on my heels, I still held on to his arm. "I'd like to meet your grandfather, Nick."

He didn't respond for a moment. "It's not easy being with him sometimes."

"I know." A cab raced by, blowing its horn.

Nick looked like he wanted to say more, but he stepped to the side and opened the door to the diner. "Come on. Let's stuff our faces."

We had a good lunch, chatting about nothing important, and Nick didn't bring up his grandfather again. There was no mistaking the fact that even though Nick and I were attempting to bring our lives together, some things were still so very separate.

And it wasn't just him.

It was me, too.

That night, I texted Roxy about Halloween at Mona's, partly out of boredom, but mostly due to curiosity. She was most definitely dressing up, but she wouldn't tell me what she was going as.

You shld come and see for urself! It will be fun!

I stared at Roxy's text, and the humming excitement from earlier returned. It would be nice to get out and do something. Since I'd moved here, I hadn't really done anything social except Sunday Fun-day, and the two times I'd gone to Mona's. I was getting tired of seeing the inside of my apartment, but should I really go to a bar? I texted that question to Roxy.

Her response made me laugh. *I didn't suggest u come and get drunk. So why not?* And a follow-up text pointed out that Avery had been in Mona's after finding out she was pregnant. I had forgotten that, but I did remember Cam stood around her like her own personal bumper car if anyone got too close.

Yeah, why not? I still wasn't too sure, so I decided to Google it, and then I immediately regretted doing so, because of opinions. Dear God, everyone had *opinions*. But the most hilarious thing I discovered, when typing out *Is it okay for pregnant woman to go*, Google autopopulated it as: *Is it okay for pregnant woman to go to a haunted house.*

What the what?

The consensus was that it was pretty much okay as long as it was safe. Mona's didn't allow smoking inside and the place wasn't wild.

Early pregnancy must affect memory, because I ended up forgetting about it until Saturday evening. Handing out candy was a total bust since only a handful of kids lived in the condo and they piled into cars and drove into the city or to subdivisions. I found myself standing in front of my closet, holding a large bowl of candy. Mindlessly searching out boxes of Nerds, I debated my options. I could sit here and pig out on sugar or I could get my ass in a car and go hang out with people.

Being pregnant didn't mean I needed to sequester myself.

And the anticipation brewing inside of me was another good reason to go. I wanted to see Nick because I . . . I actually missed him. With our opposite schedules and what was going on with his grandfather, it limited the time we could see each other. And it didn't help that neither of us was real skilled when it came to the whole relationship business. We didn't make plans to see each other like I imagined normal couples did.

I was going to change that.

Mind made up, I put the candy bowl on the counter, got changed, started toward the door, backtracked to grab a handful of Nerds for much needed sustenance for my sweet-pea-sized baby during my reentry into society.

Mona's parking lot was the opposite of packed. For Halloween, I expected it to be busier, but I could count on both hands how many cars I saw. Grabbing my beaded clutch off the seat, I headed into the bar.

A few older guys were back at the pool tables, the sound of balls clanking off one another breaking up the low hum of music. My gaze swiveled to the bar. A lot of the stools were empty. As I walked forward, I saw that Calla was in town. Her long blond hair was pulled up in a ponytail and she was waitressing, if the apron was any indication. The white T-shirt and black shorts were vaguely familiar. It was the green sticker on her shirt that gave it away. I grinned.

Calla was dressed like Sookie Stackhouse.

Then I saw Roxy standing near her.

I burst out laughing. Her hair was hidden under

a brown wig that looked like someone had taken a weed whacker to it, and her normally purple glasses were replaced with round, owlish-shaped ones. If the lightning mark drawn on her forehead with what appeared to be an eyebrow pencil wasn't a dead giveaway, the black cloak and red and gold scarf was.

"Harry Potter?" I asked as I hopped up on an empty seat, placing the clutch in front of me. "You dressed up as Harry Potter?"

She grinned as she grabbed a bottle of tequila. "You have no idea how long I've been planning for this."

Calla leaned against the bar beside me. "We went with a book theme. Of course, we were the only two people who actually followed through."

Remembering what Nick had said, I wasn't surprised. "Can you even see with those glasses?"

"Barely," Roxy chirped. "But it's worth it."

Reece walked past me, coming from the direction of the restrooms, dressed as a convict in a white and black striped outfit. Ironic. "It's kind of weird that my girlfriend is now a prepubescent boy."

"Only if you make it weird," Roxy replied before turning her big-eyed stare on me. "Glad you decided to come out. Who are you dressed as?"

I glanced down at myself. "Um . . . a lazy college student?"

"Nice," Reece replied, angling his body toward mine. "And I hear congratulations are in order."

Nodding, I was surprised to feel my cheeks heat up as Calla bobbed her head. "Yes!" she exclaimed. "God, I'm lame. Congrats! You and Avery are going to have like baby twins. Though she's a couple of months ahead of you."

That wasn't weird or anything if I thought about it. "Thank you," I said, meaning it.

Reece grinned over my head at Calla. "You're next. I keep telling Jax that."

"Oh no. I'm not open for baby business any time soon." Calla looked pointedly at Roxy. "Maybe it's going to be a little Reece or Roxy Anders next."

Reece nearly choked on his drink.

Shaking her head, Roxy wisely ignored both of them. "Soda or water?" she asked me.

"Do you have ginger ale?"

Calla clucked her tongue with sympathy. "Are you feeling nauseous?"

"Not right now, but I've been drinking so much of it, I think I'm addicted," I explained.

She glanced at the door as two women roamed in. "How has your morning sickness been? I know Avery has been having a horrible time with it."

"I've been lucky so far, because it hasn't been too bad. My mom seems to think it will be like her." The two women who came into the bar sat at one of the round tables in the center. They picked up laminated menus. "She had a fairly easy pregnancy."

"I hope for your sake it is. The stuff Avery has been telling me makes me want to swear off pregnancy for life." Calla shuddered. "With Cam traveling back and forth between Shepherd and D.C., he's missing out on all the fun stuff."

"He's still playing soccer?" I asked.

She nodded as she glanced over at the women. "Be right back."

As Calla hurried over to the customers, I glanced around the bar. Roxy placed a glass of iced ginger ale in front of me.

"Nick's back in the kitchen," Reece said, obviously reading my mind. "Does he know you're here?"

"I didn't tell him I was coming out." I sipped the drink, loving how the fizzing bubbles burst across my tongue. "I kind of decided to come out last minute."

Roxy frowned as she turned her attention to Reece. "Back up. Why would she need to tell him, Reece?"

Her boyfriend opened his mouth and then took a moment, appearing to consider what he was about to say so he didn't dig himself a grave he couldn't climb out of. I bit down on my lip to stop myself from grinning. "What I'm trying to say," he stated slowly, his eyes on Roxy, "is that he would probably just like to know where his girl is, and if she wanted me to, I could go and get him."

I was Nick's girl? Suddenly I wanted to giggle.

Roxy did not appear amused. Her frown deepened. "And why would he need to know where she is?"

He raised an eyebrow. "Maybe because . . . he cares?"

"Or maybe because he needs to realize that she's a grown woman who doesn't need to inform him of her coming and goings."

His eyes narrowed. "Maybe he realizes that she's a grown, capable woman, but he still worries about her safety."

I rested my chin in my hand, using my fingers to cover my mouth. At this point I knew they weren't talking about me. Calla streamed past us, heading for the kitchen. She shot Roxy and Reece a weird look.

"Maybe he shouldn't worry so much," Roxy shot back.

Reece sat back, crossing his arms. "Seriously?"

"Yeah. Seriously." Roxy folded her arms, mimicking him.

Before Reece could respond, a door opened on the other side of the bar and Jax walked out, and right behind him was Nick. I straightened on the stool, pressing my lips together. Calla must've said something about me being there, because Nick's gaze swung right to where I was sitting. While Jax entered the bar, Nick stalked around it, heading straight for me. I relaxed, starting to grin.

"What are you doing here?" Nick demanded.

Our little audience consisting of Jax, Roxy, and Reece froze as the worst kind of reasons bloomed in my mind at why Nick would be asking such a question. A strange slice of panic cut though me. Heat burned up the back of my neck. *"What?"*

On the other side of the bar, Roxy smirked. "Here we go again."

Chapter 19

This was so not happening again.

Nick was oblivious to how close he was to death as he placed a hand on the edge of the bar and leaned in, his face coming dangerously close. "What are you doing here, Stephanie?"

"Oh, man." Jax spun around and headed toward the other end of the bar.

I took several deep breaths. "Why would I not be here, Nick?"

His brows lifted like twin wings, but Reece cut in before he could respond. "Answer that question carefully, my friend, because I just went down that road. It was curvy."

"Yeah, we just had this conversation for you," Roxy said, her eyes sharp behind her Harry Potter glasses. "And Reece didn't fair too well."

Out of the corners of my eyes I saw Calla start toward us, but Jax tagged her with a quick shake of his head. She wisely stayed away.

Nick was ignoring everyone, though. "Why would you not be here, in a bar? You're *pregnant*."

I opened my mouth, but there were no words, so my jaw snapped back together. Nick wasn't exactly mad, more like shocked, and my irritation gave away to indecisiveness. I glanced around, and I saw Roxy looking like she was seconds away from whacking Nick over the head with a bottle of liquor.

"It's safe for me to be here," I said, my voice low. "I'm not drinking. No one is smoking. And I doubt there's about to be a massive fight with this crowd." I could feel the heat traveling from my neck to my face. "I even looked it up on the Internet. Pregnant women go out." Then I started rambling, and I didn't even know why, but I wanted to smack myself so I stopped. "I was bored. All I've been doing is sitting in my apartment, night after night. It's really lonely and I've—" Luckily, I cut myself off before I blurted out that I missed him. Right now I wasn't sure if that was wise.

"Hey Nick, you got a minute?"

I glanced over to see a heavier older man with a bald head and grease stains splattered across his blue shirt. He was standing in front of the kitchen doors, and I assumed that was the cook.

Nick's shoulders tensed as he sighed and straightened. His eyes were fastened to mine. "I'll be back in a few."

Looking away, I nodded. Nick thrust his hands through his hair as he wheeled around, walking back toward the kitchen. My gaze fell to my ginger ale. Bubbles clung to the glass wall, and I suddenly found myself so very interested in those little dots of carbonation happiness, because I could feel several sets of eyes on me. I squirmed in my seat, the muggy and oppressive feeling crowding my thoughts. I was . . . indecisive about coming here now, and I felt . . . embarrassed. Was it wrong? I mean, I could see both sides of the argument, but what I'd said to Nick had been true. All the alone time was getting to me.

"You okay?" Roxy asked.

Swallowing hard, I nodded as I lifted my gaze. "Yeah. Yes. I'm okay."

A look of doubt crossed her face as she turned to one of the guys from the pool tables. She was grabbing bottles of beer when I saw Nick step out from the kitchen. Jax walked over to him and glanced inside when Nick nodded in that direction. Calla joined them, and even though my head was caught up in its old weird brand of misery, I couldn't help but notice how Nick stiffened with her arrival. Recalling what Roxy had said about his behavior around her pecked at my attention. He obviously wasn't comfortable. That much was true, but why?

Why did it really matter right now anyway? I picked up my clutch, holding it in my lap as my gaze returned to my glass. The bubbles were less active. For the first time that I could remember, I felt out of place, and God, was that a pleasant feeling. Who knew that becoming pregnant would be such a blow to confidence? Then again, maybe it wasn't the pregnancy. Maybe it was the fact that everything in the last couple of weeks had been completely uncharted waters for me.

Being pregnant. Acknowledging that I wanted more from Nick. Attempting a real relationship. *Being pregnant.* Not being up front with my boss.

Being away from my mom. All of this was new to me.

The weight of it all suddenly landed on my shoulders, and I swallowed a sigh. Going back home and curling up with that bowl of candy sounded like a really fun idea.

"Hey."

I looked over at Reece. "Yeah?"

"Don't let it get to you," he advised quietly. "Nick's a guy. And guys are generally stupid. Trust me, I know. I'm a guy. A stupid guy from time to time."

Appreciating the words, I smiled slightly as I ran my fingers over the beads of my clutch.

When I didn't say anything, Reece continued, his voice low. "As long as I've known him, he's never been serious about anyone. He's probably going to need a substantial learning curve when it comes to not saying things that are going to piss you off."

I couldn't help but laugh at that, but my experience with real relationships was as nonexistent as his, and I wasn't over here acting like an ass. Well, I kind of acted like an ass that time I didn't respond to his text, but at least my bitchy behavior was in private.

About fifteen minutes passed and Nick had disappeared back into the kitchen along with Jax. I had no idea what they were doing in there, but when I glanced at my phone, it was close to nine. My gaze swung to the kitchen doors again, but they remained closed. Roxy was over at the other side of the bar, mixing three drinks at once.

"Hey," I said, sliding off the stool. "I'm going to head out of here. Can you let Roxy and Calla know I said good-bye? I'll text Nick."

Reece lifted his glass of what I assumed was water and eyed me over the rim. "Yeah, I can do that."

"Thanks." I started to turn.

"Drive carefully."

I nodded and then left the bar. The cool air that greeted me was a welcome respite. Once in my car, I sent Nick a quick text letting him know I was going home. The drive back was quick, and the first thing I did when I walked into my bedroom was kick off my shoes and pull my sweater off. I tossed it in the wicker hamper and then turned, planning to go back to the kitchen and reacquaint myself with the bowl of candy, but my gaze strayed to the shelf, across the spring break picture, and stayed on the picture of my father.

He was in tan army fatigues, and that's how I always remembered him. Even when he had been home, at some point I saw those tan camouflage pants. They were a symbol of him coming home and a warning that he would soon be leaving. It is possible to love and hate something so fiercely and so equally.

Reaching up, I ran my fingers along the framed photo as I let out a shaky breath. God, I missed him so very much, and I couldn't help but wonder what he'd say about having a grandchild—what he would feel. Would he have been proud or disappointed? No matter what, I knew he'd be as supportive as Mom.

I bit down on my lip as I lowered my hand. Now I really needed that candy. Tonight I was going to eat my emotions. I'd started down the hall and reached the bathroom when I heard a knock on my front door.

Frowning, I walked to the door and checked out the peephole. Surprise shuttled through me. It was Nick outside, but that didn't make sense. He was supposed to be at work. Throwing the lock, I opened the door.

"What are—?"

The rest of the words were lost in action. He stepped in, shutting *and* locking the door behind him. My heart jumped into the vicinity of my throat. Nick circled an arm around my waist, lifting me up and pulling me against his chest. His other hand folded across the nape of my neck. Within a heartbeat Nick's mouth was on mine and he was kissing me. There was nothing slow and tentative about this kiss. It was deep and consuming, and before I knew it, my arms were around his neck. I hung on to him, reeling from the depth of the kiss, of how I felt in his embrace. Like a treasure or a rare work of art. That was how he kissed, and it was like touching on forever.

Nick was slow to break the contact, but when he did, he pressed his forehead against mine. "I'm sorry," he said, and the kiss had twisted up my senses so much that I didn't realize at first what he was apologizing for. Or why he was talking. I just wanted him to kiss me again. "I didn't mean to come off as a dick at the bar," he explained, clueing me in. "I was just surprised to see you and I was worried about you being in there, in case something happened."

My fingers tangled in the soft strands of his hair. "Nothing would've happened."

"Yeah, life has a way of proving that statement wrong." His lips brushed over mine as he spoke, sending a series of shivers down my spine. "Anyway, I think I need to learn how to think before I speak."

A little smile tugged at my lips. "That sounds like a good plan."

"You think so?" His gaze was hooded as he

kissed me softly. When I nodded, I was rewarded with another lingering, blistering sweep of his lips. "Hold on."

My breath caught as the arm around my waist lifted me clear off my feet. Instinct guided my legs around his hips. I felt him then, hard and straining against his jeans. It was like a switch had been thrown inside me. When he'd kissed me, pleasure swirled tightly, but feeling him now sent a bolt of pure lust through me.

Nick started walking, carrying me back toward the bedroom as he spoke. "I didn't think."

"Think about what?" There was a breathless quality to my voice I didn't even recognize.

With his long-legged steps, we were in my bedroom within a heartbeat. "I didn't think about how lonely you've been." Before I could respond, he was kissing me again, his tongue dancing along mine. "That you're new to this town, new to work, and new to me."

Another deep, scorching kiss scattered my thoughts. He stopped in the middle of my bedroom, the hand around the back of my neck tightened, tangled with my hair. "I wanted to tell you that at the bar, but I was middle of helping Clyde hook up a new fryer. That shit was actually complicated. And when I came back out, you were gone."

"I texted you."

Nick shifted, placing me on the edge of the bed. "I didn't check my phone." Straightening, he shrugged off his leather jacket. It hit the floor with a soft thud. "As soon as I saw you were gone, I went to Jax. He let me go."

I wet my lips as he reached down, wrapping his fingers along the hem of his shirt. "You left work to come here?"

"I don't like the idea of you being lonely." Pulling the shirt over his head, he let it fall to where his jacket rested. "Fuck. I don't like that idea at all."

My mouth dried as I got a good eyeful of him. Things had been so fast and heated the night we got together that I really didn't get the time to appreciate him in all his bare-chested glory. Nick had a great body—a runner's body. Chest defined and hard, stomach rippled tautly, and hips narrow and lean. Those jeans hung way low, and my eyes followed the fine trail of hair that started at his navel and disappeared under the band of his jeans.

He kicked his boots off next, then his socks. I don't know what it was about seeing a man's feet, but there was something entirely intimate about it. Maybe I was just weird like that. "You shouldn't feel that way," he continued, drawing my gaze to his. "I don't want you to."

"I know you have a lot on your plate and—"

"Yeah, I do." His fingers went to the button on his jeans, flipping the waist open, then the tinny sound of the zipper going down sent goose bumps over my skin. "But there's time. There's a lot of time, and I'm going to start making better use of it."

His jeans dropped, and he was in a pair of tight black boxer briefs.

"I can totally get behind this use of time," I murmured.

He chuckled. "And that's why I like you."

There was a tiny part of me that wanted to demand what else he liked about me, but that wasn't what came out of my mouth. "It's been a long time since I've been kissed."

He stilled, his lips curling up at the corners. "What?"

"I . . . I haven't really kissed a guy since high school," I admitted, feeling a little foolish for blurting that out. "I know that sounds all *Pretty Woman*, but it's just not something . . ." An unfamiliar moment of uncertainty slammed into me. "God, that's a stupid thing to say right now. Can we forget I even spoke and get back to getting naked?"

"No." He shook his head. "I get it." He reached out, smoothing a hand along my cheek. "You and I . . . ? We're something else, aren't we?"

I laughed softly.

"Most people wouldn't get it, probably wouldn't even tolerate us, but together . . . we make sense."

There was a startling truth to his words, but there was also a part of me that wondered if he would've come to that conclusion—if I would've found myself here with him—if I hadn't gotten pregnant.

Then Nick was naked, and I was pretty much only capable of focusing on that. I hadn't even seen the last piece of clothing go off, but there he was, and dear God, it was like hitting the male jackpot.

A hundred percent male, he was a study of hard lines, cut muscles, and masculine beauty. He had no shame standing there in front of me, and there was no mistaking how ready he was. And his size? Whoa.

Pulse pounding, I dragged in air as he curved his fingers under my chin. With slight pressure, he urged me onto my feet. A small grin played across his lips as his hands slipped down my arms and then to the hem of my tank. Without saying a word, he tugged it up and over my head. It joined his clothing. The tips of my breasts were already tight, aching.

His gaze dipped and he made this sound in the back of his throat that turned my knees weak. "These . . ." He ran one hand over the cup of my bra, and I sucked in an unsteady breath. "You have no idea how badly I've been wanting to see these." That hand glided up, over the black lace and then under the cup. His thumb smoothed over the tip, and pleasure darted out from there, cascading into a shimmery veil of pleasure. "To touch them." His other hand snaked around my back, and with nimble fingers he unhooked my bra.

A flush spread across my skin as the bra slipped down my arms and off me. Bare to his eyes from the waist up, I bit down on my lip as I let him look his fill, and he did. He looked until I felt like he was committing the image into his memory, until that flush turned into sweltering heat.

Then he cupped me with both hands.

My back arched and a breathy moan escaped me as his fingers did crazy insane things to my senses. I reached out, placing my hand on his chest to steady myself as he explored. His skin was hot under my palm and I could feel his heart pounding.

"Nick," I breathed.

He shook his head. "I didn't take my time when we were together. I'm rectifying that right now."

Oh goodness, he really was. He spent so much time there that when he finally reached for the button on my jeans, I was nearly out of my mind. Each breath I took was shallow and a pulse had picked up, moving deep inside me. My jeans were peeled off in a daze.

Nick dropped to his knees in front of me, his hands settling on my hips. His hair tickled my skin as he placed a kiss just below my navel. "That's for the sweet pea inside you," he said, and my heart imploded in a pile of goo. "Yeah, I've been doing my own research. And this . . ." His head lowered and he kissed me again, over my center. Even with the satin between his lips and my skin, I felt the touch straight to my core. "And that's for you."

My hand was trembling as I touched him, slipping my fingers through his hair. A knot of emotion built in my throat. I knew it right then, when he'd kissed my stomach, that I could seriously fall for this guy. My heart pounded fast.

Nick lifted his head, peering up through thick dark lashes. Those green eyes were bright with heat. "I think I could spend years right here."

"On your knees?" My voice shook a bit.

One side of his lips kicked up. "As long as you're standing above me."

My laugh was dry, shaky. "You're too much."

"No. I'm not." His lips skated over my upper thigh. "I think I . . . yeah, I need to change that."

I didn't understand what those words meant, or maybe I did and I was too afraid to believe them, but then I wasn't really thinking about it because his fingers were inching the satin down my hips, over my thighs, and then they were gone and I was completely bare, just like him.

And then he explored there, with his hands and his fingers, and finally that beautiful mouth of his. My head fell back on my shoulders, and when he worked me, tasted me, my hips moved in tandem.

Nick pulled away right before I exploded. He rose, swallowing my whimper of frustration with a kiss. One hand roped my hair, tilting my head back. The kisses turned deeper, became more urgent and fierce. My hands slid over him and down, my fingers wrapping around his thickness. His hips punched out, and then my back was pressed into the bed.

His hands curved under my arms and he lifted me up, dragging me up the center of the mattress, and his mouth claimed mine. We were a tangle of arms and legs, of greedy hands and even more ravenous kisses. Sex . . . sex had never been like this before. Sure, it had been fun and I'd experienced my fair share of orgasms and good times, but this was mind-blowing, because it wasn't just about two people who wanted to get off. There was a passion in the way his lips moved over my skin, a desire in the way my hands familiarized themselves with the many dips and hard planes, and a shattering intimacy when he lifted himself up onto his forearm, his gaze holding mine as he guiding himself into me.

My hips arched and my hands clenched his arms as he began to move, slowly at first, a teasing rhythm that was just too much. I pressed the heels of my feet into his calves. My nails skated over his skin. Pressure built inside of me, and his thrusts picked up, his hot breath dancing off my cheek, the provocative words he spoke into my ear urging me on. He was on me, around me, and in me—a part of me. Skin on skin. Nothing between us. The tension rapidly spun, coiling tight and tighter.

This wasn't two people fucking.

That was the last thought at the knot in my very core bursting, whipping out. Wave after wave of pleasure crashed into me. My head kicked back and I cried his name and God only knows whatever words. I tightened all around him as he thrust an arm under me, sealing my body to his as his hips ground against mine. His other arm caged me in, holding me in place. He was moving wildly, his hips bucking, and the pressure was too much. The aftershocks shattered again and the world seemed to splinter as another release powered through me.

Nick shouted hoarsely a second before he buried his head in the space between my neck and shoulder. He stilled, his hips pressed into mine. A great shudder rocked him as I held him, and several long moments passed before he moved.

He lifted his head as my hands slid down his sides. His lips pressed against my temple, a heartbeat later gliding over my brow. There was a quick peck on the tip of my nose and then he kissed me sweetly.

And something about that lazy, soft kiss was more powerful than any of the others.

Nick eased out of me, and out of past experience I expected him to hop out of the bed and the awkward search and rescue for clothes would begin. But he didn't. With his one arm still under me, he tugged me along with him as he rolled onto his back, gathering me up so my front was pressed against his side and my leg tangled with his. We were damp and flushed, but as my cheek came down on his shoulder, there wasn't a place more comfortable. His hand idly roamed up and down my back. Neither of us spoke.

As I lay there, my heart pounding and my breaths still coming too fast, an earlier thought resurfaced. Was I falling for him?

Nick turned his head toward mine and his lips brushed my forehead.

No. I wasn't *falling* for him.

Because there was a good chance I had already *fallen* for him.

Chapter 20

*A*t some point Nick had gotten up and made his way into the kitchen, completely naked and totally at ease being so. He returned with two glasses of water, turned off the light, and rejoined me.

Curled up against him, on my side and with the comforter tucked around our waists, I was in total snuggle mode. And I was also . . . absolutely content. Although snuggling was completely foreign to me, everything about this felt right, like we'd been doing it for years. That feeling was a bit unnerving, but I didn't shy away from it. I sort of wanted to roll around in it.

Tracing the thin line of hair underneath his navel, I smiled. "Thank you."

"I feel like I should be thanking you, but I'm curious." His fingers were dancing along my back and ribs. "Why are you thanking me?"

My smile grew. "For coming over. You didn't have to do that. You could've waited. It was sweet."

"I'm a sweet guy, but don't tell anyone. I have a reputation to keep."

I laughed softly. "It'll be our secret."

Nick turned so that my cheek was resting on his arm and we were facing each other. His hand drifted from my waist to my lower stomach. "Are you excited about the doctor's appointment?"

In the darkness, I could make out just enough of the faint line of his features to tell he was smiling. "I am. I'm a little nervous, because I don't know what to really expect," I admitted.

His hand flattened along my stomach. "Sometimes it doesn't feel real, does it?"

My heart tripped. "No. And that's so crazy, huh?"

"Probably normal. I guess after we go to the doc, reality kicks in," he said. "How's your mom handling everything?"

I placed my hand over his, liking the feeling. "She's really supportive. I'm lucky. Too bad she doesn't live here, because I'm pretty sure we'd have a built-in babysitter." I paused as a thousand questions about his family surfaced. Now was a good enough time, if any, to start asking. "You don't talk about your family a lot. I remember you said your mom died. Can I ask how?"

Nick didn't respond for a long moment, and I held my breath, waiting. If he really wanted to make something out of this, he was going to have to open up. So was I. This was an important moment between us, definitely more so than what we'd just shared.

"My mom died when I was a freshman in high school," he said, and I let go of my breath. "She died of a broken heart. And yeah, I know how stupid that sounds, but after my father died, she just gave up."

My chest squeezed. I'd figured his father wasn't in the picture since Nick had said his family wasn't around, but I hadn't automatically assumed that he died. Curving my hand around his, I drew it away from my stomach and pressed it close to my chest, along with his.

"She barely ate," he went on. "Didn't take care of herself at all. Stopped going out and she basically just *stopped* everything. My grandfather—her father—tried to get her help, before he got sick. He got her into counseling, but she didn't take any of the meds prescribed. She just didn't care, couldn't deal with living without Dad. It took years." His hand tightened around mine. "I was at school. It was in the morning, and my grandfather had come to get me. After my dad died, we'd moved in with him. He'd gone out that morning to get groceries and came home and found her dead in bed."

"I'm so sorry," I whispered.

He lifted our joined hands and kissed the back of mine. Then he exhaled roughly. "I'm not sure you want to know about my father."

"I do."

Our hands lowered back to the place between our chests. Several moments passed before he spoke. "My father killed himself."

My eyes widened in shock. I had not been expecting that. Not at all.

"My family hasn't had the greatest luck, huh? My grandfather gets Alzheimer's. Mom gives up, and my dad punched out his own card. " He turned his head so that he was looking up at the ceiling. "My grandfather—Job—was a pretty success-ful businessman. So was his father. They got into the construction business around here a long time ago and they were good at it—great at it. Half the damn houses around here were built or worked on by them. When Mom met Dad and they got married, he started working for Job, and eventually Dad took over the business and things were good at first. I mean, I was just a kid back then, and I don't remember a lot, but my parents were happy. We lived a good . . . life. That much I remember."

"What happened?" I asked.

Nick's chest rose and fell with a deep breath. "My father's company was building this house while they were finishing up another. The place was pretty huge and even though Dad's company was stretched pretty thin, he couldn't walk away from the job and that type of money. The normal contractors he worked with were busy on the other home, so he hired a few new people. One of them was this electrician. Dad thought they were on the up and up. You know? I don't think he believed he had any reason to doubt the work any of them were doing. He was wrong."

His hand loosened, but I refused to let go. Another moment passed. "The electrician he hired disappeared after the house was finished. Which was common. People move around all the time. No big deal. Not at first."

Instinct told me something really bad was coming and hearing it was going to be painful.

"Come to find out, the electrician cut corners. You'd be surprised how often that shit happens. Usually it doesn't become a big thing, but his guy . . . he fucked up. The wiring was bad—real bad—and it caused the house to catch on fire." Nick swallowed, and I could feel the tension building in him. "The family that had the home built were in that house when it went up in flames. Parents. Three kids. Two of the kids died in it."

I closed my eyes. "Oh God . . ."

"Dad had insurance—liability insurance. Since the electrician wasn't around, it fell on him. Not that it wouldn't have anyway. It was his company that built that house. It was his responsibility to make sure everything was done correctly. The family sued. Rightfully. It wiped out everything except what my grandfather had. He was smart with money—with business. He separated the money he'd saved over the years from the company long before he handed it over to my dad, but it wasn't the money that got to my dad. At least, I don't think it was. Not from what I remember." His voice thickened, became hoarse. "It killed him knowing he was responsible for that family, ate away at him. I do vaguely remember him sitting up at night, in the living room. Like he wasn't even there. About a year and a half after the fire, he hung himself. Mom found him."

"God." I wiggled closer, pressing the length of my body against his. At once, a lot of Nick started to make sense. "I'm sorry. I know those two words are lame, but I'm so sorry."

"Those words aren't lame. They mean something." He turned his head toward me. "There's something else . . . and you're probably going to think it's weird."

"Doubtful," I promised.

"No. It's pretty weird. Reece is one of a handful of people who know, and I know damn well he hasn't even told Roxy. I don't even know why I'm about to tell you this."

Curiosity had a hold on me. I couldn't understand what could be so weird that Reece would know and keep it to himself, even from Roxy. "Okay," I said, searching out his gaze in the semidarkness. "Even if I think it's weird, it doesn't mean I'm going to kick you out of the bed."

He shook his head. "Well, I hope not. It would be awkward considering we're both naked."

I smiled despite the conversation. "Tell me."

He tugged on my hand a little. "You don't know a lot about Calla, do you?"

My little old ears perked right up. I wasn't a detective, but my mind immediately raced to what Roxy had said about Nick's behavior around her and what I'd witnessed. "Not really. I just knew that she hung out with Teresa when I was at Shepherd."

"But you've . . . you've noticed the scar on her face, right?"

I started to frown. "Yeah?"

Nick drew in another breath. "She got that scar in a fire. Windows blew out or something. Hit her in the face. She was one of the kids who lived in the house my dad had worked on. It was her brothers that died. And that's not all. Her parents originally owned Mona's."

Seconds passed and I had no idea what to say. Shock roared through me. "Calla doesn't know that?"

"No. And it probably wouldn't have ever crossed her mind. My father's last name was Novak, but when he died, my mother ended up taking back her maiden name—Blanco. And I've never told her. How in the fuck would I tell her? You know? When she first walked into the bar, my heart just about stopped. You see, no one ever expected her to come back here. After the fire, her father left and her mom ended up handling the bar herself, but she went downhill—got messed up on drugs and became a shit mother. She couldn't deal with losing her little boys," he said, staring at the ceiling once more. "I ended up running into Mona—that's her mom—a few years ago. She knew who I was. Said I looked like my father. It was one of those rare moments when she wasn't on something. Anyway, I was starting to take care of my grandfather, just out of college, and Mona knew what was going on with Job. She offered me a job. It was weird. I didn't need the money. Not really. Job had more than enough to care for me to be able to care of him, but it was . . . a break. You know?"

"To get away? I get it."

He nodded. "So I started working at Mona's, before Jax came around, and then when he got there, he kind of took over. The whole situation around Mona and the bar is a mess, but I think in a way, working there for her, I was kind of . . ."

"Atoning for what had happened?" When he didn't speak, I squeezed his hand. "Nick, you know none of what happened was your fault, right? And it sounds like even though your dad was legally responsible, he . . . he was a victim in this, too."

"It took me a long time to realize that," he said after a couple of moments. "I don't even know why I had my head twisted up in that. I guess just young and dumb. Anyway, like I said, I didn't expect to see Calla."

"Do you think you're ever going to tell her?"

"I don't know. Probably would've made sense if

I'd done it when she first showed up. Now it just seems weird."

"It's not weird," I told him, and when he turned his head toward me, I didn't have to see him to know there was a dubious look on his face. "Okay. It's a little weird, but I understand why you haven't. I don't know her well, but she doesn't seem like someone who'd hold something against you that you had nothing to do with."

"But how hard for her could it be to realize she's working alongside the son of the man who was basically responsible for her life being ripped apart? That can't be easy." His voice was quiet. "I just . . . I don't want to mess up her life."

Oh gosh, that hurt to hear, and there was something about those words that made me think of what he'd said earlier about being in a relationship before. Was that why he was so against relationships? Because somehow he didn't think he deserved it because of his father and the house fire? Seemed like such a leap, but the fact that Nick had felt that working at Mona's was atonement for something his father did worried me.

"You were in a serious relationship once, weren't you?" I asked.

"Yeah."

I took a deep breath. "What happened?"

"It was a girl I was seeing in college. We were serious, and for a while, I thought . . . it would be for the long haul."

An irrational surge of jealousy lit me up. The intensity surprised me, and I sort of wanted to smack myself. How could I be jealous of a girl who was no longer in the picture? Wait. Oh my God. What if he was still in love with her? My stomach dropped.

"Anyway," he continued, oblivious to my internal freak-out, "when my grandfather got sick and all that started happening, things got stressed between us. I don't think she could deal with everything I had to do. At first I didn't get to see her a lot, dealing with him. We grew apart, and then it was just over one day. It sucked, but hell, if she couldn't handle my grandfather being sick and me taking care of him, what would she have done if I had gotten sick?"

"What a bitch," I blurted out.

Nick chuckled as he let go of my hand and circled his arm around my waist loosely. "What about you? Haven't been in a serious relationship since high school?"

"I don't even know if I can say that relationship was really serious or not," I admitted dryly.

His hand smoothed up my side. "So what's your deal? You don't believe in love?"

The question caught me off guard. "I believe in love. I do. I just . . . I was never in love. Not like with my parents. They loved each other. I mean, every time you saw them together, heard them talk to one another, even if they were mad, you could hear the love in their voices. That's the kind of love I want. I just didn't settle for less."

"Hmm . . ." His hand made a slow sweep back to my hip. "You're using the past tense there, Stephanie."

My name—I really liked it when he said my name.

"Um, my dad was in the marines," I said, and it felt strange saying this out loud, because it just wasn't something I talked about often. "And he was overseas a lot. When I was fifteen, he was home during the summer, and it was great. Then he headed back over. He never came back."

Nick didn't speak as he lifted his head and

pressed a soft, chaste kiss against my forehead. I swallowed, but that damn knot was back, lodged in my throat. "He was shot, and I remember sitting on the stairs when the two officers told my mom that it was quick, that he didn't suffer. And I also remember thinking, how did knowing that help anything? Now I get it. I'm happy he didn't suffer, but at fifteen I just . . . it didn't make it easier."

"I'm sorry," he said quietly, and then kissed my forehead again. "I obviously didn't know your father, but the fact he went over there and gave his life for the rest of us, he was a good man."

"He really was," I whispered, smiling sadly. "My mom never remarried nor has she seriously dated. I don't think she ever will. Till this day, she wears his dog tags. Only takes them off when she showers. Doesn't matter what she's wearing." I swallowed again, clearing my throat. "Yeah, so, there's that."

He lifted his hand from my hip and lightly brushed my hair back from my face. His hand lingered on my cheek. "Is that a picture of your dad on that shelf?"

Surprised flickered through me. "You saw that?"

"Yeah, when I got up to get the water. I'm observant like that."

"Wow," I murmured.

"It also could've been because I noticed that bikini picture first," he admitted, and I laughed. "I mean, come on, who wouldn't notice that?"

"Wow," I repeated.

"Somehow I think your second wow was less impressed."

I laughed again, and while the seriousness of the conversation was like a third entity in the bedroom,

I felt my lips curve into a broader smile. "You can't stay the night, can you?"

"I fucking wish. I'll need to leave by three," he said, his hand moving back down, closing around my hip. He squeezed. "I don't like to keep Kira there too late if she has to head home."

"Understandable." I paused, knowing we only had a few hours left. "Are you hungry or anything?" I asked.

"No. You?"

I shook my head and was glad we weren't getting out of bed right now. I wanted to soak up the moments with him before he had to leave. It felt good having this conversation with him. We weren't just scraping each other's surfaces anymore. This was . . . this was real, and we were digging deep, going beyond the initial layers.

Nick shifted suddenly.

I squealed when he threw the comforter off us and cold air washed over my skin, spreading goose bumps. His body quickly replaced the source of heat, and I wasn't complaining when he nipped at my neck.

"Come to think of it," he said, those lips traveling over my throat and then down, "I am hungry. For breakfast."

"Breakfast?" I asked as his lips coasted over the swell of my breast. When his tongue got involved, I *so* got it. Throwing back my head, I laughed loudly, and that laughter quickly turned into gasps and moans, but that smile . . .

That smile didn't leave my face.

Chapter 21

As the time drew closer to my first real pregnancy appointment, the more nervous I became. It
wasn't a normal nervousness. More like being excited and anxious all at once. The feeling made me
want to eat things. Lots of things.

Actually, I pretty much just wanted to eat things
in general.

And I seriously didn't think it had anything to do
with being pregnant. It was like my head was using
being pregnant as an excuse to eat everything in sight.

I'd finagled a long lunch for the day of the visit
and I spent the better part of Wednesday morning
trying not to eat the last Reese's pumpkin or punch
Rick in the nuts. Every time he passed my desk, he
was staring me down like he was either picturing
me topless or my head exploding.

When it rolled around to the time for me to leave,
I locked my computer and stood, grabbing my jacket
from where I had it folded and stashed, along with

my purse. As I turned around, pushing my chair in, I saw Brock walking toward Marcus's office. I immediately looked for Jillian, because whenever I saw him, she wasn't far behind. Last week, when he stopped into the offices, she was with him, almost like his little shadow, but today he was alone.

And he did look slightly better. Last week, dark blemishes under his eyes marked his exhaustion and he'd seemed paler than normal, but today he appeared a little more like himself, with the exception of the sling his right arm was in. Although his arm wasn't injured, it helped keep the chest wall muscles stable.

"Hi," I greeted him as I shoved my arms into my jacket. "How are you doing?"

Brock gave me a tight-lipped smile. "Hanging in there. You?"

"Good. I'm heading out to lunch."

He stopped in front of the door to Marcus's office and looked over his shoulder, the movement awkward and stiff. "You meeting up with Nick?" The mischievous gleam appeared in his eyes.

Good God, I felt my cheeks start to heat as my heart did a funny little dance in my chest. I couldn't even say that was new or wonder what the hell was up with it. Every time I saw Nick or thought of him, I got all fluttery, and I was just going to fully embrace that flutter at this point, because it wasn't going anywhere. At all.

"I have a doctor's appointment," was all I said, because that was all Marcus knew, and I was pretty positive that the news of our impending parenthood hadn't made its way back to Brock.

"Ah, the doctor's," he said, reaching for the door. "I'm beginning to hate that word."

"Understandable." I buttoned up my jacket. "See you later."

Since my doctor's appointment was between Plymouth Meeting and the city, Nick was meeting me there. The drive wasn't too bad once I got out of the city, and I made it to the office with about fifteen minutes to spare.

As soon I stepped out of the car, the doors on another car parked a few spaces down opened and Nick stepped out. The flutter was there, like a butterfly was darting around inside my rib cage.

My throat was suddenly dry as I stopped in front of my car and waited for him. As he came into complete view, my gaze did a slow drift over the long length of him. I doubted there was a time that Nick didn't look good, but today he was absolutely stunning. I don't know what it was about the dark denim jeans and the black vee-neck sweater that got my girlie parts all kinds of happy, but I was wondering if we had time for a quickie before the appointment.

"Hey," Nick said, dipping his head and kissing the corner of my lips. Ever since I told him about the whole not kissing thing, he'd made it a point to kiss me. A lot. I wasn't complaining. Reaching down, he took my hand in his. "You ready?"

I nodded as I held up the questionnaire that had been mailed to me. My entire life history was on those pages. "I've done my homework."

"When? This morning?" He started toward the entrance.

Grinning, I let him guide me across the parking lot. "No."

"Last night after I left?"

I laughed. "Maybe." When he squeezed my hand,

the flutter started all over again. "It almost took me an hour. Whoever is going to read this thing is going to know me better than my mom does."

Nick chuckled as we approached the doors. Turkeys created out of construction paper adorned the glass. The creators had used the finger-as-feathers technique, and my stomach did a little tumble, because at some point something similar would be tacked to the fridge.

I simultaneously wanted to cry and laugh, jump around and throw myself on a bed.

Checking in was a breeze, and as we took our seats in the warm waiting room, I looked around. Pregnant women everywhere. Which was expected, but I was sure I'd never seen so many pregnant ladies in one place before.

And all different stages of pregnant.

A blonde across from me had a tiny bump that stretched her pale blue sweater. There was a brunette near the check-in window who looked like she was halfway through the pregnancy, her cheeks flushed prettily as she scribbled on a notepad. Next to me was a woman who looked like there was a good chance she might give birth right in the middle of the waiting room.

Her stomach was the size of two basketballs.

Nick leaned over and whispered, "Okay. This is going to sound weird, but I'm picturing you with a belly like that, and I find that kind of hot."

I turned toward him slowly and started to grin. "Seriously?"

"Yeah," he winked. "I'm looking forward to it."

"Why?" I whispered.

One side of his lips kicked. "Because it will be my

baby . . ." He placed his hand on my stomach, over the jacket. " . . . in here, and holy shit, that's a huge turn-on."

Oh. Oh. Wow.

I looked away from him as another woman sat beside the one who was still rubbing her distended belly. The newcomer could be a contender for who was going to pop out a baby first. The two immediately started chatting; they obviously knew one another, and I tried not to eavesdrop, but I couldn't help it.

"How's the swelling, Lorraine?" the newcomer asked.

She shifted, wincing as she barely lifted her leg. My gaze dropped to her feet—holy crap—her *feet*. They were so swollen she was wearing flip-flops and it was like forty degrees outside.

Yikes.

"It's gotten better," she replied.

What? That was better? I quickly looked away as the other woman started talking about how she had to take her wedding ring off. Nick leaned back, extending his arm along the back of my chair. The blonde across from us was joined by her boyfriend or husband, and he and Nick did some kind of weird male head nod at one another. I glanced around and saw the brunette openly staring at Nick.

My lips pursed.

"This is the last one, I swear," Lorraine, the heavily pregnant woman, said to her friend. "If Adam thinks he's getting another baby out of me, I will castrate him myself."

Nick pressed his lips together as his gaze flipped to the ceiling. "Ouch," he murmured.

Discreetly, I elbowed him and his lips twitched.

Turning his head toward me, he dipped his chin and kissed my temple. Swollen feet and castration forgotten, the fluttering turned into a waltz. The brunette watching him sighed.

We didn't have to wait too long until we were called back and ushered into a room, and then the questions began—the same damn questions I'd procrastinated in answering were asked, and thank God Nick was there, because I was pleased when he also got the third degree.

How were my periods? And that was awkward to talk about with Nick staring at the door. What about my habits? Any known genetic disorders? Were we interested in genetic testing?

Unsure, I glanced at Nick, who was sitting on one of the small plastic chairs. "What . . . what do you think?"

"I think it wouldn't hurt." He stretched out his long legs, crossing them at the ankles. "I say let's do it."

"All right," I agreed, resisting the urge to swing my feet from where I was perched.

The nurse smiled. "We can take the blood here for the rest of the tests, but lab results won't be back for a few days."

And the questions began once again. Have I been pregnant before? What medication was I taking, and a million and two more questions. When she was finally done, I wondered if she was as exhausted as I was.

"Dr. Connelly can do an ultrasound today if you like, along with the initial exam, and she'll try to get a picture of the baby."

My heart toppled over itself. "Yes. I would like that."

"Let's get some blood drawn and get this show on the road," the nurse said.

As she went about her business, I couldn't help but grin, because Nick suddenly found something very interesting on the floor to stare at. Only when she finished taking half of my blood supply and handed over the gown did Nick look up. He appeared a bit green around the gills.

"Dr. Connelly will be in shortly," the nurse said, closing the door behind her.

Nick's gaze moved from the door to me, his brows rising with interest. "Is this the part where you get naked?"

Hopping off the table, I slipped out of my heels. "Is this the part where you try to pretend like you weren't about to pass out earlier?"

He tipped his head back against the wall, eyeing me through lowered lashes. "Needles give me the willies."

"Willies?" I shook my head as I began to undress. "Isn't that what little boys call their dicks?"

"If that's the case, then what I'm seeing right now makes my willy very happy."

"Oh my God." A laugh burst out of me. "Maybe you coming here wasn't a good idea."

A slow smile graced his lips. "Coming here was a great idea."

Undressing and putting on the papery gown was an experience. It took a lot to convince Nick that I didn't need his help, but even though he stayed seated, the heated gaze that tracked my movements felt like a physical caress.

While we waited for the doctor, we chatted. I told him that I'd seen Brock today, and he talked about a show he'd stumbled across in the middle of the night on the History Channel and that he now wanted to marathon the season. I liked this—the idle conversation—and it was like this every time I'd seen him since Halloween night.

On the nights he had off, he came over or we went out and had dinner. Every time we talked, and each night we got to know each other a little better. We were continuously peeling back the layers.

And there was more between him and me. A lot of skin-on-skin time. Or skin against clothes. Or just the removal of the necessary clothing. Like the night on Halloween, it felt different each time, felt like *more*. Definitely not about two people getting off.

When Kira was with his grandfather, he stayed the night. And last Saturday he'd surprised me by coming by after work. I'd been half asleep when I let him, in and that night there was little conversation. Nick had lifted me up as soon as he closed the door behind him, and he had us skin-to-skin within minutes. The sex . . . the way he had pinned me against the headboard, had spread my legs and . . .

God, he . . . he took me like he was insatiable, like he thirsted for me, only me.

My mind was fully in a place where it shouldn't be when Dr. Connelly came in, and then I felt about seven levels of awkward. Somehow, with the slight grin on Nick's face, I felt like he knew where my head had gone.

Jerk.

Dr. Connelly appeared to be in her fifties. Brown hair peppered with gray was pulled back in a neat bun at the base of her neck. Fine lines reached out from the corner of her eyes and mouth. She looked like she smiled a lot, and I immediately liked her.

The appointment reminded me of a normal gynecologist visit until we got to the point the ultrasound was brought into the picture. By then Nick had scooted his butt closer to the table and was staring avidly at the screen as Dr. Connelly moved the handle. A lot of black and gray . . . blobs were moving on the screen.

"There you go," Dr. Connelly said. "Your little bun loves the camera, because we got a clear image of it."

My gaze darted from her to the screen. Uh . . . I had no idea what I was looking at. "You see it?" I asked Nick.

He was leaning forward. "Yeah, I think I do." Stretching, he ran his finger around what sort of looked like a lima bean. "Right there, right?"

Dr. Connelly nodded. "There it is."

What in the hell? I shot him a look. He could see it and I couldn't? I glanced at the doctor, who was smiling broadly at him like she wasn't immune to Nick. "I don't see it."

"That's common," she said, and the screen stilled. The picture was taken. "It doesn't really look like a baby right now. It's still so small, but the little bun is in there. Believe it or not, fingers are moving and so are the legs."

"Really?" I asked, my eyes widening.

She nodded as she started to pull away from the table. "The fingers are slightly webbed at this stage."

Nick grinned at that.

"And cool little fact for you," Dr. Connelly said. "The baby's taste buds are actually forming already."

"Wow," I whispered, floored as I stared at the screen. There were other things on the screen, dots and lines and numbers, but I focused on the blur that Nick had so easily seen. The longer I stared, I sort of saw it, and it was so incredibly tiny.

My throat clogged and I cleared it. Without having to say a word, Nick reached over and folded his hand over mine. He squeezed. "You find it yet? Or do we need to draw a circle around it with a bunch of arrows?"

"Jerk." I laughed hoarsely. "I think I see it. Looks like a lima bean, right?" My gaze moved to Nick's and was stuck, held by the softness in those light green eyes. "That's what it looks like?"

Nick nodded.

"The baby looks like a lima bean," I told him, fighting a grin.

"Yeah, but it's *our* lima bean," he said.

My lips curled up at the corners and I nodded. Yeah, it was our lima bean.

Chapter 22

*B*ecause I was a cornball of epic proportions, I'd tacked the sonogram on the fridge with a heart-shaped magnet. Sort of like when I was a kid and my parents displayed my grades. I mean, they were proud of my grades and I was proud of the lima bean.

Nick was coming over in the afternoon. Things had been rough with his grandfather the week after the prenatal appointment, so I hadn't seen a lot of him, and I missed him.

God, I really did miss Nick.

When he wasn't around, I thought about him at the oddest moments. Seeing certain things reminded me of him. Fresh, crisp scents made me think of his cologne. When something happened at work or if Roxy or Katie said something funny, I couldn't wait to tell Nick.

Relationships were weird like that, I decided.

A twinge of unease formed. Relationships were

also tricky. No labels had been tossed around. He didn't call me his girlfriend, and vice versa, but what we were doing felt like that. Except I still hadn't met his grandfather and he hadn't met my mom.

My mom would really like him. Based on everything I'd told her, about his grandfather and everything, she already did, and while I knew his grandfather wouldn't know who I was, I still wanted to meet him.

I still wanted more.

Was that what falling . . . in love felt like? I sighed. I imagined that it was what it felt like when you weren't sure if the other person felt the same way. Actually, I *knew* that was what it felt like.

I held out waiting for the perfect guy—the perfect relationship. I never fell for anyone I'd been with. Guys who had no baggage I knew of. Guys who were already firmly seated in their careers. Ironically, it was the most imperfect situation and imperfect guy who was capturing my heart.

Who *had* captured my heart.

I just didn't know where Nick stood in this. Yes, he cared about me. I could tell in the way he talked to me. Yes, he wanted me. That was obvious. Yes, he was making plans with me. Those plans centered around the baby. His words lingered in the back of my head.

We'll make the best of this.

Kind of like when life handed you ~~lemons~~ bullshit, but I wasn't a lemon, dammit, and making the best of us wasn't going to get us to the long haul, after the baby arrived and the newness of all of that wore off. Feelings had to run deeper for both of us.

I shook the troubling thoughts out of my head.

Standing in the kitchen, staring at the sonogram, I pressed my lips together as I glanced down. There was the tiniest change in the shape of my stomach. Nothing noticeable. Yet. But eventually I would be like Lorraine in the doctor's waiting room, and my feet would be so swollen I couldn't wear shoes. I started to grin as I patted my belly. Considering the way I was eating now, I was going to have a heavy belly way before I hit nine months.

Walking to the couch with a glass of OJ, I plopped down and picked up my laptop and resumed my "mommy board" creeping.

Mommy board creeping was a really bad idea I discovered by the time Nick arrived. When I let him in and he kissed me, I was so distracted by everything I'd learned that I wandered aimlessly over to the couch and sat down again.

"I thought you wanted to go out for dinner tonight?" he commented as he took off his jacket.

"I do." I picked up the pillow.

A slight grin appeared on his lips. "You going to wear that?"

Confused, I looked down at myself. Oh. I was rocking a pair of oversized sweats and an old Shepherd hoodie. "Sorry. I kind of got distracted."

He sat beside me. "With what?"

I gestured at the closed laptop on one of the pillows that I'd placed on the floor. "I got on these boards—these online forums they call mommy boards."

"Sounds interesting."

I shot him a wide-eyed look. "It was terrifying."

"What?" he laughed.

He had no idea. None whatsoever. Holding my

pillow to my chest, I stared at him. "I did learn that I had a symptom of being pregnant almost right after we conceived. My breasts were tender like two weeks after we had sex. I didn't think you had symptoms that soon, but you can." I gestured at the computer with my chin. "Did you know the nipple stimulation is the only scientifically proven method of inducing labor?"

"What?" he laughed.

"I'm serious," I whispered. "Someone mentioned it on this board and so I Googled it, because really? Like that sounds bizarre, but it's true."

Nick cocked his head to the side, his green eyes dancing. "I am more than willing to help out when it comes down to that."

I ignored that as I curled my legs up. "So then I got curious about what the baby really looks like right now, because these women were talking about how they could see eyes and stuff on the sonogram, and all I can see is a lima bean, so I started researching."

"Okay."

"And I . . . I watched this video, on how a baby's face forms in the womb, and oh my God, it was the creepiest thing I'd ever seen."

His face tensed as he leaned over, putting a hand on my bent knee as he looked away. I saw one side of his mouth curve up. "It can't be that bad."

"Oh. It was." My eyes widened. "Imagine what a clay potato head looks like. You got that image in your head?"

Nick closed his eyes and cleared his throat. "Yeah."

"Okay. Now imagine that getting all squishy, like

it's melting. And then it filling out—like remember when you were a kid and you'd put your hands on either side of your face and then smashed your cheeks in?"

He blinked several times as he looked at me. "Nah, I think I need a demo."

Dropping the pillow, I placed my hands on my cheeks and pushed forward while puckering my lips. Nick's eyes widened, and then he tipped his head back, laughing deeply. I lowered my hands. "It's not funny. Not funny at all."

"God." He chuckled.

"And then the eyes like come from where the ears should be." I shook my head. "How is that even possible? I don't even want to know, to be honest. And you don't even want to know what happens to a woman's body when they give birth." I shuddered. "I need an adult."

"You need to stop watching those videos." Moving my leg to the side, he scooted closer and then reached over. Placing his hands on my hips, he tugged me over, and I went, ending up in his lap, straddling his thighs. "And I think you need a better distraction."

I placed my hands on his chest. "I need a brain scrub."

His hands slid from my hips to cup my rear. "Did you do any research on hormones while pregnant?"

My nose wrinkled. "Not really."

"Well, you know what I've always heard?" His hands squeezed as he drew me closer and my fingers slipped up to his shoulders. "That pregnant women have an increased libido."

I arched a brow.

"It's true." He moved in, his lips brushing over the sensitive spot below my ear.

Stretching my neck, I gave him space to roam, and oh, he did, gliding those lips over my pulse. "Do you know what else is true?"

His tongue flicked over my skin, causing me to jerk. "What?" he murmured.

"Some women lactate automatically when they hear babies cry," I told him. "Even if it's not your baby. I could be walking in the grocery store and my boobs could just start spraying out milk."

Nick lowered his forehead to my shoulder, and I felt his body shake.

I dipped my chin, staring at his head. "And the longest pregnancy on record was like a year and ten days—a year, Nick. A mother freaking year."

"Steph, baby . . ." He lifted his head, smiling. "As much as your freaking out is adorable, you got to stop watching and reading stuff."

"But I need to read stuff and watch stuff. How else am I going to learn?"

"Generations and generations before us weren't online on mommy boards or WebMD." He patted my butt with both hands. "And things worked out."

I started to point out that I doubted the statistics of childbearing were better back before the invention of the Internet, but Nick kissed me, really kissed me, and when his lips moved over mine like that, there was little room to be thinking about anything else.

The kiss deepened as I slipped my hands up his cheeks, the stubble along his jaw tickling my palms. I tilted my head, drawing him into my mouth. Unbridled lust shot through my veins, and I knew if he was in me right now, I'd be ready.

"You were right," I said, kissing the corner of his lips, the slight indent above them. I dropped tiny kisses all over his face.

Nick let his head fall back. "You're going to have to be a little more detailed, because I'm right about a lot of things."

I laughed as I tasted the skin below his jaw, thrilled by the deep breath he drew in. "About pregnancy hormones. Because I'm pretty horny right now." I nipped at the space where the neck met his shoulder. "Then again, I'm always horny when I'm around you."

"It's my superpower." He dragged his hands up my sides. "Making girls want to drop their panties."

Smiling, I rocked back, watching as he lifted his head. His throat worked as his heavy hooded gaze drifted over me. "You should be careful with that superpower." Reaching down, I tugged the sweatshirt off. "Use it wisely."

His gaze dropped to my lace-covered breasts. "I'm so using it wisely right now." He lifted a hand, hooking his finger under the strap of my bra. He inched it down my arm and then did the same to the other one.

Then that same finger trailed the lace on each cup before his finger sank between my breasts, catching the material there. He pulled me toward him and his lips followed the same path as his finger.

My breath was already coming in short gasps as I reached around and unhooked the bra. I shrugged the straps off so there was nothing between his lips and my skin. His tongue glided over the rosy peak and then his mouth closed over it. My back arched as I gasped.

"Okay," I breathed as I threaded my fingers through his hair. "I think I'm going to have—" A moan broke off my words as his hand got involved, covering my other breast. "—to research if a woman's breasts are sensitive during pregnancy."

His thumb and forefinger did something wicked, and my fingers tightened around his hair. "I'm going to go with yes," he said, nipping and laving, the sweep of his tongue soothing the sting. "I just saved you precious research time."

I kissed his brow. "Aren't you just so helpful."

He cupped my breasts, lifting them. "You know, I think these have gotten bigger."

"A little."

"And these . . ." His tongue danced over the nipple of one breast and then the other. "These have gotten darker. Just so you know, I'm loving this pregnancy thing so far."

My breath caught. *Loving. Love.* Totally not the same thing I was feeling, but my little heart just soared with it. Wiggling back, I swung my legs off and stood. Nick reached for me, but I shook my head as I reached down, grabbing my sweats and shimmying them off.

"Fuck," he grunted. "No panties. Again."

I gave him a cheeky grin as I placed my hands on his knees, spreading his legs. I knelt between them, watching him as I reached for his belt, pulling it through the loop until it was unhooked.

"Stephanie . . ."

My name sounded like a plea, and I hadn't even gotten to the good part yet, which made me feel like, well, a goddess. I flicked the button on his jeans and down went the zipper. I gripped the sides of his jeans, and he lifted his hips as I tugged them down just far enough that the part I wanted was accessible.

I didn't waste time.

Stretching toward his lap, I wrapped one hand around him and took him into my mouth. Nick's hips surged off the couch as he let out a strangled sound. His hand folded over the back of my neck as I took him as far as I could. He tasted of salt and man, and as I moved my hand, I pressed my thighs together. Never before had I been so turned on going down on a guy, but I was pretty sure if I continued on this path, there wouldn't be a main event for either us.

With one last lick and a quick kiss, I returned to straddling his lap. With my hand around him, I guided him in, and his grip on my hips was tight as inch by inch I let him in. Maybe it was this position. Maybe it was the pregnancy. I didn't know, but I felt incredibly tight and my nerve endings were firing all at once at the delicious tug and pull.

Sliding my hands up to his jaw, I pressed against him as I started to move my hips, rocking back and forth slowly. The wool of his sweater teased the tips of my breasts and the rough material of his jeans rubbed my inner thighs.

There was something unbelievably hot about being completely naked while he was still mostly dressed. I think Nick agreed, based on the dirty stuff he whispered in my ear as I rode him.

My hips moved in tight circles over him, and it didn't take long before I could feel the tension building low in my belly. I reached down, placing my hands over his as I moved against him, our foreheads pressed together, our breaths hot and mingling in the space between our mouths.

"You're killing me," he said, his hands breaking my hold, sliding to my rear. "You're fucking killing me, and I can't think of a better way to go."

I gripped his arm and the back of his neck as I picked up the pace. The coil spun tighter and tighter. "Oh God," I gasped, a strand of hair falling in my face as I tipped my head back.

His lips scorched the skin of my throat. "I can never get tired of this."

Never. Never was a long time. Never was forever. Never meant love. My heart swelled as a shocking thought whipped through me, and I stilled, my chest rising and falling with shallow breaths.

Would we be here, right where we were, doing what we were doing, if I hadn't gotten pregnant?

"You okay?" Nick asked, grasping my chin with one of his hands. "Stephanie?"

"Yeah." I blinked, pushing the thought aside as I started moving again, chasing after the sweet release that I knew was just out of my grasp.

Nick guided my mouth to his and kissed me deeply as the hand along my rear moved down the center, one long finger seeking and hitting a spot that caused my body to jerk and an explosion of pleasure to occur. The release shook me as I tightened all around him. Blood pounded through me as I cried out.

He moved suddenly, and before I could even come back down, my hands were on the arm of the couch and my knees were sinking into the cushion. Nick was behind me and in me, his thrusts powerful and deep. One arm circled just below my breasts and he drew me up and back, sealing me to his chest as his hips ground into mine. He came with my name a hoarse shout.

I don't even remember moving after that, but somehow I ended up sandwiched between the back of the couch and him. My face was pressed into his sweater and my leg was thrust between his.

"God," Nick said thickly. "Damn."

I made a virtually incoherent sound as he managed to fold his hand around the back of my head.

"You still alive?" he asked.

"Mmm-hmm."

"And you're okay?"

"Uh-huh."

There was a pause. "And you're not planning on moving for a while, are you?"

"Uh-uh."

"Yeah, that's good." Nick got his arm around my lower back. "Neither am I."

I smiled in response, and though he couldn't see it, the curve of my lips felt forced, because even as my body was relaxed and blissed out, I couldn't help asking myself that horrifying question again.

Would we be here?

And there was no answer to that question. There never would be.

Chapter 23

"So are you going home for Thanksgiving or not?"

In the middle of shoving what was probably half a pancake in my mouth, I paused and looked across the table at Katie. This morning she was dressed rather calmly . . . for Katie. Her bright purple sweater was as fuzzy as a bear, but it lacked all sparkles. "I don't know yet. My mom isn't cooking. She is going to her sister's house. I'm invited, of course, but since Mr. Bowser wants me in the office on Friday, it doesn't make much sense to make that drive."

"I can't believe you have to work on Friday," Calla said. Since Shepherd was out for break, she was back home, and had joined our Sunday breakfast.

Roxy frowned. "We have to work."

"I'm working," Katie added, twirling her fork. "Working on the pole, oh yeah."

"That's because we work at a bar and you at a strip club," Calla explained. "I always thought normal jobs closed on Friday."

I finished chewing my mouthful of pancake. "He has most of the office out for the day, but they have this big project they're working on." The project was opening the academy in Martinsburg by September of next year, and they were meeting the county boards again the first week of December. "So I'm just in there to help get everything typed up."

Roxy offered me a slice of bacon. "Does that mean you get to spend Thanksgiving with Nickie Nick?"

I raised a shoulder. "I don't know. I hope so."

Calla has been told via Roxy or Katie or maybe even Jax that I was a pregnant, so I wasn't surprised that she forked over her sausage link to me. I don't know if they really thought I needed to eat all this extra food, but I wasn't complaining.

"Why wouldn't you have Thanksgiving with him?" Calla asked, and when I didn't respond right away, she added, "Isn't it just him and his grandfather?"

I stabbed the sausage. "You know about his grandfather?"

She glanced at Roxy, who also nodded. "Yeah. I know he's sick. I mean, obviously, Nick doesn't give us a lot of details about anything," Roxy said. "But I know it's just those two."

Sitting back, I wished I hadn't decided to wear jeans today. The button was now killing me. "I would like to have Thanksgiving with him, but I don't think he wants me around his grandfather. And I don't mean that in a bad way," I said as Calla's eyes narrowed. "I think he just doesn't want me to have to worry with what's going on."

"You can handle whatever," Katie said, waving her hand dismissively. "You *will* handle whatever."

An odd chill snaked down my spine. *You're going to break his heart.*

"Look, I might be nuttier than a Payday bar, but here's my advice. You want to spend Thanksgiving with him, then you spend it with him," she continued, and well, that was actually good advice. "It's as simple as that."

I almost didn't say anything, but these girls . . . they were my girls now. "I just . . . I don't know how he feels."

Roxy's brows shut up over the rim of her glasses. "What in the hell does that mean? I think it's pretty obvious how he feels. Ever since I've known him, he's never been with a girl for longer than one night."

"Yeah, but . . . but I'm pregnant."

Katie arched a brow. "No shit, Sherlock."

I shot her a look. "The thing is, I don't know if he would be with me if I hadn't gotten pregnant, and if he really cares about me and not just the baby." Saying that fear out loud was like rolling around on ice. "I'm so incredibly happy and lucky that he's on board with this baby." I patted my stomach, which was more food baby than real baby. "And that he's excited and everything, but if he doesn't really care about me deeper than being there for me, this . . . this isn't going to last."

"What makes you think that he doesn't?" Calla asked.

I looked at each of them. "He hasn't said anything that would make me think that he does, and all the plans we make center around the baby, you know? I know that sounds like a crazy thing to complain about, but I want . . ."

"You want to know that he actually wants to be

with you, with or without the baby," Roxy finished for me. "That's understandable. I totally get it. If I became pregnant before Reece and I got serious, I would wonder the same thing. I think it's a very normal concern, but how do *you* feel about him?"

My heart tripped over itself in its eagerness to gush nonstop about all my feelings. "I . . . I care about him a lot."

"She loves him," Katie quipped. "She totally loves him."

I stared at her.

"Is that true?" Calla asked.

Taking a deep breath, I nodded.

"Then talk to him," Roxy advised quietly. "Just talk to him."

I did talk to Nick later that night, when we went out to dinner, about Thanksgiving with his grandfather. At first he wasn't too keen on the idea, and it was a struggle to keep my disappointment and paranoia at bay.

"I don't know," he said, the low light of the restaurant casting shadows along the hollows of his cheeks. "There's no guarantee that he's going to be doing okay that day."

"I know that."

His lashes lowered, shielding his eyes. "I don't want you to go to a lot of trouble and then have it get ruined."

I reached across the table, poking his hand. "We don't have to go to a lot of trouble. We don't even have to do a turkey or any of the stuff. We could do the anti-Thanksgiving dinner. Keep it simple and sweet just in case the day doesn't go as planned."

"Anti-Thanksgiving dinner?"

"Yeah." I grinned. "We could make spaghetti or hamburgers." My gaze flipped to the menu as my stomach grumbled. "Mmm. Hamburgers. My vote is for hamburgers."

"And fries?"

I nodded eagerly. "I could always go for fries or tater tots."

Nick laughed. "Tater tots? Are you ten?"

"Shut up." I picked up the napkin and tossed it at him. "You are never too old for tater tots, especially the crispy kind, and if you think you are, then you're just a lame doofus."

"Wow." Sitting back against his seat, he grinned at me. "Tater tots? Doofus? I feel like we've regressed."

"Okay. How about I like to eat cylinder-shaped potatoes, so go fuck yourself?" I signed and sealed that with a bright smile.

Nick's laughter was warmth. "That's so much better."

"You're welcome." I paused. "So what do you think? I come over to your house, meet your grandfather if he's up for it, and we make hamburgers and fries? Maybe even cylinder-shaped potatoes, too."

His grin was lopsided. "That's hard to refuse."

"There better not be a 'but' attached to that statement, because I might get offended if there is."

Nick's gaze flew to mine. "Why would you get offended?"

"Um, maybe because I haven't met your grandfather or been to your house yet," I pointed out. "I don't even know where you live. Just a general idea."

He shook his head. "It's nothing . . . personal. I want you to understand that. I would love for you to meet my grandfather, but there are days when it's not . . . easy to be around him. Some days he sleeps most of the time. Other days, not so much, and it's not a walk in the park. It's a lot to handle and—"

"I'm not your ex-girlfriend."

One eyebrow rose. "I know that."

"I don't know if you do." I met his gaze. "Because if you did, then you wouldn't automatically assume that your grandfather was going to be too much for me to handle."

Nick opened his mouth but clamped his jaw shut. A moment passed and then he pursed his lips. "You know, you're right." It sounded like a lot for him to say those words, and I wasn't sure how to feel about that. "What time do you want to do this on Thanksgiving?"

A part of me wanted to be churlish, to give voice to the sour feeling in the pit of my stomach that had nothing to do with the low level nausea that hit at odd times during the day. I didn't want to do it if he didn't really want me to, but then how childish would it come across if I pulled the brakes now?

I couldn't.

All I could do was make Thanksgiving as awesome as I could and hope Nick would truly see that I wasn't going to cut and run when things got rough. That even though he was in this to "make the best of it," I was in it for the long haul.

Chapter 24

I was such a baby.

I didn't talk to him about my concerns about us, even when Sunday night would've been the perfect opportunity. But I couldn't help feeling like I wasn't grateful enough or I was being selfish for wanting to make this relationship more about me than the baby, and God, even that sounded so messed up.

Maybe this was the reason why I hadn't fallen in love before now, because as I drove to Nick's house late Thursday morning, I was convinced that when it came to love I was ridiculously neurotic.

I second-guessed so much. Like everything from calling or texting him to if we weren't doing enough couple things with other couples. I wanted to smack myself.

I also needed to stop eating everything in sight, because I was sure the extra tightness in the waistband of my jeans had nothing to do with the baby.

At almost eleven weeks, my lima bean was the size of a lime, and outside of making me want to belch every five seconds, I doubted it was the cause of the extra ten pounds I'd packed on.

At a stoplight, I glanced at the grocery bags on the passenger seat and smiled. I was going to start watching what I ate after I had my hamburgers and cylinder-shaped potatoes.

Following the directions on my phone, I easily found Nick's grandfather's house. It was on the other side of Plymouth, away from the city and on the outskirts. Suburbia. The businesses grew farther and farther apart, the subdivisions had more space than houses, and when the directions indicated that I turn left in the next two hundred feet, I found that I was driving onto a private driveway—to a house, not in a subdivision.

I don't know what I was expecting when it came to his grandfather's house as I drove up the driveway. Maybe something old? A farm, perhaps? But as the stand of trees cleared to a neatly manicured front lawn, I was surprised to be staring up at a newish home.

Slowing down, I parked in front of a double bay garage and turned off the engine. The house was a two-story, colonial style, with a massive front porch that appeared to wrap around the other side. It was the perfect porch for lazy summers, I thought, or for a baby to sit and play on.

My tummy twisted pleasantly at that thought.

Grabbing the bags, I stepped out and closed the door behind me. The sun was hidden behind fat gray clouds, and as I walked up the river rock path, there was a chill of snow in the air. When I stepped up on the porch, I noticed a wooden swing and smiled.

Goodness, this really was the perfect porch.

Nick opened the front door before I could knock, and for a moment I was sort of blinded with stupidity. He was standing in the doorway in jeans. That's all. Jeans that hung low on his hips, revealing that damn vee shape of his lower stomach. His hair was damp, curling against his temple and forehead.

"Hey," he said, grinning boyishly. "I'm running late. Just stepped out of the shower."

He sure did. A drop of water caressed the line of his collarbone and then slipped down his chest.

My pulse picked up.

Oh God, I wanted to jump him. Drop the hamburger meat and everything and just jump him, right there in the entryway of his grandfather's house.

His dark brows rose. "You coming in?"

I needed to get a grip.

"Of course." I cleared my throat and stepped inside, and because it wouldn't be appropriate to jump his bones, I stretched up and brushed my lips over his.

Nick snaked an arm around my waist, drawing me up against his damp chest before I had a chance to step back. I almost dropped the groceries as he took that kiss to a whole different level. He tasted of mint and a whole lot of sultry promises I wanted to fulfill. Like right there.

"Every time," he said against my mouth.

I had to catch my breath. "What?"

"Every time you see me, I want you to do that." His nose brushed mine as he tilted his head, kissing me once more. "I want the first thing you do is kiss me. I want that kind of hello."

Oh gosh.

My heart swelled so fast and so powerfully that when he set me back down on my feet and stepped back, I could feel actual tears climbing up the back of my throat. "I can do that," I said when I really meant, *Oh my good God, I will totally do that every freaking single time.* Turning around, I gave myself time to recover by taking in my surroundings.

The house embodied an open concept. From where we stood, I could see into a large living room and kitchen to the right, with an eat-in dining room. There was a closed door to what I guessed was a bathroom. To my left was what appeared to be a study and another closed door. The stairs heading up to the second floor were directly in front of us. Hardwood floors as far as the eye could see.

"Everything is so . . . neat," I said as Nick took the bags from me.

He laughed. "What were you expecting?"

I shrugged a shoulder. "I don't know." I followed him toward the country-style kitchen—white cabinets, gray granite everywhere. "This place is neater than my apartment."

"That is fucking true."

Laughing, I smacked his arm as he set the groceries on the counter. "Hey!"

He grinned as grabbed the packets of hamburgers and placed them in the fridge. When he pulled out the tater tots, he shook his head. "You're such a kid."

"Shut up." I leaned against the island as he placed the tots in the freezer. The house was so quiet I felt like I should whisper. "Is your grandfather up?"

"He's actually asleep right now."

"Oh." I clapped my hand over my mouth. "Sorry. I was so loud."

"It's okay." He stepped around the island and reached down, taking my hand. "When he sleeps, it's pretty deep. A dump truck could drive through the garage and he'd sleep right through it. And he's been sleeping a lot today."

"Is that a good or bad thing? The sleeping a lot?"

"It's . . . really neither." He tugged on my hand. "Come on."

Nick led me back to the foyer and past the study, to the closed door. When he opened it, I felt like a teenager again, sneaking through my boyfriend's house so we didn't alert his parents to what we were up to.

"Did you grandfather build this house?" I asked.

"Yep." He pushed the door open, revealing a large bedroom. "He always planned that at some point more than one generation of the family would be living here, so there's actually three master bedrooms. This is one of them. It has a walk-in over there. There's the bathroom." He gestured to a set of double doors to our right. "Can't complain. Lots of good space."

"Whoa." I looked around, seeing little bits of Nick. A dark shirt on the bed. A pair of boots in front of dark wood dresser. A stack of magazines on one of the nightstands. "This is nice. Where are the other two masters?"

"One is downstairs in the basement. It's virtually its own apartment—kitchen, living area, and all that." He reached out, catching a strand of my hair and tucking it back behind my ear. "The other one is upstairs. A more traditional master, I guess. It's my grandfather's room."

I turned to him, smiling as I lifted my chin. "Your grandfather built a very beautiful house."

Grinning, he backed up. "You haven't seen the bathroom yet." Wheeling around, he stopped in front of the double doors and pushed them open.

Nick stepped aside as I peered in. My mouth dropped opened as my eyes widened. "Wow . . ."

The master bath was the size of my bedroom. A Jacuzzi tub was pristine, as if it had never been used before. A slivery chandelier hung over it. The shower was large enough to fit three people, and the tan tile reached the ceilings. There was a rain showerhead.

"I could live in this," I whispered. "And I sort of hate you."

Nick chuckled as he walked up behind me, circling his arms around my waist. His hands flattened across my belly. "This house is big."

"I can tell."

He kissed my cheek. "Big enough for a family."

I started to point out that was once again obvious, but as his lips blazed a path down the side of my neck, what he was saying sunk in. Big enough for a family—for him, me, and our baby. Like ninety percent of me wanted to do a crazy happy dance in the middle of the obscenely spacious bathroom, but the remaining ten percent of me was filled with restlessness.

"Or just for a guy and a girl," I heard myself say.

Nick didn't respond as his hand moved in a slow circle over my belly. I turned around in his embrace, my gaze meeting his. I wanted to stay something, ask him what he thought about us, but the words wouldn't form on my tongue.

He lowered his head, kissing the tip of my nose before he pivoted around and went back to the bedroom. I briefly squeezed my eyes shut. When I reopened them, he was tugging a henley thermal on over his head.

What a shame.

I roamed out of the bedroom and into the study, immediately drawn to the books lining the built-in shelves. There were a lot of books, and as I made my way down the shelves, I came across several dusty photo albums.

"Oh Lord."

Glancing over at the doorway, I saw Nick standing there, arms folded. I grinned as I pulled one of the thick albums out. "What?"

"Of course you'd find the photo albums."

"It's my hidden talent." I walked over to a comfy-looking love seat and plopped down, cracking open the album. Several of the pictures were old black-and-white photos of dark-haired people.

Nick sat beside me, sighing. "My great-grandparents."

I turned the page carefully, as some of the photos were slipping out from under the film. "They look very happy," I commented.

"I didn't know them, but I assume they were."

Eventually the photos gave way to newer ones. His grandfather as a young man, smiling that half smile at the camera. "Very handsome."

"I take after him," he replied, picking up a piece of my hair.

"Have I ever told you how incredibly modest you are?"

He chuckled as he twisted the strand of hair around his finger as I kept turning the pages. "That's my grandmother," he explained when I stopped on an old wedding photo. "She passed away when I was only a couple of years old. Cancer."

"I'm sorry."

Nick said nothing as he unraveled my hair and then started to curl it again, and he remained silent as I turned the pages, eventually finally a young woman and man who bore a striking resemblance to Nick. "Your parents?"

"Yes."

My thumb smoothed over the photo of them sitting at a kitchen table. Both had dark hair and olive skin. The woman was very pretty, smiling while she held a long, thin cigarette in her hand. His father was behind her, curling an arm around her slim shoulders. There were more pictures of them. "They . . . they looked really good together."

"They did." He reached over after he stopped messing with my hair and flipped a few pages ahead, stopping on a big photo of a baby on its back, with a head full of dark hair. "And there I am. Adorable, huh?"

I grinned. "Yeah, you were adorable."

"Still am."

I snorted. "You look like you're about to scream bloody murder."

"Probably. Mom said I cried a lot. There's something for us to look forward to."

"Oh geez."

He laughed as I turned the pages, and at the tips of my fingers, Nick grew from a tiny, red-faced baby to the kind of handsome teenager who would've gotten me into loads of trouble. Along the way, I watched his parents grow until his father disappeared from the family photos and then his mother. When I reached the end of the photo album, I really didn't know what to say.

Life and loss categorized in one forgotten dusty tome.

Closing the book, I glanced over at Nick. He wasn't looking at me, but staring at the closed album. "You haven't looked at any of these pictures in a while."

"It's not . . . particularly easy to see things the way they used to be," he admitted.

I returned my attention to the black cover of the album. "I didn't look at pictures of my dad a lot, not for years after he died. It's like I wanted to . . . erase all evidence of his existence. I know that sounds terrible, but it was easier not seeing reminders all over."

He was quiet for a moment. "What changed it?"

"I . . . I missed him."

Nick took the album from me and then stood, placing it back where I found it. "You want to see if he's awake?"

Pushing up from the love seat, I nodded.

He took a deep breath. "Sometimes he gets more agitated late in the afternoon, so—"

"It's okay." Instead of waiting for him to take my hand, I took his and squeezed it gently. He led me upstairs and down the hall, to another set of double doors that were cracked open. With one hand he pushed them open, then walked in.

The room was bright and had a certain antiseptic scent to it. Everything was neat, but I wasn't really paying attention to anything but the bed at the center. Propped up on pillows was a very frail, older man who barely resembled the man in the pictures.

As Nick guided me to the chairs beside the bed,

I started to notice the other things in the room. Lap trays. Clean bedpans. A walker that appeared untouched for quite some time. Medical equipment I didn't quite understand. My gaze went back to the bedpans, and it struck me then how much Nick was really dealing with.

I wanted to hug him.

"Hey Granddad," Nick said, speaking like he'd normally talk to anyone. "I brought someone to meet you."

My heart was pounding a bit. His grandfather was awake, but his rheumy gaze drifted over us as if we weren't even there.

"This is Stephanie," Nick said, taking a seat.

I sat down beside him, my hand still in his. "Hi."

His grandfather didn't respond as his gaze slowly moved back to Nick. "She is the girl I've been telling you about. . . ." Nick paused, shooting me a small grin. "I've been telling him good stuff."

"I hope so." My stomach toppled over itself.

"Mostly," he added, and I grinned. Nick drew in a breath. "She's the girl who's going to make you a great-grandfather."

I looked over at him, surprised. Telling his grandfather about me was a surprise, and it was a downright shock that he'd spoken about the pregnancy. I don't even know why it was such a bombshell. I'd told my mother and she'd most definitely told every living person in the family by now.

"She works in the city and she eats tater tots," Nick added.

My look of disbelief turned to one of wry humor, and then I turned back to his grandfather. "I'm sure you have nothing against tater tots." Taking Nick's lead, I spoke to his grandfather like I would anyone else. "I graduated from Shepherd University last spring, and I'm now working at the Lima Academy in the city. . . ."

We stayed in there for a little while, talking to his grandfather. It didn't feel like we were having a one-sided conversation even though Job couldn't respond. The truth was, he might've had trouble understanding what we were saying, but he seemed . . . calm. He watched us with milky, unfocused eyes, but sometimes—sometimes those eyes seemed to sharpen, dart back and forth between Nick and me. I wasn't sure if those were moments of him comprehending us or if they were moments of him not knowing who we were at all.

I didn't know, and it had to be so hard for Nick to constantly be confronted with that. I ached for him. I ached for his grandfather, but I did not regret being here, sitting with Nick, meeting the man who held it all together for Nick when their world came crumbling down.

It wasn't fair—fair that a man who did so much would be knocked down by such a disease.

We didn't visit very long, as his grandfather dozed off no more than an hour into us being up there. We quietly slipped out of the room and went downstairs. The moment we entered the living room, I said, "That went well. And I think he agrees that tater tots are awesome, so—"

Nick caught my arm and spun me around, startling me. He pulled me against his chest and wrapped his arms around me, holding me against him as tightly as I had wanted to hug him upstairs. He dipped his head, pressing his cheek against mine. "Thank you," he said, his voice gruff.

I squeezed my eyes shut as I held him back. I

didn't have to ask. I knew what he was thanking me for. "There's nothing to thank me for."

"Yes. Yes, there is."

We didn't say anything after that for several moments. Instead, we stood there in each other's embraces, and I think that was better than any words we could've shared.

Much, much later, when we sat on the couch side by side, our stomachs full, there was no resisting the broad, goofy smile on my face. There was no turkey or stuffing, no green bean casserole or mashed potatoes and gravy. But there were hamburgers and cheeseburgers and delicious, awesome tater tots, and it was one of the best Thanksgivings I could remember in a long time.

$\mathcal{B}$undled up in a fuzzy hat and heavy coat, Nick and I braved the icy winds and the leftover shopping crowds on Sunday. Yesterday I'd helped put the Christmas tree up at his house, and while doing that, he discovered that I didn't have a tree. So now we were on a mission to find me a suitable artificial Christmas tree.

"No matter what was going on, we always had a good Christmas," Nick had said while rummaging through a box of meticulously packed bulbs.

For some reason it had been hard for me to picture him dragging out the Christmas directions every year and putting them up by himself. Or that he'd been the one to lovingly place all the antique bulbs back into their boxes. It was at such odds with his sultry, masculine appearance or the fact he spent three nights a week slinging beer, but then again, there was a lot about Nick that was surprising.

Now, the wind lifted the ends of my hair, tossing

it around the hat as we crossed the crowded parking lot. Once inside, Nick veered off to the right and grabbed a cart as I watched a small child teeter on unsteady feet next to a woman who was trying to fit an even smaller girl into the seat of the cart, but the little thing wasn't having it. She was kicking her legs in every direction known to man.

"That woman has her hands full," Nick commented.

I glanced over at him and then turned back to the woman, who was now trying to buckle the child in with one of those wraith-thin seat belts. I wanted to ask him how many kids he wanted to have but figured that it wasn't a Target appropriate question, and probably wasn't even an appropriate question in general considering the lack of our relationship status.

"I cannot even imagine," I finally said, watching as she picked up the toddler and started pushing the cart with one hand.

Nick grinned. "Let's do this."

The Christmas shop was in the back of the store, near the electronics section. Of course, we got distracted by the new array of tablets, then by movies and then by the books. When we finally made it to the Christmas shop, I was starting to sweat under my heavy jacket. Reaching up, I pulled the hat off and then smoothed the static out of my hair.

My lips pursed as we walked up to the trees. "There are so many and they look so real."

He slid me a long look. "That's the point."

"Shush it." I touched one of the prickly needles. "My mom always gets a live Christmas tree, so I never bought one."

Nick nudged me with his hip as he stepped around the cart. "Well, let my expertise guide you into making the right choice."

I grinned.

The wide and tall trees, the ones with frosted tips, which looked extraordinarily real, were the ones that lured me in. "I don't think that's going to fit," Nick kept commenting as I moseyed from one gigantic tree to another. "How about this one?"

My brows rose. He was gesturing at a hot pink tree. "Um. No."

He chuckled as we moved down the aisle and then stopped. "Actually this one would be perfect."

This time he was talking about a slender five-and-a-half-foot Virginia pine. I ran my fingers along the frosted tips designed to look like it was dusted with snow. "I like it. This is the one. It has cherries."

Nick glanced over at me, grinning. "I think they're holly berries."

"Aren't they the same?"

He shook his head. "No, Stephanie. They aren't."

"Ha. What—" A sharp pain in my stomach cut my words off. Pressing my hand against my waist, I stood completely still as the burning sensation eased off.

Nick stepped toward me, his eyes widening, concern etched into his features. "You okay?"

For a moment I didn't answer, because I wasn't sure, but the pain didn't return. "Yeah. I'm fine. I guess it was just a weird cramp."

He touched my hand as he glanced around. "You sure?"

I nodded. "It was just a cramp. Probably the fried chicken."

"You did eat a lot of fried chicken."

My eyes narrowed. "Not that much."

Some of the tension eased out of Nick. "You ate, like, six pieces. Two of which were mine." He paused, his sage-colored eyes glimmering. "And my biscuit. You also ate my biscuit."

I did eat his biscuit. "I was *hungry*."

He chuckled as he turned back to the tree. "You want this one?"

"I think it's perfect with its 'holly berries.'"

Bending down, he easily picked up the long, narrow box. "Look at you, such a quick learner."

I laughed as he propped the tree up in the cart, and we moved on to the decorations. As we picked out ornaments and a garland, I waited for the pain to return, and was relieved that it didn't happen again.

We headed toward the front of the store, taking a shortcut through home furnishings, which caused us to walk right through the baby section. My attention wandered over the endless sea of baby stuff.

"You want to look around?" he asked, following my gaze.

My heart flip-flopped. "You okay with that?"

He shot me a weird look. "Why wouldn't I be?"

I shrugged. "It's really too soon to even look at any of this stuff."

"You can get some ideas, though."

"You have a good point."

"I always have good points."

"Aren't you just a humble-brag." I started forward, eyeing the changing tables. "Do you really think I need one of these?"

Nick followed with the cart. "Unless you plan on changing the baby on a kitchen counter, I'd say yes."

I giggled at the image as I brushed my fingers over the white pad. A display of tiny shoes were placed near the table.

"Oh my gosh." I picked up the pair of little white Mary Janes. Both shoes fit in one hand as I turned to Nick. "Look at this! Look at how small they are."

He shook his head. "There's a part of me that can't even fathom feet that tiny for shoes."

"I know." Grinning, I bit down on my lip. "If we have a girl, I'm so buying these shoes."

"You can buy ten of them if it makes you happy."

My gaze flew to his and held. The sincerity was right there. I couldn't look away from it. Words bubbled up to the tip of my tongue and I forced myself to look away. I put the shoes back. From there I roamed to a matching dresser and a rocking chair. There was so much stuff. Car seats. Strollers of various sizes. Rockers. Bouncy chairs. Diaper genies and so many different types of baby bottles.

Standing in the middle of the baby section, I simply gawked at everything. "I think I'm going to have a panic attack," I told him, only half serious. "I mean, I need to get all this stuff. That's a lot of stuff. And where am I going to put all of it?"

Nick picked up a package of dishwasher safe bottles. "Correction. *We* need to get this stuff and *we* have room. My grandfather's house is mine. It's in the will. I had been thinking about selling it once . . . well, you know, and moving into something smaller," he said, placing the bottles back. He returned to the cart. "But seems smart to keep the house, especially with a baby coming."

I was staring at him again. "You . . . you're saying

that we—like me and the baby—could move in with you?"

He arched a brow. "No. I was talking about that guy and girl over there picking out strollers."

I was still staring at him.

"Why wouldn't you? You're right. You don't have the space. I do. It would work perfectly." He leaned on the cart and picked up my hat, twirling it in his hands. A sly grin curved his lips. "And I like the idea of sharing a bed with you."

Although I knew his mind was probably happily playing in the gutter right now, I was absolutely floored by his offer. I don't know why I was surprised. Nick had a house. I had an apartment. He had room. I didn't. And this was *our* baby.

Moving in together was a huge step, but having a baby was an even bigger one.

God, we had done things so ass backward, but I didn't care as I stood there, openly staring at him.

I love you.

I wanted to get those words out. I wanted to scream them at the top of my lungs, but once again, I couldn't get them past my tongue.

Who knew three little words would be so hard to speak?

Chapter 26

"So when will I get to meet Nick?"

My eyes widened as the subject of my mom's question swaggered out from my bathroom half dressed. Dark denim jeans hung low, showing off the vee shape of his lower stomach. While I would never ever pass up the chance to appreciate the hotness of his near nakedness, we were going to be late to dinner.

But his bare chest glistened from the shower he took, and I wasn't convinced that he was wearing any underwear. I bit down on my lip as I eyed the tightly coiled muscles of his abdomen. Desire pooled low in my stomach. My hormones could just be going crazy, but I couldn't get enough of him.

Nick had to run into the bar late Sunday morning to help move more new equipment into the kitchen. When he showed up at my place, he'd been greasy and sweaty, immediately stating that he needed to get into the shower. Which was a great idea, because we had a group date we were supposed to be at tonight, but I was . . . well, I was going to blame pregnancy hormones.

He had undressed but his shower stalled when I kissed my way down until I was on my knees before him. So the fact that we would be running late was partly my fault.

"Stephanie, honey, are you still there?"

Pushing those thoughts out of my head, I turned around and stared at my dresser. "Yeah, I'm here. Sorry. I was distracted."

Nick chuckled from behind me.

I rolled my eyes. "I don't know when you can meet Nick, Mom." Pausing, I peeked over my shoulder to gauge his reaction. If he looked like he was ready to pass out then that would probably be a bad sign, but he appeared engrossed in pulling the sweater out of the gym bag he'd brought with him. Was he purposely ignoring what I was saying? Or did it not bother him?

"Well, I think you two should figure that out," Mom insisted, and I fought a grin as I recognized her "mom" voice.

"I can ask him."

"He's there?" Mom laughed. "So that's why you're distracted."

"Mom," I groaned as I twisted around so I faced Nick. "Mom wants to know when she can meet you."

Nick glanced up as he shook out his sweater. Nice wrinkle removal technique there. "I can't really head down to Martinsburg right now. Not with my granddad," he said, and that made sense. "But if she's coming up here, I'd love to meet her."

He'd *love* to meet her. My heart did a little dance in my chest. "He said—"

"I heard him, dear. Please tell him that I totally understand about his grandfather and he's in my prayers," Mom replied. "I was thinking about coming around Christmas. How does that sound?"

Nervousness assailed me. Christmas was, like, next week, and although I was thrilled that Nick was cool with meeting my mom, the first parent-slash-my-baby-daddy meeting made me want to hurl. Actually, when I went shopping for Nick last week, looking to get him something small and special for Christmas, I wanted to hurl then, too, because picking something was harder than I'd realized. I ended up settling on a nice, durable watch. It looked pretty in its box, but now I was thinking it was kind of a lame gift, even though he'd said time and time again that he needed to get a watch.

I told Mom around Christmas was okay, and then after a couple more minutes, I got off the phone to face Nick once more.

He was still shirtless.

I arched a brow as I dropped my phone on the bed. "Are you going to go out like that tonight?"

A cocky grin appeared. "I would, but then you'd be too 'distracted' to eat."

"Shut up."

Chuckling, he walked over and took my hand. He sat down on the edge of the bed and tugged me down so I was sitting in his lap. "Nick, we need to get going," I protested. "If we don't, we're going to be late."

"We're not going to be late." He curled an arm around my hips. "We have time. And we need time." His other hand landed on my lower stomach. "How are you feeling? Are you still feeling pretty tired?"

After putting up the Christmas tree, I'd gotten hit

pretty hard with exhaustion for about three days straight, and it had been intermittent since. According to the baby sites and my check-in with the OB/ GYN, per Nick's insistence, it was fairly normal. "I'm feeling fine today. Isn't that obvious?" I teased, toying with the button on his jeans.

He grinned. "I'm pretty sure you could be half-way to a coma and still be horny as hell."

I laughed. "I'm not going to even try to deny that."

The smile slipped a little. "But seriously, I'm just worried. You were so tired last week, and you said you weren't feeling that great."

"Thank you for being concerned, but I am feeling fine," I insisted. "And if it makes you feel better, I have my next appointment Friday."

"I know." His lashes lowered to where his hand rested on my pillow. "I can't believe you haven't gained any weight yet."

I placed my hand over his. "Oh, I've gained weight. Trust me."

A look of doubt crossed his face as his fingers curled, gathering the hem of my shirt into his fist. He tugged it up, revealing my stomach. "I'm going to start feeding you Whoppers every day."

I laughed, but truthfully, I was also a little surprised by how flat my stomach still was. It had started to curve a little, but I guessed that was just bloat. My hips and ass were probably a different story. I'd looked at pictures of women who were in their thirteenth week. It wasn't obvious they were pregnant, but there was definitely a small bump.

I didn't have a small bump.

"Maybe I'll be like some women who get a bump when they're further along and not before then?"

Nick didn't answer as he bent at his waist and pressed a kiss just above my navel, causing my heart to practically implode from the sweetness of the act. When he lifted his head, I captured his cheeks in my hands and tilted his head to the side, kissing him.

The kiss was just supposed to be that, but the moment the tip of his tongue touched mine, it turned into something far more needy. Nick stood as he twisted, taking me from his lap and laying me out flat on my back.

"Nick! We're going to be late!"

He moved his long body over mine, one hand curling around my hip. "We're not going to be late."

"We so do not have time. We need—"

His mouth covered mine, cutting off the rest of what I was saying, and as his hand slipped under my shirt, slid up my skin, and covered my breast, I started to forget about the whole time issue. Especially when his agile fingers made their way into the cup of my bra, finding the tightened tip of my breast.

My fingers clenched his shoulders, digging in as he kissed the corner of my lips and then made a scorching trail of tiny, hot kisses down my throat. My pulse picked up as desire thrummed through my veins.

"Nick," I moaned, my breath catching as his fingers did something truly naughty. "We need to get . . . going."

"We will," he said, slipping his hand out from my bra. Instead of getting up, he pulled my shirt up and then hooked his fingers between the cups of my bra, tugging it down. He bit down on his lip as he stared at me. "Fucking beautiful."

I watched him lower his head to the straining nipple, drawing it into his mouth, sucking deep. "Jesus."

He chuckled, and the feeling reverberated through me. When he moved to my other breast, nipping at the sensitive skin then soothing the sting with his tongue, I knew leaving on time was going to be a lost cause.

"We need to get ready," I told him, my chest rising and falling sharply as the ache between my thighs blossomed.

"Uh-huh." He left my breast, kissing his way down to my navel. His tongue dipped in, and my hips jerked up. Before I knew it, he'd undone the button and zipper and he was inching them down my thighs. "It's my turn."

His mouth was on me in a heartbeat, and there was no tentative, slow start to his seduction. He didn't just taste me. He didn't just please me. He reveled in what he was doing.

"Yeah," he murmured against my flesh. His tongue swept across my center, heightening the tension building in my core. "We are going to be so late."

Needless to say, we were a good twenty minutes or so late getting to the restaurant, but my muscles were made of jelly and I was too blissed out to really care that my hair looked like I just rolled around on a bed.

Which was sort of what I had done.

Nick and I walked back to the large round table, and it wasn't until I saw everyone did it really hit home how weird this dinner was going to be. When Calla invited us, I hadn't thought anything about it, but now that I was seeing Jase and Cam sitting there, all I could think about was how awkward this could turn out. Nick knew I'd hooked up with them in some form or fashion, and obviously everyone at the table knew, and yeah . . . this was different.

I sat down beside Calla, forcing a smile. "Sorry we're late. Traffic."

"Traffic," Calla mused with a sly grin. "Interesting, on Sunday night."

Teresa, who was sitting next to Avery, tossed the long length of dark hair over her shoulder. "Don't worry," she said, winking. "Jase and I ran into . . . 'traffic,' too. Really heavy 'traffic.'"

Jase's eyes widened.

On the other side of Avery, sitting next to Nick, Cam's face contorted with disgust in response to his sister's words. "Come on, man. I don't want to even picture that in my head."

Placing her hand over her mouth, Avery smothered her giggle but asked, "How heavy was that 'traffic' exactly?"

Teresa opened her mouth, but Jase spoke up, "Please, dear God, don't answer that question. I really don't want Cam punching me again."

I laughed as Teresa narrowed her eyes at her older brother. "If he lays one hand on you, that baby is going to be the last Cam can produce."

"Oh dear," Calla murmured.

Beside her, Jax leaned back in his chair and eyed Nick. "They are always like this, by the way."

"Can't take my sister anywhere," Cam replied, grinning when her glare turned deadly.

"More like I can't take you anywhere." Avery elbowed him as she smiled across the table at me. "How are you feeling?"

All the eyes landed on me, and I resisted the urge to squirm in my seat. "I've been doing good. It's been an . . . easy pregnancy so far."

"She's been really tired," Nick cut in.

A look of sympathy crossed the little redhead's face. "Oh God, same here. I think I finally got to the point where I sort of feel normal, but now I feel like I'm carrying a basketball around."

"It's a soccer ball," Cam corrected, leaning over and brushing his lips across her forehead. "A beautiful soccer ball."

I eyed her. "You don't look like you're carrying a soccer ball." Actually, she looked like she had the last time I'd seen her.

Avery's eyes lit up. "Thank you for that, but that's only because I'm sitting down."

"Stand up," Teresa urged as Jase reached over, curving his hand around the nape of her neck.

She pushed back her chair and stood, and yep, there was no mistaking that Avery was clearly pregnant. Her pale blue sweater was tight, stretching across a very well-defined bump. She framed her stomach with her hands. "As you can see, a soccer ball."

I laughed. "That is not the size of a soccer ball."

"Maybe a deflated one," Jase commented.

Avery giggled as she sat back down. Immediately, Cam draped his arm around her shoulders. "It sure doesn't feel that way."

Nick's gaze tracked from Avery to me and a soft smile appeared on his face. It took no leap of imagination to figure out that he was picturing me with a bump the size of a half-deflated soccer ball. And there was also no missing the look of complete anticipation in his gaze. He really wanted this baby.

But did he really want me?

The moment that thought crossed my mind, I pushed it away and focused on the conversation. There was no way I was going to let my neurosis ruin tonight.

Nick was definitely the quietest one in the group, sitting back and just taking it in. The food arrived, and I was surprised to find my appetite wasn't up to par. I ended up eating only half of my well-cooked steak and mashed potatoes. It might have had something to do with the initial awkwardness of who we were having dinner with, but neither Cam and Jase nor their significant others batted an eyelash over my presence. Neither did Nick.

Took me a few moments to realize and fully accept that no one at this table—the only ones who had a right to have an opinion on any of it—cared about any of that. Some of the awkwardness was in my head, a consequence of previous experiences, but these people didn't care. A strange sort of weight lifted from my shoulders. It wasn't guilt or remorse, nothing like that, because no one had ever done anything wrong or to be ashamed of. It was more like a bit of the wall between me and the two girls had finally snapped in half. They accepted me and I accepted them.

The past was formally in the past.

Fatigue crept back up on me Tuesday during work and stayed throughout Wednesday and into Thursday.

So when I had to haul an armload of the new

desk calendars to the supply room, I wanted to take breaks. Maybe even a nap halfway there, between two empty cubicles. No one would notice.

According to all the pregnancy related stuff I'd looked at, exhaustion was fairly common, but I hadn't thought it would be *this* bad. All I wanted to do was sleep.

As I neared the supply room, an overwhelming scent smacked me in the nose. Heavy cologne. Ugh.

Rick was nearby.

I rolled my eyes as I pushed open the door to the supply room with my hip and stepped inside. What I saw—what I *heard*—nearly knocked me flat on my rear.

"I said *stop*—"

Rick was in the room, but he wasn't alone. His back was to me, and I could barely see who he practically had pinned against the shelf with his massive body, but I saw her small hands push at his chest. I heard him laugh like it was a joke. Skin along the back of my neck crawled.

"What in the actual fuck?" I said.

Jerking back a step, Rick whirled around, his already ruddy face turning about three shades of red. A small form darted out between him and the shelf. Jillian's face was pale as her gaze connected with mine. She tugged on the hem of her thick sweater.

"It's not what you think," Rick said, swinging toward Jillian. "Tell her it's not what—"

I stepped forward, prepared to whack Rick over the head with the heap of calendars. I was pretty sure that what I saw and what I heard was exactly what I thought. "Jillian, go get Mr. Bowser."

Rick looked like he was about to stroke out.

"D-Dad said I c-could grab some Post-it notes," Jillian explained, her brown eyes wide. Her lower lip trembled. "That's all I was doing and he—"

"Jillian, go get Mr. Bowser *now*."

"I wasn't doing anything," Rick said, puffing up his chest. "I was just talking to her."

My hands tightened around the edges of the calendars as Jillian stopped beside me, her cheeks flushing pink. "You were not trying to talk to me, you asshole."

Rick opened his mouth, but I cut him off. "Please get Mr. Bowser," I said to her.

Jillian darted out of the room as I kept an eye on Rick. Fury rose in me, but so did another bitter, acidic emotion. I knew he was a creep of the highest order, but I hadn't known he was this bad. I should've reported him to Marcus the moment he had been inappropriate with me.

"Fuck," he grunted, moving as if he was going to come at me.

I held my ground. "You take one step toward me and I swear to God I will kick your balls so hard they'll end up in your throat."

He blanched.

"You are such a creep," I said, anger lancing my words. "Such a fucking creep—a *stupid*, fucking creep. The boss's daughter?" I shook my head. Andrew was going to ninja kill him.

And it appeared like Rick also realized that, because the blood drained out of his face. A second later Marcus appeared in the doorway. I turned to him as I placed the calendars against the wall. "I walked in on this asshole—"

"Jillian told me," Marcus interrupted, his voice

scarily calm. "Stephanie, would you please leave the room. Rick and I need to speak before he gathers his belongings and gets the fuck out of this building."

Oh. Oh wow.

I left the room with a quickness.

Jillian was waiting in the otherwise empty hallway, her eyes glassy as I approached her. Her hands were twisted together. "Thank y-you for coming in. He followed m-me in there and I . . ." She trailed off, pressing her lips together.

I stopped in front of her, keeping my voice low. "Are you okay, Jillian? Did he hurt you?"

"No." She gave a quick jerk of her head.

Something horrible occurred to me in that moment. What if this wasn't the first time he'd accosted Jillian? "Has this happened before?" I asked.

Jillian looked away as she swallowed hard. "No."

I didn't believe her. "Is he why you're leaving here?"

She choked out a laugh. "No. Not at all. I . . . I better go talk to my dad." She started backing up. "Th-Thank you again. Really."

Watching her all but run out, I stood there for a moment, a thousand horrible thoughts cycling through my head. I walked back to my desk in a daze.

About an hour after Rick the Creep was escorted out of Lima Academy and Jillian had long since left the facility, Marcus opened his office door. "Stephanie, can I see you for a minute?"

I immediately pushed to my feet and went into his office, having no idea what to expect. I didn't think I was in trouble for reporting Rick, not based on how pissed he'd been and how quickly he'd handled the situation, but what if I was? What if I lost my job? With a child on the way, that would be so, so bad.

But even if this went downhill fast, I didn't regret stepping in. No way. I just wished I had said something earlier.

"Can you please close the door behind you?" Marcus asked as he rounded the desk.

I quietly closed the door and sat down on the edge of the chair in front of his desk, folding my hands in my lap.

Marcus sat down, dropping his forearms on the desk as he met my stare. "First off, I want to thank you for stepping in and helping Jillian out."

"You don't need to thank me for that," I said.

He continued. "You said something that gave me the impression that this wasn't the first time you'd witnessed his inappropriate behavior here. Is that the case?"

I nodded in agreement. "He said a few things to me that I didn't feel were very appropriate, and once he got too close to me in the elevator. He . . . he rubbed up against me." I felt the tips of my ears burn. "I told him that he ever did that again, I would report him."

"Did he bother you after that?"

"No. He stayed away from me, for the most part." My gaze flicked to the large window behind him. "I . . ."

"Say what you want," Marcus said.

I shook my head as I sighed. Guilt churned my stomach. "I just wish I'd said something the first time he was inappropriate. Then that wouldn't have happened with Jillian."

Marcus leaned back in his chair, hooking one

leg over the other. "I'm going to be honest with you, Stephanie. I understand why you said nothing. You're new here, but I hope that none of us have given you the impression that we'd tolerate that kind of behavior."

"You haven't," I replied quickly.

Marcus smiled, but it didn't reach his dark eyes. "But I do wish you would've come forward. None of us want any of our employees or their families to feel unsafe here. If something like this ever happens again, I want you to come to Deanna or me immediately. Do you understand?"

"Yes. I do."

I was dismissed after that, but the yuck feeling lingered. Part of me wanted to find Rick and kick him in the balls. The other part of me wanted to smack myself for not reporting him when he crossed the line with me. I had handled it, but my head had to have been stuck up my own rear not to realize that if he treated me like I existed purely for his entertainment, he had to treat other women the same way.

I just hoped that my initial suspicions with Jillian weren't accurate, but I did have the feeling that Rick would probably have to relocate. Not only was Andrew going to be pissed, but once Brock found out, I was betting Rick was a dead man.

On the way home, I stopped at a hamburger joint and picked up a fast dinner since I was too tired to make something. I knew the fatigue had to be normal, and I didn't mention it to Nick when he texted around seven. The last thing I wanted him to do was worry.

Besides, I had my doctor's appointment on Friday and I could bring it up then.

I didn't tell him about what happened with Rick earlier. Even though I had handled my own issues with Rick, knowing Nick, he was not going to be happy to hear about Rick's pervy behavior.

After pulling on my pajama bottoms and a loose shirt, I walked into my bathroom and stood sideways in front of the mirror. Pulling my top up, I checked myself out in the mirror. No visible bump. Not really, but I tried to imagine myself with a soccer ball.

I doubted I'd be as adorable as Avery, but my lips curved up in a smile as I slid my hands to my belly. Just the last couple of days, I'd been thinking about how I would broach the topic of my pregnancy with Marcus. It wasn't going to be easy, but I would need to say something soon.

Twisting, I tilted my head to the side as a niggle of doubt crept into my thoughts. Shouldn't I be able to see some sort of bump? Something at nearly four-teen weeks? According to the five million mother-to-be pictures I'd seen, the answer was yes, but . . .

I dropped my shirt and resisted the urge to Google more rare pregnancy issues that I could go the rest of my life never knowing about.

Walking out to the living room, I turned the Christmas tree lights off and then grabbed a glass of orange juice from the fridge and started back toward the bedroom, my sock-covered feet silent on the wood floors. It was early, but after a bearlike yawn, I was so ready for bed. I had set the glass down and reached for the remote when a sharp, stabbing pain cut across my lower stomach, knocking the air out of my lungs.

"Ouch," I whispered, placing my hand against my stomach near my left hip. "Whoa."

The pain burned as it faded off. I stood, staring at the glass of juice. My mouth dried as a horrible thought popped into my head. *Is something wrong?* Heart pounding, I waited several minutes, and when the pain didn't return, forced out an uneven breath. I was fine. The pain probably had nothing to do with the pregnancy and more to do with the fast food I'd eaten for dinner.

Climbing into bed, I shoved my legs under the comforter and picked up the remote. I clicked on the TV, flipping to the HGTV channel, and it wasn't long before I dozed off listening to couples argue over yellow walls and brown carpet.

When I jerked awake hours later, sitting straight up in bed, I wasn't sure what woke me. My throat was incredibly dry and my skin felt damp with sweat. The TV was still on, volume turned down low. I pressed the back of my hand against my forehead, but I was cool. Had I had a nightmare? Leaning toward the nightstand, I reached for the remote when the pain sliced through my stomach again. I sucked in a gasp as I froze. The pain was like period cramping, but a bit stronger. It slowly eased, but was immediately followed by a strange pressure that sat low in my stomach.

I flipped on the light with a shaky hand. Not a minute later, the pain struck again. The cramp was severe, causing my body to jerk in reflex, and before it eased off, there was a sudden wet feeling.

This wasn't normal.

My stomach dropped as I jerked the comforter off the bed and stumbled to my feet. The cramping hit again. It was like my entire stomach was inside of a fist that was squeezing and squeezing, and as soon as it lessened, it fisted again.

Turning around, I reached for my phone as my gaze fell along the bed. My heart stuttered. Panic exploded as I stared down at the mattress. "Oh my God."

There was blood on the sheets.

Chapter 27

The bright lights of the emergency room were harsh, leaving no space to hide from the reality of the situation. All I could do was stare up at those lights until halos formed around them.

Lying on the uncomfortable mattress while the nurse fixed the hospital gown and the thin, heated blanket, I didn't say anything as the doctor wheeled away from the end of the bed, the snapping elastic sound of her tugging off latex gloves cracking like thunder. Water was turned on. I wasn't waiting for her to speak, because I already knew what she was going to say.

I didn't remember driving to the hospital, which probably meant I shouldn't have driven myself, but I did remember all the bright red blood that had soaked my pajama bottoms, and the bright red blood that started to bleed through the sweats I'd changed into. I remembered the clots when I sat down on the toilet, and I remembered . . .

I bit down on my lip as the cramping returned. My hand curled along the top of the blanket. The nurse's shadow fell over me and her cool hand covered mine. I wanted to pull my hand away. I didn't want her or anyone touching me right now, but I didn't move.

"Ms. Keith?"

My gaze drifted to the doctor. She looked young. Like she could be my age. Her brow creased as she pushed the stool over to the bed, near my waist, and sat down. Her serious gaze met mine. Her gaze reminded me of the ultrasound technician who'd been in the tiny curtained off room before the doctor. That nurse had introduced himself, but once he started moving the handle around, he stopped looking at me. When he left the room, I hadn't even known if he had spoken. I thought he did. And I thought those words might've been meaningless.

"I'm sorry," the doctor said.

I inhaled through my nose as I shifted my attention to the ceiling again. My jaw ached from how tight I was clenching it, but I couldn't force it to let up. The doctor—what was her name? Williams? Williamson?—was talking again, and I missed some of it.

" . . . the ultrasound confirmed what we suspected with the symptoms you're presenting right now," she was saying, and I heard paper moving, as if she were flipping through a chart. "When you came in, you said you were nearing your thirteenth week?"

My mouth was dry as I spoke. "Friday is . . . would be thirteen weeks."

The nurse squeezed my hand.

"And you've just had your initial appointment with your OB/GYN?"

"About a month ago," I said.

The papers ruffled again, and when she spoke this time, her words were slow and careful. "Based on the ultrasound and the blood tests we ordered, it appears that the fetus has already been miscarried and what is happening right now, with the bleeding—"

"Wait." I wet my lips. "What do you—what do you mean I've already miscarried?"

"The ultrasound and the exam revealed there is no fetus. When you started bleeding, did you notice any large clots?" she asked.

Of course, the clots . . . I knew that. I'd read about the warning signs on one of the various mommy board splurges, but I hadn't thought . . .

I hadn't thought it would happen.

God.

I squeezed my eyes shut. Those clots had come when I was . . . I couldn't even finish the thought. How had I not known it was happening at that exact moment?

What if I had come to the hospital the very second I'd felt that pain?

The doctor was talking again. "It's very common at this stage in a pregnancy for the fetus to stop developing without you knowing. Sometimes it can happen days or weeks before the body starts to heal itself. That's what's happening right now."

My eyes flickered open. Had the baby been . . . gone for days? Weeks? And I didn't even know?

She was talking to me about options and what to expect, the follow-up appointments I needed to make and symptoms I needed to watch for in case everything didn't . . . didn't come out. She was rattling off all this information, and that damn nurse was still squeezing my hand, and I wanted . . .

I wanted my mom.

"Why?" I asked hoarsely.

Out of the corners of my eyes, I saw the doctor stand. "This isn't ever easy to hear or to understand, but sometimes, there is no reason, Ms. Keith. It just happens. It doesn't necessarily mean you won't be able to carry a baby, but I do suggest that when you see your doctor, to talk to him or her about your concerns. . . ."

There was no reason? No. That couldn't make sense, could it? My thoughts whirled around the things I'd read, and yes, the logical part of me realized that the body was a crazy thing that did insane things, but I wanted a reason. Pain as sharp and as real as what was cutting across my stomach expanded in my chest. I wanted to know what I did or didn't do—

The ache expanded and tears climbed up my throat, swelling in my eyes. The pregnancy hadn't been planned, but I'd wanted it. And Nick hadn't expected it, but he wanted it. We were going to make the best out of it, and within a few short weeks we were going to try to find out the gender. The hurting welled up, burning through every cell. And if the baby had been a boy, we—

I cut those thoughts off, and I shut it down, all of it down. Locked myself right up. Pushed all of it down, because I couldn't . . . couldn't deal with this right now. I just couldn't.

"Do you have anyone you can call?" the nurse asked.

"What?" I looked at her, and realized that the doctor wasn't in the room anymore. It was just us. When had she left? A cramp seized up my insides, and I fought the urge to roll onto my side.

Sympathy poured out of the nurse's expression. "I asked if you have someone you can call?"

Yes. That was what my head said over and over again. Yes. There were people to call. There was a *person* to call, but that wasn't what I did.

I didn't even know why.

That's just not what I did.

Per the doctor's suggestion, I called off work early the following morning, and with her excuse, I was able to take the rest of the week off. I told Deanna that I had the flu, but if Marcus needed anything worked on immediately, I could do it from home. All he needed to do was call or e-mail. After what had gone down yesterday with Rick, I wasn't sure how Marcus would feel about me missing work, but I didn't have any choice.

It was a very smart idea not to attempt to go to work like nothing had happened. The cramps and the bleeding were like nothing I'd ever experienced before. For a good hour after I spoke to Deanna, I was curled up on the couch, my hands flattened against my stomach and my knees curled up after I changed the sheets on the bed, removing whatever traces of the . . . incident that I could.

I didn't think about anything.

Nothing.

Hours ticked by, and any moment my brain started to drift toward what was happening, I quickly forced my attention to the TV. Around lunch my phone went off, and pressure clamped around my chest. It was Nick.

I froze, a second away from answering it. What . . . what was I going to tell him? Then I reached for the phone and, sitting up, brought it close to my chest and closed my eyes. God, he'd already lost so much in life, and he was going to be so disappointed, and I—

Without answering the call, I dropped the phone on the couch and pressed my palms against my forehead. "Stop it."

I knew there was nothing I could do about any of this. It had already happened. Lurching to my feet, I went to the kitchen to grab a glass of water. I passed the fridge and stumbled to a halt.

Held up with the corny heart-shaped magnet was the sonogram. For a moment I was simply stuck right there, not moving, barely breathing as I stared at the picture. If the doctor hadn't pointed out the baby, I wouldn't have been able to find it. The baby had been so incredibly small, the size of a raspberry.

Was this some kind of punishment since I . . . since I hadn't wanted to be pregnant? Like some kind of cosmic karma since it hadn't been planned, and I had freaked out so much in the beginning? Worrying about not being able to travel the world and stupid, pointless shit like that?

Pressure returned to my chest, and I snapped forward, yanking the photo off the fridge.

I wanted this to be over with.

I hurried back to the bedroom, ignoring the cramping in my stomach as I stepped into my closet, shoving the picture between two shoe boxes. I walked back to the living room and picked up my phone.

Mom answered on the third ring. "Hey honey."

"Hi." My fingers curled around the phone. "Are you busy?"

"Of course not," she replied with a little laugh. "Aren't you at work?"

I started pacing. "No. I have today and Friday off, because I'm not feeling very well."

"Oh no." There was a pause and I could hear Loki barking in the background. Mom shushed the dog. "What's wrong? Is it the baby?"

Is it the baby?

Squeezing my eyes shut, I drew in a shallow breath. "Um, I . . ." The words were unbelievably hard to say. "I had a really weird pain last night in my stomach, but it went away. I thought it was something I ate, so I went to bed."

"Oh," Mom whispered into the phone, and I thought . . . I thought she already knew. "Oh, honey."

I pressed my hand on my stomach, just below the navel. "I went back to sleep. I probably shouldn't have done that. I just didn't think that something was wrong, but I woke up a couple of hours later, and it was . . . I was cramping and stuff. I went to the hospital." I opened my eyes and started pacing again. "The doctor said that the ba— That it probably stopped developing. That could've happened weeks ago, I guess. I don't know."

"Honey," Mom choked out. "I'm so, so sorry. Are you—?"

"I'm fine," I cut in, wrapping one arm over my waist. "I'm actually okay."

"Honey—"

"I'm fine. I'm just going to take today and tomorrow off, then use the weekend to relax, but I'm okay.

I told work I had the flu. I guess it was a good thing that I hadn't told them before. I mean, this was probably a blessing in disguise, right?" I was rambling at this point but I couldn't stop myself. "Something was wrong and this . . . these things happen."

There was a pause, and then Mom said, "I'm going to come up there. I'm going to pack Loki in the carrier and we're going to come up there and—"

"That's not necessary. I'm okay and there's nothing that anyone can do," I told her. "I just need to spend the next couple of days relaxing."

"But—"

"Mom, I'm okay. I promise. You don't need to come up here. Okay? I'll see you at Christmas."

She didn't reply immediately. "If you change your mind, I'm just a phone call away, okay?"

"Okay," I murmured.

"How is Nick handling it?" she asked.

My chest squeezed as I forced out the words. "I haven't told him yet."

Silence.

"I . . . it just happened, and he was at work, so I drove myself to the hospital last night."

"Stephanie," she sighed wearily.

My knuckles ached. "I'm going to get off here, okay? I'll call you later."

I all but hung up on her, and I felt crappy for rushing off the phone, but I didn't want to say anything that would propel her to ignore my request for her not to come, and I didn't want to talk about it anymore, because I knew I was going to have to talk about it again.

Glancing at the clock, I knew I had time to talk to Nick before he went to work. Part of me wanted to chicken out and call him, because seeing him face-to-face wasn't something I was sure I could do.

But this wasn't the kind of conversation you had on the phone.

I texted him, asking if he could stop by. After a couple of texts back and forth—Nick wondering why I was home, and me making being vague an art form—he said he was on his way. Sitting in the chair by the small table, I waited as knots built in my stomach. The cramping wasn't so bad now, but every so often it felt like someone shoved a knife into my midsection. Part of me welcomed that pain, because I could focus on it.

When Nick showed up, not nearly enough time had passed. First look at him told me why. Wearing nylon sweaters and a thermal under his jacket, he'd been at the gym. His hair was adorably messy.

He took one look at my pale face and his hand tightened around the edge of his motorcycle helmet. "You're sick. That's why you're home." Putting the helmet on the table, he turned to me.

I stepped back, out of arm's reach. "I'm not sick. Not really. Um . . ." Avoiding his concerned gaze, I turned around and ran my hands through my hair. The limp strands tangled in my fingers. "I needed to talk to you."

"I'm here." His hands brushed along my back, and I sidestepped him. "What's going on, Stephanie?"

Walking to the couch, I sat on the edge. Since I'd already told my mom, it was easier to get the words out this time, maybe too easy. "I . . . I lost it."

"What?" Nick moved closer.

"The baby," I said, staring at my hands—my fingers. "I miscarried. I don't know why. It happened last night. I didn't even know it was happening at first. I thought it was just stomach pains. That was stupid." I glanced up to find Nick standing near the couch, still as a statue. "I don't know if it was something I did or didn't do, but I'm not . . . pregnant anymore."

Nick's expression tensed as he closed his eyes. His hand lifted and he shoved his fingers through his hair. "Stephanie . . ."

My name was harsh-sounding on his tongue, and I cast my gaze back to my hands. "I'm sorry," I whispered.

"What?" The burst of that one word drew my attention. He was staring at me. "Babe, you have nothing to apologize for." One step brought him to where I sat, and he was crouched in front of me, his hands wrapped around mine, and I thought of the nurse holding my hand last night. "God, Stephanie, don't apologize. Don't—"

"I know you're disappointed. You didn't think you'd have a . . . well, I know you wanted this."

His gaze searched mine. "I know you wanted this, too, but this . . . it happens. God." His head bowed as he brought our joined hands to his forehead. "Fuck. I don't know what to say."

The breath I drew in was shaky. I didn't know what to say either. His shoulders tensed and then he lifted his head. Those extraordinary eyes were bright, too bright, and my heart broke.

"Okay. All right." He inhaled deeply. "Do we need to go to the hospital? I can—"

"I already went to the hospital."

Nick's lips slowly parted as he stared at me, his eyes widening.

"There's nothing else that can be done at this point. I mean, not right now. I'll make a follow-up appointment to make sure everything is okay, but nothing needs to be done right now." That was the truth, and I didn't need to tell him all the . . . other details of what was happening. "You don't need to take off work or anything. I'm just going to be . . . uh, relaxing . . ." I swallowed thickly. " . . . until Monday."

He let go of my hands. "When . . . when did this happen?"

"Last night." Hadn't I said that? I couldn't remember.

Nick placed his hands on his thighs. "And you went to the hospital *last night*?"

I nodded as I smoothed my hands over my legs.

"Why didn't you call me?"

His face blurred a little as I shook my head. "I don't know."

There was a pause. "Come again?"

Why hadn't I called him? He should've been the first person I called. Granted, I'd panicked when I went to the hospital, but I should've called him once I was there or when the nurse had asked. I still didn't even know why I hadn't. I pressed my fingers to my temples and shook my head. "I didn't want to bother you."

"Bother me? Are you . . . ?" He rose suddenly, taking a step back. His hand went through his hair again. "Okay. Why would you even think that?"

I shook my head.

Nick stepped to the side, his hands settling on his waist. "Is this a real conversation we're having?"

I squeezed my eyes shut. "I didn't . . ."

"You didn't what?"

I hadn't wanted to disappoint him, because he'd lost so much. I hadn't wanted to hurt him, because he'd already been hurt enough. And I didn't know how to handle any of *this*—the baby, being in a relationship, losing the baby and Nick. I didn't know how to do this, and I had done it wrong, so wrong.

And as I lifted my gaze to him, I knew they weren't the only reasons. I'd fallen for Nick, fallen so deep, and this baby was what had brought us together—was what *stuck us* together, and now that wasn't there. He'd never said he'd loved me. No plans for the future were made that hadn't included the baby. What were we without what brought us together?

I knew I was going to lose him.

A cramp hit, catching me off guard. My hand flew to my stomach as the pain lanced through me.

Nick was immediately kneeling in front of me. "Are you okay?"

"Yeah," I gritted out.

"What can I do?" He touched my arm.

"Nothing. Just . . ." The pain let up, and pulled away as I stood. "I just need to relax for a little bit."

His hands opened at his sides. "Is there anything I can get for you?"

I shook my head. "No. I just wanted to let you know. That's all."

"That's all?" He jerked back as if he'd been pushed, and I wanted to look away. I wanted to hide, because this . . . all of this felt like my fault. "Stephanie, I don't know what to say."

Tell me that you still want to be here.

Tell me that you still see a future for us.

Tell me that you love me.

"There's nothing to say," I whispered, looking away.

"You're wrong," he said, and hope sparked deep in my chest. "We lost a baby—"

"I wasn't even thirteen weeks," I said, because it was easier not to think about it outside of that. "The doctor said it might've stopped developing weeks ago."

"Weeks ago?" he murmured, wincing.

"All I'm trying to say is that at least it happened now and not weeks from now, not when . . ." Not when I was showing or when it would be so much harder to accept and understand this.

Except it was hard to accept and understand. I didn't get it. I didn't know why this happened, and I wasn't just disappointed, I was *crushed*, and I—

"I should've been there, Stephanie. Not just so that I could be there for you, but also so that I could be there. And nothing to say? There's a lot to say about all of this. I don't know the words right now. I don't even know what to think, but . . . Fuck." He smoothed his hand over his face. His arm shook. "Why didn't you call me, Stephanie?"

I blinked. "I . . ."

"You know what? This isn't the time for this conversation."

My stomach twisted. "Why not?"

He shot me a disbelieving look. "You don't need to deal with anything else."

Here it comes, I thought. "I'm okay," I told him, straightening my shoulders. "What conversation do you want to have?"

"You're okay?"

"Yes."

His eyes flared. "You cannot be okay. You just lost the baby, Stephanie. I mean, come the fuck on. You're human. You're not—"

"I'm okay." My heart was pounding. "What do you want to talk about?"

Shaking his head, he started to walk toward the table—to his helmet. He was leaving, and panic took root in the pit of my stomach. I stepped in front of him. "Why won't you tell me what you want to say?"

"Why?" The hollows of his cheeks flushed. "Because I'm trying to be a decent human being right now, Stephanie. I'm not trying to dump more shit on your head when you don't need it right now. I'm—"

"What?" I snapped, frustration and confusion swirling in me until it turned into bitter-edged anger. "You're *what*?"

"I'm pissed! I'm fucking disappointed," he shot back, and I flinched. "How could you deal with that by yourself?" He stepped toward me, his hands closing at his sides. "How could you not think that I would've—I would've fucking dropped *everything* to be there. I mean, did you even think of me when this was happening? Did it even cross your damn mind that I would want to be there for you? For myself?"

My mouth opened but there were no words. "I . . . didn't think when I started having the pains. I drove myself to the hospital and I—"

"I get that. Okay? I can understand that part, but you wait until today to ask me to come over via fucking text message, are you kidding— Okay." He drew himself up straight, drawing in a deep breath as his entire body tensed. "I'm doing this right now. You don't need this," he said, stepping around me. "I don't need to do this right now. Okay? I need to clear my head. You need to clear your head."

I folded my arms across my waist. "I'm sorry."

Nick spun on me. "Stop apologizing, Stephanie. What happened isn't your fault." He reached out, but my body had a mind of its own. It recoiled from his words, because how could this not be my fault? His hands touched air, and the skin around his lips whitened. "What the—"

"Please just leave," I whispered. "Please. Just go."

"Steph—"

"Please." My control stretched, thinning, and then it just . . . it just snapped. "Why are you still here?"

Nick stopped moving. He might have stopped breathing, and for a long, tense moment there was nothing but silence. I closed my eyes, hearing the helmet scrapping off the table, and a heartbeat later the front door slammed shut.

Chapter 28

*N*ick had walked out, not on me, I would discover, but had simply left the apartment. He'd called Roxy and remained in the parking lot until she showed up some fifteen minutes later.

I knew this because when she knocked on my door, I heard his motorcycle roar to life.

Roxy stepped in before I had a chance to say one word. "I know what's happened, and Nick doesn't want you to be by yourself right now. *You* shouldn't be by yourself right now."

"I'm—"

"Yeah. You're fine. He said you kept saying that." Roxy shrugged off her jacket. "You might as well go ahead and close that door, because I'm not leaving."

There was a huge part of me that wanted to tell her to leave, but I was suddenly too tired to argue. Exhausted to the bone, I closed the door and then walked past her, to the couch. Sitting down, I picked up the quilt and dragged it over me, tucking it under my chin.

Roxy draped her coat over the back of the kitchen chair and made her way over. She didn't speak as she sat on the other side of the couch, and I didn't look at her. I stared at the TV screen, not really seeing it.

"I want to hug you right now," she said, and the muscles all along my spine stiffened. "But you look like you might punch me if I did."

I shook my head slowly. I wasn't sure if I was agreeing or not.

She exhaled softly. "I don't know what to say, Steph, other than I'm so, so sorry."

Closing my eyes against the burn, I gripped the edges of the blanket. My stomach cramped and it was painful, but in a way, it was no match to the complete and utter devastation I felt. "I don't get it," I said after a moment.

"Get what?" she asked quietly.

I really didn't know where I was going with any of this, but my tongue was moving and words were becoming attached to the pain bubbling up inside me. "I don't get why it hurts so much. It's not like I was even that far along, you know? I haven't even told my boss yet. Maybe I shouldn't have told anyone. I mean, I was just entering my second trimester." A sharp slice of pain cut through me. "Actually, I probably wasn't even close. The doctor at the hospital said that the ba—said that it probably stopped developing a week or more ago."

And now that I'd said it out loud, things started to make sense. The exhaustion that I felt. The loss of whatever weight I had gained. "There had been signs," I told her. I was starting to see white spots behind my closed eyelids. "Signs that I was losing . . . it, and I didn't pay attention to them. I thought they were normal."

"How would you know? You couldn't," Roxy argued. "And I know that miscarrying is common, Steph. It happens, and no one is to blame for it."

No one was to blame? I wasn't so sure. Maybe I hadn't taken the pregnancy seriously. I know I missed taking the prenatal vitamins once. My diet could've been way healthier. And what if the baby hadn't stopped developing, and if I paid attention to the pain last night instead of going to bed, could this miscarriage have been prevented?

The racing thoughts made me feel sick. I felt like . . . like I deserved this. Like some kind of punishment had been handed down. I'd messed up and I didn't even know what I'd done.

Roxy scooted closer, placing her hand on my shoulder. "This isn't your fault."

I opened my tired eyes.

"These things happen," she continued, her voice barely above a whisper. "I know that sounds lame right now and doesn't help anything, but these things do happen, Steph, and no one is to blame."

My gaze fell to the Christmas tree and my thoughts immediately drifted to the day I picked out the tree with Nick. How we'd roamed into the baby section and looked at all—

I cut those thoughts off as I inhaled sharply, but I couldn't look away from the tree. God, was that really only two weeks ago? Was the baby even still alive then?

Roxy squeezed my shoulder. "What can I do for you?"

"Nothing," I whispered.

"Do you think you can eat?" she asked, and I shook my head. "What about something to drink? Or something for pain?" When I didn't say anything, she dropped her hand. "I'm not leaving you, so you should make use of me being here."

I pressed my lips together. "There's nothing I need right now."

A moment passed. "I don't think that's true. You need Nick right now."

Sucking in a sharp breath, I stiffened.

"And he needs you right now," she added.

I shook my head again. "He . . . he doesn't need me."

"He sounded like he was about ten seconds away from losing his shit." Her eyes met mine when I looked at her. "Maybe you don't need to hear that right now, but I've never really seen Nick upset. Ever. And he was really upset."

"I don't want him to be upset." My voice was hoarse. "The last thing I wanted is for him to get hurt again. He's lost . . ." I trailed off, partly because I didn't want to share his personal business and because Katie's words rushed back to haunt me.

You're going to break his heart.

My lips slowly parted. Holy shit. Katie and her super stripping psychic power had been on point. I had thought it was crazy for, well, obvious reasons, and because this whole time I wasn't convinced that I had the power to break Nick's heart. But I did. It was the baby, I realized—losing the baby. It sounded crazy, but Katie had been right.

"What happened with Nick?" Roxy asked gently.

I drew in a shaky breath. "I . . . I broke his heart."

Thursday afternoon blurred into the night.

At some point I migrated from the couch to my bedroom, and as I lay in bed, I didn't sleep. I couldn't sleep. My mind turned over everything I had done and hadn't done since I found out I was pregnant, searching tirelessly for that one misstep I took.

Roxy didn't leave, but she gave me space, only coming into the bedroom when enough hours had past for her to pester me into eating the chicken soup that I had no idea how she obtained, because I didn't have any in the house, but that soup reminded me of Nick.

And that made the hurt so much fresher.

I thought I heard Reece's voice Thursday night, and then later I thought I heard Calla. At first I assumed I was imagining it, but then I realized dimly that Calla was home now. The semester at Shepherd was over. I prayed that she wouldn't come into the room, and she didn't.

All night long I lay awake and didn't cry. There was a vast emptiness that consumed my thoughts. I couldn't turn any of it off like I had in the emergency room Wednesday night. I just wanted it to be over—the physical pain and the deeper, sharper, and more hurtful pain.

Sometime in the quiet early morning hours, I came to the realization that I had wanted this baby far more than I ever recognized. It was like that cheesy saying, "You don't know what you have until it's gone," and that was so damn true. The burning in my throat and eyes increased.

I curled up, tucking my legs in. It wasn't fair. None of this was fair, and I hadn't hurt this badly since those two uniformed marines showed up at our front door when I was fifteen.

In the back of my head I knew I needed to pull myself out of this. I needed to get up, brush myself off, and I needed to get on with life. That's what I always did, and I would have to do it again, but I hadn't just lost the baby.

I'd lost a future.

Roxy attempted to get me to eat breakfast Friday morning, and I thought she looked as bad as I felt when she left the bedroom, her brown hair falling out of the topknot. I wanted to tell her that she didn't have to stay. She had a life she needed to get back to. I would be fine.

I was always fine.

A few minutes before eleven in the morning, I heard the door open and I was expecting to see Roxy, but it was Katie who walked into my bedroom, closing the door behind her, and I almost didn't recognize her.

Face cleared of all traces of makeup and her long blond hair pulled up in a high ponytail, she was wearing the plainest outfit I'd ever seen her in. Blue jeans and a white wool sweater. I'd never seen her so . . . low key.

Katie made her way to the bed and sat on the edge, her blue eyes bright without any of the eye shadow or dark liner. "Roxy had to run home."

My throat was dry as I spoke. "You didn't have to come. I'm just . . . taking it easy."

"Kind of hard to take it easy after losing a baby."

I sucked in a shallow breath. Apparently her normal bluntness was not missing. I didn't know what to say to that.

"You must be feeling ill," she added, hooking one knee over the other. "I know that when someone miscarries, they feel pretty shitty for a couple of days. Not just mentally. Roxy said you haven't eaten breakfast."

"I'm not hungry," I said after a moment.

She folded her hands in her lap. "You should probably try to eat something."

I didn't respond as I squirmed under the blankets. A muggy, suffocating feeling draped over me. I was embarrassed by the attention—by the fact my friends thought I needed a babysitter right now when all I needed was . . .

I didn't let myself finish that thought.

"I'm fine," I told her from my prone position on the bed. There was a good chance my cheek was plastered to the pillow.

One eyebrow rose. "I warned you."

My breathing slowed.

Katie shook her head slowly, sadly. "I just had this feeling, you know? I knew you were going to break his heart and you're doing it."

I squeezed my eyes shut. Was God smiting me or something? I really didn't need this right now.

"But I never thought you'd be this . . . stupid."

My eyes flew open. "Excuse me?"

"I mean, you're this confident, intelligent, and sexy woman. You could have men on their knees if you wanted them there. And you're fucking dumb as a bag rocks right now." She looked down at me. "Roxy told me you all but kicked Nick out of your apartment . . . after telling him you lost the baby. You know, the baby you two created together."

Something hot and uncomfortable stirred in my gut. "I know how we made the baby, Katie. Thanks. And I know I broke his heart by losing the baby, so I really don't need the reminder right now."

Katie ignored my tone and continued. "She also said he mentioned that you didn't even tell him until after you got back from the hospital. What the fuck, girl?"

My mouth dropped open as guilt moved like black smoke through me.

"You know, I get that you have these fears and concerns about how Nick really feels about you, but you have to be dumb as a motherfucker not to see the truth."

"Okay," I said after a second. "That's like the second or third time you've called me dumb, and I really don't like that or have the patience for this conversation right now."

"Too bad," she replied, eyes sharpening. "Because there's something you're not getting."

I rolled onto my back, clenching my jaw. "I think I get it."

"No. You don't." She waited until my gaze found hers. "But you will."

Exhaling loudly, I struggled to keep a grasp on my patience. "I'm really tired. I think I need to—"

"Talk about how unfair it is that you lost the baby? Or how much it hurts?" she answered for me. "We can talk about it."

"I don't need to talk about that."

She raised both brows. "That's not true. You're not okay. Talking is important. Get the anger and emotion out." She paused. "Or when you're feeling better, get on the pole. That's one hell of a workout and a great way to get the anger out."

Dumbfounded, all I could do was stare. "Are you psychic and a counselor?"

"Aren't they one in the same?"

"What even . . . ?" I lifted my hand, pressing it to my forehead. "I can't deal with this right now."

"No one expects you to deal. This is something tragic, girl. Happens all the time, to people all across the world. Doesn't mean it sucks any less. And it doesn't mean your pain is any less. You're not okay."

The air got stuck in my throat. "I am okay."

Katie shook her head. "Nope."

My eyes narrowed. "Yeah, I am."

"Keep telling yourself that."

I sat up, staring at her. "What in the hell? I said I'm okay. I'm okay, for fuck's sake."

She folded slender arms across her waist. "You can tell me that all you want, but I know better. Everyone knows better."

"Everyone knows . . ." I shook my head, painfully aware of the limp strands of hair smacking my cheeks. In that moment, I don't think there was anyone I hated more than Katie. "I can't deal with this right now," I repeated, my hand curling into a fist.

Katie tilted her head to the side. "Of course not. Who would be able to deal with this right now?"

There were no words, because, good God, we were talking in one giant, messed up circle.

A tide of violent, unstable emotions rose inside me as I reached down and grabbed the comforter. My hand shook as I tossed it off my legs. I stood, pushing my hair out of my face with a frantic shove. "I'm okay."

Katie said nothing.

The trembling danced over my fingers and rose up my arms. "I'm fine," I said, and the tide overcame me, rising up and washing over, like a levee breaking. "I'm okay." I backed up, hitting the wall. "I'm okay!"

She rose from the bed, her face crumbling as she whispered, "It's all right."

No.

That was the thing. It wasn't all right. Oh God, none of this was okay.

Something strong broke inside of me. The burning in my eyes and throat were no longer manageable. Katie's shape blurred, and somewhere, someone was screaming those two damn words over and over, and it was a lie. It was such a stupid, fucking lie.

And I'd messed up. I knew I had in more ways than I was even considering, and it wasn't okay. And I didn't know how to make it okay or where to even start. There was no manual on this, no amount of Googling that was going to fix this.

Tears streamed down my face as my chest heaved with a broken sob. Katie's arms came around me and tightened as my knees gave out and I slid down the wall, taking her with me. My head fell to her shoulder. "I'm not," I whispered. "I'm not okay."

Chapter 29

$\mathcal{I}$ finally slept.

There really was no other option for me. I'd cried myself sick, into dry heaves, and I cried myself into a mindless exhaustion that could only be cured by climbing into my bed. I don't know how long I slept, but waking up was like dragging myself out of gritty quicksand. My eyes, swollen and weary, felt plastered shut, and I wasn't ready to attempt to peel them open and face reality, face the loss of a future I hadn't known how badly I wanted until it was gone. And face the ugly truth that my insecurities concerning my relationship with Nick, valid or not, had led me to make selfish, cowardly choices when it came to involving him in what was happening. I also just didn't . . . didn't want to see him hurt, and trying to protect him from that had backfired.

I loved him and I had hurt him even more.

Like a ghost, the image of those tiny shoes Nick and I had looked at while Christmas tree shopping formed in my head, and the pain rose, sharp and seemingly never-ending. In that moment, I was never more grateful for the fact that I hadn't started shopping for anything baby related. I wasn't sure if I could bear having to return onesies or pack them away. The ultrasound picture on the fridge had been difficult enough to see.

Every cell in my body felt like I'd been through the wringer, and I really had. The last thing I wanted to do was get up, but I needed to because of what my body was going through. As I lay there telling myself to get up, I slowly became aware of another presence in the room.

A *very* close presence, like in the same bed with me. I could hear the steady breaths. While I wouldn't have been surprised if Katie climbed into bed with me, I had the distinct feeling that it wasn't her. My skin tingled as I breathed in deeply, catching a fresh scent tinged with pine.

My heart skipped a beat. The scent . . . the scent was so familiar, so right.

I held my breath as I forced my eyes to crack open, and exhaled roughly once my vision adjusted to the low light filtering in from the hallway outside the open bedroom door.

Lying in the bed beside me, on his back, was Nick.

I still had to be asleep.

Nick turned his head toward mine. Even with the lack of light, I could see the dark shadows under his eyes. When he spoke, his voice was rough. "You're awake."

Unable to get my tongue off the roof of my mouth, I started to sit up. Nick rose alongside me, his gaze never leaving my face. "Katie had Roxy call me. It's just us."

My head was still fuzzy with sleep and I blurted out the first thing that came to mind. "I have to go to the bathroom."

"Do you need help?" was his immediate response.

I shook my head. "I . . ." I was at a loss for words as I stared at him.

"I'll be waiting for you here, okay?" he said, voice low. "You need anything, yell, and I'll be there."

Pressure tightened around my chest, and I forced myself out of the bed before I lost it all over again. I shuffled to the bathroom and took care of the necessary stuff. Before leaving, I stopped long enough to splash cold water over my face and to pull my now gross hair back.

Nick was here.

He'd come back even after I'd kicked him out.

He was here.

Throat constricting, I glanced at my reflection and saw that I looked like a wreck, but I knew there was nothing I could do about that. What I looked like was the least important thing right now.

I ambled back to the bedroom, feeling like I'd aged fifty years, but seeing Nick propped against the headboard was like receiving a shot of adrenaline. Nervousness and the sweet anticipation always tied to him battled it out as I made my way to the bed, sitting down near his legs.

Nick had turned on the nightstand lamp while I was in the bathroom, and now I could fully see him. A thick stubble covered his jaw and chin, and those dark shadows under his eyes were stark. His shirt, the same one he had worn yesterday when I saw him, was wrinkled. His hair was a mess, and he looked just as bad as I felt.

His chest rose with a deep breath. "I know you don't want me here," he stated, and before I could respond, he forged on. "But I'm going to be right here. It took everything in me yesterday to walk out of that door and I don't have it in me anymore to do it again. Not after knowing what you've been going through and seeing you now. I know you're hurting. You shouldn't be alone and it should be *me* who's here for you."

I lowered my gaze as I pulled my legs up, curling them under me. "It's not that I didn't want you here, Nick. That's not the case at all."

There was a beat of silence. "I'm going to be real honest with you, Stephanie, that's exactly how it came across yesterday."

How could I explain what I was feeling and where my head was at when it was in so many places and everything was so raw? There were so many words, so many things I could say, and yet I couldn't grasp one strong thought. It was like trying to catch the rain.

Yesterday I had pushed for a confrontation, but today, right now, all I wanted was his arms to be around me. All I wanted was to be held. All I wanted was to be with the one person who shared the same pain I was experiencing.

I lifted my gaze, and Nick's face blurred as a wave of fresh tears rose.

He tilted his head to the side and his voice cracked when he spoke. "Come here."

My body moved before my brain fully registered the words. I scrambled over his legs as he sat up, his arms open and reaching for me. I climbed right into his lap, planting my face against his chest as I all but fused my body to his.

Nick's reaction was immediate. He buried one hand in my messy ponytail, and my knees bent on either side of me as his other arm circled my waist, curving his body into mine. It was like he was caging himself around me, and those tears that had welled up spilled free. I almost couldn't believe there were any left in me, but the sobs rose again, and they were so powerful they shook my body— shook his as he held on.

"That's good. That's good," he kept saying, over and over. "It's all right not to be okay. I'm not okay either. I'm not."

And he wasn't. I could feel his body trembling, and as I curled my fingers around the hair at the nape of his neck, guilt and anguish tangled together, forming a poisonous knot. "I'm sorry. I'm so sorry."

"Stephanie, baby, please don't apologize." His voice did that breaking thing again, killing me. "What happened isn't your fault. You know that, right? This wasn't your fault."

I wasn't sure if I was apologizing for losing the baby or for how I treated him during it. Or maybe I was apologizing for both things.

And then he said it. "You're breaking my heart, Stephanie. Stop apologizing. It's ripping me apart."

You're going to break his heart.

My grip on him tightened. It wasn't losing the baby. It wasn't even the way I had acted. It was this. Damn. Katie really was psychic.

We held on, becoming each other's anchor, and we shared that pain. Time became something that happened in the background. I had no idea how much of it passed before I opened my eyes and the only tears left were those that clung to my eyelashes.

His arms had stopped trembling and his chin rested atop my head as one hand trailed up and down my back, the caress soothing and grounding.

"Are you . . . not working?" I asked, wincing at the scratchiness of my voice and the lameness of my question.

"Jax gave me the weekend off, and Kira is with my grandfather." His hand curled around the nape of my neck. "I'm not going anywhere, Stephanie."

"I don't want you to leave me." I whispered those words, and it didn't kill me to admit something so vulnerable. In all honesty, it did the exact opposite. Relief blossomed, tiny and frail, but there.

Nick's hand stilled. "Why would you even think that?"

I raised a shoulder.

"Don't do that." His voice was gentle as his hand started to move again, kneading the tight muscles in my neck. "Talk to me."

My hand slipped to his chest and curled there, above his heart. "I just don't want you to leave, because I . . . I think you're going to. We got together because I was pregnant. That's why we were together. Not because of anything else, and now that's gone, there's no reason for you to keep doing this—"

"No reason?" Disbelief colored his tone.

"Well, I know you're physically attracted to me, but . . . I don't know." I sighed. "None of this is really important right now. We can—"

"That is important right now." His other hand rose, brushing back a strand of hair that had escaped the ponytail and was plastered to my cheek. "Why in the world would you think you being pregnant was the only reason I've been with you?"

When he said it like that, it did sound foolish, but our relationship had been far from normal. "You didn't want to see me again after the first night we hooked up."

"I—"

"I know you apologized, and honestly, I don't even care about that, but when you did come back around, you just wanted to be friends. There was nothing more until after I found out I was pregnant," I said, and then rushed on. "We never called each other boyfriend and girlfriend, and you said we were stuck together. That we were going to have to make the best out of this and . . ." And I trailed off, because really, what else needed to be said after that? Those were his words.

Nick was silent for a moment and then cursed under his breath. "Jesus, Stephanie, I fucked this up. I really did."

Confused, I drew back and my gaze found his. "What?"

"Shit." He lifted a hand, dragging it down his face. "Remember that night I came here to apologize for the way I acted in the bar? When I said I wished things were different between us? I wasn't screwing around then. You have no idea how hard it was for me not to see you again after the night we hooked up. I wanted to. Fuck. I wanted to more than anything I've wanted to do in a long time."

What the what . . . ? "Then why didn't you?"

He shook his head. "My focus has been my grandfather for the last couple of years, and I didn't want any other complications. I didn't have time for one." He dropped his hand. "But I'm also a fucking idiot. It's not something I realized until I got to know you. That's not a good enough excuse, but with everything that has happened in my family—losing almost all of them, and then the girl I thought I was in love with in college left me when shit got tough? Getting in a relationship again wasn't something I was looking forward to. I'm going to be honest. The idea still . . . yeah, it scares me a little."

I opened my mouth, but I didn't know what to say as I shook my head.

"I wanted to be different for you—I wanted everything to be different for you, and that was before we knew you were pregnant," he said, his shoulders hunching as he shook his head. "I just didn't think I was capable of being that person."

My brows rose. "You are."

His lashes lowered. "You know, a couple of months ago I wouldn't have been sure of that statement, and honestly, I didn't know until you came over for Thanksgiving. Seeing you with my grandfather made me realize how much of an idiot I was, not going after you the moment I left your apartment. And talking to you about what happened to my family, how it's tied to Calla. Actually saying that shit out loud helped me let it go. I should've . . . I should've said *that* to you, because I get why you'd think there was nothing else between us. I do. I should've made it clear that there was more I was feeling."

He pressed his hand to his chest. "I was feeling more for you in here, and it had nothing to do with you being pregnant."

I almost couldn't believe what he was saying. "But if I hadn't gotten pregnant, would we ever have gotten together?"

"I don't know, honestly I don't, but I like to think we would've found our way to each other." His gaze flickered to mine. "I want to believe that. I have to."

I struggled through the ball of emotion that was building again. Hope was there, swelling so beautifully, but it felt tainted with loss and with lingering, thick confusion. My lips trembled and I pressed them together for a moment. "I don't know. You were wonderful—you have been wonderful. I should've known there was more there. I've just been so . . . everything has been new to me."

"Yeah." His eyes searched mine. "Neither of us are very good at this relationship thing, huh?"

A dry, cracking laugh escaped me. "No. We're not very good at it." I lowered my chin. "But we were really good at it when we didn't even know we were doing it."

"Damn straight," he murmured, gently touching my chin. He tipped my head up so our eyes met. "Would you like to be my girlfriend? Circle yes or no."

Another hoarse laugh rattled as I lifted my finger, drawing a circle on his chest. "That's me circling yes."

Nick's lips twitched into a grin. "Maybe I should've asked you that a while ago."

"Maybe I should've asked you."

His grin faded as he leaned over, pressing his lips to my temple.

"You know what?" I whispered, closing my eyes as I tried to grasp onto that hope and almost immediately felt guilty for doing so. How could I be happy about anything right now? But at the same time how could I not be, now that I knew the man I was in love with wanted to be with me? Even if he hadn't spoken those three words, what he had told me meant so much.

He curled his arm back around my waist. "What?"

"I wish . . . I wish this hadn't happened."

"I know. I wish the same thing."

I drew in a shallow breath. "It hurts. I can't believe how much it hurts, and I can't stop thinking that I . . . I could've done something differently."

"Babe," he said, kissing my forehead, "don't let your head go there. Promise me you won't let your head go there."

Promising that was harder said than done, but that's what I did, and he cupped my cheek. "It's going to be hard. I know it is. For both of us, but you know what?"

"What?"

"We got each other. No matter what. There *is* a you and me." Nick lowered his forehead to mine. "And that is all we need right now."

Chapter 30

*W*hen I returned to work on Monday, my body was still going through the motions of the miscarriage, but my luck was twofold. The office was closed on Thursday, Christmas Eve, and didn't reopen until Monday, and I was able to schedule an appointment to get in and see my OB/GYN on the following Tuesday, snatching up a cancelled appointment.

While I was at work, I didn't allow myself to think about what my body was going through. I focused on the errands I had to run and the renovation proposal for the recently acquired facility in West Virginia. Perhaps the whole avoiding what had happened routine wasn't the smartest, but it was what helped get me through each day, and I think that it was important to take it day by day.

But I wasn't alone.

On Sunday, I had packed some clothes and personal items and followed Nick back to his grandfather's house. When he asked me to come home with him, I hadn't hesitated. Sunday night we had spent time with his grandfather and then I'd fallen asleep in his arms. His presence and his understanding of the pain kept the worst moments—the ones where guilt and doubt started to creep up—from overwhelming me. Waking up with him wrapped around me went a long way, probably more than he realized.

Then again, I think Nick did know. I think that was why he insisted I stay with him until my mom whirled into town for Christmas. He was there in those moments when I woke up in the middle of the night and couldn't fall back to sleep. Those moments when the heavy malaise twisted in discontent. I knew my body was going through a lot and it had my mood swinging all over the place, but it was also just . . . just hard as hell to deal with.

Part of me felt like I needed to spring back immediately. To move the hell along, because these things happened. They happened every day, and I was lucky that there hadn't been any major complications so far, like an infection, or that I hadn't been further along. In those dark moments in the middle of the night, it was hard to give voice to what I was feeling exactly, but I didn't have to.

Nick seemed to sense just when I needed him. Even if he was asleep, his arms would tighten around me, and sometimes, when my restlessness woke him, he would talk to me until I fell back asleep, distracting me with some of the crazy things he'd seen while working at Mona's. He was simply there for me, and I let him in completely.

And there was no denying how much I loved this man.

Mom arrived Christmas Eve morning, and after checking in at a nearby hotel, she came straight to my apartment. When she knocked on the front door, I glanced over at Nick as he rose from the couch. "You ready for this?" I asked.

A lopsided grin formed. "Of course."

I wasn't so sure as I opened the door. My mom could be . . . a lot to handle, and she all but tackled me as she rushed through the open doorway, wrapping her arms around me. I was enveloped in her warmth and vanilla-scented perfume.

Her hand smoothed over the back of my head. "Oh, my sweet girl . . ." She held me tight, and I was suddenly the little girl who just . . . just needed her mom, because now everything would be okay.

Loki's muffled bark drew us apart. Looking over her shoulder, I spotted the little dog eyeing us from inside the carrier. I lowered my arms as I stepped back. "I better get the dog before it chews its way through the metal bars."

Mom rolled her eyes, but she knew it could happen. When Loki wanted out of something, Loki got out of it. The dog could scale fences. As I picked up the carrier, I brought it into the apartment with me, closing the door behind us. I wasn't surprised that she had Loki with her instead of leaving the dog at the hotel.

She didn't leave Loki anywhere.

Nick stepped forward, extending a hand as his one-sided grin grew. "Hello, Ms. Keith."

"And this must be Nick. Now I can see why you are so distracted when you're on the phone with me and he's around." Mom eyed him as she took his hand.

He smiled as his gaze found mine. "I like her."

"Of course you do," I muttered as Mom checked him out.

"Wow. Stephanie, wow." She glanced over her shoulder at me. "I'm very proud of you."

"Oh my gosh." My cheeks burned. *"Mom."*

She chuckled as she turned back to Nick. "It is a pleasure to finally meet you." Then she dropped his hand and folded him into one of her mom hugs. I could see that Nick was surprised, but he returned the gesture without awkwardness, and I loved him even more for that. "I'm so sorry about what has happened," she said, her voice low as I bent down, unlocking Loki's carrier. "These things are never easy, but you look like you have the shoulders to carry that weight."

"I'm going to do everything I can to do just that," he replied, earning a smile of approval from my mom.

Loki scrambled out, commencing the marathon sniffing event as Nick offered my mom something to drink. Nervously, I watched them move into the kitchen as I folded my arms across my waist. They were talking about her drive up here, how long she was staying, and just general chitchat as he made her coffee. I stayed back, pretending to keep an eye on Loki as the dog darted across the couch and then jumped to the floor, racing back toward the bedroom. When Mom looked over at me and winked, my lips curved up at the corners. She didn't have to say it, but I knew she was already starting to fall for Nick herself.

Taking a deep breath, I walked over to the kitchen and my stomach twisted pleasantly as Nick drifted to my side, curving his arm around my shoulder. As my mom tinkered with the sugar and creamer, Nick leaned down and brushed his lips over my cheek.

I swallowed hard as I glanced up at him. "You doing okay?" he whispered.

"Yeah." I smiled. "Yeah, I am."

After my mom went back to the hotel with the little hooligan known as Loki, I packed a bag and rode back to Nick's house to spend the rest of Christmas Eve there so Kira, the in-home nurse, could be home for the night. Mom would be joining us at Nick's house in the morning, and it seemed like an awful big step, but Nick was chill about her coming over.

While Nick was upstairs checking in on his grandfather, I pulled the gift I'd gotten him for Christmas and carried it into the living room. With the TV off and only the flickering white light from the Christmas tree, a very mellow feeling settled over me as I sat on the couch.

It wasn't long before Nick joined me on the couch. "How's your granddad?" I asked.

"He's sleeping." He glanced down at my hands. "What's that?"

I held up the small wrapped box. "It's a Christmas present. I wanted to give it to you now."

"You don't want to wait?"

"I'm impatient. Plus it's really not that awesome a gift." I grinned when he laughed. "I mean, I suck at getting gifts. I'm not the most creative person when it comes to those things, but yeah, I just want to give it to you now."

Nick grinned as he took the present from me, slipping his finger under the edges of the wrapping paper. He peeled the paper back and made quick work of it. When he flipped open the box, I pressed my lips together. "Whoa." He reached in, lifting the watch out of the box. "This is nice, Stephanie."

"Really?"

The smile reached his eyes. "Hell yeah. I've been saying for months I need to get a watch. It's good to have one when I'm working."

"It's also water resistant," I pointed out, feeling goofy, "and . . . yeah. I'm glad you like it."

"I do." Stretching over, he placed the watch on the coffee table, and as he straightened cupped my cheek. "Thank you."

"You're welcome," I whispered.

Nick kissed me slow and sweet, his lips and fingers lingering as he drew back. "Stay right here, okay?"

"I'm not going anywhere."

His eyes held mine for a moment and then he stood, disappearing around the corner of the couch. It sounded like he was heading into the bedroom. He returned quickly, taking his seat beside me. A square, unwrapped dark velvet box was in his hand. "Since you gave me your gift, I want to give you mine."

I glanced up at him as I quietly took the box that was a little smaller than my palm. I had no idea what to expect when I popped it open, but when I saw what was in it, my breath caught.

Nestled in the box was a pair of silver dog tags. "Oh gosh," I whispered as I smoothed my thumb over one of them. My throat clogged.

"It's two of them." Reaching over, he turned one around. His name was carved into it. "The other has your name. I know it sounds kind of cheesy. Dog tags. But I saw them in the store and they made me think of your dad and how your mom wears his tags. It was kind of spur-of-the-moment thing. You don't have to wear them—"

I looped my arm around his neck and pulled him over, kissing him. "I will wear it. Every day."

"Yeah?"

Sniffling, I nodded as I sat back and looked down at them. I pressed my lips together. The gift was so incredibly thoughtful. "Will . . . will you wear the other?"

"Fuck yeah."

I laughed and my breath hitched again. Carefully pulling the tag with his name on it free, I slipped it over my neck, letting the cool metal slide under my sweater. I took the one with my name on it and lifted it. Grinning, Nick lowered his head and I slipped it over his head. He pulled his shirt loose, letting the tag with my name on it fall against his chest.

And then I smiled for what felt like the first time in days. The words came right out, requiring no effort. "I love you."

Nick froze and his shirt floated back against his skin. He started as if he was about to say something and his head swung toward mine. His lips parted. "What?"

"I love you," I repeated, holding his wide gaze. The pupils had dilated and the green seemed brighter. I couldn't believe how easy the words were to speak. "I'm in love with you. I fell for you weeks ago—months ago—and I just wanted to tell you that."

He stared at me.

"And you don't have to say it back. I don't—"

Nick's large hands clasped my cheeks and within a stuttered heartbeat his mouth was on mine. The silky soft kiss stole my breath. "Let me hear it again," he asked, his breath rough, but then he kissed me again, his tongue gently parting my lips. "Tell me."

I wrapped my hands around his wrists. "I love you, Nick."

"Christ." He rested his forehead against mine, his large hands trembling as he held my cheeks. "I never thought I'd hear you say that."

"What?" I whispered.

He slid one hand around, his fingers delving deep in my hair. "Because I never thought I would be lucky enough to hear it—to know that what I felt for you was the same thing you felt for me."

I stilled. There was a good chance I wasn't breathing. A flutter started deep in my chest. "What are you saying?"

"I don't just love you. I'm in love with you. Hell, I have been for a while, and I wanted to tell you that so many times over, but I . . . fuck, I couldn't get it out of me. I don't even feel like I deserve this."

My heart was racing so incredibly fast. Tears blurred my eyes, and the sweetest yearning blossomed in the pit of my belly, chasing away everything else. "You deserve that."

"I'm going to prove it to you, Stephanie. You have no idea." His lips met mine again, and the kiss was deeper, rawer. "And you're going to get tired of hearing me saying this. I love you. I'm so fucking in love with you, Stephanie."

"I'll never get tired of hearing that." I slid my

hands down his strong arms. "There's no way." I squeezed my eyes shut. "This is what I've been waiting for. You're what I've been looking for."

Nick's hand flexed in my hair. "You don't have to wait anymore. *We* don't have to wait anymore."

Chapter 31

Job Blanco, the kind and hardworking man who held his family together through the worst kind of tragedies, passed away peacefully, while asleep, on April eighteenth. When he slipped away early that morning, he hadn't lost his battle with Alzheimer's. No. Job had fought too long, too hard, and too bravely for him to have lost any fight.

He was simply done.

The timing of his death was not entirely unexpected. For several days Nick knew it was coming. He was still shocked when it happened, but the writing was on the wall, and while anyone would wish that was a message no one ever had to see, it enabled Nick to take the time off to be there with his grandfather.

For about a week, I spent the nights at his house, and I was so thankful that I was there with Nick, my arms wrapped around his waist, as he sat by his grandfather's bed and said good-bye for the final time.

Saying good-bye was never easy, but I think there was a relief mixed in with the grief Nick was feeling. His grandfather was no longer suffering.

In his grandfather's will, he had requested certain customs to be carried out based on his heritage, and Nick had honored those wishes, which weren't very different than the processes I was familiar with. The funeral was less than a week after his death, and he was laid to rest beside his wife and the rest of his family, which had left long before him.

The following weekend I helped Nick at the house. We cleared out his grandfather's bedroom, setting aside items that he wanted donated into one pile and little personal effects that Nick wanted to keep in another.

With spring in the air, there was something refreshing about the whole process, not just for Nick, but also for me. Windows were open. Breezy air floated through the rooms. Everything felt open and new. With each load of clothing I packed, it was like I was folding up the lingering guilt and the hurt, storing it away, because each day it got a little easier to deal with the loss of the baby. It got a little easier to accept that no one had done anything wrong, and each day both of us moved a little closer to moving on. It was a process, though, just like clearing out his grandfather's room. One where some days it felt like one step forward was actually five steps backward. Some days it was hard not to try to hide from the pain, to not give in to the what-ifs of the past and of the future.

As expected, when I met with the doctor after the miscarriage, there were no answers as to why it happened and no way to guarantee that it wouldn't happen again. We simply would not know until the next time I got pregnant. And not knowing was hard to process. It wasn't like I dwelled on it every day, but there were moments when a near paralyzing uncertainty would seize me. Could I have kids? I didn't know, but I kept telling myself that if I couldn't, it would be okay.

Like Nick had said, we had each other.

And that was what we needed.

Nick wasn't sure what he was going to do with his grandfather's room, leave it as a guest bedroom or convert it into something else.

Standing in front of the newly remade twin bed, I looped my arm through his as I leaned into him. "You don't have to make a decision right now about this room."

"You're right." He turned his head and dipped his chin, brushing his lips across the top of my messy and probably dusty bun. "I think I'll keep it like this for right now. I like it as a bedroom."

My gaze traveled across the room. On the now empty dresser, framed photos of his grandfather over the years were lined up like little memory soldiers. Leaving this room as it was for now was a good idea. "Me, too."

"Thank you for helping out. I really appreciate it." Nick pulled his arm free and then reached down, taking hold of my hand. He lifted it. "But you're filthy."

I smiled up at him. "So are you, babe."

"Then I think we need to rectify that."

My body was immediately on board with that idea. Nick led me out of the room and downstairs, to the master bedroom off the kitchen. Nick made a show of stripping off our clothes, and it took longer than necessary, but there wasn't a part of me that was disappointed in the pacing. I think, before the water was turned on and before the wispy steam filled the bathroom, he'd kissed every square inch of my body. And he wasn't done yet.

"I love your lips." He kissed me. "And those cheeks." His lips found their way there. "I love your eyes." He dropped a kiss against my brow and then started working his way down. "I love your throat."

"My throat?" I laughed huskily.

"Uh-huh. And I love your shoulder blades." He kissed my collarbone.

"You're so fucking weird."

"I'm so fucking in love with you."

My heart squeezed. It did that every time I heard those words.

He worshipped every inch of my body, and when he took the tip of my breast into his mouth, sucking deep, he drew a ragged moan out of me, stirring up powerful desire. "And I really love these."

I liquefied, ready for him to the point where it was almost painful. "Oh God."

We took our time in the shower, and I was sure that no more than a handful of minutes was actually dedicated to the whole cleansing part. It wasn't long before my back was pressed against the slippery tile and Nick was on his knees, drawing every soft cry out of me. My knees were weak and my body still trembling from a powerful release when he rose before me, the water sluicing off his bronze skin as he thrust into me, his green eyes latched onto mine in a possessive, consuming stare.

He stretched me in the most delicious way and he

held me so gently, even as his body strained against mine. Our bodies were flush, hips-to-hips, chest-to-chest. "God, you feel too damn good for me to take my time."

"Don't take your time." I skated my fingers over his skin, down his chest.

Nick groaned. His muscles trembled as he moved and my hands slipped over his skin. We quickly lost ourselves in each other, him pumping wildly, my hips meeting his, and it was no small miracle that we didn't fall and break our necks in there.

Later, much later, we lay on his bed, face-to-face, our skin long since dried as he toyed with the damp strands of my hair. "I've been thinking," he said.

I arched a sleepy eyebrow. "Congratulations."

He chuckled. "Smartass."

My smile stretched my lips. "What have you been thinking about?"

"It's kind of random." He tossed a strand of hair over my shoulder and then picked up another. "But I've been thinking of talking to Calla, telling her who my father is."

My breath caught as some of the sleepiness faded. "For real?"

"Yeah." One side of his lips kicked up. "What do you think about that?"

"What do I think?" I wiggled over to him, inching him onto his back. Straddling him, I placed my hands on either side of his face.

"I like where this is heading," he murmured.

"Shush it," I told him. "I think it's a great idea."

"You doing me on top?"

I cocked my head to the side, shooting him a bland look. "No. That's not what I'm talking about."

He laughed again, and those green eyes were lighter than I'd seen in days. "I know."

Bending over, I kissed him lightly. "I'm proud of you."

His hands settled on my hips. "Why?"

I raised a shoulder. "I just know it's going to be a hard conversation to have, and I know how much you've really been thinking about this. Talking to Calla is a huge step to just letting all of that go." I kissed him again and then sat up. "Whenever you're ready to have that conversation, if you want me there, I'm there."

"I want you there."

"Then I'm there."

One hand lifted, threading through my hair. He guided my mouth back to his, stopping just short of our lips meeting. "You know what?"

"What?"

He tugged me down so that when he spoke again his lips brushed mine. "I love you."

My heart swelled so fast it was no wonder I didn't lift both of us up to the ceiling. Those three words were words I would never, ever get tired of hearing. I kissed him again, and this time there was nothing soft or chaste about it. I whispered those very same words back to him and then I showed him just how much.

In the middle of the following week, while I was at work organizing Marcus's schedule through the up-coming summer months, Nick texted about dinner with Calla and Jax the following Sunday.

Going out with them or Reece and Roxy wasn't

something new. We double- and triple-dated often, but I knew Nick had an ulterior motive for this, and I was nervous for him, because I knew this wouldn't be easy for him. And I really, really hoped that my impression of Calla was correct, that she wasn't going to hold anything against him.

I took more time than I normally did getting ready Sunday afternoon. Sort of like hopeful primping. I got a mani and pedi with Roxy and Katie in the afternoon, then I tried out one of those green clay masks I'd bought online the previous week. Thankfully, it didn't stain my skin or do something weird. Then after a long shower, I dried my hair and artfully applied makeup.

"Artfully apply makeup" was code for putting a crap ton of makeup on but somehow managing to look like you weren't wearing a crap ton of makeup.

Moving on to what to wear, I mulled over the idea of donning a cute spring dress, but it still wasn't particularly warm, especially in the evenings. So I settled on dark blue skinny jeans, a light sweater, and eyed strappy heels I hadn't worn yet this year.

I reached up on the top shelf and pulled the shoe box down. A piece of paper drifted free, floating to the floor. Shoving the box under my arm, I bent and picked up the paper.

My breath caught.

I should've known what it was once I felt the shiny texture of the paper, but I didn't remember putting *this* in the closet. I'd probably done it when I was trying to remove all traces of being pregnant.

My hand trembled slightly as I walked to my bed. Sitting down, I placed the small photo next to me, and I didn't look at it until I had my shoes on. Then I drew in a deep breath and picked it up.

Honestly, I still didn't see a baby in the sonogram picture. It was just a black-and-white blob, but it had been my blob and it had been Nick's blob. Pressing my lips together, I gave a little shake of my head. It didn't hurt as much as it had before to see this. Confusion still existed. I would never know why it had happened and I wouldn't know if there was a serious issue with getting pregnant until it happened again, but I knew now there wasn't anything I could've done differently.

And I knew it was okay to still hurt over it.

Standing, I walked over to the shelf and stood the photo up against the one of my dad. It made sense for it to be there. Maybe one day I'd take it down again, store it away. Just like one day Nick would turn his grandfather's bedroom into something else.

One day.

Nick arrived, looking as yummy as usual in his jeans and button-down shirt. He gave a low whistle when I stepped out in the hall, closing the door behind me.

I gave him a half curtsy. "Thank you."

He chuckled as he draped his arm over my shoulder. "Weirdo."

"Whatever."

We met Jax and Calla at a local steakhouse. They were already there, seated in a booth, because we were late even though we'd left early. Nick got a little . . . frisky in the car outside my apartment and then again outside of the restaurant.

Calla shot me a knowing look as we slid into the booth across from them. Self-conscious, I lifted my hand to my hair, smoothing the waves.

Jax laughed under his breath. "Glad you guys could join us."

"I know." Nick picked up his menu, a slight smile on his lips. "You all are blessed by our presence."

Calla giggled while Jax rolled his eyes. I tucked my hair back as I peeked over at Nick and then turned my attention to her. "So what are you guys getting?"

Her brows puckered as she glanced down at the open menu in front of her. "I think I'm getting the strip."

"Porterhouse." Jax patted his flat belly. "Porterhouse all the way."

Nick tapped a finger off the center of the menu. "They have a rib-eye," he said to me. "Bone in. You know you want it."

I grinned. Yeah, I did. The waitress arrived, and once the orders were placed the conversation flowed. I'd ordered a wine, and then Nick made fun of me when I ended up getting a soda, because I couldn't eat food while drinking water or wine. It was weird and made no sense. I completely knew that.

Calla talked about what she planned on doing when she finished her nursing degree. Having transferred to one of the local colleges to get it, two of her transfer credits hadn't been accepted, so she'd be taking summer classes to finish up. Jax mentioned the plans he had for a small remodeling of Mona's bar. He wanted to strip out the old floor and get rid of the tables and chairs. There was one topic I knew they wouldn't bring up, because of what had happened to us, so I knew it would be up to me to cross that bridge.

After taking a sip of the Coke, I placed it next to my plate. "You guys have seen the pictures of Avery and Cam's baby, right?"

Calla's gaze shot to mine and she nodded. A moment passed. "I've never seen a baby before with so much red hair."

"She could be a Weasley sibling," I said, placing my hands in my lap. No one had sent me the pictures at first or brought it up around me when Avery went into delivery a week shy of nine months. I'd seen Roxy showing Katie two weeks ago, and then after a few days I got Avery's number from her and sent her a congratulations text. After a few back and forth texts, I got a picture of the tiny baby girl.

Avery and Cam's child was gorgeous.

Jax chuckled. "Don't tell Cam that, because I think Avery tried to name her Ginny."

I laughed. "But Ava is such a beautiful name."

"Fits them, I think," Calla agreed, smiling tentatively at me.

From what I gathered from the bits and pieces I'd heard from everyone, Avery's delivery hadn't been easy, and there were some complications. I didn't know the details and I hadn't felt comfortable asking for them. I was just glad that in the end they were a happy family of three.

"What are you planning to do with your grandfather's house?" Jax asked as he picked up the beer he'd ordered.

"My grandfather left the house to me, so it's mine and it's free and clear," Nick explained. "I'm not sure what I'm going to do long-term, but for right now, I'm going to keep it."

"It's a great house," I threw out.

Jax nodded. "Hell yeah it is. You're sitting on a nice nest egg."

"Yeah." Nick leaned against the booth, stretching

his arm along the back. His fingers brushed over my hair, then played with it, but his posture had shifted. He stiffened, and I knew he was about to drop the bomb on them.

I reached over, under the table, and placed my hand on his knee, letting him know that I had his back.

"There's something I wanted to tell you guys," he began. "Something I probably should have said a long time ago."

Jax's brows knitted as he glanced over to a confused Calla, and then he said, "Okay. You've got my curiosity. What's up?"

When Nick's attention shifted to Calla, I wished I'd had the foresight to order a second glass of wine. His shoulders lifted with a deep breath and then he said, "Blanco is my grandfather's last name—my mother's maiden name—but my father's last name was Novak."

Calla blinked slowly as her face paled a little. "Novak?" She sat back, her hands falling into her lap.

Beside her, Jax frowned as he stared across the table. "Wait a sec. Novak was . . ."

"Novak Construction," Nick confirmed quietly.

"Oh my God." Calla's hand rose toward her cheek, but she stopped short of touching the scar.

My chest squeezed when Jax reached over, wrapping his fingers around her wrist, gently pulling her hand back down. "What are you saying, Nick?"

Nick exhaled roughly and then told them everything—about his father and the electrician he hired, and what his father eventually had done. He told Calla that her mother had known who his father was and that he'd been shocked when he'd first seen Calla, never expecting to see her walk into the bar.

When Nick finished, Calla gave a little shake of her blond head. Several moments stretched out, and I began to fear the worst, but then she finally spoke. "Why didn't you say something sooner?"

"I don't know," he replied, and then said, "Actually, that's a lie. You were dealing with a lot then and I didn't want to add to it. I didn't want to mess up your life any more than—"

"Wait," she interrupted, her eyes widening as she held up a hand. "Why would you mess anything up? What happened to my family wasn't your fault. I mean, you had to be just a kid then."

Nick sucked in a ragged breath while a strong jolt of release burst through me. Jax nodded in agreement. "She's right. You had nothing to do with any of that."

"But knowing who my dad was has to be a shitty reminder," Nick protested. "That can't be easy."

"It's definitely surprising. I am a little shocked, but I'm so, so sorry to hear what happened to your father and mother," Calla rushed on, her blue eyes shining. "I know what it's like to lose someone, and that couldn't have been easy on you."

Nick closed his eyes. "You're apologizing?" His voice sounded strangled, and I squeezed his leg. "There's nothing you need to apologize for."

"There's nothing you need to apologize for either," she insisted, her voice ringing with sincerity. "I get why you didn't say anything, but I want you to know that knowing who your dad was doesn't change the way I think of you."

"I . . ." Nick's voice was hoarse, and I leaned into

his side. The arm around the back of the booth curled around my shoulders. "That's a . . . major relief to hear."

"Part of me wants to punch you for thinking that it would change a damn thing," Jax said.

Nick chuckled as he dragged his other hand along his jaw and then dropped it on the table. "Yeah, I sort of want to punch myself, but once so much time had passed, it just became harder to say something."

"I get that." Calla reached across the table and squeezed his hand. "You know, what happened— the fire? It destroyed a lot of lives. Not just mine or my family, but yours, too." Her gaze flickered to mine. "A tragedy is a tragedy, no matter what, but I've learned that it doesn't define who we are and it doesn't weaken us. It makes us stronger. It took me a long time to figure that out." She glanced at Jax and smiled. "I had help in that department."

Nick's arm tightened around me and I rested my cheek on his shoulder. I smiled faintly at her and whispered, "So did I."

Chapter 32

*A*n older dark-haired woman who was sitting in the front row of the ballroom bounced the cooing four-month-old baby on her knee. The tuffs of red hair were a dead giveaway.

Ava Hamilton was absolutely adorable in her little white dress and headband. She had lost her shoes and one sock at some point, and I wasn't sure how long she was going to last before those giggles turned into cries, but I had grabby hands. I wanted to hold the baby. There was a dull twinge in my chest, but it was . . . it was okay.

The woman holding her reminded me of Teresa, all dark hair and bright eyes, and I figured she must be the groom's mother—Mrs. Hamilton.

I watched Ava's chubby fingers open and close as she grasped at air until a tall older man caught my attention. He was walking down the wide middle aisle that separated the two sections of chairs, his stride stiff and awkward. The cut of the man's black suit and even his trim hair screamed money.

His steps slowed as he approached Mrs. Hamilton. She looked up, shock splashing across her pretty face before she replaced the surprise with a smile. Her lips moved but I had no idea what she was saying.

The man was staring at Ava, and all I could see was his profile. His face was pale, his expression taut, and his shoulders rigid as he knelt beside them. Mrs. Hamilton turned Ava toward him. She said something and the man nodded. Then she handed Ava over to him.

My breath caught as I watched him take the baby in his arms and hold her close to his chest as if she were something very fragile. Mrs. Hamilton was speaking to him, but I had the impression that all the man heard and saw was Ava. His hand trembled as he smoothed it over the wisps of red hair.

"Who is that?" I asked.

Beside me, Roxy squinted as she looked up front. "I don't know," she said as I straightened the hem of my lilac skirt. "I've never seen him before."

Whoever the guy was, it seemed he must know either Avery or Cam pretty well. Eventually he handed the baby girl back to Mrs. Hamilton and then rose. He walked back up the aisle, his movements less strained.

I sighed as my gaze flicked back to Mrs. Hamilton. "I want to hold the baby," I said.

"I'm sure she'll let you," Roxy replied, straightening her glasses. They were blue today, matching her dress.

"I've never met her so I think it's totally creepy for

me to just shuffle up there and be like, 'Can I hold the baby,' while making grabby hands at the kid. I'd probably make her start screaming bloody murder."

Roxy giggled. "Good point."

I pouted, but before I could change my mind and make an utter fool out of myself while traumatizing a wee baby, the guys returned from whatever they were doing, which I'm sure involved giving Cam an incredibly hard time.

Nick sat beside me as Reece took his seat on the other side of Roxy. Although I'd already seen Nick in his suit, I couldn't stop myself from checking him out, because he looked so damn good all dressed up.

He leaned into me, stretching his arm along the back of my chair. Tipping his chin down, he whispered into my ear, "If you keep looking at me like that, we're going to miss the wedding."

"And why would we miss the wedding?" I whispered back.

His hand curled around my bare shoulder. "Because we'll be making use of that room upstairs we rented for the weekend. Or the nearby bathroom. There's also a closet down the hall that'll give us enough room."

I bit down on my lip, enticed more than I should have been by that idea. "You are so bad."

"And you . . ." He kissed my temple. " . . . are freaking gorgeous in that dress. Have I told you that yet?"

My lips curved up as I reached over, wrapping my hand around his. "Yes. A couple of times."

"Well, add one more to that list." He squeezed my hand. "You look stunning."

Reece sighed. "You two are going to give me diabetes."

"Shush it." Roxy planted her elbow in Reece's side. "You're just as sickeningly sweet, so don't even pretend."

I laughed, mainly because Reece didn't deny it. Somewhere behind us, music started playing and the heavy wood doors opened. We turned in our seats as Cam made his way down the aisle, looking as handsome as always. His normally messy hair was styled and he looked good in his black tux with light blue accents. As he passed us, Nick fist-bumped him.

I turned to Nick slowly. "A wedding fist bump?"

"Seemed legit," was his response.

Shaking my head, I giggled, and then had a huge aw moment, because Cam stopped by his mother before he went to the archway decorated with blue roses and baby's breath, bent down and gave his baby girl a big mushy kiss on her chubby cheek.

"Damn," Roxy murmured. "There just went my ovaries."

Reece sent her a long look.

"What?" she whispered. "I can't help it."

Grinning, I watched as the bridal party made their way down the aisle. First up was Jase, Cam's best friend, and Teresa, Cam's sister, and both of them looked like they stepped off a runway. There couldn't be any couple as striking as those two were, and I figured they would be married sooner than anyone expected.

Next was Brit and Ollie, and my smile spread seeing them. Wearing the same pale blue strapless gown as Teresa, Brit was stunning with her cap of blond hair, but it was Ollie who stole the show. Somehow, even in a tux, he managed to look like he was at the beach. His hair was shorter than when he was in college, but he still had that surfer look about him. They separated once they reached the archway.

Calla and Jax were next, and of course they were absolute perfection. With Calla's long blond hair and his darker features, they were like night and day, the perfect complement.

Then there was Jacob, looking as freaking smooth as always as he came down the aisle with his boyfriend. I'd met him the night before, and he was the exact opposite of Jacob—quiet, a bit more reserved, but it was so obvious those two were in love.

Jacob joined the bridesmaid, and even though he was in a tux that matched the guys, he looked damn good standing there.

The final addition to the wedding party was Brock "the Beast" Mitchell, which probably made Cam's fanboy heart soar. I had no idea Cam had gotten to know Brock that well or if it was a favor to him. Obviously Brock was out of the sling, but he hadn't come back to the academy full-time yet. There had been complications in his recovery.

I didn't recognize the super tan chick with him, and I was kind of disappointed that he wasn't there with Jillian. I don't even know why I wished for that. I hadn't seen Jillian since the day in the supply room. As far as I knew, she never came back to Lima Academy after that.

Once the bridal party was in place, the bridal march began and Avery appeared. She was a beautiful bride. Her long red hair hung in smooth waves around her freckled face, and even from where I sat, I could see the sheen of tears in her eyes. Her dress was simple Grecian style and perfect for her.

I couldn't believe she'd had a baby a handful of months ago, because she looked amazing as she glanced up at the man beside her. It was the guy who earlier had talked to Cam's mom and then held Ava. Now I knew the answer to who he was.

Avery's father.

He escorted her down the aisle as we rose. Before she reached her soon-to-be husband, Avery stopped and cupped little Ava's cheek, bending to press a kiss against the top of her head. The baby gurgled happily in response.

"And there goes my heart," Roxy sighed. "Gone. Along with my ovaries."

I pressed my lips together to stop the laugh from escaping as Avery's father handed her off to Cam. It would've been a strange laugh—part humor, part sob. As I watched Cam's mom turn Ava so she was facing her mother and father, the ache returned, piercing my chest, and I had to remind myself that it was okay. Someday it would happen.

Nick squeezed my hand, and when I glanced at him, his gaze searched mine intently, and I knew he felt where my head had gone. I gave him a smile, and he tugged me against his side with an arm curled along my back.

The ceremony began, and the words were really just a blur as Cam Hamilton and Avery Morgansten finally tied the knot. It was beautiful, and I had to fight back tears more than once.

"The rings?" the officiant requested.

Ollie stepped forward, and in his hands were two

tortoises. One had a pale blue ribbon around the shell, the other had a black ribbon. Rings were secured to both. I had no idea where he had the turtles the entire time, and God only knew with Ollie, so I didn't want to give that too much thought.

"Oh my Lord," I murmured, grinning.

Nick chuckled.

"I want turtles at my wedding," Roxy whispered to Reece.

Someone, I'm assuming him, choked.

Gasps and giggles gave way to laughter as Ollie lifted the tortoises and then walked them over to where Cam and Avery stood. They couldn't keep a straight face as they retrieved the rings amidst laughter, and then Ollie returned to where the groomsmen stood. He'd bent, placing the tortoises into something I couldn't see. Then he wheeled back around and gave a flourished bow. On the other side of him, Brit rolled her eyes.

Cam's hand shook as he slid the simple band onto her finger. "Will you spend forever with me?"

Avery's voice trembled as she spoke, sliding the ring onto Cam's finger. "I will spend forever with you."

Tears filled my eyes, and I looked over at Nick. Our gazes collided and held as a tear snuck free. Without saying a word, he smoothed his thumb under my eye, chasing the tear away, just like he had chased away all the pain and guilt, and opened a future I hadn't necessarily planned for but eagerly anticipated.

The officiant was speaking again, but I didn't hear the words. I barely registered the cheers as Nick lowered his mouth to mine, kissing me softly, and in that kiss were all the words I had so desperately wanted him to speak all those months ago.

Tell me that you still want to be here.
Tell me that you still see a future for us.
Tell me that you love me.

Nick had spoken the words before, many times in the last couple of months, but they were also promised in that kiss, and that promise spelled forever.

At Avon Books, we know your passion for romance—once you finish one of our novels, you find yourself wanting more.

May we tempt you with . . .

- **Excerpts** from our upcoming releases.

- Entertaining **extras**, including authors' personal photo albums and book lists.

- Behind-the-scenes **scoop** on your favorite characters and series.

- **Sweepstakes** for the chance to win free books, romantic getaways, and other fun prizes.

- Writing **tips** from our authors and editors.

- **Blog** with our authors and find out why they love to write romance.

- **Exclusive content** that's not contained within the pages of our novels.

Join us at
www.avonbooks.com

An Imprint of HarperCollinsPublishers
www.avonromance.com

Available wherever books are sold or please call 1-800-331-3761 to order.

FTH 1013

*G*ive in to your Impulses!

These unforgettable stories only take a second to buy and give you hours of reading pleasure!

Go to *www.AvonImpulse.com* and see what we have to offer.

Available wherever e-books are sold.

AVONIMPULSE

IMP 0811